"This is your family and home, not mine and Bryce's."

"Stop it. This is your home, and I'm pretty sure my dad would adopt you and Bryce if you'd let him." Tyler held up the Bible. "I think this is the greatest gift my dad has ever given me, and he used you to get it to me."

"That tells me he is suffering, too, and doesn't know how to talk about it. You both are so stubborn."

"I'm thinking you might be right."

He wanted to lean in and kiss her. She had made it clear she had no room for a man in her life, especially one with his lifestyle. He held her there in the starlight, time moving like a dream. What if he changed his plans?

He moved back, breaking all contact. The moment was gone.

"Good night, Karly. Thank you, and tell Dad I'm all right. Tell him I'm better than I was a month ago."

And I have you to thank for that.

A seventh-generation Texan, **Jolene Navarro** fills her life with family, faith and life's beautiful messiness. She knows that as much as the world changes, people stay the same: vow-keepers and heartbreakers. Jolene married a vow-keeper who shows her holding hands never gets old. When not writing, Jolene teaches art to inner-city teens and hangs out with her own four almost-grown kids. Find Jolene on Facebook or her blog, jolenenavarrowriter.com.

Renee Ryan grew up in a Florida beach town where she learned to surf, sort of. With a degree from FSU, she explored career opportunities at a Florida theme park and a modeling agency and even taught high school economics. She currently lives with her husband in Nebraska, and many have mistaken their overweight cat for a small bear. You may contact Renee at reneeryan.com, on Facebook or on Twitter, @reneeryanbooks.

A Texas Christmas Wish

Jolene Navarro

&

The Doctor's Christmas Wish

Renee Ryan

LOVE INSPIRED

INSPIRATIONAL ROMANCE

Recycling programs
for this product may
not exist in your area.

LOVE INSPIRED®
INSPIRATIONAL ROMANCE

ISBN-13: 978-1-335-28497-6

A Texas Christmas Wish & The Doctor's Christmas Wish

Copyright © 2020 by Harlequin Books S.A.

A Texas Christmas Wish
First published in 2015. This edition published in 2020.
Copyright © 2015 by Jolene Navarro

The Doctor's Christmas Wish
First published in 2015. This edition published in 2020.
Copyright © 2015 by Renee Halverson

This edition published by arrangement with Harlequin Books S.A.

For questions and comments about the quality of this book, please contact us at CustomerService@Harlequin.com.

Love Inspired
22 Adelaide St. West, 40th Floor
Toronto, Ontario M5H 4E3, Canada
www.Harlequin.com

Printed in U.S.A.

CONTENTS

A TEXAS CHRISTMAS WISH

Jolene Navarro

This book is dedicated to all the students who have sat in Studio 115 and Studio 201. I learn more from you than you will ever learn from me. Especially the teen parents who are working so hard to build a future for their young families. The cards might be stacked against you, but that doesn't mean you can't get your own happy ending.

Acknowledgments

I'm living a dream.
There are so many people who make this dream come true. First, the best agent, Pamela Hopkins, who muddled through my dyslexic musings and found a story. Thank you for your support.

To an editor, who always knows exactly how to make a story better. Thank you, Emily Rodmell, for giving me the opportunity to write for Love Inspired.

To my nephew, Jackson Ward, for staying up late and going through airplane crashes with me. May you never have to use your knowledge. You're making your Poppy proud.

And to my brainstorming partners… you feed my soul.

Peace I leave with you; my peace I give you.
I do not give to you as the world gives.
Do not let your hearts be troubled and do not be afraid.
—*John* 14:27

Chapter One

Karly turned the wipers to the highest setting, but they didn't help much. She knew the ranchers in Clear Water, Texas, were celebrating after the long drought, but she just wanted to get to her new home without drowning.

New home. If everything worked out the way she planned, her young son, Bryce, would be celebrating Christmas in a real home for the first time ever. Last Christmas they had been living in her car. At church, deacon Dub Childress had always made her feel welcome. Now he was recovering from a stroke and broken arm—and it was her turn to help him.

On the huge plus side, if she could pull this off, no shelter or cheap hotel for them this year. But would she be able to care for Dub and his house? She didn't even finish high school. Doing some research on stroke patients online might not be enough.

Deep breath in...out. She made herself relax. This past year had brought so many changes, and with the help of her new church family, she was free of bad relationships. Hopefully no one expected her to cook. She could clean. She was very good at cleaning.

The rain pounded the roof, making it hard to hear anything else. In the backseat, Bryce finally calmed down. Her five-year-old son hated storms—or any loud noise. She leaned forward, her knuckles white around the steering wheel. God had gotten them through worse storms.

Glancing in the rearview mirror at her son, she continued the game. "Let me see. Is it your baby picture on my visor?"

Kicking his feet against the passenger seat, Bryce grinned at her. His smile shone through the dark, dreary day. "Yes! Now it's your turn."

"Okay…let me see… I spy something…blue and white."

Bryce gasped. Karly turned back to see what startled him. He pointed to the road in front of her.

"Airplane."

Squinting to see through the heavy rain, she saw it, too. "No…" She blinked to clear the image, but it was still there. A small aircraft hovered over the road. The spinning blades on the nose of the plane headed straight for them. The wings tilted from one side to the other as if trying to balance on the air.

Instinctively, she hit the brake and jerked to the right, taking them through a muddy ditch. The car bounced over the rocky terrain. Their seat belts were the only thing that kept them in place. The boxes and bags weren't so lucky.

After a hard stop just short of a barbed-wire fence, she looked back at Bryce, reaching for him, needing to touch him. "Are you okay?"

He twisted in his booster seat, pulling himself around as far as the seat belt would let him go. "It's an airplane." He looked at her for a second before pointing around the overturned boxes in the back. "An airplane on the road."

Sure enough, the small airplane she had just lost a game of chicken to sat on the opposite side of the county road, tangled up in the tall game fence.

Through the back window, in the gray, water-blurred scene, Karly saw a figure run toward them. She slowly filled her lungs, making every effort to breathe and stop the shaking of her hands. Eyes closed, she counted and relaxed each muscle.

Thank You, God, for protecting us. Please get us to our new home safely.

A tap on the window caused her to jump. A drenched man stood outside her car. Rolling the window down, she was hit with rain. She cupped a hand over her face and found Tyler Childress staring at her.

Tyler pulled his leather jacket over his head to block her from the onslaught of rain. Leaning closer to her, he looked into the car. "Is everyone all right? I'm so sorry. Cattle were on the airstrip and I thought I could make it to the field, but the pressure came in low."

"We're fine. A little shaken up, but fine. Tyler Childress, right?"

"Oh, no." He smiled—the smile she heard the women of Clear Water sigh over whenever they gossiped about the good-looking son of Dub Childress. Wild and impulsive, but good-looking as all get-out. This phrase was repeated often. "We didn't go to school together, did we? I'm horrible with names." The rain started dripping off the sides of his jacket.

"No, we've never met. Why don't you get in the car and out of the rain?"

He gave a quick nod and ran in front of her car as she rolled up her window.

Reaching across the seat, she pulled the lock up, then started stuffing bags and containers in the seat behind her. The off-road adventure had scattered their worldly possessions throughout the car. They would have to re-pack everything. Tyler slid into her '97 Volvo wagon. The space got a lot smaller with his tall, well-built body. He looked like a pirate just rescued from a shipwreck.

She focused on her hands. He was dangerous, the kind of man that could bring trouble to her new, safe world.

Carefully tucking her leather-bound Bible into the console, she ran her fingertip along its spine. It was a gift from her church family at her baptism six months ago. The idea that she now had people who cared about her and Bryce still felt a bit surreal. And with this man now beside her, it was a good reminder.

Dub's son reminded her of all the bad choices she had made based on wanting to be rescued by a knight in shining armor. This job her pastor offered her was more than a way to repay kindness or even make money. It was an opportunity to make a stable future for her son. An opportunity she couldn't afford to waste.

Tyler adjusted himself in the passenger seat and slammed the door to the storm outside, his long legs not quite fitting. He looked too big for the small space, like a jack-in-the-box ready to pop out if someone pulled the roof open. Her car had a new scent now, a clean mas-culine fragrance.

"Would you mind following me over to the county airport?" He pointed his perfect chin to the turnoff about fifty yards ahead of her.

"Oh, sure." *Stop trying to smell him.*

"Thanks."

"Hi! I'm Bryce. I like your airplane!"

Tyler turned and held out his hand to her son. "Hi, Bryce. I'm Tyler. Glad to meet you."

Karly tightened her lips, forcing herself not to say anything as she watched Childress's reaction when he realized her son didn't have a right hand to shake, only five unformed digits right below his elbow. Without hesitation he laid his hand flat, palm up, on his other hand. "Give me five? Hope I didn't scare you."

"No, that was fun!" He leaned forward to slap their guest's hand.

Karly was a bit surprised by Bryce's enthusiasm. Most of the time, he pulled back from men and he never wanted to meet someone new.

She had to admit that Tyler's nonreaction automatically bumped him up in her opinion no matter what everyone said about him. Bryce's dad had taken one look at their son and walked out of the hospital and never came back. Of course, he had been a seventeen-year-old boy already scared of being a father.

Tyler might be a late coming home, but she didn't know his story and it wasn't her place to judge. She'd been hired to do a job. Keeping a safe distance from this good-looking adventurer would be best for them all.

She placed her hands over her son's short active legs. "I'm sorry about the small space—we might be able to move the seat back a little bit." There wasn't much room available with all the stuff she had wedged between the seat and Bryce.

"No worries." He chuckled and winked at her. His

clear blue eyes matched his father's perfectly. "I've been in tighter places. Besides, we aren't going far."

She put the car in Reverse and hit the gas, but all that happened was the whirling sound of a spinning tire. She gripped the steering wheel and tried again, pressing harder on the gas pedal.

"Whoa. You're just digging in deeper. Go forward."

She gritted her teeth against his short demand and reached up to shift gears. His hand stopped her. The touch startled her, and she jerked back.

He didn't even seem to notice her reaction. "Hold on. Let me put one of those branches in front of the tire." Without waiting for her to agree, he sprang out of the car. Running hunched over, he gathered some of the larger limbs that covered the ground on the edge of the cedar break. Climbing back into the car, he nodded. "Now go forward. Keep the pressure on the pedal nice and steady."

Holding her breath and sending a quick prayer, she followed his instructions. After a few bounces, they were back on the road. She couldn't help giving him a big grin. "Thank you."

"Well, it was my fault you ended up in the ditch."

With a slow U-turn on the highway, she headed back toward his plane.

"Are you going to be able to drive the plane to the airport?"

"Yeah. I think a wing is damaged, but it can move across the ground without a problem. The Kirkpatricks aren't going to be happy. I think I ran through their fence a couple of times back in high school." With one hand on the door, he turned to face her. "You don't mind following me to the hangar, do you? I'll need a ride to town."

"Town? You're not going to the ranch?"

"You don't need to drive all the way out there." He glanced over her stacked and labeled boxes. "You look busy. Do you need help?"

He didn't know she had been hired to stay with his dad? She made herself stop chewing on the inside of her cheek. She hadn't even introduced herself.

"I'm Karly Kalakona. I was hired as the new house-keeper and to care for your dad after he had the stroke. I'm heading to the ranch anyway, so it's not a problem. I've never been to the ranch, so it would be great if you could show me where to go. I mean I know where the ranch is, but once on the ranch I have no clue." *Stop rambling, idiot.* No, she reminded herself, no more name-calling. Be kind to yourself.

She held her expression neutral as his eyes narrowed. The space in her old Volvo seemed to get smaller and warmer. The heavy raindrops hitting the roof was the only sound for what seemed like hours. Taking his hand off the door, he turned and looked straight at her. Karly pushed her dark hair back.

"You're moving into my dad's house?" His friendly tone had been replaced by a sharp edge. "Who hired you?"

"Uh… Pastor John Levi. He was married to your sister, Carol, right? He told me he still helps your dad with the ranch." Silence. Tyler stared out the windshield. She was getting the feeling he was not happy. "Is there a problem?"

He shook his head. "I just thought…" Instead of finishing the sentence, he sighed and looked back at her. "How do you know John?"

"A little less than a year ago I started attending his church, and a few months later they helped me get out of a bad situation. When your father had his stroke, Pastor John asked if I would be a live-in assistant. Your father had always been a great support to me so I really wanted to repay all the help I found here in Clear Water."

"You look really young for a nurse."

"I'm not a nurse."

"Do you have nursing exper—?" Flashes of lightning flooded the car with white light, followed by a rolling boom of thunder. Bryce cried out, covering his ears. She reached for him again.

"It's okay, baby. We're safe."

"Hey, big guy, have you ever gone bowling?"

Bryce looked up at Tyler and shook his head. Karly couldn't keep from raising her eyebrows. Bowling? What did that have to do with anything?

"Well, I'll have to take you so you know that's what it sounds like. A giant marble ball hitting a bunch of wooden pins. Sounds scary, but it's actually loads of fun."

"Really? I wanna go, Momma. I wanna go bowling." He looked at his new hero. "When are we going?"

"Now, Bryce, I don't know. We have a lot of things to do and you just got your braces off." She cut a glance to Tyler. "Between the surgeries and physical therapy, we have to be careful of the activities we pick." She didn't want Bryce disappointed in the things he couldn't do. She wanted him to focus on what he could safely accomplish. "We have to get moved into our new home and get you back in school."

"Yes, ma'am." His narrow shoulders slumped. Well, at least he wasn't crying.

"Sorry, big guy. Your mom's right. We gotta get you all settled in. Then we can make plans. Right now, I've got to get my plane to the hangar."

Her son perked back up. "Can I ride in your airplane?"

Tyler considered her. His eyebrows rose.

Great, he was going to make her be the bad guy again. "Sorry, sweetheart, you would have to get out in the rain. I need you to stay with me in the car."

Tyler reached across the back of his seat and tugged at Bryce's foot. "Hey, we'll do it another day. I promise." He grabbed the door handle, jumped out of the safety of her car and darted through the rainstorm to his plane.

She had a feeling she might be headed down a road she had not planned. With a sigh, she watched her son focus on every move Tyler made. Karly saw a joy on his small face that she hadn't seen in a good while.

Her son should know by now that a pretty package wrapped in easy smiles and good manners could be masking a monster.

Unfortunately, Tyler Childress would not be the first man to break his promise to them.

Blinded by heavy rain, Tyler pushed the Piper back from the tangled fence. Hopefully, none of the Kirkpatricks' stock would test the damaged wire. He needed to call Henry and let him know. Yeah, so much for proving to his dad he had managed to become a responsible adult.

He could hear Dub Childress's voice now. *Don't start*

with the excuses, son. Somewhere along the way your choices put you in this position.

The argument already played in his head. An argument he needed to avoid. Yes, he'd procrastinated coming home, had buzzed the house one too many times and flew needless circles over town. By the time he'd headed to the airstrip, the storm had hit and livestock had escaped one of the ranches, blocking the only way to land.

So no excuses, Dad. It was my fault I ran a young mother and her child off the road.

With the plane turned in the right direction, he climbed up and pulled the door shut to the cockpit. He wished he could just stay there—his favorite place in the world. A place he was in total control.

Behind the seat he pulled out a towel. With a quick rub through his hair, he tried to stop the dripping, at least. He had so much mud on him, keeping the interior clean was a lost cause. Much like his relationship with his dad. Maybe this time he would manage…

Eyes closed, he stopped the pointless words. Clear Water was the last place he wanted to be. He knew he should have been here sooner, but every time he and his dad walked into the same room there was a fight. His mother had said it was because they were so much alike. He didn't buy that.

He was nothing like his dad. *Obstinate* didn't even begin to describe the old rancher. He was as hard to move as the rock that held the hills steady. Now that his mother and sister were dead and buried, there wasn't anyone to soften the blows between them.

His fingers tightened around the controls. How did his father do it? How did he stay at the ranch and live in the home where memories of his mother and sister were in every corner? The silence of things they would never say, or moments they would never see, contaminated everything.

Tyler rolled his head back and took in a lungful of air. When had he become so melodramatic? He needed to get the plane in the hangar, call Henry about the fence, not to mention find out why his dad and John had gone ahead and hired someone without waiting for him. He had told them they needed a certified nurse.

Instead, he found a single mom barely out of her teens and a kid with special needs moving in on the ranch. One of John's lost sheep. His dad would do anything for John Levi, the perfect man who had married his sister.

Karly and Bryce had *charity case* written all over them. So how was he going to handle this without a fight? Could he kick a single mom and her kid into the streets?

Easing the battered wings over the cedar post, he turned the plane onto the narrow asphalt road that led to the county airport. He had vowed not to say or do anything to get his dad upset, but that plan was already rolling downhill and picking up speed.

The discussion to sell the monstrosity of a ranch would have to wait at least a couple of days, if not weeks. First, he needed to get a certified nurse in the house so he could go back to his own life without worrying about his father.

He parked the plane in the small hangar right next to his dad's plane, a vintage Mustang. The faded gray Volvo station wagon pulled in behind him. Maybe she could stay on as a housekeeper and he could get an agency to do daily nurse visits. Firing Ms. Karly Kala-kona would not be an option, unless she was lying about who she was and were she came from.

The clouds lit up again, and thunder shook the old metal walls. Scanning the building, he found nothing had changed. Half of his childhood happened in the barns, the other half here in this metal hangar. His father had spent hours teaching him to fly. It was a passion they shared and had brought them together—until Tyler had announced he wanted to leave the ranch and make flying his life, not just a hobby.

He forced his jaw to relax. The muscles burned from the tension. Pulling a duffel bag from the back, he glanced over at the plane he'd learned to fly in as a kid. Things had been so much easier back then. He hoped his dad was okay. He had to be.

Tyler stepped out on the concrete, stomping some of the mud off his boots. He checked a few damaged areas on the right wing before heading to the car.

In the gray Volvo parked behind him, Karly smiled. She was saying something to her son. He had to admit she was a dark-haired beauty. Not his usual type. There was sweetness mixed with a spine of steel. Like his mom and sister. He froze in midstride.

His dad wouldn't dare. One of their long-standing fights the past few years was about Tyler's love life. Every time Dub called, he told Tyler he needed to settle down with a solid family kind of girl. His father hated every woman he brought to the ranch. They all spent more time estimating the value of the ranch than appreciating the raw beauty of the land.

A knot formed in his gut. He wouldn't put it past the manipulative old man to use his health crisis as a means to play matchmaker. One more attempt to get Tyler to do what his father thought was best for the Childress name.

Karly opened her car door and stood. She was taller than he expected.

"I called the ranch and told Adrian that I picked you up and we're heading that way now."

"Adrian?"

"De La Cruz, one of the trainers." She looked at him as if he didn't have a brain. "He has a little girl about ten. I was told you went to school with him."

"Adrian works for my dad? When did that happen?" Surprise made his words sharper than he intended.

"Um… I don't know?" Her stunning eyes went wider, and her fingers tightened on the door frame.

Way to go, Childress, scare the girl. Why was he barking at her? "Sorry. I've been gone too long, and it's been a long day." He made his way to the passenger side of her car and folded into the tight space. She smelled like his mother's kitchen during the holidays. Now she was making him think of Christmas cookies before Thanksgiving.

Four weeks. Surely he could manage four weeks without yelling at his dad or getting tangled with the new hired help. He knew right away that Karly was not the kind for a casual relationship, and that was the only kind he had managed to have the past ten years. He lowered his gaze to the worn leather handle of his bag.

Definitely *not* looking at the exotic tilt of her dark eyes with hints of gold, or the silky ponytail that swung when she talked. No, none of that caught his attention. *She's a mother, Tyler. That alone should make her invisible.*

Chapter Two

For most of the ten miles to the ranch, Karly sat forward, her tight muscles sore from strain. She wasn't sure what made her the most nervous, the storm or Tyler Childress.

The gossips adored talking about all the trouble Tyler got into while in high school. People loved to gossip—the more scandalous the better. She tried not to pay attention, but now that he was next to her she had to wonder how much was true.

Pulling through the stone pillars, she glanced up to the wrought iron archway where the letters spelling *Childress* boldly stood, surrounded by silhouettes of horses in motion. If things worked out, this would be their new home for the next year. Enough time to get Bryce's physical therapy done, some of the medical bills paid off and a bit of breathing room to figure out where to go to next.

Living out of her car was getting old. She needed a plan and Bryce needed to be in school. This was the perfect job for her—that was, if the younger Childress didn't kick them out.

He had spent the whole trip staring out the window. She'd glanced at him. He didn't seem to want to be here. Maybe he would be leaving soon. "So how long do you plan on staying?"

He shrugged. "I've taken the next month off. I need to speak with the doctors tomorrow, figure out what Dad needs and when he can come home."

Oh, no. He hadn't been told. "Pastor John is bringing him home this evening."

With his elbows resting on his knees, Tyler pressed the palm of his hands into his eyes. "John's bringing him home today? I thought he had at least another week in the hospital."

"The nurses can't keep him in bed, and he tries to leave every few hours. He tells everyone he's walking home."

She drove around a cluster of twisted live oak trees. At the end of the narrow asphalt drive, the redbrick ranch house sprawled long and low behind a shaded yard of lush, green carpet grass. She slowed down and took a moment to find her breath.

A home. A real home that Bryce was going to get to live in, hopefully, for the next year. She blinked a couple of times to stop the tears from spilling down her cheeks. Tyler would think she was crazy if she started crying. *Thank You, God.*

"Are you okay?"

She didn't dare look at him. "Yes. I'm just not sure where to go. I haven't been to the house before now."

He pointed to the right. "Go to the back. We'll pull into the garage and unload from there." Facing her again, his blue eyes intense. "I don't get it. Dad doesn't have a way to leave. He can't drive, and from what I understand he can't walk that well, either. So why is John bringing him home?"

"He told the pastor that if someone didn't drive him home he'd start walking. Your father seems very determined to get back to the ranch. So Pastor John's giving him a ride. They should be here within the next couple of hours." She skimmed the area around them, avoiding eye contact. "He's leaving AMA."

He threw his head back against the seat. "Seriously? A man with brain damage and a broken arm is allowed to leave against medical advice and no one calls me? That's what AMA means, right? Against medical advice."

"I believe that's what it means." She didn't know what to say.

"Great. And no one thought to hire a real nurse?" His voice low as he stared back out the window.

"Horses! Momma, look. Horses!"

The drive forked. To the left, a couple of large barns, two outbuildings and several pens made what looked like a small resort for horses. A sharp right put them in front of a giant wooden garage door that belonged on a fortress. Rich wood and large wrought iron hinges brought to mind another time and place.

"Can we go see the horses? Please, Momma."

"Bryce, it's raining, and we need to get set up. Besides, the horses are off-limits. You cannot go to the barn area without me. Do you understand?"

"But, Momma…"

"Bryce." She lowered her chin and looked at him through the rearview mirror.

"Hey, we need to help your mom unpack the car.

Well, maybe repack first, then unpack and find out which room is yours."

"Oh, I can take care of—"

"I'll be in a different room? Is it far from yours, Momma?" Worry filled his young eyes. He had seen too much in his short life, and it was her fault.

"Right next to mine." Sleeping together had become their norm since the night Officer Torres had arrested Billy Havender, her last life blunder. *No more mistakes.* "Bryce, it'll be okay. Pastor John told me our rooms are connected through a bathroom."

"You're in my sister's room?" His Florida Key blues narrowed. How did someone have eyes that blue without contacts? She didn't think he wore them. She hadn't thought about whose room she would be living in. The offer of a salary, plus room and board, had been all she'd needed to hear.

"Pull up. I'll run inside and open the door." His voice was gruff as he looked away again.

"Oh, Pastor John gave me the remote." Digging it out of the console, she hit the button. The left door slid to the other side instead of overhead. As she pulled into the large space, the feeling of crossing the threshold into a special world washed over her. What if she couldn't do the job that was needed? What if they didn't let her stay? She stopped herself. *No self-doubt allowed.*

The concrete space was large enough to hold three cars along with a workshop. Currently only a large silver Suburban with the ranch's logo sat in the opposite end of the garage. Color-coordinated boxes lined the organized shelves, sorted by shape and size. She skimmed over her car, filled with a hodgepodge of boxes she had saved from the drugstore Dumpster.

Nothing organized or coordinated about her. Maybe she *had* made a mistake. Taking a deep breath, she studied the most precious thing in her life, the reason she'd taken this opportunity. *Bryce.*

"Are you ready for our new adventure, Bryce?"

"Can I go pet the horses?" He blinked. "Please?"

Tyler opened Bryce's door in time to hear the word *horses.* "How about we help your mom get your stuff in the house? Then I can take you to the barns and introduce you to the stars of the Childress family."

"Oh, I'm not sure that's a good idea. He's never been around large animals." She didn't want to come across as the No Patrol, but Tyler was making all sorts of promises and probably didn't realize how serious a five-year-old took his every word.

Bryce started struggling with his seat belt. Another roll of thunder shook the walls.

"Hold on, baby. I'll come help." She made her way to the other side of the car.

Her son glared at her. She paused. He had never glared at her before today. They had always been a team.

"I'm not a baby. I can get out of the car on my own, and Tyler said we could see the horses."

She realized she'd embarrassed her son in front of his new hero. Karly glanced at Tyler. He shrugged his shoulders, the wet T-shirt plastered to his skin. He mouthed "sorry" from behind Bryce's back. She put her attention back on her son.

"First, you call him Mr. Childress. Second, I know you can get out of the car on my own. I just needed to get my bag so you won't step on it. Third, the horses will have to wait."

Tyler crossed to the other side and started pulling

out trash bags full of their clothes. She bit the inside of her cheek.

Do not apologize for your lack of luggage. You have nothing to be ashamed of, Karly Kalakona. "I'm sure this is the most unique baggage you've seen as a pilot." Her laugh sounded stiff to her own ears. She kept one eye on Bryce as he climbed out of the car, his legs still not at 100 percent.

"You'd be surprised." Tyler's voice brought her back to him. "This looks like the luggage I used when I moved to college. Aunt Cora gave me a matching set, but I took it back to the department store for the cash and used dependable Hefty bags. My mom got so mad. The best part is when you're done you can use them for cleanup and they don't take up any space."

But she was a mom, not a kid moving away from home the first time. Growing up, she'd gone from feast to famine. During a con, her stepfather, Anthony, had always insisted they travel with only the best. He would spend thousands of dollars, then take everything to a pawnshop when they ran out of money.

Things were different now. She paid her own way. And she didn't need to waste time thinking about her stepfather. That was the past. "I can get our stuff if you could point me to the right room."

"No need, I'm here and I know the way." He pulled out one of her free book bags full of makeup and hair supplies. "Here you go, big guy, can you carry this for me? That's pretty heavy. Do you think you can handle two?"

"The doctor said I'm strong now. I can carry three."

Tyler winked at her. "Oh, I don't know, three is a lot. What do you think, Mom?" Tyler handed Bryce a lightweight grocery bag before picking up a small plastic container with a sealed lid.

"I can do it. Mom, watch!" With the straps across his shoulders, he tucked the box under his arm.

"Good job, Bryce." At the look of pride on Bryce's face, a piece of her heart twisted. She popped open the tailgate and stuffed clothes and toys back into the boxes. Tyler was by the door, slipping off his muddy boots. The wet jeans had mud on them, too. It couldn't be comfortable. "Tyler, the large tub stays in the car. If you would just show me the way, I can get the rest of our stuff. I'm sure you want out of the wet clothes."

"Oh, don't worry about me. I'm a river rat. I love the rain."

Bryce giggled. "I want to be a river rat."

Great, now she had to worry about him going to find the river on his own. She followed Tyler and Bryce through a huge washroom. When he led them through a large open kitchen, she paused. It was bigger than any apartment she had ever lived in during her entire life.

It was unreal, the kind of home she had only seen in a *Country Living* magazine. The smoothness of the long gray-and-black granite counters begged to be touched. A beautiful pine table with eight chairs sat opposite an island. Four stools hugged the counter.

The kitchen had two sinks. Everything was clean and fresh, from the white cabinet doors to the dark wood floors.

Well, except for the two bananas in a ceramic bowl. They were covered in black dots. She should throw them out.

"Mom! Come on."

He didn't even know they had just stepped into another world, a world where they didn't belong. *Thank You, God, for giving me such a resilient child.*

She looked at the desk with a shelf full of cookbooks above it. She would need those books.

Ramen noodles cooked to perfection were the extent of her skills in the kitchen. She had a feeling this family wasn't the cheap noodle crowd.

Tyler stepped back into the kitchen. "Sorry, I guess I should have given you a tour first."

She shook her head. "No, I'm fine. I was thinking I should throw away the bananas before Mr. Childress arrives."

Bryce came up to the table and wrinkled his nose. "Gross."

He chuckled. "Oh, yeah, I didn't even see them. Dad has one every morning with his breakfast. Always made me eat one, too." He put the bags down and took the overripe fruit to the other side of the room. With a tap of his foot, a trash bin rolled out from under the counter.

"Cool." Bryce went over the hidden trash container and opened it with the same motion Tyler had used, staring wide-eyed, as if he had discovered a treasure.

"Don't let me forget to take that out. We don't want to compact rotten bananas."

Bryce nodded as if he understood what Tyler said. "Okay."

In a few long strides, Tyler had the bags of their clothes back in hand, with Bryce right behind him. As he moved under a large archway, he looked back at her. "This is the family room. The dining room and living room are on the other side."

There was so much to see. Two cream-colored sectionals anchored the spacious room. A million shades of blue pillows invited her to sit and get lost in all the comforts. There were pictures on every surface. Pictures of people, horses and airplanes. An ornate pool table sat in the far corner next to a wall of glass doors. This house invited you to stay and enjoy living. Three double doors led outside.

She hurried to catch up with Tyler and Bryce, who had disappeared down a dark hallway. She glanced at the wall. More pictures. Many of a young girl and boy riding horses or playing sports. She had never seen so many award plaques in one place. They stretched down the long hall, covering the wall along the way.

Tyler's voice interrupted her thoughts. "Sorry about the overkill. Carol always called it Mom's Hall of Mortification."

"Is this it?" Bryce stood in front of a door. Tyler nodded, but didn't make a move to open it. Bryce looked up at the man beside him and adjusted the straps on his shoulder. He glanced at her, then back to Tyler. "Can we go in?"

Drawing in a deep breath, Tyler nodded, still staring at the door. *Oh, this is his sister's room.* "Hey, you know what? We can put everything in the family room and figure this out later. Maybe there is another room I'm supposed to move into."

"No, it makes sense you staying here. You and Bryce are next to each other, and my dad's room is close." He turned to point to the opposite wall at the end of the hall. "That's his door."

He still didn't seem all that sure about it. Of course, he also wanted a trained medical professional, not an uneducated single mom.

"Go ahead. Open the door, Bryce. You do the honors. It's your mom's room for now."

Her little man switched the box to his shorter arm and turned the knob. For some reason she held her breath. When was the last time anyone was in this bedroom?

"It's locked." Bryce glanced up at Tyler.

This was getting awkward. "I'll just take our stuff to the fam—"

"No, no. The key is up here." He set the bags down and went to the door at the back of the hall. Stretching up, he ran his fingers along the top of the door frame. "Here you go." He handed the Allen key to Bryce. "I'll go get more of your boxes."

"Are you sure?" She ended up talking to his back. "Don't take out the large green tub. It stays in the car." She wasn't sure he had heard. Bryce fumbled a bit with the key, then turned the knob before flashing her one of his I-did-it smiles.

She took a deep breath and smiled back. It was just a door, an ordinary door, so why did she feel so heavy walking through it?

"Wow! Mom, the bed is huge and purple." He tossed the bags on an overstuffed armchair. "Look how big the windows are, and it has a seat."

She stepped into a fifteen-year time capsule. Every teenage fantasy of being a normal girl with a family and school friends came to life in the room. Purple and silver ribbons hung from the corner of the curtain rod, the silk mums were coated in a fine layer of dust. The cream-colored walls were covered in poster frames that held collages of a high school girl's memories. Sports, dances, horses and local and international mission trips were highlighted in each of the five poster frames.

"Who are all these people?" Bryce was studying the pictures.

"This is Carol, Tyler's sister. All the other people are her friends. She's also Rachel and Celeste's mother." Carol hadn't been much older than she when she had been killed in a car accident, leaving behind two small daughters, a young husband and a whole town that loved her and still missed her. She looked at the laughing girl who'd thought she had a lifetime in front of her. Somehow she had managed to accomplish more in one short life than Karly dreamed of doing.

"Oh, look at these, Momma." He picked up a model horse from the purple dresser. "These are cool. I hope my room's not purple, though."

"Here're some more boxes." She heard Tyler's voice from the hallway, but by the time she had gotten to the door he was already gone again.

"Momma, what's that word?"

She went back into Carol's room. "What word, baby?"

"Momma, I'm not a baby." Then he pointed to a poster, purple, of course, on the wall. "Go An-gore-as! What's an Angora?"

She shrugged. "Not sure. We'll have to ask Tyler."

"Can I see my room?" He lowered his head and whispered. "Please, anything but purple." He opened the door to the bathroom that connected the rooms. "If I don't like it, your bed is big enough for both of us."

"Yes, it is." She just wasn't sure if there was room for them. In this home. This substantial house was big enough for them *and* Tyler, though.

"Cool, Momma! Look." He tilted his head back to look at the ceiling, slowly turning. Airplanes of all sizes and shapes hung from the clear wires. Two-tone blue, with a touch of red, made the room inviting and all boy. Baseball and football equipment packed the spaces between the books on the shelves. Posters of Texas teams and colleges covered the wall.

The strangest was the leather halter and bridle hanging on the headboard. Bryce started going through the closet, pulling out some sort of sports jersey with a large nineteen on it. "Do you think it's Tyler's?"

"Hey, what have you got there?" Tyler stood in the doorway, leaning on the frame.

"Oh, I'm sorry." She took the shirt from Bryce and put it back. They'd intruded into his world; now he found them digging through his closet.

"I'm sorry, Mr. Childress." Her little boy took a step back, his head down.

Towering over her small son, Tyler reached past him and pulled out the shirt. "You can wear it. It's my basketball shirt from my seventh-grade year. We got new ones, so coach let us keep them." He slipped the jersey over Bryce's head. "In just a few years, you can be a fighting Angora."

"I can't play basketball." He held up his short arm. "I only have one hand."

"You only need one hand to dribble." He rubbed Bryce's dark hair.

Karly crossed her arms and stopped herself from saying anything to Tyler. She wished he would stop telling her son all the things he could do. She was sure he meant well, but he didn't understand all the complications.

The joy in her son radiated from his grin. "So what's an Angora?"

This time Tyler laughed out loud. "A goat with long, wavy white hair and curled horns."

She had to laugh at Bryce's horrified expression. "A goat?"

"Yeah, a goat, but most people don't even know they're goats. They're different and they're tough, able to survive through harsh conditions."

Maybe she had more in common with the school mascot than she thought.

"What kind of conditions?"

"Sorry, he'll ask you questions all day." She came up behind her son and pulled him against her. "Bryce can stay with me. This is your room."

"Hasn't been my room for years." He ran fingers through his damp hair and looked around. "The times I came home, I slept in the bunkhouse."

Bryce's big eyes went even wider. "Bunkhouse? Like with cowboys?"

"Yep. Speaking of which, since you live on the Childress Ranch now, we need to find you a cowboy hat and boots." He stepped into the closet and pulled a black hat from the top shelf. "Let's see if this fits." The cowboy hat wobbled a little bit on Bryce's head, but it wasn't too bad.

"It fits, Momma. Look! I'm a cowboy!" He turned back to his new champion. "Can I stay in the bunkhouse, too?"

"Sorry, partner. Have to be nineteen to live in the bunkhouse. You can stay in my old room and be a cowboy in training."

Karly's phone vibrated. Looking at the name, she saw it was the call she had been expecting. "Hi, Pastor John." She noticed Tyler stiffen, his jaw muscles flexing. "Yes, we're here. Tyler's here, too. I picked him up at the airport." He raised an eyebrow. She was not going to explain the almost head-on collision over the phone. "What do you need me to do? Okay, see you in a while."

Sliding the new phone back into her pocket, she took a deep breath. "Your father will be here soon. They're turning off the highway now. Are there any more boxes in the car?"

"Nope, got them all. Left the tub. Why is no one calling *me* about *my* father?"

Her stomach knotted. She hated conflict. "I don't know. Maybe because you'd been out of the country and they weren't sure when you'd be here." She shrugged. "I'm going to make sure your dad's room is ready. Tyler?"

He had started bringing boxes into the room. "Yeah."

She swallowed. "Pastor John said to tell you he was glad you were here, but…to remind you that your father needs to be in a stress-free environment."

Anger clouded his blue eyes, making them darker. "What does he think I'm going to do?"

With a shrug, she headed for the door. "I don't know. Bryce, come on."

"Momma, please. I want to help Mr. Childress."

"Hey, partner. Call me Tyler. With my dad coming home, it'll get confusing if you call us both Mr. Childress. Anyway, I'm really not much older than you. Just ask my dad."

She still saw a bit of a mischievous look in his eye, ready to cause trouble.

"He can stay and help me. I need those strong muscles."

Bryce giggled.

"Okay, but be careful. You just got the braces off your legs." She looked at Tyler, hoping he understood her concern.

He nodded. "We'll be careful." He looked back at her. "So why didn't you tell them I ran you off the road and crashed into a fence?"

She pulled at the end of her ponytail. "It's not something we need to talk about now or over the phone. You'll have time to explain it to your dad if you want to tell him."

With one last glance at her son, she nodded and headed to the master bedroom. She couldn't even imagine how that room would look in a house that already overwhelmed her.

Her stomach hurt. What was she going to do if this didn't work out? Tyler was hard to read. One minute she felt he wanted to get rid of her, the next he was being all sweet to Bryce and helping them unpack.

And what had she signed up for? She had no medical experience outside of taking care of Bryce. Not only that, she didn't even know how to cook real food. *God, if this is going to work, I really need You. I feel so unprepared for this job. Not to mention Tyler Childress...*

Chapter Three

Tyler set Karly's last box down next to his old closet. He stared at the door to the bathroom, the door that connected the two rooms. A numb spot started spreading through his chest. Simple, walk through the bathroom and into her room.

Carol's room.

It was just a room. A room full of memories from a girl that no longer lived in this world. Gone.

At some point his father should have packed away all her old stuff and gotten it out of the house.

He looked down at the small boy now playing with an old box of Lego pieces he'd found forgotten in the closet. What was he going to do about his former brother-in-law's project? Karly and Bryce obviously needed a safe place to stay. As a single mom with a special needs child, she would be limited in her job opportunities. Especially here in Clear Water.

He crouched down next to the dark-haired boy. "Need some help?"

Bryce tucked a block between his elbow and ribs

in order to attach another with his hand. "Nope. I got it." He dug through the box and picked a yellow brick.

Up close, Tyler noticed the scars on his forehead wrinkled with concentration. He totally understood John and his dad wanting to help these two, but they weren't even from the area. At least, he'd never seen her before. And he'd remember her.

What did anyone really know about Karly? He doubted anyone had thought to run a background check on her. Or vetted her skills. Tyler needed to know that when he went back to Colorado, his father would be in good hands with a professional.

Bryce slumped over, his head landing on the soft rug next to the bed. In a panic, Tyler swept him up and moved as fast as he could to his father's room. "Karly?" He made sure to keep his voice calm and quiet.

"I'm right here." She stepped out of the master bathroom. Her eyes went a bit wider when she saw Bryce in his arms.

Rushing to her, he met her in the middle of the room. "He was playing. Then, without any warning, he just fell over."

Long, graceful fingers gently pushed the fine wisp of hair that had fallen across her son's forehead. The smile and soft chuckle from Karly eased his pounding heart. It couldn't be anything dangerous if she was happy. When she raised her warm eyes to look at him, his breath stopped somewhere around his heart.

He had seen more beautiful women than he could count, but something about Karly Kalakona made the world stand still. Not good. His world needed to keep moving.

He swallowed and looked down at the tiny being in

his arms. He had been around a great deal of children, many of them sick, some even dying, but he'd never actually held them so close. "He's okay?"

"Yeah, he does this when he doesn't get his nap." She shrugged, then leaned in to kiss the small forehead. "With the packing, driving in the storm, the excitement of the plane and meeting you, then a new house and a room of his own, he just crashed once he sat still for a minute." Her hand went to his lower arm. "I should've thought of it before he passed out. Do you want me to take him?"

"No, I've got him. I'll take him back to his room." Making his way down the hall, he sensed Karly close behind him.

"Are you sure it's all right for us to be in these rooms?"

He nodded to the bed. "Like I said earlier, I haven't slept in here for years. Turn down the quilt, and we can tuck him in."

After laying Bryce down, Tyler took a step back, allowing Karly to settle her little man in a bed that looked too big for him.

Turning away from the mother/son moment, he left.

He had to shut off the memories of his sister climbing into his bed while their mother read to them, and sometimes their dad would join them. Every night ended with prayers. He shook his head, clearing out his thoughts. He was such a loser, going down that road. It was a dead end.

"Tyler? Karly?" John's voice called out from the laundry room.

Tyler moved to the kitchen area. "We're here. Putting Bryce to bed." His father was home. *Remember,*

Tyler Childress, nothing is worth upsetting the old man over. He might need God's help with this one, not that he expected any break from that quarter. Some habits were just hard to kill.

He took a breath and looked behind John. "Where's Dad?"

John ran his fingers through his hair. His usual open expression was closed and clouded with something Tyler couldn't read.

"Tyler, this is not going to be easy, but I need you to stay calm and not start any fights."

Stepping into the garage, he saw a frail man struggling to get out of the SUV and leaning heavily on the door. That could not be his tall, robust father.

"Dub, I asked you to wait until I got help." John's easygoing voice sounded exasperated.

"I. Am. Not a…kid."

Tyler heard some other words mumbled, but he couldn't make them out.

"Dad?" That man could not be his father.

He had been on an international flight when Maggie, their neighbor, had called him with the news. She'd told him it was only a small stroke. When his father had gotten on the phone, he hadn't even wanted Tyler to come home. He had sounded almost normal during that conversation. "Is everything okay? Has something else happened?"

Dub grunted and John sighed. "When he gets tired, it's harder for him to speak or move." John gave Dub a pointed look. "It's been a long day, and arguing about everything doesn't help. Rest, Dub, you need to rest."

Turning away from Dub, John pointed to the back

of the ranch vehicle. "Tyler, there's a wheelchair in the back. Can you get it out?"

"Sure." He moved without much thought, the cold concrete on his bare feet keeping him in the present. This weak man could not be his strong, hearty, stubborn father. Was he worse than he had been led to believe? Was he going to die sooner rather than later? He had been told his mom had a year. A year that turned into three months.

He glanced over the backseat as he pulled out the wheelchair. What if his dad didn't get better? Thunder rumbled in the distance, the storm passing on to the east.

"What's...all the...mud?"

"Sorry, Dad. I'll clean it up. Karly's car got stuck. I helped her out. I took off my boots before I went in, so I didn't track mud in the house. I'll get her car washed and the floor cleaned." He wasn't a twelve-year-old anymore, so why did he start acting like one around his father?

"Karly is... She's...she's a good girl." Dub made some growling noises. "Be...be nice."

The subject of the conversation appeared in the doorway. Miss Sunshine herself.

"Welcome home, Mr. Childress." She glanced around the garage, appearing nervous.

This wasn't going to work out—they needed a professional nurse if they were going to get his father healthy again.

Tyler unfolded the chair next to the passenger's door. His father shook his head and pointed, his fingers shaking. "I...ain't sitting...in...that."

John took a deep sigh, but his voice was firm. "Dub,

I don't have much time. I told the girls I would pick them up from 4-H. If you fall, think how embarrassed that will make you feel." He glanced up to Tyler. "The doctor said falling might be the biggest danger to his recovery." He cut his gaze back to Dub. "Remember, we had a deal. If I brought you home early, you'd let Karly help you. That's why she's here. If you don't let her help, she won't have a job."

She came up behind them. "Is there anything else I need to do? All the equipment that was ordered has been placed in his room. I made the bed. Pastor John said you'd be ready to rest and build up your strength."

John held Dub's arm and eased him into the black seat. Tyler just stood there, useless. Once Dub was settled, his son-in-law went back into the vehicle. "Here are some premade dinners Maggie packed for y'all. With moving and getting everyone settled, she was worried you wouldn't have time for cooking. Here, Dub." He placed the bags on Dub's lap. "You can drop this off as you go through the kitchen."

"Tell her thanks." Karly smiled at John before leaning forward. "Ready, Mr. Childress?"

"Karly, Tyler, the occupational therapist is scheduled to be out here for the first home visit Thursday. That was the earliest they could get out here on short notice. I have a folder with all the instructions and tips. Things to look for."

Karly nodded, then smiled at his dad. Bending low, she whispered close to his ear. He mumbled something and she laughed. "I'll take him in to check out his room."

Tyler couldn't form a word. He knew he had words, lots of them, but they had all left.

John spoke again. "Thanks, Karly. Behave, Dub."

"Tyler, the doctor said—" John started, but he couldn't let him finish. How had his dad convinced them to bring him home without a medical professional?

"He can't stay here. He's too weak. We have to get him in assisted living."

"Really?" John's eyebrow shot up. "I wish you well with that move. I couldn't even get him to live with me in the house he grew up in, right here on his ranch." John reached inside the SUV and pulled out a red folder. "Here's all the information the hospital gave us. The contact numbers for the speech therapist, physical therapist and the occupational therapist. You'll need to set up times for the PT and speech. The speech therapist can also help with any eating problems he has."

"We need a professional nurse. Karly can't handle all this medical stuff, and I gotta leave in a few weeks."

"Karly will be fine. Besides, we tried to talk your dad into a home health nurse, but he didn't want a stranger in his house. He agreed to Karly, and I trust her. She also needs this opportunity to get her life on track. It's a win-win for everyone, Tyler." John reached over and gripped Tyler's shoulder. "I know it's hard seeing your dad like this, but you need to rely on your faith. God's in control, Tyler. There's a plan."

Head against the wall, Tyler stared at the ceiling. He couldn't look at John, the pastor his sister had married. His sister's husband, who would soon be married to someone else, to their old neighbor, Lorrie Ann Ortega. "What if I don't like the plan?" Too many of his plans had been ripped apart. "You can't just blindly fumble through life waiting for God to answer prayers.

Dad needs more medical care than Karly can provide. When I talked to Maggie, she said it wasn't that bad."

"For a stroke, he's fortunate, but it's still a stroke. The doctors said there is no reason he won't have a full recovery, but they won't be sure for some time as to permanent damage. If he does fully recover, it could take up to two years. And there's also the broken bones. They just need rest and time to heal."

"Two years? I don't have that kind of time." He pressed his back against the garage wall, sliding down to the floor. He buried his fingers in his damp hair. His grip tightened, wanting to pull all the strands out of his scalp. "Sorry, that was completely selfish. I just want my dad back. What about the horses? The ranch? What am I going to do?"

John sat next to him. "For now we have to take it one day at a time. With work and focus, the doctors believe you can have your dad fully back. The fear of losing him, any part of him, was hard to deal with today. Seeing him was a shock." John put his hand back on Tyler's shoulder. "That stubbornness of his can help him get better. It's also that pride that can get in the way of his recovery. He's not going to change his mind about where he lives or who lives with him. In Isaiah, we're reminded, 'For I hold you by your right hand—I, the Lord your God. And I say to you, "Don't be afraid. I am here to help you."' You're never alone, Tyler. God is here. I'm close by if you need anything." He patted his should a couple of times and stood. "The girls want their uncle over for dinner soon. They miss you." With that, he left.

Tyler's throat was dry. He needed something to drink. How did John manage to stay so positive? His sister's husband had more reasons to doubt the promise of a happy ending than anyone else.

Making his way to the master bedroom, a fog filled his head. In his parents' room, the huge oak four-poster had been replaced with a hospital bed. Karly was tucking the edges around Dub, just like she did for her son. From the soft snores, it appeared his dad had fallen asleep as fast as Bryce.

"Karly?"

She turned with a yelp; her hands went to her chest. "You startled me."

"Sorry." He nodded to his dad. "He's asleep?"

Karly looked at his father with a soft smile. "Yeah, as soon as I got him still he was out."

"We need to talk." He knew he sounded short and he would be better off at least trying to use some of his charm, but right now he was too raw to care.

"Okay." She nodded, her big eyes begging him for something he didn't know if he could deliver.

"I'm going to take a shower first. I'll meet you in the front living room in about fifteen minutes."

She just nodded again.

He steeled himself against any weakness she brought out in him. His father's needs came first.

Chapter Four

After checking on Bryce, Karly went back into her new room. Unpacking again, she hoped this time they would get to stay for longer than a few months. With one hand she gently opened the top dresser drawer to start putting her few belongings away. Pens, hair clips, rings and other random items cluttered the space.

Oh, my. She took a deep breath. Carol's belongings were still in the dressers. She reached down to the bottom drawer and pulled on the handles. The clothes smelled musty. Shutting the drawer, she sighed.

Putting her back to the dresser, she scanned the room. The closet was probably filled with Carol's things, also. She didn't feel right moving anything. When Pastor John had told her to take this room, he must not have known his late wife's teenage life was still here.

"Wow." Tyler stood at the open door. "It looks as if she could walk in any minute." His triceps flexed as he crossed his arms, the loose T-shirt and jeans in contrast to the tension in his stance. Dark blond hair still damp from his shower curled at the base of his neck.

She had no clue what to say. "I'm sorry. I can move my things into your room."

"You mean Bryce's room. No. When Carol left for college, Mom wanted to clean out the room for sewing and crafts, but my dad wouldn't let her. He said it was Carol's room and would always be Carol's room. Then Mom got sick." He walked over to the dresser and picked up a trophy with a horse on the top. "I think it's time to clean it out. Man, this was from seventeen years ago."

He put it down and picked up another relic from his sister's childhood. Silence lingered as he went from one dust-covered item to the next.

She understood loss, but she didn't have a house full of memories. She'd always wanted something of her mom's to hold. Tyler had a whole house of memories of the people he loved. It didn't seem to make it better. "So you lost your mom before Carol's accident?"

His back to her, Tyler nodded and set down a picture frame. "Yeah, eighteen months."

No one had talked about all his losses when they talked about Tyler Childress. They loved to recap all his wildness and scandals. "I'm sorry. Were you still in school?"

This time he turned away from the dresser and walked over to the faded purple-covered bed. "When Mom died I was in Florida, at flight school." He looked around the room. "We could put the old clothes in your bags and donate them. All the other stuff can go in the boxes." He pulled the bedcover up at the corner and folded it over, starting to strip the mattress. "I think the room is ready for a new comforter, also. There are plenty of newer ones in the hall closet."

"Oh, no… Everything can stay."

He raised one eyebrow and grinned at her. "So you like the purple-people-eater theme." He walked to the other side of the bed. "Really, it should have been done years ago. Carol would do it herself if she was here."

"What about her girls? They might want some of their mom's things." Habit stopped her from saying more. She always made a point not to dwell in the past, and she never talked about it. He folded over the stuffed comforter, shoulders slumped as if a heavy weight pushed them down. Biting hard on the inside of her cheek, Karly resisted the urge to put her arms around him. She couldn't go there, but maybe she could ease his pain in another way. At this rate she would be eating the flesh inside her mouth. "Right after my sixth birthday, I lost my mom. The same age Rachel was when her mom died. I dreamed of having something, anything of hers. I don't know anything about her other than she was from Hawaii."

"So your parents are from Hawaii." He placed the purple comforter in the window seat. "That explains your last name." He walked back across the room without looking at her.

"It's my mom's name. A lot of people think I'm Hispanic."

"What about your grandparents, your father? They didn't share anything with you?"

He picked up her bag of clothes and dumped them on the bed. He didn't have much sense of personal space. Another reason to not get emotionally involved.

She rushed to the bed and started gathering the articles he had scattered on the bed. "I can get my clothes."

"I'm using the bags to clean out the old clothes." He paused.

"You could have asked."

He moved to the dresser, pulling open the one with all the trinkets first and closed it just as quick. Reaching for the next drawer, he looked at her. "We need to make room for your clothes." Without looking, Tyler pulled out the next drawer and dumped the contents into the black plastic bag. He did the same with the three long drawers, his jaw locked and his posture tense.

He nodded to the bed. "Go ahead and put your clothes in here and I'll get the ones hanging in the closet."

"Tyler, we don't have to do this now."

He shook his head as he opened the closet door. "It should have been done a long time ago." His face took on a hard look as he pulled clothes off the hangers and crammed them into the now-stuffed trash bag. "My dad goes on as if they're coming back. He won't change anything."

"If you really love someone, I would think it's hard to get rid of their things."

He stopped and looked at her. "You said you didn't have anything of your mother's. How did that happen? How did you lose her?"

She shouldn't have brought it up. He wouldn't understand all the holes in her life. "She just died. One morning Anthony took her to the hospital. I never saw her again. The next day, my stepfather put me in his car and we left town." And from that day forward traveling became the cornerstone of her life. Anything given to her got pawned.

What if her mother had lived? Would they have left Anthony? She couldn't change the past, only her fu-

ture. This was why she never let herself think about it.
She took her eyes off her list and peeked at Tyler from
under her lashes.

Tyler looked at her as if she was crazy. "You left
town with your stepfather? What about your father,
grandparents?"

"No, there was only my stepfather. I don't even know
my bio dad's name and my mother didn't have any family."

With sharp motions, he stuffed the clothes into the
plastic bag and tied off the top. "I can't imagine not
having any family." After grabbing a box off the top
shelf, he turned back to her. "There's still some stuff
in there, but you can hang your clothes for now." Tyler
left the room.

He confused her. She went ahead and put a few of her
things in the dresser. The long skirts she loved wearing
were wrinkled from being jam-packed. Shaking them
out, she took them to the closet and hung them on the
faded pink silk hangers.

Tyler returned, this time with a stack of blankets and
sheets and a smile. "Here you go. I'll take the purple
monster to the laundry room."

Karly went to one of her boxes and dug out a spiral
notebook and her green pen.

Lists—she liked making lists, organizing the things
she had to do, learn and schedule.

She also needed to make a plan in case the worst happened and she lost this job. She'd been afraid of that earlier, when Tyler said they'd needed to talk. *Pray for the
best but prepare for the worst.* So far the worst seemed
to follow her around, but it was time for a change.

Eyes closed, she took a deep breath and centered

herself with God. He put her here. He would give her the tools she needed to make this work.

In the laundry room, Tyler started the washing machine and stuffed the old comforter into the hot water. He rubbed the palms of his hands deep into his eye sockets. How did someone not have any family? There had been days when he thought life would be easier without one. But if he truly thought about it, he wouldn't know who he was without his parents and sister.

He hoped taking Carol's things out of her room wouldn't upset his dad. Why did he want to act as if she would be coming back? The muscles around his chest tightened.

Running both of his hands through his hair, he filled his lungs and let the air out with a harsh sigh. He walked back through his mother's kitchen to his sister's room.

His dad was so stubborn. The whole house looked exactly the same as the day his mom died. Dub Childress was a stubborn fool, but he always got what he wanted. He always won.

Well, Dad, you can't beat death. Mom and Carol are gone and they aren't coming back.

He walked right past Carol's room, his old room, and straight to his dad's. Stepping through the door, he leaned his weight against the door frame. The hard, breathing bump in the hospital bed was his dad. They had a chance to get this right. Tyler wasn't going anywhere until he knew his dad would be walking, talking and laughing again.

His family had been hit hard; first they'd lost his mom, then Carol. When was the last time he'd heard his dad's laugh?

The ranch was too much for him alone. He had to convince the old man to retire, maybe even sell the place. First, he had to make sure his dad had the care he needed.

He walked over to the edge of the practical steel-framed bed and noticed his father had kicked one foot out from under the covers. He had always hated being completely covered, insisting he needed air.

Tyler shook his head. The edge of the bed gave under his weight as he sat next to his dad. He thought of all the nights his dad had tucked him in after saying their nightly prayers. With his left hand he reached for his father's shoulder. He didn't remember the last time he even tried to talk to God. "God, Dub has been a faithful servant to You. He did the best he could with a son that wouldn't listen. Give me a chance to make this right. Amen." He leaned over and kissed the side of his father's forehead. "I'm here, Dad. Together we will get through this and you'll be as good as old."

With a nod to his sleeping father, he turned and made his way to the other problem he had to figure out. Karly and Bryce.

Chapter Five

~~

Stopping at his sister's door, Tyler took in the small changes in the room. Karly sat in the window seat, just like Carol. But the similarity stopped there. Where his sister had charged into the world with a fearless walk, Karly's movement reminded him of a cat his mom had once rescued, slow and cautious, wary of strangers.

With long, graceful fingers she tucked a lose strand behind her ear and wrote in a notebook. He moved to the walls cluttered with Carol's memories and dreams and started taking down a framed collage of photos.

He knew it was irrational, but a drive to get the stuff of his sister's life off the walls and put away had taken hold of him. Why had his dad left this room untouched for so long? It was just another reminder of the conversations that would never happen.

Karly left the window seat. "What are you doing? I thought you said we needed to talk."

"We do, but you don't want to look at pictures of someone else's memories. I was going to put them in the garage for now."

She smiled at him. "I don't mind."

He doubted that, and raised one eyebrow.

"Really." Stepping closer, Karly ran her fingertips over a group of pictures from pep rallies and school dances. "Growing up, I moved a great deal. I love your sister's pictures. Maybe I could put them in an album for her daughters. Have they seen the pictures?"

"I'm sure Rachel did when she was smaller, but I don't think Celeste has ever been in here." He scanned the room. "We should at least pack the mums away."

Her full lips turned up at the corners. He saw a gleam in her dark eyes. "Leave them for now. I really find them fascinating. Where did the idea of a huge flower and tons of ribbon and glitter come from anyway? While we were in Dallas, we went to a homecoming game. The flowers were so pretty with all the bells and glitter. I imagined getting one from a secret admirer. Of course, I never did."

He was getting the feeling her childhood was in stark contrast to his sister's experiences. Or she was just sharing those anecdotes to get his sympathy. Wouldn't be the first time, so why did it seem to be working tonight? "If you don't want to take anything else down, let's go to the living room. We can discuss what you will be doing and what my father needs." With one last look at Carol's celebrations he walked out, not checking to see if his dad's new project followed.

Karly stopped herself from pulling on her earrings. She needed to trust God, not fret over Tyler and his motives. "Sure." She made an effort to smile at him as she picked up her notebook and tucked her pen into the spiral.

There was more to Tyler Childress than the local

gossip talked about. Details missing that would make him a whole person. The way he reacted to Bryce told her he had some experience with kids—kids with differences. But she had a bad habit of seeing the good in the worst guys. Tyler was pulling on all those old heartstrings. The ones she should not trust.

Walking back through the hall, she smiled at the name. The Hall of Mortification, Carol had called it. She couldn't imagine growing up in a town that knew your grandparents, a town where you belonged, even if they remembered all your mistakes.

Plaques lined the walls. She tried to picture the life that collected these awards: homecoming court, rodeo queen, football captain, basketball tournament MVP, valedictorian, even honors for choir and grass judging.

Who knew you could win a state championship by knowing grasses? The wall carried on in an endless line of best of this and that. Carol's name seemed to be on most of them, accomplishments that surpassed her own childhood fantasies. These were the kind of growing-up years she wanted for Bryce. He might not be able to play sports, but once he recovered from the surgeries for his foot, he could have a school and friends and be involved in so many things.

The awards pointed to a bright future that had been cut short. Tyler had lost his mom and sister, but he seemed to forget he still had a dad and a home where he belonged.

Passing through the kitchen, she walked into the front living room. It screamed Texas ranch. The leather sofa and chairs were just the beginning. Everything else was made from wrought iron and antlers, including the huge square coffee table and all the lamps. Area rugs of assorted cowhide warmed the stone floor.

Tyler stood in front of the biggest stone fireplace she had ever seen. Over the rough wood mantel hung a painted portrait. Six people, three generations, all wearing white shirts and jeans, stood in front of the cypress trees that lined the Frio River.

She recognized Dub Childress, younger but with the same stubborn jaw. Next to his older sister, Carol, Tyler looked to be about ten with a roguish grin. The older couple had to be Dub's parents, Tyler's grandparents. All the men in the family had the same look, although Tyler's frame tended to the leaner side.

Tyler's mother, however, surprised her.

In the photo, her lips were pressed closed as if she was fighting laughing out loud, and her eyes gleamed with the same glint Karly had initially seen in Tyler's gaze. Tyler's mother had one hand on her son's shoulder, anchoring him in place. Her other arm was entwined with her husband's, keeping them linked.

It was a portrait that showed a happy family—and what was gone.

All of a sudden the collection of achievements lost their shine. Now Tyler stood alone. She knew how that felt, but was it worse or better to have it all, only to lose it?

Tyler continued to look up at the oil painting. "She was always laughing." He glanced at Karly for the first time since she walked into the room. "Dad would get so mad and ask if she took anything seriously. She would just laugh and tell him life was short and he was too solemn. She would tease him until we were all laughing." He turned back to his family.

Silence lingered.

Karly pulled on the colored beads that hung from her right ear. "So you're a good mix of your parents?"

He turned to her. Surprise stamped on his face. "Why would you say that? We just met."

"True, and most of that time you have been very serious, but I've also seen you make light of situations that could have been tough, like you not fitting in my car or when I got stuck in the mud. Plus the way you work with Bryce—you made a game out of him being scared and gave him your old basketball jersey." One thing life had taught her was to watch the way men reacted to difficult situations. It told a great deal about their character.

He had turned his back to her and continued to stare at the portrait. Maybe that was why God had put her here—not for the job and home for Bryce, but to help Tyler see how much he still had here on the ranch in his life if he wanted it.

She gave herself a mental shake. She could not fall into her fix-him mode. Bryce and their future needed to be her focus.

She sighed. Silence always made her nervous. "By the way, you were great with Bryce. Thank you for not making a big deal of his arm. Most people get uncomfortable and don't know how to act. You made his day when you gave him jobs to do instead of ignoring him. You seem to have experience with kids like him." Okay, she needed to stop talking.

Silence. Again she fought the urge to fill it. Finally he moved to the sofa and nodded to her. She guessed it was an invitation to sit down. Tucking her long skirt under her, she sat. Perched on the edge of the giant leather sofa, she waited for him to talk. Pen in hand, she posed to take notes.

And waited.

His gaze scanned the room before coming back to her. "I have a friend that works in the burn unit at a hospital in Houston. The kids like it when I stop by in my pilot uniform and talk about flying. We've done a few Make-A-Wish trips with the airplanes, too. Many of the kids are missing limbs. Bryce's looks more like a birth defect than an injury."

She nodded. "The doctor said his arm got tangled up in the umbilical cord, so it didn't fully develop. It happened below the elbow, so he has most of his arm. He's also had surgeries on his foot. That's why he limps now, but he will fully recover from that. Bryce's needs won't in any way interfere with my working here."

"Other than your son, what is your medical training?" His intense gaze locked her in place.

Karly made herself breathe. He had every right to ask her that question. Her first instinct was to lie, to say whatever she needed to say to keep this job, this home. She swallowed and clenched her hands.

Her stepfather had taught her to lie so well it was as natural as breathing, and she always had to fight the impulse to give the expected answer, but she had made a vow to tell the truth no matter the consequences. "I don't have any. Pastor John is the one that came to me with the idea that I could help out. I know I can keep the house clean and watch over your father, make sure all the appointments are set up and he gets to them. Help him move around and take care of all the little things."

Leaning forward, Tyler kept his gaze on her. "My dad's health comes first. Do you have a résumé?"

The taste of blood hit her tongue. She relaxed her jaw, but her lungs would not let up. Unable to talk, she shook her head. *A résumé?* She had never needed one before. She didn't have enough education or experience to even fill half a page.

Well, she could fill a page with all her job bouncing, but washing dishes, laundry, serving coffee and cleaning kennels didn't count in the real world. This was it— less than twelve hours and the best opportunity she had ever been given would slip out of her grasp.

A loud knock caused them both to look toward the kitchen. Tyler stood.

"Tyler? Karly?" It was Adrian De La Cruz.

Karly had met the horse trainer at church when she'd joined a single parent group he led. He seemed to like her and support her working for Mr. Childress. And his appearance was putting a stop to a bad conversation. "We're in here, Adrian."

Rounding the corner into the kitchen, she bumped into him. He grabbed her arms to steady her. Adrian was shorter than Tyler, instead eye to eye with her own five-foot-eleven height. He smiled, causing the lines around his golden-brown eyes to deepen. "Whoa, where're you going in such a hurry?" Stepping back, he chuckled and looked over her shoulder. "I'm not used to women running from Hollywood here."

"Hollywood?" She glanced at Tyler.

"That was pretty boy's nickname. No matter what he was doing, he did it in style and loved an audience." Adrian laughed. "Always had the girls all worked up. The rest of us poor slobs had to wait for the fallout."

"That's not how I remember it at all." Tyler held his

hand out to shake, but Adrian pulled Tyler into a hug and slapped him on the back.

"Good to see you back in town. Sorry about your dad, but I know he'll get through this. Too stubborn to do anything else, *que si*?" Flashing her his open, friendly smile, Adrian winked at her. She couldn't help but grin back at her friend. She was already feeling better.

So why didn't she fall for guys like Adrian? The solid, hardworking and easygoing family man. As a single dad, he loved his daughter above all else. She looked at Tyler from under her lashes. She had some kind of messed-up genes when it came to picking men.

"So you've left construction to get back in the horse business? Riding bulls again?" Tyler leaned a hip on the counter and crossed his arms, pulling the cotton shirt tight over his shoulders.

"No bulls for me, but Mia's ten now so I have a bit more freedom, and the construction jobs took a dive a while back. Your father was looking for a part-time trainer, so it was good timing. Are you going to stick around? There are some big shows coming up and we're not sure what we should do. Your dad is pretty hands-on and was still riding."

Tyler sighed. His jaw flexed. "There are a lot of decisions that need to be made, and Dad is in no shape to be running the ranch."

Karly needed to leave the room. She nodded to the men. "Excuse me." She moved in between them, making her way to the refrigerator. Maggie had sent a casserole. It just needed to be heated up.

But standing in front of the stainless-steel, professional-looking gas stove, she had no idea how to start it. What if she blew them up?

"Karly, you're the reason I came over," Adrian called out to her.

Sweat beaded up on her lip and heat crept up her neck. She couldn't even heat up a premade dinner. "Me?" Oh, great, what had happened now?

"Yeah, Pastor John called me." He turned to Tyler. "He said he tried calling you. Anyway. He was going to show Karly around but in the rush to get his girls he forgot. He wanted to make sure you got settled in and that you had the password to the desktop here in the kitchen." He turned behind him and sat at the desk. "He said the computer was yours to use. I'll write it down here. He also said there was a binder with all the accounts and important information in the desk." Opening the cabinet, he pulled out a black binder. "Here it is."

"All of the accounts? He is handing all of his accounts over to her?" Tyler's hard voice was back. He took the binder and started looking through it.

She didn't blame him for the distrust. "I'm sure not all. He said I would be doing the shopping for the house." Pastor John had also encouraged her to use the computer for online classes. He'd thought it was for college classes, for her dreams of being a PT assistant, but he didn't know that she first had to get her high school diploma. She'd tried to finish that using the computer at the library, but their hours were limited and she'd had to refresh every forty-five minutes. Now she could actually start and work on it while Bryce slept or was at school. It was another blessing.

She would not cry. No crying in front of the men. They wouldn't understand.

"Were you going to heat up some dinner?" Tyler asked before turning to Adrian. "You want to stay and eat?"

"No. Thanks. I'm heading home. Anything else you need from me before I leave?"

She forced a laugh before asking what she hoped sounded kind of like a joke. "Are there instructions on turning on the oven? I've never used one like this." Should she admit she really didn't even know how to cook in general?

Without hesitation Adrian moved next to her and turned a few knobs. A pop indicated the burners were lit and ready.

"Gas can be scary if you're used to electric." He reassured her with a friendly smile. "Oh, I almost forgot. The other reason I came over is to make sure you were still coming with me to Uvalde this Sunday."

Tyler narrowed his eyes. "Y'all are dating?"

Karly gave a quick "No."

Adrian laughed. "I wish. She has turned me down every time I've asked. We have a teen-parent meeting every other Sunday."

"Teen-parent meeting?" Tyler raised his eyebrow. "Aren't you a decade past being a teen parent?"

"Feels more like three, sometimes. But we're mentors to the teens. You know, the been-there-done-that sort of thing. It's one of the outreach programs the churches do as a community program. Karly just started and she's already making an impact."

"I'm more like the example of what not to do." She tried to laugh, but there was too much truth to be really funny. She looked at Tyler, not sure if she should take a day off right after starting. She hesitated.

Adrian shook his head. "That's not true." He shrugged. "Anyway, they don't want perfect people. Just someone that understands. Do you want me to pick you up?"

She glanced at her new boss. "Do you need me to stay?"

"No, I'll be here. You kids go off and have fun." Tyler gave a tight smile, arms crossed over his chest.

"So are we on?" Adrian held his arms out.

She nodded and smiled at him. She enjoyed working with the young parents.

"Good." Looking at Tyler, he started backing out of the kitchen. "I'll be back tomorrow, Tyler, and we'll talk about the upcoming shows. Night."

The back door shut and she was alone with Tyler again.

Tyler watched Adrian leave. Karly said they weren't dating, but Adrian seemed a bit territorial. They were both single parents, so it made sense they would be interested in each other. Adrian was a good guy. He had given up his rodeo career in high school to be a parent to his daughter. So why did the thought of them being together bother him?

"We never actually talked about your experience or skills." His voiced sounded grumpy even to his own ears.

She stopped messing with the foil on the casserole pan and looked at him. Her multicolored eyes causing him to think about things he shouldn't be thinking about, like how soft her lips would be against his fingertips if he reached out and touched them.

"Tyler, I'm sure you figured out I don't have the education or experience you expect, but I'm a hard worker.

I care very much for your father, and I'll do whatever needs to be done to help in his recovery."

"What were you doing before this job came up?"

"Serving coffee and lunch at the drugstore. And just so you know, I have had a string of odd jobs like waitressing, cleaning and working at car washes."

"You worked at a car wash? I've never met anyone that actually washed cars for a living." He leaned against the counter opposite of her. "How did you end up in Clear Water? Not exactly a hub for jobs."

She closed her eyes for a moment, then turned and put the pan in the oven. With her back to him she continued, "I moved here with Billy Havender."

"The youngest Havender?" He tried not to sound disgusted, but a Havender? "Is he Bryce's father?"

"No." Now she sounded disgusted. Taking a deep breath she faced him and gripped the edge of the counter. "No." She blinked. "I take it you know the Havenders?"

"Yeah, I went to school with the older ones. I didn't really know Billy. He's the only one that ever left town."

A few strands of long dark hair had slipped out of the ponytail, and she twisted it around her finger before tucking it behind her ear. "He seemed to be the answer to my prayers. He asked me to marry him. I thought it would be good for Bryce…and he promised that I could go back to school and that I would love Clear Water. He had big plans to make money with his brothers."

"They run a delivery business, right?"

She nodded. "That was about a year ago. They sold the trucks. They were going to do guided tours and hunts. But things didn't work out like Billy had wanted. His brothers, well, they…"

"Were lazy drunks who beat each other up more than they worked?"

Her hand covered her mouth. He smiled at her. He hoped it was a gentle kind of smile. Laughing was so much better than watching her trying not to cry.

"It got bad and I tried to leave. Without money, family or friends you can feel trapped. And Bryce had just had surgery on his foot. One night Billy lost it—yelling and throwing things. He had taken my car keys. I didn't know what else to do so I called 9-1-1 on Billy's phone." She picked up a rag from the sink and started wiping the counter.

He just sat there, not sure what to say.

There had to be so many details she was leaving out. "So what happened?"

"The anger between the brothers escalated and started trickling down to Bryce and me. I had to get Bryce out of there even if we had to walk all the way into town. He still had the braces on his legs. We hid in the cedar break around the back of the house. Billy yelled and screamed, looking for us inside the house."

For a moment Karly couldn't go on. *Just give him the facts. Don't get emotional.* "I could hear doors slamming. In a rage he set the house on fire. The Havenders claimed it was an accident, but I couldn't stay there with Bryce." Her hands started shaking, reliving the fear that Bryce would be hurt. "When Officer Torres arrived I ran with Bryce to his car. He got us to a women's shelter." Moving back to the sink, she rinsed out the towel and draped it over the faucet. That was the night she had prayed so hard to God. Prayed for Him to take over and lead her. "The town basically adopted us, helping me find odd jobs. I volunteered with the youth program, and they have been helping with Bryce so I could work. Pastor John and the whole congregation, including your father, gave me a second chance."

She sat on the stool across from him. "I needed a place to live and a steady job. I was thinking of packing my car up and going to San Antonio when Pastor John asked me if I was interested in working for your dad. He said the stroke was mild and I would be responsible for keeping the house and his appointments. That is how I got this job." *Please, God, let Tyler see the truth.* They were safe now. God had protected them. She relaxed her hands and rolled her shoulders.

"I know we look like a charity case, but I'm not telling you this so you'll feel sorry for us. Everyone in town knows the story, and I'm sure there are different takes depending on who you talk to. I want you to know that I'm working on building a solid future for Bryce. I'm going to give this job everything. It's a chance at a real future I can build for my son." She looked down at her hands. Fingers twisted in a knot. A deep breath expanded her chest.

He leaned in closer and touched her. One large hand covered both of her hands.

He could see that look of steel and determination in Karly's gaze. A heavy feeling twisted his heart. If everything she said was the truth, he couldn't imagine the battles she had fought to survive. He had no clue what to say to all that.

Karly saved him from talking. "I'm here to focus on your dad, Bryce and getting my education."

He leaned back and put his hands in his pocket. "Fair enough. My dad is not an easygoing man, as you probably know already. Now that he's recovering from a stroke, I can guarantee you *difficult, stubborn* and *grumpy* are just a few of the words that'll describe him. But from what I saw briefly today, he seems to like you and trust you with the house. But can you handle his ups and downs?"

"Pastor John warned me that Mr. Childress might challenge the most even-tempered person. I'm committed to be here. I won't leave. Well, as long as he doesn't hit or yell at Bryce." She smiled with a feisty spark in her eyes. "Or burn the house down. If he tries to set the house on fire, I'm gone."

Oh, so she had a dark sense of humor. "Fair enough. So we have a deal?" Tyler could see why John and his dad wanted to help her. His dad thought women were like Tyler's mom and sister, and he would even believe them over his own son. But in Tyler's experience, most women did whatever it took to get ahead—lie, steal or cheat.

He held out his hand to shake on it. "One last thing." Soft fingers wrapped around his hand.

"Yes?" She looked at him with absolute seriousness.

"Don't lie to or in any way use my father. You'll be gone, and John will have to find you a new place to live. Got it?"

"Got it."

Chapter Six

"Oh, no, no, no, no." The rice boiled over the side, causing hissing and popping from the burners. She had headed to the kitchen this morning with plans of starting breakfast. After her talk with Tyler last night, she wasn't sure if she should be worried or reassured that she was doing the right thing. She tested some of the rice. It was still hard. She reduced the heat.

She remembered her mother making it with sugar and butter. How to make rice was one of the things she never got to learn from her mom. Rice seemed so simple and a good breakfast for Dub.

That plan had gone south rather quickly. She stirred the foaming mess only to discover rice stuck to the bottom. The back door opened and closed. Male voices reached the kitchen before the men appeared. Karly looked around frantically.

Did they eat breakfast here before going to work? Her stomach dropped. Tyler entered the kitchen and winked at her before making his way to the refrigerator. Well, at least he seemed to be in a good mood.

"Mornin', Karly." Jefferson, Dub's lead trainer and

ranch foreman, nodded at her as he placed his hat on the counter. "Good seeing you here."

"Thanks, sorry about not having breakfast ready." Maybe they wouldn't notice the mess and the rice would be fine. "I'll need to go to the mercantile to restock the fridge."

"You might want to be careful. We had rain all night, and the crossings are running high."

"I'll take you in the ranch truck." Tyler pulled something wrapped in white paper from the bottom freezer and stuck it in the microwave.

Adrian came in through the garage door. "Man, it's a mess out there. Some of the roads have been washed out, and it looks like we might get more rain." He paused and smiled at Karly. "So where's the pancakes and sausage?"

Jefferson nodded. "We usually have eggs, bacon and potatoes. I don't smell any coffee, either. Where's the coffee?"

"And don't forget the homemade cinnamon rolls. Connie always had fresh ones ready for us every morning." Adrian had never looked so serious. "So mean of Connie to up and move to Dallas after taking care of us for the past six years."

Coffee? Cinnamon rolls? She was in over her head. A cold sweat broke out over her skin. She took a deep breath and reminded herself she could learn to do this. They were staring at her, waiting.

Coffee. She'd learned to make it at the diner. She looked for the pot. In her panic she really couldn't see anything. She'd thought she would be helping Dub around the house. He was weaker than she thought, and now a roomful of men were looking at her, expecting her to know what she was doing.

Left unattended, the rice boiled over again. This time the fire alarm went off.

"Guys, that's enough, leave her alone." Tyler's voice stopped her downward spiral. He laughed as he waved a towel under the alarm. Jefferson took the rice off the burner and flipped the fan on.

Was Tyler laughing at her? She swallowed and glanced at the men. They were all laughing. A hand on her shoulder caused her to jump. It was Tyler. She took a step back, putting distance between them. The room went silent.

"Karly, they're just teasing you." He moved into the pantry. "Adrian, make the coffee. I'll cut up potatoes. Karly, if you would start the sausage, we can make breakfast tacos."

"Momma, what's wrong?" Peeking around the edge of the archway from the family room was Bryce, his dark hair sticking up in every direction. The fear in his eyes twisted her gut. The sweet voice sounded small and unsure.

She rushed to her son and picked him up. "Everything is all right, sweetheart. I lost track of the rice." She kissed him on the cheek and tried to smooth the mess on his head. "So sorry about all the noise. I was making breakfast."

"You tried to make rice again?" If his face wasn't so cute, she'd be offended.

Jefferson pulled a skillet out from under the island. "I used to eat rice for breakfast growing up. My mom put sugar, butter and cinnamon in it."

"Hey, why don't you get the little man ready for the

day?" Tyler stood at the island with a knife in one hand and a potato in the other. "We'll take care of breakfast."

"Okay. I'll check on Mr. Childress again. I'm sure all the racket woke him up," With Bryce on her hip, she turned to leave the kitchen.

"Momma, why are there so many people in our new house?" His voice so low she could barely hear him. He was back to the shy, uncertain boy. "Do they all live here?"

"No, they work on the ranch. They just came to check on us our first day." Or check up. It seemed Tyler wasn't the only one that had doubts about her abilities. Pastor Levi had told her she wouldn't have to feed the crew.

A thumping on the walls in the hallway got everyone's attention. "Dad?" Tyler ran past her, the first to move to the noise.

Karly followed and found Dub Childress on the floor sitting against the wall.

He growled at his son. "I don't need an…an aud… people staring at me."

She turned to look at the men behind her. Jefferson nodded and headed back to the kitchen. Adrian reached for Bryce. "Come on, Cowboy, let's get breakfast made." Her son slid to the floor and looked at her. With a nod she reassured him it was all right.

"Dad, let me take you back to your room. You know you can't leave the bed without your walker. I can help you clean up and comb your hair."

"I don't need a walker or a lousy nursemaid, boy." Dub struggled to stand without putting any weight on his broken arm and shoulder.

"Then, I guess I'll fire Karly so she can find another job." He stood over his dad with his arms crossed.

Karly's heart thumped against her rib cage. Were they back to her not being good enough?

"You can't fire Kar-Karly." Dub struggled to stand. Tyler just stood there and watched him.

She moved in to help. "Tyler?" What was he doing?

"Then, are you going to let her do her job? Because if you're not, we can save the money."

She gave her arm to the elder Childress and tried to not glare at Tyler. Why was he being such a jerk to his dad?

"No. She stays. Kar-Karly, can you get my wa-walker?" He leaned all his weight on the wall, but he was standing.

She patted him on the good arm. "Call me Kar." She looked at Tyler. "I'll take care of him, and we'll join you in the kitchen."

"Okay." He put his hand on his father's shoulder. "Dad, please don't be stupid because of pride. You're all the family I have now. We need to get you back one hundred percent, but it's going to take time."

Dub stared at the other wall, not looking at his son. He placed his shaking hand over Tyler's and patted it a couple of times, the only indication he heard a word from the younger Childress.

She left them alone and retrieved the walker. By the time she got back, Dub stood alone. He tried to smile at her. His clear blue eyes glistened with moisture, but his jaw remained firm. Helping him move forward, she stayed next to him. "Thank you for this opportunity, Mr. Childress."

He nodded. "Ty's got a good heart. Needs a good woman to help him grow up."

She laughed, ignoring the flip in her gut at the

thought of being Tyler Childress's woman. "I think he's grown up just fine. I hope you're not playing matchmaker because I'm not on the market, and your son has a complete different taste in women—he's not into the homeless single-mom type."

"His type?" He stuck out his tongue and made a gagging sound. "Needs someone like you—strong, caring."

Now he was going to make her cry. "Thank you for the kind words, but my card is full already with two marvelous males. Let's get you ready for the day."

When Tyler walked back into the kitchen, the image of Karly gently helping his grumpy dad filled his thoughts. He stopped at the table before he even noticed his brother-in-law, John, had joined the men. The smell of burned rice was being pushed out by the sizzling breakfast sausage and coffee. He would never admit to the guys that he hated drinking coffee, but the smell always brought him home. His dad drank two pots a day, all year long.

The window over the sink was open, and he could hear the rain hitting the metal roof.

Bryce sat on the counter next to the stove with a pair of tongs in his hands. He flipped a tortilla on the cast-iron griddle and watched it puff up before turning it to the other side.

Tyler didn't think Karly would be happy. "I'm not sure if your mom would be cool with you that close to the burners."

John had arrived and stood close to Bryce with a mug of coffee in his hand. "Morning, Tyler. I said the same thing but got outvoted."

"He's a ranch cowhand now and has to do his share, right, Cowboy?" Jefferson ruffled the kid's crazy bed hair.

"It was Jefferson's idea." Adrian shrugged. "You can tell he doesn't have kids yet."

"I can help!" Bryce threw the next one on the burner and tossed the cooked one in the tortilla warmer before covering it with a towel. "Mom used the microwave to heat them up. They don't get puffy and brown when you do that."

Tyler thought she might have a fit if she saw Bryce sitting so close to the flames and hot grease. He decided to intervene, grabbing the tyke by the waist to move him away from the burners. "You did a great job. So you already have a nickname, Cowboy?"

Some of the sausage popped out of its frying pan. "Ouch!" Bryce yelled as the grease hit his short arm.

"What happened?" With perfect timing, Karly rushed into the room and grabbed her son. "Tyler, what are you doing with my son next to a hot stove?"

He closed his eyes and groaned. Looking around at the other men, he raised his eyebrows and held out his hand palm up. His dad shook his head as he settled into a chair at the table. All he got from the peanut gallery was a bunch of smirking faces before they all of a sudden needed long drinks from their coffee.

He tried to reassure Karly. "It's just a tiny flick of grease."

She glared. He sighed.

"Momma, I'm fine. I helped cook the tortillas the real cowboy way."

She turned on the water and checked his whole arm, pushing the T-shirt all the way to his shoulder.

"Momma, it doesn't even hurt."

"You're okay this time, but you're too young to be working around a hot burner."

Adrian started filling the tortillas with the potato and sausage mixture. "I'll take some for later. I need to get back to the barns." Obviously familiar with the kitchen, he pulled some foil out from under the counter and wrapped a few tacos up tightly. "Welcome to the ranch, Karly, and you, too, Cowboy. When you have time you'll have to come out and see the horses. We have a couple you can even ride. Thanks for the tacos and coffee."

"Here, let me top off your coffee before you go." Karly took the coffeepot across the room and gave Adrian one of her beautiful smiles as he thanked her and left the house.

John made a stack of breakfast tacos and set them on the table. "Are you going to join us, Jefferson, or are you leaving us for the horses, too?"

"Someone has to get the work done around here." The lead trainer laughed and snatched a couple of the tacos from Tyler's plate. "I'll be back later to talk about our plans for the upcoming shows and auction. We can set a new schedule that works for you, Dub." He looked at John for an answer. Tyler gritted his teeth, reminding himself it was natural for them to look to his brother-in-law, since he lived here on the property. Almost ten years had slipped past since Tyler had gone to the barns.

Nodding, John smiled at Dub. "We'll figure out the best time and get back on a schedule." He stood and shook Jefferson's hand. "Thanks for holding down the fort. Hope to see you Sunday."

"Maybe," Jefferson muttered. With a wave he headed out through the family room.

Karly stopped him. "Do you want to take some coffee to go?"

"I'm good. We've got more in the barn."

"I want to go riding!" Bryce stood in his chair.

"Bumper stays in the seat." She pointed to his bottom. "We'll talk about visiting the horses later. Your tortillas are good. Here, eat them before they get cold."

"So, Dub, now that we have Tyler and Karly here, we need to talk expectations and schedules." John took a healthy bite of the soft taco.

"Are you hungry, Dub? I made some rice." Karly stood.

"Uh, it didn't make it." Tyler made a face, his nose wrinkled. "Sorry."

"Here. You should be able to eat this." John put a small bowl of oatmeal in front of Dub. With his right arm in a cast up to his shoulder, he couldn't use it. He grabbed the spoon with his left hand but dropped it. He tried again. This time he got the hot cereal on it but it all fell off before he could get it to his month. With an angry grunt he threw the spoon down. Tyler closed his eyes. His father was going to make this difficult.

Karly bit hard on her bottom lip. Should she offer to help? Her gut told her Dub would not appreciate the assistance.

Bryce moved to the empty chair on Dub's left side. "I only have one hand to use, and it can be hard to do things. My mom said it took me twice as long to learn to eat because I'm right-handed." He held up his short arm. "But I don't have a right hand, so I have to use my left. It takes practice, and sometimes I drop things. That's okay because I'm working hard."

Comforting warmth filled Karly. She had said those words to Bryce so many times. To hear him repeat them to Dub made her throat a bit dry.

Tyler picked up his taco with his left hand, keeping his right under the table. He laughed when most of his filling fell out of the bottom. "I never realized I relied on both hands to eat." He tried to get the egg and sausage back into the flat tortilla. He folded it back over and tried to pick it up again.

"Mr. Tyler, if you use your little finger to hold the bottom rolled up, the good stuff won't fall out." Bryce demonstrated and the men at the table followed his example. Karly wanted to take a picture to capture the memory.

From the corner of her eye, she watched Dub's reaction. With the attention off him, he tried again. After a few more tries, he managed to take a bite. She noticed John and Tyler stayed focused on Bryce and their own plates of food, avoiding any eye contact with Dub.

"John, would you like some more coffee?" If nothing else, she could serve coffee.

"That would be great. Thanks, Karly." John held up his mug and nodded to her.

"Tyler, do you want more?"

"No, no. I'm good."

Dub laughed at something Bryce said, and John put another taco on Bryce's plate.

Tyler got up and disappeared into the walk-in pantry with his cup.

"I'm going to school today?" Bryce looked at her with anticipation sparkling in his eyes.

Was he really ready? What if he didn't make the friends he thought he would make? What if the other kids made fun of him and he had to sit alone on the playground and cafeteria?

John picked up the empty plates. "I promised Dub I would keep him updated on our men's Bible study. Why don't y'all take Bryce up to the school and talk to them about getting him registered. You can get some groceries, and when you get back we can set that schedule. Karly, we don't expect you to be here twenty-four hours a day."

"Oh, I don't have anywhere else to be and I'm so blessed to be able to live in this beautiful home. Whatever you need, just let me know."

Tyler came out of the pantry, the steaming mug in his left hand. He took a sip from the cup that was empty just a little bit ago. That was weird. Why didn't he want her to serve his coffee?

"This is much harder than I thought it would be," Dub winked at her son. "Bryce, you are a very gifted boy."

"Oh, no. I just practice a lot. You can do it, too, Mr. Childress, it just takes practice. And sometimes you want to cuss, but my mom won't let me. Since you're a grown-up, I guess you can if you want." He looked at Pastor John and turned red. "You should never cuss."

Dub grabbed Bryce's shoulder. "You are one wise cowboy. So glad you're here."

John ruffled his hair, and Bryce had the biggest smile on his face.

Hope surged through her. This would work. She could do this and give Bryce the kind of life she'd never had, never even knew could be real.

Now, if they could stay here long enough for her to get her high school degree and become a physical therapist assistant… She could actually be in control of her own future, no longer living out of her car. She could have a real home and a real life. Away from the roads her stepfather's lies had put her down.

Sometimes she played with the idea of going back down those roads on an apology tour. It wouldn't serve any purpose, though. Most of the people they'd conned hadn't even known they had been swindled. She had to remember God's promise. *For by grace you have been saved through faith. And this is not your own doing; it is the gift of God.*

Chapter Seven

Tyler had been home for five days, and a steady routine had been set up. The different therapists had been
out to visit his dad, and Karly seemed to be able to keep
it all organized and even got his dad to cooperate. He
and Jefferson had hired a couple of local kids to help
around the ranch, mainly to put miles on the horses and
rebuild some damaged fences.

The floods had messed up the roads, and Tyler had
taken charge of seeing them repaired. Karly's car was
too low to safely make the crossing. Somehow he ended
up driving Karly and Bryce into town every day and
taking her when Bryce was done with school for the day.

The one thing he had not done was walk through the
barn doors. He knew she was there, but his guilt still
ate at him. Her beautiful legs would be scared, legs that
used to move with unbelievable quickness. Her days of
cutting and winning were over because of a stupid dare.

All he wanted to do was go back to Denver, back
to flying, back to the life he had created for himself.
This morning, like all the others, Karly started gathering plates off the table. She scraped the leftover eggs

onto one dish. There was something about her simple meals he liked. He looked at his dad, then John. John shrugged. "Dub, you won't be able to make it to the Houston show. You have to focus on getting better and not rushing."

Tyler ground his back teeth. The same argument about Dub going to Houston had happened at least twelve times in the past five days. It started every morning over breakfast. If not for Karly's calming presence he was sure it would have been worse.

This would be a perfect time for his dad to look at retirement. No way should he be getting back on a horse. "John, I took four weeks off work. Do you think I'll need more?" He looked across the table at his father. Dad did appear a bit stronger this morning, but he could barely feed himself. "Maybe I could switch to domestic flights and stay here in between trips."

Dub's scowl deepened. "I… I'm fine. Karly and Bryce are gr…good. You do not need to stay."

Tyler glanced at Karly, who had joined them at the table. But her innocent appearance didn't mean he'd lost his reservations about her being in complete control of his dad and the house accounts.

When he'd asked Sheriff Johnson about getting a background check done, everyone had seemed offended that he would question Karly's integrity. Everyone liked her and defended her. There was some unwritten rule about saying anything bad about her. But she'd be the perfect con artist if she wanted to make easy money.

Even worse, Adrian and John had already pulled him aside at different times and warned him about messing with her, as if they believed the rumors from his high school days. They both knew him better. At least, he'd thought they did.

Tyler pulled his attention back to his dad. Where in the argument were they? Oh, yeah. He sighed. It was time to drop the *R* word. "It's not about me, Dad. What about retirement? Maybe this is a good time to evaluate the ranch and how to go forward."

"Ret…ret…ugh. The ranch? What do you mean, Ty?" A heavy frown pulled on his dad's brow.

Karly stood up. "Excuse us. We need to get ready for the day. Come on, Bryce."

"Yes, ma'am." As Karly's son left the room, each of the men said goodbye to him,

With them gone, Tyler took a deep breath and went back to the conversation. "Dad, we have to be realistic. What if you have another stroke? We could use this time to look at the ranch's future. I have no interest in living here or being burdened with the running of a ranch this size. You need to focus on your health."

"Well, if that's the way you feel, it's good I gave John…the power of attorney." His dad glared at him. "John has final say on any decisions, and I'm leaving his girls the ranch."

Tyler couldn't breathe, couldn't move his arms.

He'd never seen this coming—to be cut out of the will. Someone had reached into his chest and twisted all his internal organs. "You really hate me that much?"

His dad sat back, shaking his head. "Nothin' to do with that. You would sell the ranch the minute I couldn't stop you."

"But I'm your son. You already gave the old ranch house to him." He flung a hand at John. "He's marrying Lorrie Ann Ortega." He looked over at John, the perfect son Dub hadn't been given by birth. He didn't appear any happier about that news than Tyler. "Did you know?"

John shook his head. "I knew he gave me power of attorney in case he got worse and couldn't make decisions, but I didn't know about the ranch. Dub, I don't think this is a good idea."

"It's good." He looked back at Tyler. "Son, you didn't want to ranch or anything to do with the horses after you destroyed your mare." He paused and took some deep breaths. "Carol loved this ranch. She wanted her chil…kids to grow up here." Another pause. "She had de…de…was moving home when she died."

"What?" He turned back to John. "You had decided to move here before Carol's accident?"

John's face lost all color. He ignored Tyler, his gaze locked on Dub's. "You knew she was leaving me?"

Tyler's world shifted under his feet. "Carol was divorcing John?" He turned to his father. "And you still gave him Granddad's house." He wanted to hit something or someone. Fists clenched, he stood, causing the chair to scrape across the floor. He paced to the far end of the kitchen and back. Carol had been more than his sister. They'd been best friends. Or so he'd thought. All the anger from losing her swelled and pushed at his head, threatening to break him.

"She was leaving you, and had never even called me?" When had they grown so far apart?

"Tyler."

He ignored John. Moving to the pantry door, he thought about taking off. Going to the airport and never looking back.

John moved in front of him, trying to make eye contact. Tyler bit down hard until his jaw hurt. He wanted to hit John. Fists thrust into his pockets, he turned away from the pastor. A man that had hurt his sister. Tyler waited for a few seconds before facing him again. "What did you do to her? Why was she leaving you? She loved you so much."

John ran his hand over his face. "My music career had taken over. I'd lost focus. She was setting me straight." He took a step closer. "Tyler, your grandparents' house belongs to the girls, your nieces, not me."

That didn't help. Blood pounded through Tyler's veins, slamming into his ears. "How can you do it? How can you live knowing you hurt her?"

"I lived with the guilt for over five years. Why her and not me? She was the better parent, the better partner, the better everything. I don't understand, but I have faith that we are all held in the hands of God."

"You don't deserve to be happy." His legs felt numb. "She's gone, and now you're guilt-free and ready to move on and love again." Tyler slammed his clenched fist into his own chest. "My sister is still dead."

"Ty, there is a part of my heart that will always belong to Carol. She will forever be a huge part of my life, of the man I am today. I can't park my car there. She is the mother of our girls. I have to move forward for the sake of Rachel and Celeste if nothing else. To live out the purpose God has for me." His voice dropped. "Why did Carol die so young?" Sadness masked his face. "In this lifetime we'll never understand, but I have faith that God is in control of all our days."

All Tyler wanted to do was scream at the unfairness of it all and tackle John. Yeah, take him to the ground in a good old-fashioned fistfight, just like he did back in high school when he got mad. The small part of his rational brain thought to keep him from making the situation worse. The last thing he needed to do was take down the town's beloved pastor.

"Boy, settle down. She wasn't divorcing him." Dub tried to stand.

John rushed to his side. "Dub, it's okay. Tyler just got some shocking news."

"She was coming to the ranch…to wait for him." He looked at his son-in-law, grief and love embedded in every line on his face. "She didn't know what to do. I'm so sorry. I told her to come home…and you would follow. It's all my fault."

"No, we all make our own choices." John patted Dub's hand, a sad smile on his face. "I did follow her immediately. You never said anything, so I didn't think anyone knew. But this isn't about me. Tyler's upset and needs—"

Dub took his eyes off the perfect son and turned back to Tyler. "Those are Carol's babies, your nieces. They have every right to live on this land. It's what she wanted. As far as I'm concerned, they'll inherit the whole thing." Hard coughs rattled Dub's chest.

Fear squeezed Tyler's lungs. With a new urgency, he moved to the other side of his father, kneeling. He laid his hand on the old rancher's back. "Dad, I'm sorry. I promised myself I wouldn't get in a fight with you." He tried to laugh. It sounded weak even to his own ears. "Just relax."

"Death doesn't scare me, boy. At this point I have more people I love in heaven than I do here on earth. I'm not going to stop living out of fear of dying."

"Thanks, Dad. That makes me feel better." With that

bit of sarcasm, Tyler sat back on his heels and pressed the palm of his hand against his forehead. Pushing his hair back with his fingers, he looked at his dad, trying to figure out where he went wrong. How had they ended up hurting each other again?

The wretched ranch. To him it was a heavy stone, too full of memories, but to his dad it was everything.

"Now, see, that's the problem, son. You are too sensitive. I love you. You just don't need me anymore." One last weak cough, and then he turned to John. "Would you mind getting my Bible? It's by my bedside."

With a warning glance at Tyler, John left the room. That hurt. What did he think he was going to do, start yelling again?

"Son, you're not alone. You have John and the girls."

How did he tell his dad it hurt too much to be around the girls? It hurt to be around the barn and remember all the stupid things he couldn't undo or change.

"They need to know their uncle. You have memories of their mom no one else can share with them."

Tyler bit his lips. His chest burned. Managing a nod, he started to stand. He needed to get away and breathe. He had been so busy at the ranch he hadn't even gone to the airport. "I need to go check the airplane for damage."

"Damage?"

With a groan Tyler hung his head. He hadn't told his dad about his spectacular arrival.

"With the storm, some cattle were loose on the county airport and I couldn't land on the airstrip. The upper level pressure was coming in too fast. I was shooting for the Kirkpatrick pasture, but Karly was on the road and the airplane coming in low scared her."

He took a breath. "Anyway, she panicked, ran off the road and I ended up in Henry's fence."

"Her car?"

"It got stuck but it's good. She's the one who brought me here."

"The fence?"

"I called Henry and told him. I already got the supplies ordered at Bergmann's Lumber."

"Karly is a real nice girl. She got in some trouble with that youngest Havender boy, but she's always volunteering at the church. Just like your mother and Carol."

He sat and narrowed his eyes. "Dad, please tell me you're not trying to set me up. She's a single mother."

"She's a hardworking one that will do anything for her son. She has a strong faith in the Lord. Family is im-im…key to her, and she told me she always dreamed of living in the country being part of a com…small town."

"So she reminds you of Mom and Carol. Does that make her girlfriend material?"

Dub sighed the heavy what-am-I-going-to-do-with-you kind of sigh. "It makes her a life kind of girl."

"Really, Dad? You don't think I'm responsible enough to make decisions about the ranch, but you want me to go out with this perfect female with a child?"

"You are a good man, Ty. You just need—"

"To grow up and find a good Christian woman." He finished his father's often-said words.

"You are the last Childress." Dub slammed his fist on the tabletop. "I want to see you married with children before I die. I need to let your mom know you'll be fine."

"Emotional blackmail. Nice, Dad." He sighed, standing and looking out the window. From there, he could see the barns. Adrian had one of the yearlings in the round pen. "You have never liked any of my girlfriends."

"I don't think *you* liked any of your girlfriends. You never dated anyone of them longer than three months."

"I don't find Ms. Karly attractive. I don't want to date her. I definitely don't want to marry her. I'm not even sure I trust her to be working here, let alone live in the house."

A noise at the entryway caused him to turn. He closed his eyes and suppressed a groan.

John and Karly stood there. Her mouth was slightly opened, and with her dark hair in a ponytail he could see the tops of her ears turning red. John had one eyebrow raised as if to say, *I told you to behave.*

Karly gave Dub a stiff smile, refusing to look at Tyler. "We just got off the phone with the therapist." She pointed to John. "They called to tell me they needed to move your visit to the morning." She moved next to Dub. "I told them that was fine. We'd be here."

Tyler hated it when his temper got the best of him, which tended to only happen around dear Dad. Now he had to apologize. Would it be too immature of him to blame his father?

He snorted at his own thought. Turning to Karly, he found her looking at him with hurt in her eyes.

He gave her his best smile. "Are you ready to go to town?" She moved to help his father, acting as if she didn't hear him.

He was fascinated by the tenderness and strength in her every move. How did he apologize without telling her the truth? There was no way he could tell her she was the kind of beautiful that was real. The kind a man imagined seeing every morning. He couldn't go there. It was too dangerous.

Really, she was too attractive and real for his peace of mind.

He didn't want to see Karly as a woman he could date. She needed a man that wanted to stay in one place and be part of this tiny, nosy community. Or else she was just like all the other women he'd dated—and it came down to how much he was worth moneywise. He wasn't staying. From the time he was eighteen, all he'd dreamed about was leaving. Why did his father insist he should marry a girl that wanted to live here when all he wanted was to be somewhere else? His father didn't get him; he hadn't in over ten years. The old man was crazy.

"Tyler?" Dub's rough voice pulled him out of his stupid coil of self-pity. "Son, don't be so rude. We were talking to you."

Flexing his jaw, he looked up from the wooden floorboards. "Sorry."

"You should take Kar to town." His father's steel-blue gaze glared at him.

Hadn't he just offered to take her? What had he missed? He looked back at Karly.

"I can take you to town to drop Bryce at school. I told Bryce I'd take him to see the airplanes."

"Thank you for the offer, but it hasn't rained since I arrived, and the water is down. I don't want to be a bother. I'll take my car." She picked up empty coffee cups and carried them to the sink.

"It's not so much the high water as it is the roads

and crossing. Your car might not make it. Let me take y'all to town."

She started shaking her head.

He swallowed a chunk of his pride. "I'm sorry about what I—"

She waved her hand at him. "Don't worry about it."

Dub coughed. When she rushed over to him, he held up his hand, coughed a couple more times, then laid his hand on her arm. "Let Ty take you to town in the ranch truck. I'll feel better."

She glanced at him, then over to John, who nodded. Tyler rolled his eyes. It was just a trip to town. "Are you and Cowboy ready?"

Nodding, she turned. "Let me get him."

His father sat back and gave John a lopsided smile. Somehow he had lost another round to his dad. Why did he even bother?

Chapter Eight

During the morning trip to school, Bryce had chatted all the way. Other than that, the easy conversations she and Tyler had developed over the week disappeared. Today he hadn't come in for lunch or for a visit with his dad.

Karly rubbed the worn leather key chain between her thumb and index finger. Sometimes the action soothed her. Not this afternoon.

He didn't like her at all. His charm was a lie, like every other man she had ever been attracted to. *Slow learner* might be the biggest understatement regarding her. He wanted her gone.

Dear Lord, remove this fear. I know I'm in Your hands, but it's so hard to relax and not worry.

Tyler's rumbling voice from the driver's side drew her out of her thoughts. "Dad makes me so angry sometimes. I really need to apologize about what I said. I didn't mean—"

"Tyler, it's okay. I haven't given it another thought. I'm not interested in you, either. I do want you to know I really care for Dub, and I wouldn't do anything to hurt him. You love him and you worry about him. I get that. That's what good families do. It's okay. Believe me, I have thick skin."

She rested her forehead on the window and started playing with a hoop earring.

He cleared his throat. "You shouldn't have to have thick skin." He eased the big truck into the main highway. "You seem anxious about something. Relax. If you're not worried about my opinion of you, then it must be Bryce. He'll be excited today, the same as he was the past three days. You left him with Mrs. Farris, and she's a great teacher."

She snorted and rolled her eyes. He acted as if he knew her. "Yes, I worry about Bryce." Tyler's life consisted of grand adventures with safety nets. He couldn't understand. "He refused to wear the prosthesis for his arm. Physically he's behind in his development from kids his own age. I'm not sure he's ready for school." Even she heard the whining in her voice. With a sigh, she closed her eyes and prayed again. Turning her worries over to God didn't come easy for her.

"He's more than ready. You're the one not ready to leave Bryce." His left hand lay over the top of the steering wheel while his right arm relaxed across the back of the bench seat. "He'll be fine. Probably better than fine, he'll have another great day and be excited to tell you about it when we pick him up."

He was probably right. She scooted closer to the door, as far from him as possible. Even his hands were perfect—long fingers, the bones at his wrist slightly protruding, looking all masculine. It irritated her.

She sighed. Her reaction to him was what really irritated her. She was finished with relationships, finished with being Cinderella to every prince that came along and promised a happy ending if she just followed him. Happy endings were fantasies and charm was overrated.

He studied the road for a while. The sound of the diesel engine filled the silence in the cab as the rain-drenched countryside slipped past them. He looked back at her with his eyes narrowed in thought, maybe even suspicion, as though he was trying to figure her out. "Are you willing to get your hands dirty?"

Fear froze her stomach. Did he know about her past with her stepfather? She had told the counselors she felt dirty, as if she couldn't get her hands clean, no matter how hard she worked to be good. Pastor John told her she was new and clean with God, but he didn't know everything, and it was hard to believe all she had to do was ask for forgiveness. Would all the people they hurt agree that she was new and clean?

She looked at her own hands, twisted in her lap. Anthony was in her past. Her stepfather could no longer use her; he was out of her life. And she needed to stop being consumed by the guilt, a guilt that led her to overanalyze the simplest of statements. Lifting her head and taking a deep breath, she looked over at Tyler.

Prayer. She would be better off in constant prayer instead of focusing on fear.

After a long moment of silence, Tyler started talking again. "Jake asked me to help with building the village for the Christmas pageant. He said they're not sure yet where they're going to have it this year. It would be good for Bryce. I'm picking up supplies today for Jake. It can be dirty work, recreating Bethlehem."

"Okay." Not that he actually asked her permission. She sighed. Just going along didn't make her weak, she reassured herself. The people pleaser that lived in her heart always got her in trouble.

Tyler pulled off Main Street and parked behind the two-story limestone Bergmann's Lumber building. It had been years since he had walked through the back door at Bergmann's. When he was a kid, the selection of nails alone would keep him entertained while his father picked up supplies for the ranch. Old Mr. Bergmann always had butterscotch candies on the counter. Even though the former owner had passed on, the bowl full of candies still sat on the old wooden counter. Tyler popped one in his mouth. He handed another to Karly. Stan, along with two of his four daughters, ran the store now.

A golden Lab met them, sniffing their hands and its tail wagging.

"Well, I heard you had come back to town!" Samantha Bergmann walked from the power tools. "How's the world treatin' you? How's your dad? Hi, Karly." Sam gave Karly a hug before leaning against the counter.

"He's as stubborn as ever."

Sam laughed. "Good, then, he'll be back in the store soon. Miss him. Jake said you'd be swinging by to get the Christmas pageant materials."

"I'll let Dad know you said hi. Yes, I have the truck in the back."

She reached through the handmade soap display and grabbed a walkie-talkie. "Joaquin, Childress is here to pick up the Bethlehem stuff. Over."

A crackling sound came over the speaker. "The truck kind of told me that, but thanks." The voice speaking back sounded heavy with sarcasm.

She rolled her eyes. "You know I can fire you. Over."

"Try it. Ooover."

"He drives me crazy."

Tyler had to chuckle. "Joaquin Alvarez? He still riding bulls?"

"Not this month, but I'm sure he'll go back. He always does. I don't know why Daddy has to hire him every time he comes back to town with some broken bone."

Tyler grinned. "Do I owe you anything?"

She went to the other side of the counter and flipped through a notebook.

"So you've gone high tech?"

She laughed. "Dad doesn't trust what he calls 'those internet things.' Dani has a computer upstairs, but Dad refuses to use it. He says he's never lost a notebook. Here it is. There is a balance of eighty dollars. I was told to send it to the church."

He imagined the church had a tight budget. "I'll get it." He handed her his card. "So Danika's not here today?"

"She ran to town. She'll be sorry she missed you. Just the other day we were talking about you." As she ran the charge, she gave him a squinty look.

"What?" He glanced down. "Do I have something on me?"

"I was trying to decide if what I want to tell you is something I should tell you so you don't get caught by surprise, or is it just drama and gossip?"

"Sam, you're making it too complicated." He signed the paper she gave him and handed it back to her. "Is anyone going to get hurt?"

"You again, maybe. You know for the record I always said she was a liar." She handed a candy to Karly. "Here, take this to Bryce. Bring him to the store. Kids love it here."

"You're going to say that, then change the subject?" This was why he hated small towns…well, one of the reasons. No matter how old you are you're still Dub's son, the wild one. Everyone knows your business or they think they do.

Sam glanced at Karly. "It's Gwyn Peterson. That's Tyler's high school girlfriend. I never liked her." She adjusted a display before looking back at Tyler. "She's back and she has a couple of sons. With you being back on the ranch, it's brought up the old stories. I'm sorry."

"Neither one of them are mine, no matter how old they are. Is that what people are saying? This is ridiculous." He wanted to leave, drive to the airport and take off.

"I know. The only reason I'm telling you is her youngest son is in Bryce's class. I hear you've been going with Karly to pick him up, so you have a good chance of running into her. If you're prepared, it would give the talkers less to talk about. The other boy is about ten and had red, curly hair." She shrugged. "You know, like all the Havenders, but the boy's last name is Peterson. Just wanted to give you a heads-up."

He shook his head. "Yeah, thanks. I'm going to help Joaquin load up." He turned to Karly. "When you're ready, I'll be in the truck."

Karly shadowed Tyler up the short, uneven steps that went to the back door. The Joaquin person that she had heard on the radio was not anywhere to be seen, but the truck bed was full.

Tyler got in the cab and slammed the door. Once she buckled up, he started the engine. His jaw flexed.

The mother in her wanted to soothe his hurt. "Gossip can be hurtful."

He snorted.

There had to be something she could say that would be more helpful, but couldn't think of a thing. She hated the silence. "So you think Bryce can help build the Christmas village? He loves helping. You're great with him."

"Were you ever accused of something you didn't do?"

"No." She had done plenty with her stepfather, but somehow they had gotten away with all of their scams. "Sometimes the world isn't fair."

"That's the understatement of the year." He turned the wheel, taking them off Main Street to the school. "That was the worst part. Not her lies, but my dad believing them. He got mad at me."

"Your father believed her over you?"

"I shouldn't have had to tell my father I didn't do it. He should have known I would never…" His knuckles turned white. It looked as if he was going to rip the steering wheel off its column. "My parents got in the biggest fight. That's when I moved to the bunkhouse and waited to graduate so I could leave for Florida."

He took a deep breath and exhaled. "Sorry. I don't know why I let the old history get under my skin."

"The past has a way of messing with the future if we let it. We're supposed to turn it over to God, but our brain or maybe our pride doesn't want to go along with that plan."

"I don't get God's plan. Most of the time I hate it."

Karly sighed. "The hardest part for me is letting go of my own understanding. But it seems the more I don't try to understand the clearer some things get. Not all things. Some things I just don't get and never will. If I had my way, Bryce would have been born whole. People joke about counting all their fingers and toes, but Bryce doesn't have his. For the longest time I battled guilt over that. What did I do wrong? For most of his life I blamed myself." She sighed and twisted her fingers. "Anytime you're different, it makes life harder, but maybe if it's harder up front, then it can actually be easier." She was talking too much. Turning away from Tyler's stern face, she looked out the window. "You don't have to have all the answers, just faith."

The school came into view. A few parents had already started lining up in the pickup area. The kindergarten building and playground were on the edge of the campus that housed pre-K through twelfth grade, a place Tyler had spent his whole childhood.

She wanted to point out all Tyler's blessings. If he didn't want to see them, he wouldn't, even if she listed them. She didn't want to give him another reason to be angry with her.

"I've meet three of the Bergmann girls. They all have been supernice to me. Your father said you had dated one of them in high school. That must be strange, seeing old girlfriends every time you're in town." Karly was looking out the window, trying to keep her voice casual.

He shook his head. "We didn't really date. I was too afraid of getting stuck in Clear Water to get really serious about anyone." Another reason his father should have known Gwyn was lying. "They were just friends. I went to homecoming with one of the twins and prom with the other, can't really tell them apart. All I remember is wearing a tux and walking in a parade thing. Plus, I think I'm related to over half the families in town." He gave her a wink. "Didn't feel right dating a cousin, no matter how distant. How about you? Did you ever date a cousin?" His anger evaporated and the charmer was back. She might like him better, however, he was the one she didn't dare trust.

Shaking her head, she finally looked at him. "No, no cousins. Just street thugs and toads I tried turning into princes."

He pulled into the parking lot between the fine arts building and the football field. Bryce ended his day in art or music, so they had gotten in the habit of waiting there for him.

"I can't imagine growing up in one house and going to one school my whole childhood." The statement came out as a wishful whisper. Opening the door, she stopped midway. "Are you going to stay here?"

He flashed the smile that made her knees go numb. "Nope. Apparently, the whole town is brimming with anticipation." He nodded to the pickup patrol. "Might as well get it over with so they can move on to another hot topic. They might get bored if we wait too long." He got out of the truck and winked at her again. "It's all about timing, you know."

Elbows on the silver hood, he leaned back and propped his boot on the bumper. The elementary students started filing out of the buildings. They were released before the "big kids," as Bryce called them.

Moving next to Tyler, she kept an eye on the door. "You had to have good memories growing up here."

Tyler scanned the campus and looked back at her

with a lopsided grin. "Yeah, some of the teachers would tell you I had too much fun. I remember waking up excited in the morning. Between sports, the horses and flying, there wasn't enough time in the day to do it all. I had some great friends. I took for granted that I got to go to the same campus as my big sister. Fortunately for me, everyone loved her, so they put up with me by default."

"I doubt that very seriously. There's Bryce." Her little guy dragged his backpack behind him, his head down. Something had happened. Putting her hand over her heart, she could feel the blood rushing. This had been her fear. She would send him out into the world and he would be hurt.

She moved toward him, but Tyler stopped her.

"I suggest you get the world-has-ended look off your face and smile. Greet him as if everything's good. Let him tell you what's wrong, and we'll go from there."

Nodding, she knew he was right. If she overreacted, it would only make everything worse. She waited with a smile planted on her face.

"Tyler?" A female voice called from the other side of the parking lot. The women approached them slowly before stopping about five feet from them. "It is you."

Petite, with jeans and silky blond hair in a short, stylish cut, she was the exact opposite of Karly.

Leaning close to Tyler's ear, she whispered, "I suggest you get the world-has-ended look off your face and smile. Greet her as if everything's good." She straightened and smiled at him.

He actually threw his head back and laughed, a deep, authentic laugh. Cocking his head to the side, he whispered, "If half the town wasn't watching, I'd kiss you right now." He stepped forward with his beautiful smile in place and let Gwyn give him an awkward hug.

All Karly could think about was the idea of a kiss he had just put in her head. *Oh, no, girl, don't even go down that rocky road.*

Gwyn said, "I heard about your dad, so sorry. Such a dear man. So what are you doing at the school?" Her gaze slid over to Karly.

Her voice sounded like a country-and-western love ballad.

Tyler put his strong hand on Karly's shoulder. The idea of a kiss popped up again.

"This is Karly. Karly, Gwyn. We are here to pick up her son, Bryce."

Bryce had finally dragged himself to her side. Pulling him close, she ruffled his hair and focused on her son. "Hey, Cowboy." She hoped using his new nickname would cheer him up.

Gwyn smiled. Karly saw the moment she noticed his missing hand. Pity filled her eyes and she looked away. "Well, it was nice meeting you. Tyler, tell your dad hi for me. My son, Cooper, is on the playground. Bye-bye." And she was gone.

"Come on over here, Bryce. I've had a hard day and feel like going for some ice cream."

Bryce's whole face lit up. "At the drugstore? When Mom worked there, she would give me a strawberry shake if I was quiet and didn't bother the customers."

Tyler opened the back door for her son and casually helped him up. "Then the drugstore it is. How was your day?"

"Julie and Corina made fun of me because I wear Velcro shoes. Mom, if we tie the laces real tight can I wear regular shoes? Or what about boots? Can I get a pair of cowboy boots?"

With everyone buckled in, Tyler started the truck. He checked the rearview mirror and made eye contact with Bryce. "You're a cowboy. I know we have extra boots your size around the ranch somewhere. How's that sound?"

"Really? Great."

"And about the girls. They probably tease everyone. I went to school with people like that. For some reason they get a kick out of putting others down. If it's not about your arm, it's big ears or crooked teeth. I imagine you're not the only one in Velcro shoes anyway."

He nodded. "They laughed at Cooper 'cause he has funny hair. They also said I couldn't be in the Christmas pageant. The rule is to carry the candle with both hands. They said I couldn't do it." He looked as if he was going to cry.

Her heart twisted in a tight knot. "Maybe they have to use both hands, but you have a lifetime of using one hand. We'll talk to Pastor John."

"Mom, you always say nice stuff about me. They might not let me in the pageant. Maybe if I use the arm you got me, they'll let me."

Tyler winked at her. "Hey, I was talking to John, Pastor John, and he asked me if I thought you could lead the angels this year. I said without a doubt, no one would be better."

The truck came to a stop in front of the old drugstore. "Hey, Cowboy, I figure if the Statue of Liberty can hold up a torch with one hand, so can you. Ready for a giant strawberry shake?"

"Yeah!" With his precious smile back, Bryce bounced out of the backseat.

Tyler turned to her at the base of the steps. "Hope you don't mind that I offered ice cream. I should have asked first. I'm not used to requesting permission." He held out his hand and helped her up the old lopsided cement steps. On the sidewalk, he picked Bryce up and tossed him in the air.

Her son's laugh melted all the knots right out of her heart. "Higher! Higher!"

"Your mom is giving us that look to behave in public. I think she needs two scoops of ice cream."

"Chocolate! Her favorite is chocolate."

"Then chocolate it is for the best mom." With another wink he opened the glass door to the vintage black-checkered floor and red vinyl stools at the long counter.

"Come on, Momma. You are the best, and Tyler says it, so it's true."

Why did he have to do that? Make her sure he was like all the other selfish jerks, then treat Bryce with such thoughtfulness and respect. And to cap it off, he'd put the idea of kissing him in her mind. *Please, God, if this is a test, show me the right answers.*

Chapter Nine

That night at the dinner table with his dad, Tyler tried to focus on the positive, but when Dub started in on how one careless act could ruin a whole life, he couldn't take it anymore. Why did Dub still treat him like a stupid kid? Pushing away from the table, he stood. Without another word he stomped out of the kitchen. Okay, so he was now acting like a hotheaded eighteen-year-old again.

He stopped on the edge of the concrete patio and looked across the land that had been in his family for generations. Running his hands through his hair, he locked his fingers behind his head. Why did he do this? Why did he let his dad get to him?

Early on, Dub had fought Granddad to add the barns and refocus the ranch from cattle to his renowned cutting horses. Granddad wanted to stay with cattle and goats. At one time Tyler had shared his father's dream, too, until he'd turned it into a nightmare.

The sun was setting; colors of red, orange and yellow streaked over the hills and burned through the trees.

How could the place that brought him so much peace also be the greatest source of torment?

He didn't want to be here. Not without his sister and mother. Not after the one stupid act that had destroyed his dream and the legs of his favorite horse.

Moving across the yard, he walked to the caliche road that led to the barns. Twisting the leather cords and horsehair bracelets around his wrist, he let his mind drift to places he usually avoided. His top-of-the-line quarter horse, Jet-Set Lena. She had been part of that dream. A mare that he had bred and raised. At the age of three she had already collected trophies and purses.

They had been an unbeatable team on the circuit, until his senior year when he'd allowed Gwyn to convince him to take out his father's plane at night for a stupid death-defying stunt just because she was bored. Alcohol had been involved, too, the reason he never drank these days. He had been seventeen, and that had been the beginning of his life spiraling out of control.

The next day he'd broken it off with her. In pure high school drama, she'd retaliated by spreading lies about him.

The barn door stood before him. Horses moved in their stalls, some munching on their hay. Eyes down, he looked at his boots. They toed the threshold. One step and he would be back in the world he didn't deserve to be part of anymore.

He gazed into the dark corridor. Was she there? His sister had told him they'd saved Lena, but there was permanent damage to her legs. He closed his eyes and took in the smells and sounds of the barn as the horses settled in for the night. Crickets mixed with the soft sounds of the stables. Leather, hay and horses filled his senses.

Jet-Set Lena, his horse. He remembered picking her name and filling out the paperwork to get her registered. He was so proud of her. Then the stupid move with the airplane that ended her run to nationals. She had been one of the best cutting horses people had seen in decades.

He took a step into the barn. Curiosity and bids for attention brought several heads out over the half doors. Tossing forelocks along with low nickers pleaded for him to come to their doors. Scanning the line of stalls, he found her. The big bay pushed at her door. The perfect white diamond on her forehead was partially covered as she threw her muzzle in the air and whispered to him. She seemed to remember him, too.

"Are you still talking to me?" He gently touched her muzzle with the back of his hand. She had always been a bit bossy. Standing in front of her, he could barely breathe. She looked bigger, and her red seemed a little lighter, but her eyes still held keen intelligence and warm understanding. He didn't see any trace of blame or resentment. With her neck stretched, she tried to nip at the pocket on his shirt. She remembered where he would hide her treat. He laughed and took a step closer, running his hand under the curved jaw. "Hey, girl. How've you been?"

He needed to tell her he was sorry, but the words got lodged in his throat. Leaning his forehead on the crest of her neck, he patted her shoulder. "If I could go back and undo that night, I would." He closed his eyes.

A force of warm air came from her nostrils as she bumped her forehead against his chest. Laughing, he rubbed behind her ears. "I promise I'll bring it tomorrow. Tonight I'm hiding from dad. You know how he is." From the time she was a few weeks old, she would push at him until he did her bidding. She'd trained him as much as he'd trained her. "Lena, girl, I'm so—"

"Is that your horse?" Bryce's voice caused Tyler to jump back.

Why did he feel guilty? He looked past the boy to the door. "Hey, where is your mom? Does she know you're out here?"

He crossed his full arm over his short arm and glared up at Tyler. "My mom is helping your dad to his bedroom. You and Mr. Adrian said I could ride, but everyone keeps forgetting."

He dropped his arms and walked to the horse. The mare stretched her neck and lowered her muzzle. Bryce touched the velvet nose. "Is she yours?"

"She used to be."

"What's her name?" The small hand reached up to rub her forelock.

"Jet-Set Lena, but we call her Lena. You didn't answer my question. Does your mother know you're out here? More than once she told you to stay away from the barns."

Bryce groaned and rolled his eyes. Tyler made sure not to laugh, though it was hard. This little boy had his own ideas of what he wanted, no matter what his parent thought. Tyler could identify.

"Rolling your eyes won't help," Tyler said. "We need to get you back to the house."

Bryce stepped closer to the horse. "Lena? That's a pretty name. Why is she not yours anymore?"

"I messed up and she got hurt." He held his hand out to the little boy. "Come on. We can talk to your mom and set a date for a ride."

Bryce paused. "Why do you get so mad at your dad? Your dad is the best."

"Yeah, well, we bring out the worst in each other sometimes. Sometimes dads and sons just don't get along."

"I wish I had a dad. I'd make sure not to fight with him." Big dark eyes looked up at Tyler, completely innocent.

That drove a stake straight to his gut. What did he say to that? He waved his fingers. "Come on, let's go before your mom discovers you're—"

"Tyler?" Karly's voice had an edge. "Bryce?"

"We're here." Tyler tossed his head toward the door. "Come on, Cowboy."

"Oh, I couldn't find you. What are you doing in the barn? I told you to never come out here alone."

"I'm not alone, Momma. I was petting Tyler's horse."

Heated eyes and a stern frown stared Tyler down. This wasn't good. "We were just coming back to the house. Is Dad okay?"

She shook her head as if he was an idiot for even asking. Marching forward, she reached for Bryce's hand. "It's time for your bath."

"Momma, Tyler said we could go riding. Please?"

"It's dark outside and time for bed."

"Not now. In the morning. I don't have school. It's Saturday." Short legs hopped to keep up with his mother.

Tyler followed, wanting to make sure they got in the house without a problem. "We could go in the morning, Karly. John will be over to do the weekly Bible study with Dad. I could take you out to see the ranch on horseback. It's the best way to see it."

"Those animals are big, and we've never ridden be-fore."

"We have some gentle rides. I can ask Jefferson. He used to keep a couple of babysitters on the ranch."

She stopped at the edge of the porch and looked up at him. He lost his breath for a moment. The last rays of sun filtered through the tree and highlighted her face. In her natural beauty she took the image of all other women right out of his mind. Maybe it was because she didn't try. She didn't even seem to know the power she possessed with those eyes and lips. He'd seen oth-ers wield them like weapons. She was more than he expected.

He took a step back. *Get a grip, Tyler.*

He was just going crazy from being on the ranch for so long. Karly blinked and frowned at him. Women didn't frown at him. Maybe that was it. He was caught up in the age-old game of chase. She ran; he followed. The pursuit had him intrigued. Yeah, he needed to stop.

"Momma, please."

"What's a babysitter?"

It was his turn to blink. "Babysitter? Oh, they're horses that you can put the youngest kid on and they'll just stand there until you lead them. They'll follow an-other horse at a slow pace. They are also called bullet-proof. Completely safe for a new rider."

"Momma, you said I could ride. Please. Please?" Her son held her hand and bounced around.

She sighed and glared at Tyler. "Okay, what time?"

He smiled back. Yeah, he'd take the heat for this one. The smile on Bryce's face was enough. "John should be here around 9:00. That will also give time for the sun to be out and warm up a bit."

"Yay! I'll get to wear my new boots and hat. Thank you, Momma, thank you." He ran inside, then popped his head back out the screen door. "Good night, Mr. Tyler, and thank you. I'm going to get my clothes ready for tomorrow."

"Bryce, I'll be there is a minute for your bath. Don't go to bed yet." Karly wrapped her arms around her waist. "Are you sure Bryce can handle one of your horses? They look huge. They have really big teeth."

He nodded. "It'll be good. I'll have Adrian pick the horses for you and Bryce, since it's been years since I've worked with any of them."

"Why?"

He shoved his hands into his pockets. "Why what?" Maybe if he played dumb she'd drop it.

"You've been blessed with growing up in this incredible ranch, given this loving father and you seem to resent it all." She tilted her head and gazed at him. "Why has it been years since you've ridden any of the horses or been in the barn or even slept in your own room? I really don't understand."

It was so close to what Bryce had said earlier, Tyler looked away. The sun was completely gone now, leaving stars hanging in the dark purple sky. The stars always made him think of his mom and Carol.

Where did people go when they died? Did they know what was going on back in their old lives? Did his grandparents, mother and Carol know how much he missed them? He snorted. His mother would be telling him to stop acting like a spoiled brat. Was that how Karly saw him? Spoiled and ungrateful? He grunted. If he was honest with himself, she might have a point. Being honest hurt.

"There is nothing quite like a night sky in the country, is there?" Stepping out from the porch and standing closer to him, she looked up at the same sky he had just been lost in. "I'm sorry. I don't have a right to question or judge you. I don't know the whole story. Thank you for taking us to the drugstore today and letting Bryce ride tomorrow. I know he is more than excited. I just get worried that he'll get hurt, but little boys get hurt sometimes."

He watched her eyes scan the starry night. No makeup, no manicure, no artificial highlights in her hair. The women he dated spent hundreds of dollars on their upkeep each month. He'd be surprised if she had spent a hundred dollars in her lifetime.

The more he got to know her, the farther away she seemed from a money schemer. She had access to all the accounts and she was actually more conservative than his dad. And her cooking had even gotten better. Maybe he had been wrong about her motives.

"So what are you plans once Dad gets better?"

She turned toward him, the porch light backlighting her so he couldn't make out her expression. She shrugged. "I hope he keeps me on as a housekeeper long enough for me to go to school and get some sort of degree. Physical therapy assistant would be my dream job. I could stay in Clear Water and work here or Uvalde or even Kerrville."

When she lifted her eyes back to the sky, he could see her profile. Her full lips definitely brought kissing to mind. He shook his head and turned back to stargazing, also.

If she was an opportunist who was here to take advantage of his dad's trust, then he needed to get rid of her before he left. But he was starting to have a hard time believing she wasn't everything she claimed to be—a hardworking mother who cared about the people around her.

Close enough to him that he could smell her perfume, she sighed. "I need to go and make sure Bryce gets his bath. Night, Tyler."

"Night."

The screen door shut softly. Then he heard the lock click. He headed to the bunkhouse. Hitting the wood step, he paused and took in the endless sky one last time. The Big Dipper was easy to make out, and tonight the Milky Way looked as if someone had scattered crushed diamonds across the sky.

Loneliness had never felt so heavy. He needed to get back to flying. Traveling the world was so much easier than worrying about family.

The morning chill went right through Karly's light crocheted wrap. Bryce didn't seem to notice the cold. He jumped from rock to rock that lined the drive to the barns. The cowboy hat wobbled on his head. The idea of her little boy on one of the ranch's big horses made her stomach roll. She wasn't sure she could trust Tyler to keep him from getting him hurt.

"Bryce, stay on the path. The rocks might be loose."

He jumped from the rock and ran to the barn door, only stopping to pick up his hat when it flew off. Shoving it on his head, he took off running again.

"Bryce! Slow down." He ignored her. "If you get hurt you won't be able to ride."

"Momma, hurry up. They are waiting for us."

She closed her eyes for a moment. *God, please give me the fortitude to raise this little boy You gave me.*

"Momma!"

With a sigh she opened her eyes and directed her attention to the barn. Tyler stood behind her son, a huge grin on his gorgeous face. That was the reason the women in town loved talking about him. But the perfect teeth, perfect jawline and perfect dimple on his right cheek were just a small part of his charm. His bright blue eyes made him even better looking. It just wasn't fair. What was God thinking?

Today he looked all cowboy, from the off-white hat to the dark brown boots. His jeans were crisp and clean, a starched line down the front center. Was he for real? She had on her Goodwill hiking boots and hand-me-down jeans, soft and faded from heavy use by the person who'd owned them before her.

"I want a white hat like Tyler's! The good guys wear white hats."

She narrowed her eyes. "Bryce."

Tyler took off the hat and ran his fingers through his dark blond hair. "Mine isn't really white, it's more of a light beige. That makes me a not-so-good guy." He lifted the black hat off Bryce's head and put his hat in its place. The hat was so big it hit below his nose.

Was Tyler a good guy? Could she trust him with her son's safety? He had her so confused, and she hated that feeling.

"I can't see!" When Bryce shook his head, the hat almost spun.

Tyler laughed and put the hat back on his own head. "Well, a cowboy needs to be able to see if he's going riding."

Adrian joined them, a steaming cup of coffee in his hand. "So you're actually doing this?" He took a sip and looked at Tyler over the rim.

Bryce jumped up. "Yes."

"Are you sure it's safe?" She had to ask Adrian. He understood the fears of a parent.

Tyler clicked his tongue. "You really don't trust me?"

She kept her eyes on Adrian, ignoring Tyler. She couldn't afford to worry about his hurt feelings.

"Yeah, we have a couple of horses that won't do anything but walk behind or beside the mare Tyler is taking." His gaze cut to Tyler. "You're riding your mare, Lena, right?"

Tyler crossed his arms, and his jaw tightened and released before he spoke. "She's not mine anymore. Nope, I hadn't planned on it."

"She loves going over the ranch, and she's missed you. The others will follow her."

Tyler frowned. "What about her knees? The damage was bad."

"Yeah. But as long as you don't ride her hard or fast, she's fine. Taking her on the trails will be good for her."

Tyler nodded, but he didn't look happy.

"What horse do I get to ride?" Bryce looked down the long corridor. "Can I ride the white one?"

"Lancelot would be a good choice for you. He's a dapple gray. I was thinking your mom could ride him, but he would love giving you a ride. This big guy likes kids." As if the horse knew they were talking about him, the gelding stretched his neck over the door and gave a low nicker.

For a moment Karly couldn't breathe. "He is...he's huge."

Adrian headed toward the horse. "He's a gentle giant." He rubbed his muzzle with one hand as he grabbed the halter on a nearby hook with the other. The large animal lowered his head and let Adrian slip the halter over the soft ears. "The smaller horses sometimes have the biggest attitudes. So we got a horse for Cowboy. Now one for you."

She didn't want to do this, but no way was she going to let her son go riding across the ranch without her. "Maybe we could ride in the arena. That would be fun, right?"

"Momma." Bryce's eyes couldn't look any bigger.

Tyler moved farther down the stalls. "We're going to start there. Make sure you can sit without falling off." He turned and walked backward. "Karly, if it looks as if y'all can't sit on the moving horse, we'll stay in the arena." He stopped in front of a stall. No friendly head popped out to greet him. "What about Tank? Will he do for Karly?"

"Tank?" Karly asked. "That sounds a little, um… violent."

Adrian laughed. "He's the perfect trail horse—slow, steady and strong. Running or even trotting is not in his vocabulary."

Tyler had disappeared into the stall. She stepped closer, surprised at her own excitement at seeing a horse she would be riding. Adrian walked past her with the massive gray horse, Bryce right next to him. "Stay close to me. Never jump or run around a horse. And make sure they see you. Never sneak up on them." As they headed down the alley way he kept instructing her son on horse safety.

"Here ya go." Tyler led the most beautiful, unique

horse toward her. He was white with red spots covering from head to, well, hoof. The dots on his rump were the biggest.

"What kind of horse is he?"

Tyler slipped a halter over the horse's ears. "An Appaloosa and quarter horse mix." He led the gelding into the wide corridor and stopped in front of her. "He's one of my sister's rescue horses. Tank, this is Karly. Hold your hand out flat. Like this." He held his hand flat, palm up. The horse flared his large nostrils and pushed at Tyler's hand. Reaching up, Tyler patted his neck. The horse wasn't tall like the white horse, but his chest was wider.

Karly held her hand out. "Hi, Tank." When she started to pat his thick neck she saw the scar, broad and long at the base of his neck. "What happened?" She touched the old wound, deep and painful looking.

Tyler ran his hand along the long back. "Our local 4-H horse club, which Carol was president of, helped local authorities with animal abuse cases. Tank was found on a five-acre lot on the edge of the county line with a chain embedded in his neck." The horse nudged him, and Tyler chuckled. "He wasn't even a year old. Out of five of the horses found, two couldn't be saved. Tank needed surgeries to remove the chain that had basically grown into his neck, it had been on him for so long. My sister adopted him and Dad paid for the surgeries, of course. She tried to run barrels with him." He scratched the gelding under his jaw. "He would do anything for her, but he hated running, so he became one of our trail horses that guests could safely ride. And he has a great calming effect on our more high-strung horses. No matter how long he has gone without being ridden, he is always ready to go—no drama, just a slow, steady pace."

She had never felt such a connection to an animal before now. She wanted to hug him and promise that everything would be fine from now on. No one would ever hurt him again. He had found a safe home here at the Childress Ranch.

"How can people be so cruel?" she whispered as she moved even closer to the gentle eyes that looked at her with such acceptance and trust. She swallowed and blinked. Tyler would laugh at her if she started crying. She laid her cheek against the horse's jaw and stroked his neck.

"Selfishness…greed or just plain ignorance. We need more people like my sister to do good…be good." Heavy emotion clouded his voice. He coughed. "Come on, let's get him saddled up."

Nodding, she stepped back so they could move forward. "You seem to do some of your own good works. Not many people spend their free time with kids at a hospital or making sure the dreams of little boys come true, despite their mothers' concerns."

"Hey, us little boys gotta stick together against mothers that want to tape us up in Bubble Wrap."

At the end of the passageway, she saw Adrian's ten-year-old daughter, Mia, stood with Bryce next to the big horse with a saddle. Bryce was intently listening to everything Adrian told him.

"Momma, Adrian said he would take me to the arena when you got here. Mia's going with me. Can we go now?" He spoke soft and low, but the eagerness in his eyes gave his excitement away.

Looking at Adrian for reassurance, she bit the inside

of her cheek. Her little man looked so small standing next to that giant of a horse. Maybe this was a bad idea. Even if the horse had perfect manners, he could trip, or Bryce could just lose his balance and fall.

Adrian nodded. "Mia, will you take him to the tack room to get a helmet that fits? Get yours, too, so you can ride alongside of him in the arena."

Tyler frowned. "A helmet. I've never worn one."

Bryce turned back to them, the same expression as Tyler's on his face. "I'm a cowboy. I don't want a helmet."

She turned to Tyler, ready to have it out with him when she noticed Adrian looking at him with one raised eyebrow. Tyler rolled his eyes and sighed.

"And that was stupid of me." He flipped the lead over a post. "Come on, Cowboy, we all get to wear helmets today." He smiled down at Bryce and took his hand. "I've got to get Tank's saddle anyway, so you can help pick out a helmet for me, and we can get one for your mom, too."

"Okay." Bryce kicked at the gravel just as Tyler had done.

She groaned. Just when she thought she was safe from creating a Prince Charming fantasy about him, Tyler had to go and be all noble again. It was not her job to redeem the prince. She had gone down that path too many time and gotten lost. Redemption was God's job.

Warm air brushed her arm. Tank nudged her with his soft velvet muzzle. She scratched him under the jaw like she had seen Tyler do earlier. The big brown eyes closed in total bliss. Karly smiled.

Tank had found a happy ending and a forever home here on the Childress Ranch, so maybe she could, too.

Looking back toward the tack room, she knew she had to keep any wild ideas about Dub's son firmly locked down.

She could do this. She could give her son the safe home and normal upbringing she'd never had as a child. With God's help, she could do this for Bryce and for herself.

Running her hand down Tank's neck to his thick scar, she realized she was about to ride a horse for the first time, something she'd never dreamed of doing in real life. It was just like Pastor John told her—leaning on God made her stronger.

She was no longer the scared little girl who needed someone to take care of her. She was strong, and she was going to ride a strong horse that had survived horrible people.

She smiled at Tank. She was a new person in God.

Chapter Ten

Tyler rode alongside Karly while she grew comfortable sitting on a moving horse. "Remember to keep your heels down. It feels awkward at first, but it helps with balance and keeps your weight distributed. Makes it easier on the horse, too."

The serious look never left her face as she concentrated on everything he told her. He knew she heard when she gave him a quick nod, and he watched as she shifted her weight.

"A horse can feel your tension. Tank loves taking it slow on the trail, so relax and you'll both enjoy the ride." Tank kept his head down and moved carefully, with an easy pace, as if he knew he had a first-timer on his back. His sister, Carol, would be so proud of her rescue horse. She loved all the horses. Noble bloodlines and big wins hadn't impressed her.

His sister had given him a hard time about staying away from the barns, especially his mare, Lena. Maybe she would be a little proud of him today, too. "Doing great, girl." Her ears flicked back and forth, listening to him and all the other noises around them. This beautiful animal hadn't deserved the career-ending injuries she had endured because of his recklessness. "I'm so sorry, Lena, girl." He gave her two strong pats on her neck.

"Did you just apologize to your horse?" Karly pulled up closer to him.

Embarrassed, he nodded. She looked at him as if he was crazy. "When I was dating Gwyn, I let her talk me into something stupid, something I knew was wrong and dangerous. I took my father's plane out at night without permission and buzzed the pastures. The horse spooked and ran into a barbwire fence and off a bluff. Her front knees were a bloody mess, and without sound legs a cutting horse is finished. I ended a brilliant career." He stroked her withers. The mare twisted her neck and nudged his boot.

Karly laughed. "I think she's forgiven you."

"It appears that way." He patted her again.

"A few weeks ago Pastor John said sometimes the hardest part of forgiveness is accepting what we have already been given. I struggle with that, too." Karly's face relaxed in a genuine smile, and he loved the light in her eyes. It reminded him of Christmas Eve when the world was perfect.

"This is incredible." She leaned forward and ran her hand along Tank's neck "Do you remember the first time you rode? How old were you?"

"I must have been…" He concentrated, trying to remember. "I don't know. There are pictures of me with my dad when I was less than a year old, and I've seen pictures of me riding solo when I was about three or four."

She gave a short laugh, as if she was mocking him. "You had a childhood every kid dreams of having." She shook her head and grinned. "You're such a brat and you don't even know it, do you?"

"Momma! Look!" Bryce yelled.

Adrian was jogging at a slow pace in the deep sand, Bryce's big gray trotting alongside with Mia and her horse on the other side.

Slowing down, Adrian walked his horse toward them. "Bryce is a natural. His balance is great. I think we should let him go around the arena with Mia." He looked at his daughter. "No trotting, just a nice easy walk around the railing."

Mia nodded and guided her horse to the rail. Bryce and the big Lancelot followed. Karly's son looked over his shoulder, reins in one hand, just like Mia, and smiled so big Tyler thought his skin would rip.

"Look, Momma! I'm riding all by myself."

Humbled by the look of joy in Karly's eyes, Tyler's heart twisted. He had always taken the horses and this way of life for granted. He watched the muscles in her slender throat work a bit before she answered.

"You look great. Pay attention to where you're going." Her gaze went to Adrian. "So you think it will be safe to go on the trail?"

"Oh, yeah. He's good, and that horse won't let anything separate them." He patted Tank. "Y'all have fun. I'm grabbing Mia and heading over to the other barn. We have some two-year-olds we're prepping for show."

Tyler looked at Karly. Oh, no, her eyes looked suspiciously moist.

"Thank you, Adrian," she said. "You've helped a dream come true, that I didn't even know could happen."

"Not a problem." He gave Tyler a quick nod and started off toward the kids.

Tyler wanted to point out that he was the one that set up the riding date and got the horses. He was the one taking them over the ranch, but that might make him appear to be the brat she had already accused him of being.

Adrian was a good guy and helpful, too, so he just needed to get over himself. It wasn't as if he wanted to impress her anyway. He would leave that for Adrian.

Adrian and Karly would make a great couple.

He swallowed down the burning acid the thought brought up and planted a smile on his face. "Y'all ready to see the ranch you can only see on horseback?" He pulled on the unfamiliar feel of the strap to the riding helmet.

"Yes!" Bryce practically bounced out of his saddle. "Where are we going first?"

"Follow me." Guiding the horses out of the arena, Tyler headed to the north end of the ranch, to the highest point.

Half an hour into the ride, Bryce's questions had slowed to about one for every three minutes. Tyler constantly did little checks on Lena's gait. Adrian had reassured him the ride up the hill would be fine for her, even good exercise. In his mind he could still hear her screams as the fence snapped and she tumbled to the dry creek bed below the small cliff. Closing his eyes for a minute, he tried to erase the image of her lying on the rocks, tangled in the fencing, bloody and broken. Riding her was like meeting up with a good friend after years of separation. He glanced over at Karly, who was leaning forward slightly, whispering something to Tank. The soft morning sun along with the cool breeze playing with the loose strands of her hair created an image

of the perfect woman. The picture hit him hard in the
gut. The most amazing part was she didn't even know
how beautiful she was.

"Mr. Tyler, why are the trees up here fat and wide,
but the trees along the cliff below were all superskinny
and tall?"

Tyler chuckled. Three minutes must be up. "The tall
trees are fighting for sun, but the trees up here need
water, so they cover the ground by being low and wide."

"How do you know all this?" Karly paused and
looked around her. Sweeping valleys nestled in the ma-
jestic rocky hills. Spots of yellow and orange stood out
among the surrounding evergreen. Tyler had forgotten that fall was his favorite time of year on the ranch.

He shrugged. "Doesn't everyone learn this stuff in
school?"

She turned a bit red and looked down at the ground.
Way to make her feel stupid, Tyler. "Actually, I take
that back. I learned almost everything I know about this
place from my father and grandfather. Granddad was
not only a rancher, but he was also a teacher at the local
junior college. He taught botany and taxonomy. He said
he wanted me to know everything about the land I was
born to." Man, he missed his granddad.

"What's a taxes-money?" Bryce stumbled over the
new word. "Tax-on-tomy."

"Taxonomy." Karly helped with the new word.

"Taxonomy." Bryce smiled and repeated the word
several times.

Karly turned to him, her nose crinkled up. "Is it
where they stuff animals?"

Biting down so he wouldn't laugh, Tyler kept his face
impassive. She would take his humor as an insult, and

he didn't want her to feel any worse. He shook his head. "That's taxidermy. They sound kind of the same. It's the classification and cataloging of plants. We would spend hours out here when I was little, gathering samples and pressing them so he could track any new species that invaded."

"Oh, look!" Bryce's excited yelp caused Karly to jump. Tyler turned his attention from her to the area Bryce was pointing to. They were reaching the top of the ridge.

He'd forgotten about the Childress Christmas-tree lot. Well, maybe not forgotten, but locked away. Had he come this way on purpose?

"Christmas trees! Just like in the books." Bryce turned to Tyler. "I didn't know Christmas trees grew on your ranch."

"They're piñon pines…they're normally a little farther north, but my great-grandfather didn't want a cedar in his house, so he transplanted these. Growing up, we would come pick trees for the houses."

"So we can pick a tree? Mom, we get to have a tree this year. A real, live tree we can decorate and everything, like in the stories with tinsel and lights and stuff."

"Bryce, this isn't our house or our trees." Karly looked at Tyler.

The longing he saw pressed his heart. All the things he took for granted were fairy-tale fantasies to her.

"I'm sorry, Tyler. I—"

"Don't apologize. Bryce is right. It's time to trim up the lot. It's been too long since a tree was brought down the hill." For a moment he could hear his sister's laughter as they darted around the trees. "Even as grown-ups Carol and I would argue about which tree was the best.

My mom would give us a fifteen-minute warning, then bribe us with hot cocoa and cookies. While we were distracted, Dad cut down the tree he wanted." He laughed. That stopped him cold. Since his sister's death, memories of them just made him angry, not laugh.

Karly reached out and touched his arm. "Are you okay?"

"Yeah, just remembering the good times."

"You should bring your nieces up here and share those memories with them. Do they pick a tree out?"

"I don't think so. After Mom died, most of our traditions slipped away. At the time I was finishing school in Florida, and Carol lived in Houston. It was just easier to forget."

"I want this tree!" Bryce was circling Lancelot from tree to tree.

"Bryce, these belong to the Childress family. They're not our trees. You can't just—"

"I like that one, too, Cowboy. You think we should get Rachel and Celeste to help us? They can get one for their house, and we can get one for ours."

"Ours?" A faint whisper from behind him caused him to twist in the saddle and look over at her. She wiped at her face and gave him a forced smile. When had he started thinking of the ranch house as "ours"? That surprised him. For the first time since he'd left at eighteen, the idea of living on the ranch entered his head. He could almost see himself living here with Karly and Bryce.

Oh, no. No. No. No.

He cleared his throat and turned back to Bryce. "What do you say, Bryce? Should we bring the girls up here? We can do it the weekend after Thanksgiving. I can make hot cocoa like my mom's and we can get your…uh…" He thought of Karly's last attempt at cookies. "Maybe we can get Maggie to make us some cookies." Hopefully she didn't notice his slip. Last thing he wanted to do was hurt her feelings.

Bryce raised his hand to the sky and shouted. He looked as if he had so much energy his small body could not contain it all. Tyler remembered those days. It had been a long time but the feelings were coming back.

"I have one more place to show you before we head home."

Lena took the lead again and brought them to the highest point on the other side of the tree line.

He stopped once the panoramic view of the valley and hill, with miles of uninhabited Hill Country, came into view. The bend of the river looked like a thin ribbon from this high up. He heard a gasp as Karly joined him. For a moment the only sound to be heard was the conversation of nature. Birds, water, wind moving through the trees. Tyler lost his own breath.

How could he have forgotten the magnitude of this land? He loved flying over the hills, but to sit here on horseback was a whole other perspective. He was part of the soil and trees. His great-great-grandparents had stood on this land and sacrificed in order to build a future for their family.

"Wow." Bryce stood in his stirrups. "Is this all yours?"

Tyler chuckled. "Granddad used to say it was God's country and we were blessed with the responsibility to take care of the land." He leaned closer to Bryce and pointed to the river. "Our property runs about a quarter of a mile along the river, then goes up the hillside there." He moved his finger to the opposite side. "To there. This is the far north end of the ranch. We used to own everything all the way to that hill over there, but I had a great-uncle who sold his share. That didn't make the family happy."

"This is truly amazing, Tyler. I knew the ranch was big, but this is beyond anything I could imagine. How could you not want to live here?"

He shrugged. So many others had asked him the same question. "I don't know. Since my mom and sister died, it just isn't the same." He paused. "I think the horses are ready to go home."

"Sure. Thank you so much, Tyler. I don't know what I was expecting, but this by far exceeded it all."

"I love the Christmas-tree spot!" Joy radiated from Bryce's voice. "I hope it snows for Christmas, just like the stories you read to me, Momma. Snow on the trees!"

Tyler laughed. "Sorry, Cowboy, but it never snows in the Hill Country before January. Most of the time not even then."

That bit of news didn't dim the young face. "It could. Momma says, 'You never know' all the time." He made his young voice go higher as he imitated her.

Karly's laughter sounded as sweet and pure as the crisp fall air. "That is true, Tyler. You just never know."

There was no way to stay immune to their happiness. "Where does all that optimism come from?"

She laughed. "One thing life has taught me—if you keep getting up, you might actually get where you want to go, and of course with God there is always hope. So for this special Christmas I'm asking for snow."

"Yay. And a horse. I want a horse, too, Momma."

Now it was Tyler's turn to laugh at the expression of horror on her face.

He couldn't resist. Pulling up his horse, he leaned closer to her and whispered, "You never know. You just never know."

For the first time in a long time, he smiled at the thought of reaching the barns and going home. Karly was not his usual type, but maybe his father was right. He needed a new type.

From atop her new best friend, Karly saw the ranch house drawing closer. Dub and Pastor John waved from the porch. A bright red cardinal flew from the dark leaves of the giant oak tree in front of the barn door.

"Momma! Did you see that red bird?" Bruce turned in his saddle to watch the bird land on another tree. "She's so pretty."

Tyler chuckled. "That's a he. The females are gray." Pulling up his horse next to Bryce, he leaned down and pointed to a nearby tree. "See over there. Close to the trunk, on the bottom branch."

Bryce squinted. Karly also looked closer, scanning other trees before finding the gray bird. She was almost the same color as the tree bark.

A gasp came from her son. "I see her! Why does she have the boring color?"

Tyler sat up and patted Bryce's back. "His job is to attract her attention, and once he has it she blends in with the trees and their nest while he keeps the predators away. If anything dangerous comes near their family, he'll draw then away. Her color helps hide the nest from predators."

Was he like the red bird, all flashy and beautiful

but loyal and protective of his family? Or was he like all the other men in Karly's life, making promises they didn't keep?

Stopping his horse outside the big barn, Tyler twisted in his saddle. "Well, guys, are y'all ready to go get some lunch at the house?" He swung his right leg over the saddle and dismounted. With a grimace, he moaned as the saddle creaked. "These legs aren't used to sitting in the saddle for so long." He patted Lena's neck and ran his hands down her front legs.

Grabbing the saddle horn, Karly tried to copy his action. Her leg cramped and got stuck midmotion on the back of the saddle. She gripped the horn tighter, not sure whether she should go back or forward. "Ow, ow, ow!"

"Karly, let me help you." Tyler's hands were on her waist. "Go on and bring your leg down. Karly?" His deep voice was too close.

She tried to beat down the giggles. She really did try, but they took control, bursting out of her. "This is ridiculous."

"Momma. Are you okay?"

A giggle bubbled up. She couldn't believe she was stuck on a horse with Prince Charming helping her get off. "Yes, it just looked so easy and now I'm stuck and…can't stop…giggling." She felt the warmth of Tyler's hand on her shin and calf through her blue jeans. He gently brought her leg over the back of the saddle.

"Now, easy does it to the ground." His voice had an edge, sounding as if he was working hard to not laugh at her as she tried to put weight on her leg but couldn't.

"Ow." She hopped on one leg. "It's cramping."

He bent down and kneaded her calf. "Point your toes up. That'll help stretch the muscles."

She tried to remain stoically silent. She looked down at him. "It's better."

Yeah, he was laughing at her.

He stood and stepped back, and they both started laughing.

"That wasn't how I pictured my dismount. I thought it would have been more—I don't know—graceful."

"Oh, it was graceful, all right. Are you good?"

She nodded.

"Then, let's get these horses rubbed down and turned out to pasture."

Bryce had no problem getting off his horse. He seemed to be flying. "Can I go tell Pastor John and Mr. Childress about the Christmas trees?"

"Bryce! Slow down or you will get hurt. I'd rather not end the day in another visit to the hospital."

Tyler caught him in midflight. "First, we need to get the saddles off. How about you bring me a caddy with the brushes? Then you can go tell them all about it." He took the helmet off Bryce and led Lancelot to the cross ties. "And remember, you always walk around horses. No running. You don't want to spook them."

"Yes, sir."

She watched as he started taking saddles and blankets off the horses. "What can I do to help?"

He pointed at Bryce's smaller saddle. "Take this one. I'll grab the other two."

In his hands the saddles looked light, but it took both of her arms to hold the smallest one. The smell of leather and horse was strong. He tossed the blankets on top of the saddles. She started coughing. They smelled like sweating horse. Ugh, not as nice.

He laughed again. "You got it?"

She nodded, not willing to admit she wasn't so sure. He took the time to show her and Bryce how to brush the horses down. In no time they had the horses groomed and the tack put away.

"Can I go tell them now?" Bryce bounced with energy.

Karly nodded and put the oversize cowboy hat back on her son's head. He ran all the way to the house.

"Are you sure you aren't the one who should talk to them about the trees?"

He gave her that lopsided grin. "I think it's better coming from your little guy than me. I'm sure it would turn into some power struggle between my dad and me."

"I don't get why you fight so much. He brags about you all the time."

He crossed his arms over his chest, feet planted wide. With one eyebrow raised, he stared at her. He acted as if she was making it up. He didn't say a thing, just stared at her.

"He does. You can tell by all the pictures and stuff all over the house that he loves you."

He shook his head and moved to her Appaloosa. Not that the horse was hers. She had a problem of getting attached too fast and needed to stop it.

"Why would I lie about your father loving you?"

"I don't know. To get on my good side?" He handed the lead rope to her. "Take Tank and I'll get Lancelot. We'll turn them out."

With the rope in hand, she followed Tyler. She loved the sound of the hooves on the concrete. Tank nudged her with his muzzle, the long whiskers tickling. "What, big guy? Thanks for the ride, it was fun." They came to a stop.

Tyler opened a gate and slipped the halter off the white gelding. The horse lunged forward into the pasture, his mane flying. He stepped back and motioned her through the gate. "Can you take his halter off, or do you need help?"

"I've got it." Tank lowered his head and waited for her. She gave him one last pat on the neck before turning him loose. Slower, he followed Lancelot. Together they started running.

"They love the cooler weather, and getting the saddle off makes them frisky."

"I could watch them all day." She stepped up on the bottom rail and leaned over the fence. "How could you ever leave this place?"

He gave her a half smile. "There is a big world out there ready to be explored. I felt like a ten-foot tree crammed into an eight-foot room."

"Well, I've seen the world, and it made me feel small and invisible."

His gaze traveled over her face. "I can't imagine you ever being invisible."

Her eyes looked down before going back up to make eye contact. "I love it here in Clear Water. I want to make it our home. Thank you for showing us the ranch today. It was truly a fantasy come to life." She tried to laugh, to lighten the seriousness of her mood, but it sounded flat to her own ears.

He took a step closer and pushed back a strand of hair playing with the breeze. "You're welcome. Thank you for reminding me of the places I had forgotten. It was fun seeing it through new eyes."

He focused on her eyes, then moved down to her lips. The space between them closed. She relished the warmth of his strong hand as his fingers entwined with hers. His thumb traced circular patterns in her palm. Gentle and kind. She savored the feeling. He whispered her name.

He was going to kiss her. She leaned into him. Their lips touched. A soft pressure as his other hand went up her arm. He pulled back and she felt herself follow. Oh, she was in trouble. This was not what she needed.

She closed her eyes and took in his cologne, clean and fresh. His large hands cupped her face, and his kiss went deeper. The hands became a force holding her in place. Suddenly they didn't belong to Tyler. Another had taken his place. Someone from her past.

Trapped. Her lungs forgot how to work. A cold sweat tightened her skin.

Forcing her mind back to the present, Karly gritted her teeth and moved back. She pushed the palms of her hands against his chest. "Tyler, stop." She closed her eyes and took in one deep breath, holding to the count of five and letting it out.

"Karly?" His hand went to her shoulder. "Are you okay?"

"No." She pulled back, raising her gaze to meet his, reminding herself it was Tyler. He wasn't going to hurt her, not physically anyway. "We can't do this. I… I work for your dad. You're leaving soon. There are so many reasons why we shouldn't be kissing." Her treacherous heart was in battle with her mind and body. It started listing the reasons he was a good person and why they should be kissing. "No."

He stepped back and put his hands up in surrender. "I didn't argue with you."

"I'm sorry, I was actually yelling at myself." Hearing a cardinal sing, she looked up. The male was gone, leaving the drab-colored female alone.

The horses now grazed in the pasture. She searched for something else to distract her. Anything but Tyler and those eyes that promised more than they could deliver.

"Hey, it was one of the best mornings I've had in a really long time. I went a little overboard. Sorry, I know I'm not your type."

"My type?" She wrapped her arms around herself and looked toward the house. "That's the problem, Tyler. You are too much my type. Good-looking, charming and always on the move. I have to focus on Bryce's future. I can't get distracted and derailed again with a false promise."

"Did you just lump me in with your past boyfriends? With Billy Havender?" His jaw was working. He slammed the latch down on the gate. "Just for the record, and despite what my father and half of this town think about me, I would never ever abandon a child or hit a woman."

"Tyler, I didn't mean it th—" She was making a mess of this conversation.

"I get it. I won't touch you again." He started walking back to the barn. "I'll see you later."

How had she turned this wonderful day into an argument? No, she needed to stop taking the blame for other people's moods. She'd said no, and if that upset Tyler, it wasn't her fault. She had to break the bad habit of trying to keep everyone happy. She leaned against the fence and watched the horses. *God, how do I do that while still being a nice person?*

* * *

Karly tried calming the conflicting emotions battling it out in her mind. Dub had his granddaughters sitting with him on the porch swing. Pastor John and Bryce sat on the chairs on either side of the small table.

Dub looked so happy. "Bryce was telling us about the find y'all made today."

She nodded. "I hope it's okay with you that Tyler offered to cut down Christmas trees for the house."

Celeste wiggled in her seat. "I want to go see them! Can we go, Daddy?"

Pastor John nodded and smiled at his daughter. "I'll have to get Tyler to show us where they're growing. I didn't even know about them. It sounds fun."

"There are Christmas decorations stored in the attic. It's about time we got them down and spruced up this old house for Christmas. It's good timing, since we'll be hosting the pageant this year. Oh, look, here comes the prodigal son." Dub laughed at his own joke.

By the look of his scowl, Karly didn't think Tyler found it funny.

"Uncle Tyler!" His six-year-old niece, Celeste, ran and jumped off the top step with complete trust that her uncle would catch her.

"Hey, monkey, not everyone wants you climbing on them," Pastor John told his daughter.

With one arm around her waist, Tyler ruffled her hair with his other hand. "She's good." He lifted her a little higher, adjusting his niece on his hip as though it was an everyday occurrence. "What's this I hear about the annual Christmas pageant being here at the ranch? Are you sure that's a good idea with Dad needing to recover?"

"What, you don't think I can handle a little show on my place?" Dub struggled to stand.

Karly moved to his side.

"No, Dad, it's just a lot of people coming and going, and knowing you, you'll want to be in the middle of everything." He faced Pastor John. "I thought it was at the church?"

"Last year Lorrie Ann turned it into a live Nativity with animals. We used the unfinished youth building, but it's finished now. Everyone wants to keep it outside, so I thought about the covered pavilion here on the ranch. Carol had told me it was used for the huge company picnics before y'all sold the business."

Dub nodded and settled back down. Karly sat next to him and patted his leg. She leaned in and whispered, "Dub, you have to stay calm."

He gave her his charming smile and patted the top of her hand. "Tyler, you can help with the construction of the village. Since you're getting a tree from the hill, you can also get all the decorations from storage. These kids are going to have the best Christmas ever."

"Uncle Tyler, can I help get the decorations?" Celeste wiggled down.

"I want to help, too." Rachel, at eleven, was more reserved, but the sparkle on her face revealed her own excitement. "Bryce can help, too."

Tyler laughed. "All I did was offer to get a tree from the hill, but how can I tell you guys no?"

All three cheered. Celeste danced across the porch and stopped at the door. "Can we go get them now?"

Pastor John picked her up. "Slow down. It's not even Thanksgiving yet."

With a heavy sigh, she laid her head on her dad's

shoulder. "Bryce, since you're in kindergarten you get to be a singing angel this year. I did that last year, but I'm in first grade now, so I get to be in the chorus."

Bryce slumped, his feet swinging. "I only have one hand to carry the light."

Pastor John put his hand on the boy's small shoulder. "I was hoping you would lead the group. Do you think you can do that for me?" He gave Tyler a quick wink.

"Yes, sir!" Bryce sat up straight. "Mr. Tyler, you were right."

She really wished she could hate Tyler. Life would be so much easier. "How about some lunch?" Karly helped Dub up and wrapped her arm under his. "All this talking has made me hungry."

Dub nodded. "So you had a good time on the ranch with Tyler?"

"Yes, sir, you have a beautiful ranch."

And a beautiful son who will break my heart if I let him.

Keep your goal in sight, Karly. You need a solid and safe future for you and your son. That means no Tyler Childress.

Chapter Eleven

The therapist had been at the ranch all morning working with Dub. Now he and Bryce were napping, leaving Karly to explore the small wooden box of recipes
she had found in the back of the pantry a week ago, the
day after their ride.

Curved on the top lid was "Happy Mom Day to the
Best Mom. Love Tyler." The crude writing melted Karly's heart every time she looked at it.

Each index card was written in the same graceful
cursive. Notes and doodles gave insight into the personal family connection for the most important recipes. She pulled the sugar cookie recipe again. Two little
hearts decorated the upper corner with Dub's and Tyler's names written next to them. She had tried making the cookies three times now and found new ways
to fail each time. She had one week until Thanksgiving to get all the recipes perfected. Today she would
get the cookies right.

The last pieces of the village were going up today
and everyone was bringing a baked good to celebrate.
She wanted to take the cookies. She read each line and

followed the directions. With the oven preheated, she slid her first batch into the stove. Setting the timer, she went to the computer to read over the study guides for her GED classes. Number one on her list was to get her high school diploma. She found the dates the test was given in Uvalde and circled them on her calendar.

She had ordered her birth certificate, and as soon as it arrived, she could finish signing up for the classes. That process hadn't been easy. Karly had known her mother was Hawaiian, and now she knew she herself had been born there, too. Anthony had also changed her birthday a couple of times. She'd had to do some digging to get the document she needed to pave the way for her future.

Karly jumped at a noise behind her.

Adrian stepped back. "Didn't mean to frighten you. We knocked on the door. What has you so engrossed you didn't hear us open the back?"

On the other side of her, Tyler leaned over and looked at the screen. "GED classes?"

Karly turned off the monitor. The timer on the oven went off. Saved by the bell. Using the mittens, she pulled out two sheets of cookies. So far so good. They didn't look burned.

"I have perfect timing. Nothing better than cookies straight out of the oven." Adrian pulled a flat wire rack from the bottom cabinet and set it next to the stove top. "Here's the cooling rack."

Tyler had a spatula ready. It wasn't fair that all the men on the ranch seemed to know more about cooking than she did. "What are the two of you doing at the house together at this time of day?"

"Picking up Dad's tools for the finishing touches on

the Bethlehem village." He nudged a cookie with the edge of the spatula. "I talked to the therapist. He said Dad's recovery is going well. Is he napping?"

At the thought of Dub, she smiled. "He said he needed to do some reading, but when I checked on him he was sound asleep. He still insists he doesn't need a nap. He's talking about going to the barn in the morning to check on the horses."

A scowl on his face, Tyler turned to Adrian. "I'm not sure he's ready to go traipsing around the barn."

With a shrug, Adrian scooped up a cookie. "I found he does what he wants, whether he should or shouldn't." He popped the cookie in his mouth and immediately choked, his eyes widened and she could see his throat working.

Tyler's reaction was just as bad. His jaw muscles tightened, and his face did a couple of weird contortions. On his way to the refrigerator he grabbed two glasses. "Want some milk?" His voice sounded as if it had gravel in his throat." Glasses in hand, he passed one to Adrian "Um…what did you put in the cookies?"

She glanced at her latest attempt. They looked so good. Picking one up, she studied it. They couldn't be that bad. The cookie looked perfect. "I followed the recipe." Taking a bite, she spit it out in her hand. "That's horrible." She wanted to cry. Why did every mother in the world know how to make a simple cookie but her? What was wrong with her?

Adrian finished his milk. "My guess would be you used baking soda instead of baking powder. Mia did that once."

"There's a difference?" Karly was horrified they had seen her failure.

"Okay. I can try again." Tyler went to grab another cookie.

"Karly, really, it's okay if you can't cook. Everyone has different skills. These aren't *that* bad." Adrian shook his head as he lied to her.

"I'm a mother and housekeeper. I should be able to bake a cookie." Both men had a panicked look in their eyes. She was so close to crying and they knew it. Taking a deep breath, she relaxed. Giving them her best smile, she gathered up the offensive treats, took the one out of Tyler's hand and threw them in the trash. "I'm okay, guys. A bad batch of cookies won't ruin my day." She made sure to give them her biggest smile. "No worries, no drama with this momma."

Tyler looked at her as if she had gone crazy. Adrian patted her on the back.

"Really, Karly, you are great at other things, like working with the teen parents. The kids were asking about you last Sunday. Tyler, she's a natural. She needs to think about joining our program full-time. We'll buy the cookies."

"Thanks."

Both men still looked a little lost. "Go get your tools and go build something. Bryce and I will be out later for the costume rehearsal. I'm fine. I promise it takes more than a few awful cookies to bring my world down."

The men headed out the back door as she grabbed the flour. She was going to make these cookies if it was the last thing she ever did.

Before she could start mixing, she heard the door open again. She sighed in frustration. Tyler came back into the room. "Hey, I forgot to give you the mail. You have something official looking from Hawaii."

She gasped. This was it, her birth certificate. Her hand had a slight tremor to it as she took the FedEx envelope from him.

"Are you okay?"

She looked at the envelope, then back at him. "It's my birth certificate. I've never seen it before." Blood pounded in her ears.

He moved closer. "How have you not seen it? How did you… The classes. You need it to get your GED."

She nodded. "I'm so sorry. We moved so much I never finished school. I want to… I mean, I need to fix this if I'm going to build a safe future for Bryce."

"You. Are. Amazing." He looked at her as if he believed that.

"I thought you would be mad or appalled. I'm a high school dropout. I haven't done anything right." She had spent weeks in fear of his reaction if he found out. Now she stood in front of him and waited.

Thrusting his chin at her, he smiled. "Open it."

She took a deep breath and pulled the tab. Carefully, she pulled out the sheet of paper. Tears welled up in her eyes and her throat burned. With trembling fingertips, she touched her mother's name. Laura Kalakona Morgan. Her mother had been married to someone else other than Anthony. She looked at her father's name. Philip Morgan. Her father's name was Philip Morgan. Her name was Karly Kalakona Morgan. She shook her head. A drop of water landed on the paper.

"Here." Tyler took the paper from her and wrapped his arms around her. She had a father. A father named Philip Morgan. "My father is Philip Morgan. I never knew that." Was he alive? Had he abandoned her and her mother the way Bryce's father had done to her?

She stepped back from Tyler. "I'm sorry. I wasn't expecting to get all emotional over my birth certificate. I'm a mess."

"You just saw your father's name for the first time. Seeing your mother's name, too, after all these years. You're perfectly normal. You just found out you might have family in Hawaii."

She had even thought of that. "No. Even if I do, they didn't want me." They had left her with Anthony.

"How do you know that? Because your stepfather told you?" He raised an eyebrow.

She adjusted her ponytail. "Good point. Right now I have to focus on getting my GED and getting ready for Thanksgiving. You do realize it's only a few days away."

He laughed. "From what I understand, we are going to John's place. Lorrie Ann and her family are going to be there. With the Ortegas there that means Maggie, her aunt, will be in charge, all we have to do is show up and eat. Stop worrying about everything. Get signed up for your classes and come see the work your son has done on the set." He gripped her upper arms and looked her right in the eyes. "Are you okay? Do you want me to stay?"

Shaking her head, she said, "No."

"Are you sure?"

She smiled at him. "Yes, I'm sure. Seeing my parents' names caught me off guard. Go on. I'm sure they're wondering where you went off to."

He gave her a quick kiss on the forehead, a simple gesture that almost brought her to her knees.

"I'll see you out in the pasture, right?" He started walking backward out of the kitchen.

"Yes, we'll be there." Now she had to get those family cookies done if it was the last thing she did. Family. She might have family in Hawaii.

God, what do I do with this information?

The cool breeze brought the smells of evergreens and coffee as it ruffled through her hair. She tossed her favorite red poncho over her left shoulder.

Katy waved from the tables of baked goods and coffee. "Karly, over here!"

"Mom!" Bryce waved as he ran with the other kids.

For a moment she watched him.

He ran. Like a boy without a care in the world. She closed her eyes and thanked God for all the blessings He had brought to their lives.

Katy Buchannan, the mercantile owner, stood with Lorrie Ann and newlywed Vickie Torres. Her friends—there wasn't a better word. They also made the best sweets from scratch. She had thrown away her last baking attempt. Her platter was filled with pigs in a blanket. Precooked meat and croissants from a can were her meager offerings.

She was a cheater. Hers would be the last to go, after all the homemade baked goods had been devoured.

Lorrie Ann took the plate. "Thank you for bringing these. They'll balance out all the sweets."

Vickie grinned and shook her head. "I can't even look at another cookie, let alone eat one." She laughed. "Words I couldn't imagine ever saying."

Katy hugged her. "You're so smart, bringing something other than cookies or cakes."

Returning the hug, Karly snorted. "You're all so sweet to not mention I couldn't bake an edible cookie to save my life. Consider these canned croissant and little sausages my public service."

Stepping across to the table, Katy laughed. "You're so funny. You know the guys will expect them every time we have food from now on."

"They want the good stuff. Not my heat-and-serve fast food."

Vickie pushed the platter back to her. "Just take these over to the guys and see how many are left when you come back here."

"No, no. Really, no one even needs to know I brought them." One day she would actually bake something she would be proud to serve, but not today.

Karly shook her head. These women were crazy, which worked for her. Otherwise they might not be her friends. She smiled and looked at the women standing in front of her. For a moment joy vibrated throughout her whole body. Bryce was running and playing, and she was talking with her friends. Vickie had an eyebrow raised in a challenge.

Katy's lips were pressed tight in a silly grin. She nodded. They acted as if she was on a mission. Rolling her eyes, she palmed the platter in her hands and turned to march off to the men.

On the other side of the building, Tyler laughed. Not that she had been watching him the whole time. He lifted the wood over his head. Officer Jake Torres, Vickie's new husband, had the other side.

Tyler's dark shirt pulled across his back as the muscles of his shoulders bunched and flexed. Together the men hoisted it onto the post while two others used nail guns to anchor it in place. He turned and found her staring at him.

She swallowed and looked down at the pigs in a blanket. She looked up, but this time sought out Pastor John, avoiding Tyler's intense stare that saw too much. She was so embarrassed about the scene she created earlier. "Are you ready for a break?"

Adrian laughed. "We've barely started, and you're already trying to feed us?"

She nodded to the table where her friends, the wives of many of the men standing around her, stood. "They either think you're brave enough or desperate enough to eat these pigs in a blanket I made."

"Are they mad at us?" Tyler leaned against the post with his arms crossed and winked at her.

"There is that option." She shot back at his grinning face.

Adrian approached her first and took one. He turned it over, checking all sides before popping it in his mouth. There was a hushed anticipation. Karly held her breath. Would he need a drink to wash it down? Oh, she should have brought drinks.

He leaned closer and grinned at her before grabbing a few more. The other guys yelled at him. "You can't have them all."

Hands reached for the plate, and before she could blink they were all gone. The men chewed and grinned.

"These are good. You've been holding out on us."

"Do you have more?" Tyler asked.

She laughed. She had been so worried about not being able to bake. Who knew she could have won them over with canned dough and baby sausages?

"Hey, Ty, stop staring and be useful." Jake gave Tyler a shoulder bump as he went back to work.

Tyler put his hands into his front pockets. "Red's a good color on you."

The spark in his blue eyes made her desire things she was too smart to want. "I think your friends need you."

He shrugged. "I'd rather do what I'm doing." He tilted his chin up. "You've been hiding your skills. Will you make more when we get home?"

Who knew she would feel so empowered just from cooking something they all liked and wanted? "Anyone can unroll a can and wrap dough around little sausages." She was being silly stupid for being so proud of the fact he liked what she had cooked.

"Will you make them for Christmas Eve at our house? My mom had standard dishes, but she was always looking for something new." His voice was so low she barely heard him. "It's been a long time since I spent Christmas with family."

"At our house?" She kept her voice low to match his.

Tyler's clear blue eyes held a trace of sadness that was in contrast to his beautiful smile. For a moment it was just the two of them.

"Yeah." The grin finally reached his eyes. "Will you make more?"

"Of course."

"Hey, Ty! Did you come to help? If you wanted to talk to Karly, you could have stayed home and done that," Adrian yelled at them.

"I'm being summoned." He winked. "Later."

"Later." She stayed there and watched as Tyler joined the men. Before the day was done, they would have a biblical village built in the Texas Hill Country. And she might lose her heart.

Was that a good thing or a bad thing? Maybe she

should talk to Lorrie Ann. She knew Adrian or Pastor John could help her. She took a deep breath and headed back to the women. Humming a song, she looked for Bryce. He was running with a long piece of material draped over his head.

She couldn't stop the smile even if she had wanted to. This was the life she wanted for her son. A community they belonged in; friends they could trust. There were moments in life when everything came together in a perfect moment. God was good.

Heading to the tent, she saw a man she didn't recognize had joined the group of women. He looked familiar. He threw his head back and laughed out loud—a deep hearty laugh that made others want to join in even if they didn't know why he was laughing. She stumbled on a rock. He was tall with thick dark hair mixed with the perfect amount of gray. The gray was new.

He turned, his gaze locking on her. "Karly, baby! Surprise."

Ice. Ice took over her veins. Her heart stopped. The lungs that had just been breathing forgot how to move. She fell into a black hole, blood leaving her legs. Something hit her. In a dream state she looked down. The plate she had been holding lay shattered on the ground around her boots. Pieces too small to be fixed.

"Karly?" Vickie was the first to reach her. "Are you okay?" She started picking up the broken pieces.

Bryce. Her gaze went wild trying to find Bryce. She wanted to grab him and run. Her car was back at the ranch house. She needed to get there.

"Karly?" Lorrie Ann stood on the other side of her. Her hands on her arms. "Karly?"

"I wanted to surprise you, baby girl." Her stepfather

stood before her, his charming smile in place. Anthony reached out and tucked her hair behind her ear.

She stepped away and focused on the chucks of plates on the ground. Vickie took the pieces from her shaking hands.

His eyes became moist. "It's been too long. I'm so sorry it took me so long to find you." He took her into his arms and enveloped her in a bear hug, holding her so close she fought to breathe. He leaned back with his fingers wrapped around her arms. She stepped out of his reach. "Look at you. You look so much like your mom at the same age. It took me so long to find you. And you have a son." He smiled and wiped a single tear off his cheek. "I have a grandson." He looked to the kids. "Which one is Bryce?"

No, no, no were the only words she could find in her brain.

"I can't believe how fast I was able to find you here in Clear Water. I checked into a cabin, and the first person I asked knew where to find you." He flashed the charismatic smile that put everybody at ease.

Her? A deep chill radiated from her bones to her skin.

She blinked and looked at the people she trusted. People she loved. They were smiling. A few even had tears spilling over lashes.

"Oh, I love reunions. This is so amazing."

Karly wasn't even sure who spoke. Everyone crowded around her. A hand landed on her left shoulder. She jumped and turned. Tyler stood there. His blue eyes grounded her. "Karly? What's going on?" His steady gaze moved from her to the man standing before her. Her long-lost stepfather. Oh, no. She was going to be sick.

Anthony reached inside his jacket and pulled out a worn picture. "I've kept this next to my heart ever since the day I got it." He held out a picture of Karly at nine years old, bald. Those were the days he had kept her head shaved, allowing people to think she had cancer.

Vickie gasped. "You never told us you had cancer as a child."

She couldn't breathe. Unable to talk, she shook her head.

Maggie laid a warm hand on her, questions in her soft brown eyes.

Sweet Katy had tears in her eyes. "How horrific."

Tyler put a gentle hand on her back. "Karly?"

Maggie tightened her fingers around Karly's arm. "You've been through so much. I'm so glad God brought you to us."

Surrounded by Maggie's fresh, clean smell gave Karly a moment to collect herself. These people were truth and love. She needed to get Bryce and go home, except it wasn't her home. She closed her eyes and took a deep breath. Maybe she wasn't meant to have a home, but her son needed one. "Where's Bryce? I don't see my son." The world became a fuzzy blur. She needed to breathe before she passed out. "Tyler, I don't feel well. Can we go home now?"

Anthony tried to haul her into a side hug. "Oh, that's a good idea. I would love to see your new home. You could give me a ride and we can talk in private. You live here on the ranch now?"

She pushed against him and moved closer to Tyler.

"Um… I don't know." How did she keep him from tainting the best place she had ever lived?

Tyler shifted to her other side, standing between her and Anthony. "Hi. I'm Tyler Childress. Karly works for my dad. She actually lives at our house, and Dad's not feeling well. He's not up for company."

Oh, she loved him.

"Tyler!" Katy punched him in the arm. "They haven't seen each other in forever."

He kept his gaze right on Karly. She saw either confusion or concern in his gaze, maybe contempt. She just wasn't sure. Whichever it was, she was grateful he'd given her a way out of here.

Maggie hugged her. "Katy, I think this might be too much." She looked at Anthony. "I can take you back to the Pecan Farm. I'm sure you're tired after that long trip."

Tyler wrapped his arm around her shoulder and pressed his lips right above her ear. "Let's get Bryce so we can head home." He shot one quick glare at Anthony before he left to find Bryce, his fingers anchored in hers.

Anthony kept pace with them. "Karly, I've been searching for you since I found out you ran away from the Walters." He paused and made eye contact with each of his audience members. "I had gone to Peru on a mission." He went into storytelling mode. She didn't want to hear any of his stories. They were lies, all lies.

She followed Tyler. The bad boy promising to rescue her. Not again. She couldn't fall into the pattern of expecting someone else to save her.

Life was unpredictable. Proof—her ugly past stood in the middle of her current life. After working so hard to get her life on track, she was right back where she started.

She'd always made a point to stay in the background—to stay hidden. Clear Water had given her a false sense of security. She'd gotten too comfortable.

They got Bryce. "We need to go home." Holding out her hand she waited for his small fingers.

"Momma, we haven't practiced yet." As he complained, he took her hand and followed her and Tyler.

Maggie met them to the truck. "Karly, are you okay? I should have called you before I brought him out."

"No, you're fine. I just need time to explain everything to Bryce. I haven't seen Anthony since I was fifteen. I'm just not sure what I'm feeling right now."

Maggie hugged her, a long tight hug. "Something is wrong. You let us know if you need anything. We're here for you. Remember God has you."

Karly allowed the truth to seep into her veins. "Thank you." Leaving Maggie's warmth was a hard thing to do, but she had done harder things. She was about to do the most difficult thing she had ever done.

In less than an hour Clear Water would be in her past. "Maggie, thank you for everything. I can't put into words how much you and so many of the others have changed my life."

Maggie patted her cheek and turned back to the crowd. Karly helped Bryce into the ranch truck.

Buckled into the booster seat, Bryce touched her hair. "Momma, I don't want to go."

"We have to go, Bryce. I'll explain it later." He was going to be so upset when he realized they were leaving town, the ranch, the horses, Dub and Tyler. She would be leaving Tyler.

Tyler drove in silence. He didn't ask one single question. That made it easier not to cry as she watched the horses in the pasture. He was taking them back to the house she had foolishly believed could be a real home for them.

Once again, Anthony had stolen Christmas. It was as if she was nine years old all over again.

Tyler parked the truck. Words bounced around in his head, but he didn't know which ones to use. Something was wrong, something big. Less than an hour ago, she was flirting and laughing. Now she acted like a scared kid, as though she was about to run.

"Karly?"

Facing him, she raised an eyebrow in question.

He had her attention. Now what? "Are you okay?" Well, that was brilliant.

"Just in shock. I haven't seen or heard from him in over eight years. We didn't part on good terms. He never went to Peru." She was out of the truck before she even finished the last sentence. Bryce had climbed down from the side step.

Crossing in front of the truck, he noticed the tension in her whole body. Instead of her usual graceful movements, each effort appeared stiff.

She pulled Bryce through the door. "Sweetheart, I need you to get the red backpack under your bed and put your favorite things in it. We are going on a road trip."

"Momma, we can't. I have school tomorrow, and I didn't even get to do rehearsal today. We have a Thanksgiving party at school. We can't leave, Momma."

She knelt in front of him, eye to eye. "You know our plan? When I say to go you go, without question."

Bryce looked at Tyler, fear in the little guy's face. "Did you do something to Momma?"

Without even a glance at him, she brought Bryce's face back to her. "It has nothing to do with Tyler. You have to trust me. You know how we have an emergency plan. We keep supplies in the car ready to start a new adventure. Well, today we are hopping in the car and seeing where God takes us."

He pulled back, anger radiating off him. "No, Momma. I prayed for God to give us a home and a horse and a real family. God gave us them. I don't want an adventure. I want to stay with my friends." Tears started rolling, and he wiped them with the back of his sleeve.

"Shh." Karly used her thumb to clean his cheek. "It's going to be okay."

Tyler couldn't stand by and watch this train wreck happen without trying to pull her off the rails. "Hey, Cowboy, will you do me a favor? In your room, under the bed there are boxes."

The little boy nodded. Trust and intensity burned bright in his eyes.

"I need you to find a Bible. It's brown leather and has the name Samuel Childress engraved on the front. Will you do that for me and bring it to me? There's something I need to show your mom."

"Will you tell her God wants us to stay here?"

He roughed up Bryce's hair. "I try not to speak for God, but I'll see what I can do. Okay, Cowboy?"

"Yes, sir." Small shoulders slumped, he stalked off down the hall.

"You still need to pack your bag," she called after him. "Or we'll leave without it."

Once Bryce was out of earshot, Tyler turned to her. "What are you doing?"

She went into the pantry and pulled a box from under the cabinet. "I'm going to take some food. Please make sure it gets deducted from my last paycheck."

Tyler leaned a hip on the opposite counter and crossed his arms over his chest, watching as she frantically packed dry food items.

"And where would I be sending this check?"

She groaned and covered her face with her hands before going back to grabbing crackers, cereal and canned tuna. "I don't know. I have your number. I'll text you in a couple of days."

With the box full, she darted past him and went to the computer desk. Opening a drawer, she started moving things around.

"What did he do?" Because of the way she was reacting to her stepfather showing up, the worst scenarios kept running through his mind. "Did he hurt you? You're not a kid. We can go to the police."

"What?" She paused and looked at him.

"Did your stepfather hurt you? Is that why you're running?"

A flash drive went into the box. "No. No, nothing physical. I… He just… I have to leave. There is nothing the police can do anyway." The hallway was her next goal.

Tyler cut her off at the pass. "Karly, slow down, take a deep breath and tell me what's got you frightened. You running like a scared kid."

"Please let me by."

Instinct drove him to take her hand and lead her to the living room, away from her frenzied packing.

"Tyler, let me go. I don't want him in my son's life. This is why I have the suitcase in the car ready to go. We never know how our life will change, but I do know if we leave now I can be out of the state by morning."

"Why? What did he do that makes you bolt out of the life you're building here with your son?"

She turned on him, anger flashing hot on her cheeks. "You, Mr. Childress, with your safe home and bunkhouse, do not know what it's like." She actually snarled the words and flung her hand toward the door. "You, with adoring parents and a sister, a town that loves you no matter what you've done, would not understand what it's like to be alone and…" Head down, she turned away from him and buried her face in her hands.

"Karly, you're right. I had those things. It doesn't change the fact that you can't just run away. This has become your home, Bryce's home." He gently held on to her upper arm, wanting to hold her in place. "Look at me."

She turned her face away and looked down.

He held his ground but spoke softly, afraid if she left, that would be it. He would never see her or Bryce again. Suddenly the pressure on his chest made it hard to breathe. They were underwater, and he needed to get them to air. "Your stepfather can't be in your life without your permission. If he's hurt you, then we need to talk to Jake or the sheriff."

"No, it's not that. Stop calling him my stepfather." She made eye contact and poked his chest. "It's so easy for you. You still belong here, even though you left. You might hate Clear Water, but you still belong. Your father and you butt heads because you're so stubborn, but he would never use you to hurt other people. You know he loves you."

"This isn't about me and my father. Your step— Anthony can't hurt you now. Whatever he did happened when you were a child, right?" One step closer to her and he gently wrapped his fingers under her chin, making sure he had solid eye contact. "You're not a child anymore. You have friends that will do whatever you need. This is your ground. We are your family. Don't let him run you off."

One big tear slid over her bottom lashes and trailed down her cheek. The scared look faded as he watched hope flutter to life in her eyes.

"Don't run." He waited. What else could he say? *Please, God, give me the words.* "Do you trust that God brought you here for a reason?"

Shutting him out again, she closed her eyes and turned her head. But no attempt was made to leave. The muscles in her arms still trembled, but she stood in front of him.

"Karly?" In his heart he knew they were being tested and his job was to find the right words to help her face her fears. "I ran. I ran from the grief. I ran from the pain. I ran from the memories. I ran from everything I knew because it was easier than staying and fighting. You have so much to fight for right now. Don't let him take that from you."

"What if I'm not strong enough?" She blinked a couple of times. Then her eyes focused on him. "What if he makes everyone believe him? He's good at that."

"Recently you were telling me to have faith that God will take care of all my needs—that I didn't have to be in charge and have all the right answers. You don't have to be strong enough if you believe that God put you here. We can't handle everything. We weren't meant to. God has you, Karly. Let Him be strong enough."

She nodded. "'Forgetting what is behind and straining toward what is ahead, I press on toward the goal to win the prize for which God has called me Heavenward in Christ Jesus.' I say it every night."

"Karly, don't let the past stop you from the future God intended for you."

She took a deep breath. "I'm not going to let him steal another Christmas from me or Bryce." Her gaze searched his as if she found something she hadn't expected. "Thank you, Tyler." She smiled. "You're not as bad as everyone says." Then she gave him a weak smile.

Air filled his lungs. He had made it to the surface.

A half laugh came from his throat. "Yeah, well, don't tell anyone. I don't think I'm ready to be the full-fledged prodigal son. I might give Dad another stroke."

Dismay stamped on her face and she slapped him on the shoulder. "Tyler!"

"What, too soon?" He rubbed the back of his neck and winked at her.

"You're horrible." But the small laugh took any insult out of her comment. She stood still for a few moments.

Tyler held his breath, afraid to spook her. He wanted to pull her into his arms and tell her he would take care of everything. She had stopped packing for now, but the real problem had not been addressed. She didn't trust him to help her. He ran his fingers through his hair and rubbed the back of his neck. Could he blame her? He wasn't sure he trusted himself.

Her shoulders lifted, then fell. "I'm going to tell Bryce to stop packing."

As she walked past him, he grabbed her hand. "Karly, seriously, you can tell us anything. You're not alone. You've got Maggie, John, Adrian at your side. Dad would do anything for you. Don't think you have to do this without help. Whatever it is that had you running can't be bigger than your friends or your faith. Okay?"

She nodded before turning away and heading through the kitchen and down the hall to his old room. The room that now belonged to her son.

Well, he got her to stop packing. Why did he feel so hollow? He'd convinced her to stay, while he knew he would be leaving in a couple more weeks. Faith. He had told her that her faith was bigger than her problems. Where had his faith gone? Half of the time when he talked to Karly, all he could think of was reaching down and kissing her. That was what the heroes did in the old Westerns he had watched with his dad. But she had made it clear she didn't want his kisses, and he was no one's hero. The best plan of action was to stay away from her.

She had run into the mercantile to pick up some plates and cups for the Thanksgiving dinner tomorrow, and now she found herself cornered in the back between the glass doors and Anthony. She scanned the store but didn't see anyone.

He leaned in close. To anyone else it might look like an affectionate move. She stepped back. "Don't touch me."

"Karly, what's wrong? Come on. You're not a highstrung teen anymore. I can see you've grown up. So what are your plans for Thanksgiving? You gonna be serving those rich ranchers?"

"It's none of your business." She turned to go around him, but he slid in front of her.

"You're a mother now to a beautiful little boy. My grandson's an amazing kid. I can see why people are tripping over themselves to help you."

"Bryce is not your grandson. I'm not going to let you use Bryce the way you used me when I was little." She turned to step around him. "I take care of everything we need."

"Oh, I'm sure you do. You were always so resourceful after we lost your mother." His hand gripped her upper arm.

With a hard jerk she pulled her arm away from him. Her lungs froze, burning when she tried to take a breath. "I gave you a good life, and people loved helping us."

With a hard jerk she pulled her arm away from him. Her lungs froze, burning when she tried to take a breath. She no longer a six-year-old who had to rely on him.

He nodded and smiled at her as if to reassure her. "I've been looking for you ever since you ran away. I took you in and raised you when no one else wanted you. You've been very ungrateful, Karly. It being Thanksgiving and all, it just isn't right."

"The way we lived was wrong. You took money from people by lying to them."

"I showed you the world. You got to swim with dolphins and ride elephants. Here in Clear Water you're just a maid, cleaning up after other people. That little boy of yours is a gift. You could have more. Better things."

"I'm not interested. We also lived in horrible conditions, at times not even knowing when we would eat or get evicted. You are not welcome in my life."

"You're the only family I have left, and I'm getting

older. I made mistakes in the past, but I did the best I could do. I kept you fed."

"Then, why do I remember mornings waking up hungry but you had a new bottle of whiskey?"

"I had a bit of a drinking problem, but I never hurt you. I never hit you."

"No, you didn't. You also never told me about my family in Hawaii. My father, Philip Morgan. Why did you tell me there wasn't any family?"

"Your father was dead before you were born. I saved your mother."

Dead. That was her fear, but what if he was lying? No one had come looking for her. "You need to leave. There is nothing for you here."

"I'm not leaving empty-handed. You live on that big fancy ranch." He moved in closer. "I imagine you have access to some nice funds. And all the good church people are already talking about fund-raising when I told them how you're struggling with medical bills, but too proud to ask for help. You don't even have to steal or lie. These people are ready to open their wallets to you and poor little Bryce. You're sitting on a gold mine."

"Karly?" Tyler's voice from the front of the store had never sounded so wonderful.

"I'm coming!" She grabbed the bag of cups and a jumbo stack of plates. The pretty ones she wanted were out of her reach, so she settled for the ones closest to her, hitting Anthony with them in the process. "I'm not taking anyone's money." Paper goods in hand, she shoved past him and marched to the front. She would find a way to get him out of town or she would have to leave. She didn't want to leave.

Tyler looked at her than glanced to the back of the store. "Are you okay?"

"Yeah."

Vickie came out of the back and rung up her goods. She went to pay, and Tyler stopped her.

"I'll pay for it."

"No. I can pay my own way." She knew she sounded harsh, but she could take money from anyone. "Maybe I shouldn't go to Pastor John's house for Thanksgiving. It's all of the Ortega family."

He chuckled. "I think you might be considered more of a family member than me."

She handed the cash to Vickie. "Then, I'm paying my own way."

Vickie winked at her.

Tyler put his wallet back into his back pocket. "Fine, but you really need to stop this nonsense about not being part of the family. And remember to be careful what you wish for. You just might get it."

Chapter Twelve

Tyler had survived his first family Thanksgiving without his sister. He had expected the emptiness of her absence, but it surprised him that he'd really enjoyed being around the people had had grown up with. Watching Karly soak up the traditions and smiling through the whole chaotic event had made it worthwhile. Rachel was growing up and looking more like Carol. He really needed to be around more.

This morning he had headed straight to the barns, needing something to center him after all the emotional ups and downs yesterday. He ran his hand along the smooth coat of the young stud, Lena's only foal, Lena's Jet-Setter.

Working the three-year-old in the arena took him back to the days he'd ridden Lena. More important, he got away from the emptiness of being surrounded by family but missing the most important ones, the ones who were gone.

They had bred Lena once, but the added weight had been too hard for her at the end, so they would only have one foal from her. He was a champ. The young stud had challenged him and embraced the action. The horse was the best of his dam and sire. Tyler could change his schedule in order to make the Houston show. He patted the horse's neck. "Jet, your dam outshone them all the year I took her."

"Are you thinking of riding again?" Dub walked into the barn with his walker, Karly close behind. "You had a gift and now you've buried your talent. No good ever comes out of that, son. It's been too long, Tyler. It's time to come home."

Untying the lead, Tyler walked Jet to his stall. "Karly, should Dad be in the barns?"

"The therapist said—"

"What? You can't talk to me, son?" His dad's voice sounded gruff.

"Dad, I promised John I wouldn't start any fights." Securing the latch, Tyler went back and retrieved the saddle and blanket. "So no, I'm not going to talk to you about my life. We just don't agree. Leave it at that." The door to the tack room got stuck so he kicked it, probably harder than he needed to.

He heard his dad shuffle closer. He closed his eyes for a bit. Man, he'd never thought Dub Childress would ever walk with anything other than an I-own-the-world swagger. Of course, he'd also thought his mother would live longer than the three months.

"Son, don't take your anger out on an innocent door." His bigger-than-life father stood in the doorway, not so big at the moment. "I wanted to go for a walk and I also need to talk to you, but you didn't come in for breakfast. I'm forced to come track you down."

After making sure the saddle and equipment were

clean and secure, Tyler took a deep breath and turned to his dad, who had been waiting patiently. "What about?"

"It's time we got the Christmas decorations out of storage. I want Bryce and Karly to have a real Christmas, the kind we used to have when your mom was with us. She'd like that."

"Dad, I only have a week before I have to go back to Denver."

"Then, all the more reason to get it done today." Without waiting for a reply, his dad turned, hitting the frame with the cane and stumbling a bit before Karly steadied him. "We'll be at the house waiting for you."

Tyler busied himself with making sure all the tack was in perfect alignment until laughter brought him out of the tack room. After his eyesight adjusted, he found his father was showing Bryce how to hold the apple slice in his hand to feed Tank. Together they moved to the next stall and were greeted by Lena. The years slipped away, and he was the little boy learning about the horses from his dad.

"Tyler?" Karly approached from behind him. A worried expression caused lines in her forehead.

"What's wrong?" He leaned a shoulder against the door frame and stuffed his hands into his pockets. "My dad giving you problems?"

"I know how you feel about pulling memories out of closets. You don't need to help get the decorations. I am more than capable of moving some boxes and stringing lights. I'm running into town so I can pick up a tree. You don't need to go cut one down."

"I already promised the girls and Bryce I would take them out to pick out the tree. I don't break promises." Did she think he was irresponsible, also?

"Okay. So you get the tree and I'll get the boxes." She gave him a tight smile before turning to leave.

"Karly, is everything okay with your stepfather?" Stupid question. He already knew the answer.

She stopped, but didn't turn around. "He is not my step-father. Anthony wants to spend time with Bryce. I told him no. I'm still trying to figure out what to do next." As she tilted her head back, the ponytail, long and silky, touched the base of her back. Her laugh sounded forced and dry. "I was a high school dropout and pregnant by the time I was seventeen. I have no right to judge anyone, not even him. Maybe he did the best he knew how."

He moved to stand in front of her. Wanting to cup her face in his hands, he settled for eye-to-eye contact. "Don't let him off the hook. Look what you've accomplished. It's amazing. I really don't know how you do it. You have every reason to be bitter and blame the world. Instead, you find the beauty in everything and you keep going. You're worried about my feelings over getting some old decorations out of storage."

He took a deep breath and clinched his jaw. What he really wanted to do was kiss her, but he had promised not to touch her again. So he took a step back and offered her his gratitude for helping him see the beauty of the ranch again. "My mother would be heartbroken that those boxes collected dust when they could be creating joy and memories. You are doing us a favor. All of us."

Shifting her gaze to the barn door, she took a step back. "Your father wants to go to the café and meet some of his friends. It's good that he's willing to go out in public. The therapist says he's recovering at a phenomenal rate. Some people just want to hide and wallow in their misery. You don't have to worry when you head back to Denver and to your flying."

Where was his brain? He was standing here thinking of kissing her while he also made plans to take off. "That's good. It'll make it easier when I leave for my trip."

"Will you be coming back?"

"In four days. I asked to be switched to domestic flights so it will be easier to be at the ranch between trips, if Dad needs me."

"Okay."

They stood in silence for a moment.

She turned toward the house. "Well, I guess I need to get going. Dub says we have to leave at four on the dot."

Falling into step next to her, he wanted to say something but was not sure what needed to be said.

"Tyler, are you sure about taking Bryce to get the tree? Maybe I can get Maggie to take your father to town."

"I know how protective you are about him, and I won't take his safety lightly. John and the girls will be with us. We'll have fun. I think it might be good for him to do this without Mom hovering."

"You're probably right. Thanks for convincing me to stay and giving Bryce a great memory."

"Not a problem." He wished she would let him do more, but to what point? He was leaving Clear Water as fast as he could, and she wanted to grow old here.

The world looked different from behind the steering wheel of the ranch truck Dub insisted she use to drive him into town. It made her feel empowered and a little scared that she might roll over something without even knowing. Dub's chin fell against his chest. He'd assured her he was strong enough for the short day trip, but he fell asleep almost as soon as they started driving back home.

She smiled. Something about the strong, stubborn man sleeping was endearing. He worked so hard to take care of the people he loved.

Of course her traitorous mind took her to Tyler, standing in the barn, putting his feelings aside to make sure Bryce would have his own special memories. She'd thought he might kiss her again, but instead he had moved away from her.

She had a feeling he wouldn't make a move after she'd made him promise not to touch her again. He never broke a promise. She would have to be the one to kiss him.

What was she thinking? Ugh. He was leaving and she was determined to plant roots here. Her brain needed to have a good sit-down chat with her heart. She didn't have time to mess with a relationship, especially one that was doomed from the get-go.

Easing the truck through the ranch gates, she felt as if she was coming home. "Oh, Dub." A gentle touch woke him up. "Look."

On the front porch of the brick ranch house, Tyler, Pastor John, Bryce, Rachel and Celeste stood around a large Christmas tree leaning against the window. Tyler had his hands on his hips. Bryce mirrored the stance. They scowled at the tree.

"What are they doing?"

Dub laughed. "They forgot to measure the tree and it's too big for the house. They always look smaller out on the hillside. Park in the front drive."

The group all turned and looked at the truck. As she pulled up to the circular drive, the kids jumped off the porch. By the time she had the beast in Park and the engine killed, the two girls had Dub's door open.

Celeste, the youngest girl, grabbed her grandfather's hand. "Grandpa, Uncle Tyler has to make the tree smaller. Ours was almost as tall but it fit in our house. It didn't look so big in the pasture."

"Momma." Bryce flew off the top step and ran to her. "I got to pick out the tree. Tyler said it was the best he's ever seen, but now it won't fit in the house."

Pastor John followed the kids, his face a bit red from the wind. "It's been a great day, and now that the reinforcements are here, the girls and I are meeting Lorrie Ann to decorate our tree."

"But, Daddy, Grandpa just got here!" Celeste had her arms around her grandfather.

Dub squeezed her. "Y'all come over for dinner tomorrow night."

Pastor John took his daughter's hand. "Why not come over and we can serve all of you?" He smiled at Karly, making sure she knew they were invited, too.

If he knew the whole truth about her past, would she still be welcomed?

Tyler cleared his throat. "Before you go, I noticed a box we got from the attic you should have before you leave." He held the door open for everyone to come inside.

Once in the living room, he picked up a red-and-green plastic box with Carol's handprints on the side. Tyler kept his face expressionless as he handed the box to his brother-in-law. "Mom kept a box with all of our school-made ornaments. I thought the girls would like to put them on your tree."

Celeste ran to her father's side. "I want to see them!"

Pastor John tucked them under his arm. "We will, monkey, as soon as we get home. Thank you, Tyler." His eyes full of compassion, he hugged Tyler with his free arm, patting him on the back.

Tyler ducked his head. "You should have had them five years ago."

"All in God's timing." He glanced at his oldest daughter. "I think this is the perfect year to hang these on our tree in our new house. What do you think, Rachel?"

She nodded and went to hug her uncle. "Thank you."

She kissed him on the cheek before stepping back, tears in her eyes—eyes that were so much like Carol's it used to be hard to look at her. Now it made him smile to see a bit of his sister alive in her daughter.

"Yeah, thank you, Uncle Tyler!" Celeste leaped up on him. Arms around his neck, she gave him a loud kiss. Hopping down, she hugged her grandfather, then headed for the door. "Come on, guys. I want to see the ornaments Momma made when she was little."

Laughing, Pastor John followed his daughters. "Ty, you're good at distracting kids. It's a skill. See y'all tomorrow."

Dub snorted. "It's because he's just a big kid himself."

Tyler rolled his eyes. "I'm going to get the tree ready for the house. Bryce, you want to help me while your mom gets the decorations unpacked?"

"Cool, can I use the saw?"

"Bryce—" Her concern was cut off.

"Sure, we can take turns. I'm sure my arm will get tired." He looked at Karly, his boyish smile melting her a bit. "We promise to be careful. Right, Cowboy?"

"Yeah, Mom, we promise." Joy lit up his face.

"I'm counting on it." She needed to work on saying no to those smiles.

"They'll be fine." Dub's gruff voice brought her back to the job at hand. Boxes, at least twenty, stood in the entryway and in the living room.

"She loved decorating for Christmas. Half of the boxes are her nativity scenes. She had everything marked and labeled. Let's start with those."

"Are you sure you don't want to take a nap, Dub?"

"I don't need you to worry about me. I'm fine. I'll nap after we get this stuff out. It should have happened before today, but I didn't have any reason."

Was Tyler being home the reason, or her and Bryce? She made sure he had the walker beside him as they started to unwrap all the memories of the Christmases past, one piece at a time.

They all stood back and looked at the tree that was about six inches from the ceiling. "Dad, do you think that's enough room for the star?"

"Yep, you did good." Dub ruffled Bryce's hair. "For your first time, you did a fine job. Lights go on first."

"Do we need to get new lights?" Tyler frowned at the two piles she had made of the tangled strands.

"I already tested them. These are the strands that are still working. There was a whole container of lights. I think we have more than we need."

Picking up the coil closest to him, Tyler grinned at

her. "Childress Christmas rule number one. No such thing as too many lights."

Bryce's eyes went wide. "There are rules? What's rule number two?" He took the end of the strand Tyler handed him.

"Music! We can't trim the tree without Christmas music and hot chocolate."

Dub had moved to the built-in cabinet. He fumbled opening a CD case. "I've got the music. Kar… Kar, you can make the hot chocolate and popcorn."

"Can I trust you guys alone?"

"Momma, you have to follow the rules, and that means hot chocolate!" He turned back to Tyler. "I've never decorated a real tree. Once we made a tree out of paper. In the shelter someone brought a tree in but it was already done. We didn't get to put anything on the tree, so I don't know what to do."

Tyler's lips curved, but not in his usual charming smile. This one was softer, sadder. "Dad and I had one job." He lifted the tangled cord of Christmas lights. "To get the lights on the tree while Mom and Carol made the drinks and cookies. Once the tree lit up, we would all hang the ornaments—well, I would hang one or two, then wander off for something more active. Mom and Carol made sure things were perfect."

"O Come, All Ye Faithful" sounded from the speakers.

Dub had his back to them, his fingertips on a framed picture of two small children standing in a Nativity scene, dressed as biblical characters. In a soft voice, he said, "Us boys did the lights every year and Cindy would have us rearrange them until they were just where she wanted them." He turned to face them. "I never saw the difference, always looked the same to me, but it made her happy." He started singing along as he got more photos out of the box of Christmas past and placed them on the mantel.

Karly pressed her hand against the frame of the archway. She needed something to anchor her to the ground. This was the Christmas she had always dreamed of during the years she'd spent in a car or hotel with Anthony on the way to another town, another con.

These were Dub and Tyler's traditions, traditions that had been so painful for them they had packed them away, letting dust and cobwebs claim them. They were not her memories. She had no right to be here and intrude on their family rituals.

Bryce stuck out his tongue, concentrating on every word Tyler said. The cord looped around his short arm as he used his left hand to drape the lights along the branches. She pulled her phone out of her back pocket. Even if they didn't really belong to this family event, she wanted to get pictures of Bryce decorating the tree. There was no telling when they were going to have this opportunity again.

The flash gave her away.

"Momma!"

Tyler leaned closer to him and wrapped the lights around Bryce and made a face. Bryce started giggling. She clicked several more. Dub laughed as he sat in the large wingback chair.

Straightening, Tyler rolled his shoulders as if they were stiff. "Do you need help with the hot chocolate?"

"Oh, no." She had been so caught up in the moment she forgot about the drinks. "No, no, I can do it."

Tyler raised one eyebrow and glanced down at her

son. Bryce made a face and gave her his worried look. "Are you sure, Momma?"

Fist on hips, she glared back. "Just because I can't bake doesn't mean I'm completely lost in the kitchen. Get the lights on that tree and I'll be back with the best cocoa you have ever dreamed of drinking."

With that last bit of false bravado, she spun on her heels and marched to the kitchen. Now, if she could actually pull it off, she would feel so much better. She had practiced the recipe she found in the box. So far it had been too thick or too thin, and who knew milk burned so easily? If mistakes were the best way to learn, this batch should be perfect.

She came back after her second attempt with a tray full of steamy mugs and a bowl of popcorn.

Dub slept with his chin resting on his chest. The tree held silver, red and green Christmas ornaments, each reflecting the lights in multiple directions. "I'll Be Home for Christmas" played. Tyler had Bryce lifted on his hip, helping him put a silver icicle-shaped adornment deep into the center of the tree.

Quietly she set the tray on the coffee table and lifted her phone out of her pocket to take another picture. How had she found herself in the middle of this dream?

Tyler put Bryce on the floor and put his finger to his lips with a nod toward Dub. Bryce nodded back and smiled at her. She started adding ornaments to the branches.

Tyler picked up his mug and one of the picture books now on the table. With a jerk of his head, he motioned for them to follow him to the tree, where he lowered himself to the floor. Bryce sat down next to him. When she didn't follow right away, they both turned and looked at her, waiting.

Unable to stop her smile, she got her drink and sat with crossed legs next to Bryce. "What are we doing?"

"Before we finished we always took a moment to read the story of baby Jesus and enjoy our hot chocolate."

Bryce rested his elbow on her thigh, sipping on his drink. Her hand lay on his back, feeling the rhythmic beating of his heart. The Christmas story had never sounded so good. Tyler's strong, steady voice made her think peace could come to the world. Even the little corner she lived in now.

Chapter Thirteen

Dub was awake by the end of the story. He moved to the tree. "There is only one thing left to do. Tyler, why don't you lift Bryce up so I can hand him the star."

"Me? Really?" Bryce asked.

"Yes, you." Tyler picked him up and placed him on his shoulder. Dub handed him the star. Taking pictures helped Karly control the emotions that threatened to turn to tears.

After the star topped the tree, she started gathering up the boxes and paper.

"Momma, look! I found another box in the bottom of this box."

Laughing, Karly turned to Tyler. His smile went flat and he stood like a statue, frozen.

She glanced at Bryce. Her son had already lifted the lid, and disappointment made him frown. He looked up at her. "It's just a bunch of paper things."

He pulled one out of the box. A smiley-faced angel spun on a red string. The wings were made from two silver, small handprints sprinkled with glitter. On the back, large, lopsided letters spelled out Carol's name and a date.

Dub waved Bryce over to him. "Every year, beginning with Carol's first Christmas, Cindy would make angel wings from all our handprints. Then she did it with Rachel for her first three years. Tyler threw a fit when he was eighteen. Said he was too old to be making handprints." Dub held up an angel with large wings. According to the back, Tyler was six when he had made the ornament. "Do you remember that?" Dub lifted another out of the box, a tiny one made by the newborn Rachel. "Can't believe Carol's baby girl is heading into her teen years. The years just slip by, don't they?"

Bryce looked over the edge of the box. "Do you put them on the tree?"

Karly glanced at Tyler. His jaw clenched. "Tyler?"

He shook his head and turned to the door without a word. The screen door slammed behind him. Silence echoed in the room, and Dub sighed.

"Mom, did I do something wrong?" The wonderful moment had been sucked from the room as if someone had popped all their party balloons.

Dub patted Bryce on the head with his good arm. "Oh, no, son. Some things we're just not ready for tonight."

"Bryce, these bring back memories that make Tyler sad."

"These don't go on the tree?"

"Not tonight." Dub handed her the box of childhood mementos. "I think Bryce and I should end the evening with a Christmas movie."

Bryce looked at Karly. "Can we, Momma?"

"Sounds like a great idea."

"Why don't you go check on Tyler? I want to make sure he's all right, but if I go it would make it worse." He shrugged. "We'll just fight."

"Oh, no, I don—"

"Please, Karly. I need to know he's okay, and I can't talk to him. With Bryce's help I can get the movie. Right, Cowboy?"

"Yes, sir." Bryce hugged Karly. "Is Tyler missing his momma and sister?"

She tightened her arms around him and kissed him on the top of his head. One day he would be a teenage boy taller than she was, with his own dreams and goals. She hugged him tighter for a moment. "Yes. I'm going to check on him. You good with a movie?"

Dub started to list movies as Karly slipped through the door. There was no telling where Tyler had gone off to, but she hadn't heard any of the trucks, so he had to be in walking distance.

Turning to the steps, she came to a sudden stop. He stood right there, at the edge of the light, looking out into the darkness.

"Tyler?" She laid her hand on the back of his shoulder.

His muscles tightened.

The sounds of the night mingled with his heavy breathing. What could she say to make this better? "I'm sorry." Well, that was lame.

He pulled away from her and sat on the top step. "No need to be. Is Bryce okay? I didn't mean to upset him."

"He's good. Your dad pulled out a collection of Christmas movies."

The night temperature had dropped to about fifty. Her sleeveless T-shirt wasn't much coverage in the cool breeze. Instead of going in and getting her wrap, she sat next to him and rubbed her hands over her upper arms.

Tyler sighed and took off his long-sleeve plaid shirt. He covered her shoulders, leaving him in a T-shirt. "What are you doing out here?"

"Your father's worried about you." Her heart broke for him, but that wasn't information that needed to be shared.

"More like he's mad at me for acting like a child and ruining the evening for you and Bryce."

"You didn't mess up anything." Through the door, she heard Bryce laugh at the movie. Bumping Tyler with her shoulder, she smiled. "See? They're fine. I'm sorry we upset you. Do you want to talk about the hand-print angels?"

"No." Since hung in the air between them.

"Thank you for having Bryce help with the tree and the lights. I can't explain how special this evening is for us."

"I'm glad." His voice was husky. "You have a special little boy there, and he is going to grow up too fast, so memories are good."

No longer able to hold back, she reached for his arm. His skin was cold, now that he was only in his short-sleeved shirt. "Just like you were a special little boy for your mom. She would want you to be happy."

He pulled her closer. Tucking her hands between his hand and chest, with his other hand he gently rubbed back and forth over her wrist.

"Every year of my life we made those handprint wings for her angels. It was one of the traditions she loved the most. Carol got married and we still did them. When Rachel was born, she became the center of the universe. When I was eighteen, I thought I was too much a man to make paper angels with my baby niece and sister. I refused." Untangling their arms, he pulled away. He planted his elbows on his knees and rubbed his palms against his forehead. "I was a self-important jerk."

"Oh, Tyler, you were a teenage boy. Your mom understood that." This time she put her arms around this grown man, thinking of Cindy's baby boy. "She loved you."

A deep moan came from his chest. "That was her last Christmas." Like a wall that had been causing too much pressure, he crumbled against her. His face pressed into her hair, and her skin became wet with his tears. Deep, wrenching sobs escaped from his chest. Each one tore her heart into a million pieces.

Instinct had her rocking back and forth. She hummed softly while his grief poured out of him. There was nothing to say that could fix this kind of pain, but she laid her cheek against his hair and smoothing the small curl behind his ear.

Her own tears fell. She loved this man, but she couldn't go further. It wouldn't be good for either one of them. So she pulled him as close as she could, praying to absorb some of the pain chained in the depth of his darkness.

He quieted.

Now she wasn't sure what to do. From her experience, men didn't like being vulnerable. It tended to make them angry. Angry men lashed out. She pressed her lips against his head, then slowly scooted away, giving him space.

Clearing his throat, Tyler sat up and wiped his arm over his face. "I'm sorry."

"It's okay." She stood. "I'll get you something to drink."

He nodded, keeping his back to her. No fireworks or blame, just sadness.

Tyler was so different from the other men in her life. He might not shout it out, and he even claimed to have some issues with his faith, but he had been raised to be a man of God, and it was obvious in so many of his actions. Surrounded by his scent, she pulled his shirt tighter around her. How could he not see he was full of goodness and love?

Maybe that was just what she wanted to see—a golden boy who could sweep her off her feet and give her a happily-ever-after.

That was dangerous territory. On that thought, she rushed inside, letting him have time to collect himself.

Tyler rested his forehead on his palms. His head hurt. He lifted his face and gazed across the front pastures. *God, I don't understand why You would take them both so early.*

John's sermon from the previous Sunday ping-ponged around his head. *God is our refuge.* "That's so easy to say, but how do you live it?"

So many times his mom told him not to fear any troubles of this earth. He scrambled for any of the verses she used. How could he forget her favorite verses?

Whenever he started worrying about something that was all-important to him at the time, she would tell him not to fear. He looked through the treetops.

Even if the mountains slipped into the heart of the

sea. First his mother had been his mountain, then his sister. How did he learn to live again once his mountains slip out of his life forever? The greatest mountain, his father, was crumbling. He'd lose him one day, too. What would he do then?

"Tyler?"

Her soft voice was a light in the dark. "Hey." He turned to make sure she felt welcomed back. "You have hot chocolate? You are a true gift."

"Here's your shirt." She handed him his plaid button-down. She had her wrap on now. "It's gotten colder."

He took the top from her and slipped it back on over his T-shirt. "We might actually have a winter this year." Taking one of the mugs from her, he noticed she had something else tucked under her arm. "You are multi-talented. What else have you got there?"

"Oh, I told your dad you were fine. When I came back through with the drinks, he stopped me." She sat down next to him and pulled a black leather book out. "He wanted me to give you this. He said you could keep it if you promised to use it every day."

At first he couldn't believe what he saw. His mother's study Bible. Without touching the gift she held out to him, he looked back up at her. "Are you sure he told you to give this to *me*?"

She nodded. "Is something wrong?"

"No." He took the Bible, running his hands over the worn leather before opening the pages. Her handwriting was scribbled along the margins, verses highlighted. He turned to Psalm 46 and read it out loud. "'God is our refuge and strength, a very present help in trouble.'" He took a deep breath.

Her warm hand slipped under his arm, holding him,

giving him a level of comfort he had not allowed anyone to give him for ten years.

Continuing to read out loud, he could hear his mother. "'We will not fear though the earth should change, and though the mountains slip into the heart of the sea.'"

The world was silent.

"Tyler, that's beautiful."

"It was one she used all the time when dealing with me."

"That's the kind of mother I want to be to Bryce. Thank you for sharing that with me."

"Karly, I'm so sorry about earlier. I've never lost it like that—and over some stupid paper ornaments." He tried to laugh it off, but his voice sounded hollow.

"Oh, they're not stupid." Tears glistened in her compassionate eyes. "They are the kind of things I wish I had with Bryce, and one day he'll be a teenage boy and won't think they're so cool. Your mother knew that, Tyler. Don't let that guilt stay with you. You gave her so many wonderful memories of being your mom. They're all over the house and in boxes. I think they're even in the Bible she used as she prayed for you. You don't doubt she loved you, do you?"

"No, but I didn't love her as much as she deserved."

"As one mother of a son speaking for another, she wouldn't want that guilt around your shoulders."

Closing the book, Tyler touched the embossed name on the lower right corner. "I can't believe my dad gave this to me."

"I think he's just as lost and lonely as you are when it comes to the loss of your mother and sister. Maybe even crying together would help, at least talking about it."

"My father never cries. It's a weakness. A man moves forward. You have to get the job done. No time to cry."

"You can't tell me he hasn't cried over the love of his life and his daughter. I don't believe it. Maybe he told you that because he was told the same thing. Maybe in order to move forward together you need to cry together...your earth shifting and your mountains slipping away."

He rubbed the back of his neck. "Maybe."

"Do you want to pray?"

He nodded, but his throat was so dry words clawed their way out. "That would be good. Can we pray silently?" He coughed.

The hand on his arm moved to his hand. She intertwined her fingers between his. "Sure." She lowered her head, and her lips started moving.

He just watched at first. Not a single real prayer had passed his lips since he was eighteen. The sounds of the night calmed him. *Father, God, please forgive me for being silent for so long. Thank You for not giving up on me, for not leaving me, even though that's what I deserve.*

Eyes closed, he poured everything out from the past ten years. He had stopped talking to God during his senior year in high school. When his words finally stopped, Tyler paused and gave God time to speak to his heart, just like his father had taught him.

Time had no ownership of this moment. He sat and spoke with God. With Karly sitting beside him, Tyler lifted his head and looked at the stars scattered across the sky. The light from the living room was at his back, lighting a place that his heart wanted to call home again.

He stood and offered her a hand. "I think it's getting late. Probably time for the two inside to go to bed. Karly, thank you."

"Tyler, I'm really sorry for setting it all in motion. I know how emotional bringing up the past can be. This is your family and home, not mine and Bryce's."

"Stop it. This is your home, and I'm pretty sure my Dad would adopt you and Bryce if you'd let him. I think John said something about it being in God's timing. Well, this unquestionably has God's stamp on the delivery." He held up the Bible. "I think this is the greatest gift my dad has ever given me, and he used you to get it to me."

"He's suffering, too, but doesn't know how to talk about it. You're both are so stubborn."

"I'm thinking you might be right." His gaze moved over her face, from her eyes to her lips and jaw back to her eyes. He wanted to lean in and kiss her. She had made it clear she had no room for a man in her life, especially one with his lifestyle. She knew what she wanted, and it didn't line up with his plans. He held her there in the starlight, time moving like a dream. What if he changed his plans?

He moved back, breaking all contact. The moment was gone.

"Good night, Karly. Thank you, and tell Dad I'm all right. Tell him I'm better than I was a month ago." *And I have you to thank for that.*

The house sighed as it settled in for the night. She walked through the dark kitchen into the living room, now a winter wonderland. After their movie watching, Dub and Bryce were all tucked in, and Tyler had left for the bunkhouse. She settled on the sofa with her notebook and Bible. Nighttime was a perfect time to work on her classes and get organized for the next day. It had become her favorite time to pray and reflect on what happened during the day and what goals she still had before her.

She tucked her feet under her skirt. The soft leather sofa engulfed her as she stared at the lovely tree that now stood in the room surrounded by an eclectic collection of nativity scenes. The notebook lay unopened in her lap.

Her phone vibrated. The sound surprised her, and her heart hammered against her chest. Calls at this time of night were never good. "Hello?"

"Karly." Anthony's voice had a slur to it. How did he get her number?

"Anthony, I'm not talking to you. And don't call me again."

"Wait. I want to take my grandson shopping. I want to spend time with him."

"No. Don't call me again. And he's not your grandson." As she hung up, she could hear threats and yelling.

Pulling her knees up against her chest, Karly closed her eyes and prayed for wisdom.

Chapter Fourteen

It had been five days since Tyler had left for his first trip. He had said he'd be back today, but today was about to disappear. So much for keeping his word. What hurt the most was seeing Bryce's disappointment when Dub and she had picked him up from school today. He had gotten used to the routine they had fallen into with Tyler. She sighed and clicked to the next page of the article she was reading for her class.

Who was she trying to fool? She hated the way she missed Tyler, missed seeing him in the kitchen and going into town with him. He would eventually return to Denver permanently and go back to his international flights. Why was she so weak?

Her phone vibrated. She closed her eyes and refused to look at it. Anthony would not stop calling. So far she had been able to ignore him, but he was wearing her down. She just wanted him to leave. The thought of all the people she had come to love finding out about her past made her want to curl up and cry. Her phone vibrated again. Without looking at the screen, she ignored the call.

An hour later she stood and stretched. It was almost midnight, and she needed to get to bed. Thank goodness tomorrow was Saturday. They could all sleep in and be lazy until they headed out for the Christmas pageant.

Headlights flashed across the living room wall. Had Anthony followed through on his threat to come to the ranch? She picked up the phone to call 9-1-1. She was not going to deal with him. Glancing down, she saw she had missed several calls and messages from Tyler. Was he in the driveway?

The front door opened. It had to be Tyler. She went to the living room as he stepped into the house. Gently he shut the door and turned.

He smiled. "Hello, stranger."

"You're late." She wanted to be mad at him, not weak in the knees.

"I know. There was a storm on the east coast that knocked me off schedule, then I couldn't catch a standby out of Houston. Anyway, I got here as fast as possible." He glanced at his watch. "I have five minutes before midnight, so technically I made it." He moved closer to her. "Did you miss me?" He wiggled his eyebrows. "I stopped by to leave some stuff for Bryce. I thought I could put it on his nightstand so he'd see it when he woke up."

"What is it?" She crossed her arms.

"Jealous I don't have something for you?"

"No."

He grinned at her. "How about a welcome-home kiss?"

"No."

He laughed. "You are downright adorable."

She shook her head while completing a full-on eye roll.

"Can I put these in Bryce's room?" He held up a handful of blue Jolly Ranchers and some postcards.

"Sure." She followed him through the dark house to the hallway.

Tyler eased the door open and slipped into his old room. Her heart always turned a bit gooey when she saw her little boy sleeping peacefully. As Tyler laid out his gifts, Bryce shifted.

"Mom?" He rubbed his sleep-crusted eyes.

"It's me, Cowboy." Tyler kept his voice low.

Bryce jumped up. She had never seen him wake up that fast. "Tyler!" He stood on the bed and launched himself at his hero. "I was afraid you wouldn't come back."

She stifled a gasp. He hadn't said anything to her.

Patting his back, Tyler hugged the boy. "You're too important to me to not come back. Isn't there something big going on tomorrow night, like a Christmas pageant? I wouldn't miss it for anything in the world." Tyler moved Bryce to his hip. "I remembered something Carol and I would do after we decorated the tree. You want me to show you?"

"Yes!" Bryce slipped down to the ground.

He glanced at Karly as if he expected her to say no. She turned to go back to the living room.

Tyler moved past her and stretched out on the rug under the sparkling tree. Bryce didn't hesitate dropping to the ground beside him. "Hurry, Momma, this is cool."

On the other side of Bryce she lay on her back and joined them under the tree.

Bryce asked Tyler a thousand questions about his trip and where he went, the places he saw and the people he met. After declaring he wanted to be a pilot, too, her son fell into a sudden quietness. Which meant only one thing. She looked over at him. Yep, he was sound asleep.

"I'll take him back to bed. You stay here." Tyler carefully gathered the small body of her baby up against his chest and carried him back to the bedroom.

Alone under the tree, she watched the twinkling lights reflecting off the shiny surfaces of the ornaments, creating a kaleidoscope of color on the ceiling. It felt so right having him home. That was so wrong.

He scooted under the tree, his hands one thin tinsel width from her. The warmth of his skin had her fisting her hand in order to resist the urge to make contact.

"Thanks for letting me bring him out here. I know it's late, but I really missed him."

She kept her gaze on the ceiling. Had he missed *her*?

"You said we needed to talk?"

He turned to his side, a grin as bright as Bryce's on his face. She tried not to think what news would make him so happy, but her heartbeat accelerated in anticipation.

"I have some news for you. You know how you're afraid to contact your family?"

Dread filled her. Her rapidly beating heart wanted to stop. "Tyler, what did you do?"

"I found them."

She tried to get away. He laid his arm across her waist.

"You had no right. It was my decision to reach out to them, not yours. And what if they don't want to meet me?"

He whispered against her ear. "But, Karly, what if they do want to meet you? Which they do."

"What?" Her head jerked toward him, searching his

eyes for a lie. "Why would they want to meet me now, after years of not wanting me? I can't meet them. My life is a mess. I dropped out of school, had a baby and an ugly string of bad choices."

"You're amazing."

Her eyes widened. "You're crazy." She looked into the beautiful, clear blue eyes and found no deception or ruse, but then again, she never did. She was such a fool to fall for the same stupid lines.

"Karly?"

"I can't do this. I can't meet them yet. I can't let you or the promise of a long-lost family distract me from what I have to do. Bryce has to be my focus." His body moved closer to her. All she had to do was turn and she would be in his arms. She bit the inside of her cheek and scooted away from the illusion of security.

"Karly, we'll talk about your family when you're ready. I did what I thought was right." He followed her, and his warm hand rested on her forearm. "You're strong, but you don't have to do it alone, Karly. How many times have you started over when your world fell apart?"

She touched the needles above her. They tickled her fingertips, making her think of Tyler's scruff—something she had no business thinking about.

"I didn't have a choice. My son depends on me. I have to make things right for him." An ornament with Tyler's little-boy face caught her attention. He had made it clear he didn't want to be on the ranch.

Karly sighed. "For most of Bryce's five years, we have ended up in shelters during Christmas. When he was three we actually spent Christmas Eve in my car. I made a promise that one day I would give him a real holiday—that he would never feel rejected or used by people who should love him. I wanted to give him a real family. I made the mistake of thinking Billy was an answer to my prayers, but my habit of leaping into someone else's arms, ready to be rescued, just got us in more trouble. I am Bryce's family. I'm all he has."

"Maybe it was an answered prayer," Tyler whispered.

"How could my relationship with Billy be an answered prayer?" Tyler had gone off the deep end in more ways than one.

He chuckled. "Not that part. You made some bad choices by putting your trust in the wrong person."

"Thanks. If you're trying to make me feel better, this is the worst pep talk ever."

"Your choices might have been the wrong ones, but God still got you where you needed to be. He got you here to Clear Water. I trusted the wrong people, also. The worst part is I wasn't the one hurt. I let Gwyn convince me to take my dad's plane out one night after we had been drinking. She challenged me to fly as low as possible without touching the ground. I did and scared the horses into stampeding. Because of that stupid stunt, my horse was injured and almost killed. The next morning, I broke it off with Gwyn. To get back at me she told everyone I had gotten her pregnant and that was the reason I left her."

"Tyler, that's horrible."

"The worst part is it seemed most people believed her. Even my dad believed her. I had never even touched her. She lied, and people believed her over me." They fell into a long moment of silence. "Instead of looking at myself, I blamed everyone else, even God." He turned his head and looked at her. "I'm tired of living with this anger inside me." A rough edge coated his voice.

Karly reached over and touched his hand. His fingers slipped between hers and softly squeezed. The twinkling light reflected off the blue in his eyes, making her think of the time Anthony had conned a family into taking them to the Florida Keys. The water had been an unreal blue, just like Tyler's eyes. He might have had the kind of family life she could only dream about, but everyone had a story. The pieces of his weren't as perfect as they appeared from the outside.

"Your mother would want happiness for you. So does God." How had they gotten so serious? "So you're saying my road full of potholes brought me to this perfect place?" She glanced away from the lights dancing across the ornaments and studied their hands. Nestled against his skin, her hands looked small. She'd never really thought of herself as overly feminine, but next to his large hand, pure masculine in their form, her smaller hand looked downright soft and girlie.

With a sigh she turned away from their connection and looked up through the branches, to the star on top of the tree. If she didn't get control of her thoughts and stay focused on her goal, she would end up making another bad choice. She pulled her hand away from his warmth. His comfortable embrace might be what she wanted, but it was not what she needed. "So you're saying that despite my bad decisions God still was in control and got me where I needed to be in this moment?"

He grunted or maybe laughed; some sort of masculine sound came from his chest. "I think so. John's better at this deep thinking and purpose-of-life stuff than I am." He turned his head and looked right into her eyes.

"Something about being under a Christmas tree in the dead of night makes everything else clearer. Thanks, Karly. I didn't even know how much I missed this."

Tyler wanted to see the world, but she had seen enough. All she wanted was a home to raise Bryce and a place where people knew her name.

Tyler wanted to reach out and take her hand back into his. It had been a perfect fit. She had made him think about things he avoided with every fiber of his being. Air was hard to find. He needed to get out of this living room, back to the bunkhouse, back to Denver, back to the skies. If he stayed here much longer, he might start thinking about being a part of Karly's life on a permanent basis, and that would mean moving back to Clear Water.

Scooting out from under the tree, Tyler avoided touching her. "Tomorrow is the pageant." Sitting up, he draped his arms over his knees. "I can take you flying Sunday after church." He grinned. For the first time he was actually looking forward to church.

"When do you leave again?" Pulling herself up, she sat cross-legged. "Are you going back to Denver?"

"For now I've switched to domestic flights. I can put my schedule on the calendar. They are mostly trips of three or four days." He stood, looking down at her. The lights highlighted her cheekbones and the soft curve of her lips. When had she become the most beautiful woman in his life? He cleared his throat. "Sunday after church?"

"I'm not sure. Maybe we should forget it." Karly wrapped her arms around her knees, pulling herself into a tight ball.

"Everyone should see the Hill Country by air at least once. The other day I told you I would take you, so Sunday we'll go up."

With one sigh and a roll of the eyes, she stood. "Tyler, you can't make people do what you think they should do. If I don't want to fly, I'm not going flying."

"Sorry. I didn't mean it that way." The pictures of his family, his dad and his granddad, proud men, seemed to be staring at him from the portrait on the wall. They loved their family and thought they knew what was best for everyone. He chuckled. "I'm starting to realize my mom might have been right."

She tilted her head. "About what?"

"She claimed the only problem between me and my dad was that we were too much alike."

"Oh, yeah. She knew you both very well. What took you so long to figure out she was right?"

"It might be that stubborn pride I get so mad at my dad about." He shrugged. "Anyway, I would love to take you flying on Sunday. I'll be back if you want to do it later. Or not at all. That's fine, too." He grinned. "See, I can be agreeable."

She looked down at her fuzzy socks, then back up at him, tucking a strand of long hair behind her ear. He wanted to do that. He wanted to run his fingers along that silky strand of hair and pull her close. Holding her felt so right, even though it shouldn't. She wasn't his to hold.

"Good night, Karly."

"Night, Tyler."

Karly bit the inside of her cheek as Tyler made his way to the back door. Could she trust him to help her?

She had made a vow to stand on her own feet, to take care of any problems without expecting to be rescued.

Or, like the Childress men, was she letting pride get in God's way?

She rushed through the kitchen, trying to reach him before he made it to the bunkhouse. "Tyler!"

At the edge of the patio, he stopped and turned to her. "What is it, Karly?" His charming smile melted her heart. "So you want to go flying?"

She stared at him, then at the moon playing hide-and-seek behind the tree branches. *Just say it. It doesn't mean you're giving him your life.* Focusing on his face she took in a deep lungful of air. "I need help."

The smile was gone, and his eyebrows formed a V. He moved closer to her. "What's wrong?" He took her hand into his.

"My stepfather, he's telling people that they need to start a fund-raiser for Bryce. He wants to use Bryce the way he used me. He said he would leave town if I gave him ten thousand dollars. I thought of selling my car, but it's not worth that much. I need help telling him to leave town." There she said it.

He stiffened and pulled away. "So you want money?"

"No, I—"

"Really? Is this the routine? You come into town and get people to trust you, then he follows and, bam, you got the money? Do you always pretend you don't know you had family in Hawaii?"

She stepped back. His words confirmed her greatest fear. If people knew the truth, they would doubt her, look at her with suspicion. "I don't want your money. Never mind." She needed to find a way to do this on her own anyway. "Forget I said anything. Good night,

Tyler." She turned to go back into the house. *God, please let me know what to do.*

Tyler stopped her from going through the door. "Karly, I'm sorry. When I heard *money* it was a knee-jerk reaction. Which makes me a jerk." His fingers gently touched her cheek. "How can I help?"

"This was a mistake, Tyler." Closing her eyes, she wrapped her arms around her middle. "I just want to avoid drama. I hate conflict."

Strong arms came around her, pulling her against him. "Conflict can't always be avoided. We can't let the bad guys win."

"Anthony told me over and over again that my mother didn't have any family. I just want him out of my life. I thought maybe you could go with me. I'm not sure what to do. He keeps calling, following me around town." She moved away from him. Needing some space to sort out her emotions and thoughts, she moved to the rocking bench. "He actually hasn't done anything wrong here, and all the other stuff happened years ago. I can't go to the police."

He followed and leaned against the column next to her. "When he showed up, you were ready to run. I don't understand why your stepfather would keep you from your mother's family."

"Anthony is manipulative and selfish. I wasn't allowed to go to school. He told me I had cancer." She pulled her knees up to her chest and wrapped her arms tight around them. "For the longest time I thought I was dying, but at about eleven I realized he had never taken me to the doctor. We would live in some small town for six months to a year, then we'd take off. He would con people into providing exotic trips for us so I could—" she made air quotes "—'recover' or get a last wish granted. Once the money ran out we moved to another town in another state. He never hurt me or even hit me. He just made me feel so ungrateful." Her stomach hurt. "There were so many people who wanted to help. When I was little I loved the attention and gifts, but as I got older I realized we were lying to them and taking their money. I couldn't get the dirt off me."

Her muscles ached. Standing, Karly walked over to the edge of the patio, pulled her jacket tight around her middle and searched the sky for answers. Why had Anthony kept her from her mother's family and, if he'd lied about them, what else had he lied about? She didn't like thinking about the past. She definitely never talked about it.

"Karly, I can't even imagine that kind of life." Tyler joined her. He stood right outside the light coming from the house. He stared out into the night, not looking at her. Good. If she didn't see any judgment it made it easier to keep talking.

"When I started questioning him, things got ugly. It wasn't as easy to use me after I outgrew the little girl role. Somewhere in my early teens, he started dating older women. Women with money and no family. I couldn't take it, so I ran away." She sat down. The thin cotton material of her long skirt was not much protection against the cold concrete step.

"He's a con artist who used a young girl." He sat on the step below her, close enough to touch if she wanted to. "He needs to be in jail."

"At sixteen, I thought a boy I had met was my Prince Charming. He even had a white car. I was so in love and such an idiot. Well, as you know, that didn't work out, either."

"Karly, you can't give Anthony money. He'll just want more. I'll go with you in the morning." He reached for her hand. "The day he showed up I told you to not be afraid to ask for help. I know you want to be strong and independent, but I don't think God ever intended for you to do everything all alone." He laid his warm hand on her knee and gave her a slight squeeze. "It's not a sign of weakness to need help." He shook his head. "And you call *me* stubborn."

She gave him a weak smile. It wouldn't change his mind if she tried to explain how scared she was of falling into that old pattern. Tyler made it easy to slip back into believing she could have a happy ending.

Tyler smiled. "Okay, tomorrow morning we go talk to Anthony. Tomorrow night we go to the pageant. Sunday after church we go flying."

"Sounds like a deal." Then he would be gone. For the safety of her heart and sanity, she needed to plant that fact firmly in her brain. Thinking about talking to Anthony unsettled her nerves. She hated conflict, but sometimes there was no way to avoid it.

Chapter Fifteen

The temperature had actually dropped below freezing, which was unusual for this time of year. Karly had on the heaviest jacket she owned. She adjusted the scarf around her neck and focused on the sound of her boots on the cabin steps as she made her way to Anthony's door.

She stopped. Standing in front of Anthony's rental, she felt a cold sweat break out over her skin. Right behind her, Tyler looked all cool and confident in his black leather jacket.

If she'd been alone, she would have already run for the hills. With an encouraging smile, Tyler nodded to her. *Please, God, give me the words and the perseverance I need to get this done.*

One more step and she knocked on the door. Three solid knocks. Tyler rested his hand between her shoulder blades as if gently holding her in place so she couldn't give in to her desire to flee.

The door swung open. After a flash of surprise, Anthony had his best smile in place. "Karly, I'm so happy to see you." He nodded to her partner. "Tyler, right?" He stepped back. "Come in, come in."

"No, Anthony," she said. "I'm here to tell you I'm not giving you any money and you are not getting anywhere near my son. You will be leaving Clear Water by the end of the week."

His smile fell and his gaze shifted to Tyler before coming back at her. He reached for her shoulder, but she stepped back before he made contact.

"Don't touch me."

Tyler moved closer, cutting Anthony off from her.

"Karly, what did you tell him?" He relaxed with his hands in the air as if to surrender, then smiled at her new bodyguard. "She does lean toward the dramatic. I mean, look at her choices. You can't believe half of what she says."

"I've learned to believe everything she says. You'll find most of the town does, also." Tyler's normally warm eyes where hard as steel.

Anthony glanced at Tyler, then back to Karly. "I can't leave now. I want to see my grandson. Remember how we used to travel to the greatest places? We can do that again. You don't want Bryce growing up thinking this place is the whole world."

"Actually, I do. This is my home, and Clear Water is full of good people that I want to be in my son's life. I won't argue with you. If you're not gone by the end of the week or if I hear you are talking to people about fund-raising, I'm going to the sheriff. There is nothing for you here."

"I haven't done anything wrong."

"Goodbye, Anthony." She turned and headed back to her old car, her heart beating so fast she could hear it.

Pulling out of the Pecan Farm, Karly took a deep breath. "I did it. Usually, if the con's not easy, he'll leave."

"I hope so. Maybe you should go ahead and call the sheriff. Let him know what's going on."

"And tell him what? Over fifteen years ago Anthony shaved my head and took money from people? Anyway, it would just be his word against mine. I'm a high school dropout that has had some trouble with the law and ended up as a runaway and teen mother."

"You don't feel safe, but this town loves you and Bryce. You're not alone, Karly. Just give the sheriff a heads-up. There might be more he can do for you or not, but you should talk to them. You don't want him moving on to the next town to con other people."

"You're right. I'm not used to trusting anyone, especially the law." She bit her lip. "At one point, because I was so young and homeless, they talked about putting Bryce in foster care." She wasn't that girl anymore. She glanced at Tyler. He was looking out the window, so she couldn't see his reaction.

"But you kept your family together," he said. "You did what you had to do to take care of your son. He's happy and well adjusted. You've done a great job. Better than I would have done in the situation." He put his arm on the backrest and placed a hand on her shoulder. "I know you want to be strong and do it on your own, but asking for help from the right people doesn't make you weak."

She gave him a quick glance. He looked so intense, as if he needed her to believe what he was saying was the absolute truth. "You're right. I'll talk to the sheriff. I should see him at church on Sunday."

Tyler's phone vibrated. Checking it, he looked back at her and grinned. "Christmas secret project is ready. Let's head home."

"Secret project. What is it?"

"Well, if you knew, it wouldn't be a secret, would it?" He started singing along with "All I Want for Christmas is My Two Front Teeth."

She couldn't help but laugh. "I don't really like surprises, and you have all your teeth."

"I didn't in first grade, and every time Dad picked me up from school he would sing the song as loud as he could. Carol would join him. I was so embarrassed." He sang the chorus with full gusto one more time before smiling at her. "I wasn't sure how to go about doing the secret project, so I asked Lorrie Ann, John's fiancée, if she could help. She has everything set up at the house to make the angel handprints, like my mom did every year. I thought it would be great to do with Carol's girls. Rachel has them for her first two or three years. It makes a good Christmas memory for Bryce and you, too. With the pageant later today I wasn't sure we could get it done."

"Are you sure about this?" She didn't want to see him so hurt again.

"Mom would be heartbroken if the tradition didn't carry on to the next generation. I threw a fit as a teenager, but I'm not a kid anymore. I want to do this for my mom, the girls and you." He looked out the window. "I want it, too."

"I love the idea, Tyler." He was making it so hard not to love him. He was just being nice to her, she told herself. It didn't mean anything else. She gripped the steering wheel.

She was strong. Her faith was larger than any of the monsters from her past, and she could walk into her future alone. Tyler would move on with his real life, and she would be here where she wanted to be with Bryce. A soft rain started falling. "I'll Be Home for Christmas" started playing on the radio.

Tyler laid his head back against the headrest. His baritone voice joined the music. He turned his head and winked at her. "Come on, sing with me."

That was safe, so she did. As she drove toward the ranch they sang about home, dreams and Christmas Eve.

The kitchen had been transformed into a kid's craft corner. Newspaper covered every surface, and cinnamon filled the air. Lorrie Ann stood at the center island rolling out dough. Laughing with Rachel was a tall, lanky boy who Tyler thought was Vickie's son, Seth. He could believe she was married to Jake Torres now. And there was talk of the two kids having a budding relationship. There was no way Rachel was old enough for a boyfriend. He wondered if John knew the boy was here.

Karly bumped him with her shoulder. "Stop glaring. They're friends." Her voice was low, and the softness of her breath fluttered across his cheek.

"You should know that boys at any age cannot be trusted, and girls fall for their stupid lines." He knew he sounded grumpy, but the thought of anyone hurting his niece hit him hard.

The humor left her eyes. Oh, now he regretted the words. "Karly, I—"

"You're right, but she has a family that loves her and is watching out for her. If you're so worried, maybe you should stick around." She charged away from him into the middle of the mess.

"Maybe I should," he said under his breath before following her.

Celeste reached across Bryce to get a cookie cutter. On the other side of Cowboy was a little blond girl he didn't recognize. She had to be Vickie's youngest. Music mingled with laughter as the kids worked. Dub sat at the table, a cane leaning against the table. Where was his father's walker?

"Hey, guys. Are you making cookies?" Tyler inspected the creations.

"Uncle Tyler!" Celeste jumped from the stool she had been kneeling on and threw herself at him. He swung the bundle of energy around. He wished he greeted life with half of the joy she did every day.

Lorrie Ann pushed a strand of her dark hair out of her face with the back of her hand. "Not in the kitchen, guys. I thought while we were waiting, it would be fun to make dough ornaments before we do the handprints. It turned out to be more complicated than I thought, but we're having fun."

The kids all agreed. Celeste shook her head. "It's not compli…complicated. It's messy and fun! They smell like cinnamon. This is our last batch. I made hearts."

"Momma, I made a horse. I also made sheep and a camel. From the Christmas story of baby Jesus. They're in the oven."

"Oh, the horse is wonderful, Bryce." She looked at Lorrie Ann. "Can I make one?"

"This is our last batch. I didn't make very much dough. Here, use the extra to make your ornament." The timer went off. "Okay, guys, put your last ones on the tray so I can put them in the oven." As she took out the baked ornaments, she glanced at Tyler. "Vickie called. She and Jake had some last-minute errands for the pageant. I told her it wouldn't be a problem for the kids to hang out with us. I know this is a special activity, so I hope—"

"Mom used to invite our friends over and everyone made their own handprints to take home. It's all good. Hey, Dad, how are you feeling?"

"I'm going to read." Dub struggled to stand.

Karly left her dough and rushed to his side. "I think you might have done too much the past couple of days." She supported his arm.

"I'm fine. I just want to lie down for a minute and read." As he shuffled out of the room, he stopped by Celeste. "Make me something pretty." He kissed the top of her head.

Lorrie Ann hustled around the kitchen organizing and directing the kids. "Okay, clean up all the tools, and we'll wash them before we start the next project."

Tyler looked at Karly's dough. She had started making a *B*. He picked up the extra and made a *K*. With the fork, he gave it wavy lines. Adding dots with the butter knife, he finished it with a hole on top for a ribbon and put the date on the back.

"Oh, you made one, too." Karly had walked up behind him.

"It's for you. To go with the one you're making." With the letter on his flat hand, he held it out to show her.

Long graceful fingers covered her mouth as she gasped. Wide eyes teared up.

"Karly, it's just a letter." His voice was hushed. He hadn't meant to upset her.

She shook her head and raised her gaze to his. "I've… No one has ever made me a Christmas gift before. I mean… I know it's not a gift, but it's for Christmas and it's for me… Ugh." Pulling her bottom lip between her teeth, Karly stopped talking.

"Finish your *B*, then you'll have a memento from your first Childress Christmas." Moving to the other side of her, he placed the *K* on the cookie sheet with the other creations of the day.

Gathering everyone around the table, Lorrie Ann started the kids making their handprints with white paint.

Tyler's heart skipped an extra beat as he helped Celeste. His mother and Carol would be delighted and perhaps a little proud of him.

His tongue out, Bryce pressed his left hand on the dark blue paper. "Mom, my angel will only have one wing, or can I use my left hand again?"

Celeste reached over with her clean hand and touched the end of his short arm. "You should use your short arm, than you'll have an angel perfect for you."

"I don't know." The doubt in his voice twisted Tyler's heart.

"Bryce, I volunteer in a hospital where several of the kids are missing hands and arms because of…accidents." Fire seemed a little too dark for this crowd. "Each year they send out thank-you cards, and they have all sorts of handprints and most didn't include five fingers or palms. So make wings with each of your hands. Over the years your mom will get to see how much you've grown as your angel gets bigger."

"Okay." He dipped his short arm in the paint and pressed the end of his arm onto the paper, the five tiny undeveloped fingers leaving their own unique mark. He looked up at Karly. "What do you think, Momma?"

She smoothed down some of his curls. "I think it is the most beautiful wing I have ever seen."

Five-year-old eyes rolled. "Momma, you're just saying that because you're my mom."

Everyone laughed. "No, really—"

"Oh, no!" Lorrie Ann was digging in a bag. "I forgot the glitter at the house. Y'all need to start on the faces and cut out the gowns. I'll go get the silver glitter. I'll be right back."

"Lorrie Ann, it's fine. We don't need the glitter." Tyler had always kind of hated the glitter anyway. "I don't see what difference it makes."

"Tyler Childress, I can't believe you. This was your idea, and every year the wings are covered in silver glitter. I'm going to go get it."

He had to laugh. This was so something his mother would have done, and it had to be perfect, even if no one else even noticed the difference.

After she left, everyone worked in silence for a few wonderful minutes. The kids, focused on drawing the faces and cutting out the gowns, had stopped talking.

"Uncle Ty," Rachel started, then paused.

"What is it, Rachel?" Tyler asked.

With a heavy sigh, she sat her scissors down before looking up at him. "Do you think Mom would have liked Lorrie Ann?"

"Your mom actually knew Lorrie Ann. We kind of grew up together being neighbors. She liked her. Your mother liked everyone."

Seth finished cutting his white paper. "It's weird thinking of your mom and Lorrie Ann knowing each other before y'all were even born. Now she's marrying your dad. I would guess she didn't see that one coming."

Rachel rolled her eyes and elbowed him in the ribs. "I'm serious. Do you think she would want Daddy to marry Lorrie Ann? I mean…" She studied her handprints for a few heartbeats. "I mean, is it okay that Daddy loves Lorrie Ann?"

Tyler walked over to Rachel and put his arm around her shoulder. His gut told him she was really asking if it was okay that she loved her dad's future bride, but he didn't know how to reassure her, because he had his own resentment against Lorrie Ann. Carol would be disappointed in him.

Bryce spoke up. "Moms always want the people they love to be happy. Right, Momma?" He looked up at his mom with total love and trust. No matter what she claimed, despite their rough beginning, she had found a way to protect him from the worst of life. She had no clue how remarkable he found her.

She smiled at her son before giving her attention to Rachel. "He's right. Your mom would want you all to be happy. You, your dad, Celeste, even your old uncle Tyler."

Seth coughed. "It's okay to love more than one parent." His voice was so low they all leaned in to hear him. "Doesn't mean you love your dad or mom less."

The boy might get to stay around after all. Tyler squeezed Rachel's shoulders.

"I think God brings people into your life when you need them." The room dropped into a thick silence. Seth focused on the face he was drawing, not making eye contact with anyone. "Sometimes your own parents can't be what you need and you get other people to love you. Doesn't mean you don't love them. They just can't be there for you."

Oh, man, he had forgotten the kid's father, Tommy Miller, was in jail for beating up Vickie. Seth had been the one to call the police. He would hug the kid, but suspected he wouldn't appreciate the show of affection.

Tyler moved to help Celeste cut her wings. "You know your mom was the kind of person who wanted everyone to feel welcome. She rescued horses and made sure they had homes. She would have wanted your father to love again, too, to have a full house. Moms will do anything for their children's well-being. Rachel, don't overthink this or feel guilty. I know it's what my sister would have wanted."

His mom had always said her joy came from her children being happy. Was *he* happy?

Chapter Sixteen

The past month was like a dream, from a Thanksgiving family dinner to the Christmas pageant. She took a million pictures of Bryce leading the kindergarteners with his light held high, singing one beautiful Christmas song after another. When the pageant was over, Derek, the drummer boy, told Bryce about a famous drummer with the same type of arm as his and showed him some moves on the drum. Now her son had gone from wanting to be a pilot to being a drummer. She smiled and looked at the pictures on her phone. Next week he would probably want to be something else.

Now the dream continued. Karly settled into the co-pilot seat and watched Tyler checking things on the outside of the small aircraft. He had said the weather was perfect for flying. Texas weather was crazy, from freezing cold to the sixties in less than twenty-four hours.

Her phone went off. Thinking it might be Bryce, she checked it.

Nope. It was Anthony. With one swipe she dismissed it. Her excitement now sat in her belly as dread. Why had he called?

Tyler climbed in next to her. "What's wrong?"

"Nothing."

"Danger...danger." Tyler clicked his seat belt, then put on headphones. "Really, when a woman says 'nothing,' I was taught to take cover." He checked a few things before looking back at her. Brow raised, he waited.

"Anthony called. I didn't answer."

"Good. Maybe he was telling you goodbye. Whatever it was, you didn't need to hear it." He turned back to the plane. "Remember, he is not allowed to ruin your days. Speaking of family, have you emailed your grandmother?"

She gave her head a strong shake. "I'm ignoring anything that has to do with extended family. I'm focusing on flying over the most beautiful country."

Good energy bounced off him. Excitement in his eyes indicated how happy he was to be in the cockpit of his father's airplane. Of all the traveling she had done with Anthony, this was the smallest plane she had ever boarded.

He flipped a few switches and wiggled his eyebrows at her. "Ready to soar?"

Her stomach dropped. "I'm not sure."

"No worries. I was trained by the best. I promise, you couldn't be any safer."

The engine started, and he turned the Mustang to the single runway. A few small bounces didn't seem to bother him, so Karly relaxed the grip she had on the door handle. There was no getting out now while they picked up speed. She leaned back as the plane lifted from the ground.

All of Tyler's focus was on the plane, his hands steady as he pulled it higher into the sky. She could already see the town of Clear Water nestled in the center of the hills.

The landscape rolled out over the endless horizon, the hills becoming smaller as they climbed. The sky was a clear blue. Not a single cloud muddled the view.

No ties to the ground; nothing to weigh her down. She understood why he loved it so much. Above the earth, everything looked perfect and small, as if she could cup the whole county in her hand.

"Want to see the ranch?" He winked at her and banked left, away from any evidence of humanity. Endless green with shades of golden brown showcased the Texas Hill Country. This was home.

"Beautiful, isn't it?" His head was turned to the window. He pointed out a few landmarks.

A small sputtering of the engine surprised her. She glanced at Tyler. He was frowning at the instrument panel. He tapped on one of the dials.

The plane made a weird lurching motion.

"Karly." His voice was calm. The kind of calm people used to keep everyone else from panicking.

"Tyler." She matched his tone and reminded herself to breathe.

"We're going to make an emergency landing on the ranch. I know the field, but it's going to be rough. We'll be fine. Trust me, okay? The best you can do is stay calm and exit the plane as soon as we land."

She made herself breathe. "Okay, I trust you, but I'm going to be praying, also."

"Good plan." He focus was intense. His whole body seemed to be flying the plane. The engine cut in and out, then went silent. Her body became empty of all blood. Spots danced in her sight, so she closed her eyes.

A weightlessness took over her body, making her feel as if she had lost all control of her muscles.

"Breathe, Karly. If you pass out, I'm in trouble. Breathe."

She sucked in as much oxygen as she could get through her nose. She did it again. It helped.

"That's it." His voice sounded so calm. "Keep breathing and be ready to get out of the plane. We're going to land on the ranch."

She always imagined a plane would nose-dive if the engines stopped working. Instead, they were floating, gliding in the eerie silence. Her phone beeped. She had a message. Maybe she should call the house and leave her own message for Bryce.

Please, God, guide Tyler and the plane so I can hold my baby again.

"Karly, take this." He pulled a paper in a page protector out of the door pocket without taking his eyes off the skyline. "It's a checklist. Read the items on the back to me." His voice was a scary monotone. No trace of his usual charm or carefree easy attitude existed.

"Engine fire? We're on fire?" She looked out the window.

"No, the one under that. Engine out. Read each line slowly so I can make sure I got everything." He talked as if it was a grocery list.

She started reading. Pronouncing each word carefully. Most of it didn't make sense. She finished the last line and looked at him, afraid to look out.

"Perfect. We're in good shape. I need you to open your door." He opened his and it started bouncing against the frame.

"What?" Did he want them to jump?

"It's so we don't get trapped inside the cockpit when we land. I promise it's safe. Breathe, Karly, and open your door. Then put your head down and cover it with your arms. It's going to be rough, but we're good, okay?" His breathing sounded hard and controlled.

She did what he asked but kept her eyes closed the whole time. She didn't want to see how close they were to the ground. She braced herself for the unknown.

The first hit was a shock. They went from weightless peace to being slammed against the seat belt. Tossed to the side, her head hit something hard, and she saw spots. She made herself as small as possible and pressed her eyes and lips closed. Bryce was all she could think about. She wanted to cry and scream. She tasted blood. Tyler didn't need her distracting him, so she clamped her jaw harder.

Her body snapped in the opposite direction as they hit the ground again. She lost count of the bounces that almost pitched her out of her seat. She dug her fingers into her scalp and curled tighter into herself.

Chaos reigned, and she lost track of up and down. Just as suddenly, the world stopped and everything went silent. Her body was pressed forward into the strap of the seat belt, making breathing difficult. But she was breathing. That was good. She clasped her arms tighter over her head. She could move her feet.

"Karly?" Tyler's voice sounded as if he had swallowed gravel. "Karly?" An urgency he didn't have before edged his voice. He reached over and pushed her hair back.

Raising her head, she blinked to clear her vision. She saw mud and grass instead of hills and sky.

"Karly, are you okay?" His hands went from her

hair to her face to her arms, then returned to her hair. He cupped her face.

She was alive, and so was Tyler. "Yeah. I'm good. It's hard to breathe, but I'm good." She braced her arms on the dashboard in front of her. "We're hanging in midair."

"It's okay. We ended up nose in the dirt. Brace your feet on the front of the floor panel and push back. I'll get your seat belt."

He reached across her, his body creating a warm cocoon. She wanted to hug him close and stop her body from shaking. When had she gotten so cold?

"Plant your feet and push up." He pushed open her door. "Can you stand?"

"I think s-s-so." Her teeth chattered. They were safe on the ground, and she was falling apart. "What's wrong with me?"

"Adrenaline rush. Now that you're safe, your body's reacting." He stroked her hair, his voice low and soft. "Do you want me to go around to your door and lift you out?"

She closed her eyes and took a deep breath. "No, I'm fine." She planted her feet and pushed back into the seat.

As his arm reached across her waist, his face was a whisper away from her ear. His breath reassured her as it went in and out, touching the skin over her cheekbone. "That's my girl. I couldn't have asked for a better copilot."

With a click, the pressure against her middle and chest was relieved. Grabbing the control panel, she kept her balance.

He disappeared, his warmth gone. The shaking started again. How was she going to climb out of the cockpit? He reappeared at her other side. "Hang on. I'm going to level the tail so it's easier for you to get out."

Twisting around, she watched Tyler check some items on the plane. Then he disappeared again. Her head started hurting. With a slight recoil she found herself sitting in the correct position again. The world had righted itself. Well, Tyler had righted the plane anyway.

Less than ten feet away a thick line of trees edged the pasture. On the other side was a drop-off. They had survived. Tyler had safely landed the plane without an engine in the middle of the ranch. Tears hit her arm.

Now she was going to cry?

His arms were around her. He lifted her out of the plane and carried her to the tree line. A duffel bag over one shoulder, he sat her on the ground. He knelt next to her and pulled out a blanket and a bottle of water.

Wrapping her in the thick flannel material, he looked at her with the saddest look she had ever seen on his face.

"Tyler, what's wrong?"

"Other than I almost killed you? Nothing." With one twist he opened the bottle and handed it to her.

"You saved us. You landed a plane without an engine."

"You handled dropping out of the sky like a pro, Karly. I don't know many people who would have stayed that calm. Drink."

After following his command, she pulled out her phone. She needed to hear Bryce's voice. Her son reminded her of the reasons she needed to stay strong and rely on God. Not Tyler Childress, no matter that he truly had saved the day. "I want to talk to Bryce. Just to say hi. I need to hear his voice." She looked at her phone in confusion. "I have eleven voice messages? I'm not sure that many people know this number."

Looking at her phone, Tyler put his hand on the small of her back. "Are they from different people?"

She called her voice mail. The first recording was Anthony sobbing so badly it was hard to understand him. "Please don't…don't get on the plane. I'm so, so sorry. Too much to drink. I promise to never drink again. Don't get on the plane." All the blood rushed from her body. She wasn't sure where it went, but she was empty. The next two were Anthony crying and apologizing. Then the sheriff. The last one was from Pastor John, who wanted them to return his call as soon as possible. Her eyesight blurred. Tyler took the phone from her and pulled her into his arms.

His voice calm, he rubbed her back while he called Pastor John. They must have been so worried. She wanted to curl up in his shirt and absorb warmth. Anthony had tried to kill them. It was all her fault. She should have left when he first showed up.

Tyler went quiet, and his other arm came around her. They just sat there, her fingers clinging to his jacket. His cheek pressed against the top of her head.

"We survived, Karly. The sheriff has Anthony in custody. He turned himself in. John is on his way to pick us up."

She nodded. This was all her fault.

Tyler took a deep breath and reminded himself to stay calm. He rubbed his hands over her back. "This is not your fault." All he wanted to do was hold her. The idea of her hurting tore at his gut. He couldn't even think of what else might have happened today. Somewhere in the past month, she had crept into his heart in a way that made him fear she would always own it. He'd thought love would come at him with trumpets blaring.

Somehow she had quietly made him aware of the empty holes in his life. Now what did he do?

He didn't need to burden her with his emotional mess. She had a clear plan for her life, and it didn't include a guy like him. It seemed the more you loved someone, the harder it was to actually say the words out loud. Or maybe he was just a coward.

For the first time, he truly understood what it meant to put someone else's happiness before your own. Yeah, he had totally and absolutely given her his heart. He might as well rip it out and hand it to her. Now he was being all stupid and…in love. He pressed his lips to her forehead. He had promised not to kiss her again, but surely that didn't count. At least she had stopped crying.

A heavy diesel engine broke the silence. The ranch truck came to a sliding halt, throwing dirt from under the tires. John rushed out from the driver's side and wrapped them both in a tight hug. "Tyler. Karly. We were frantic. Are you okay?"

"She's fine. We're fine."

John stepped back, and Tyler saw Dub standing by the truck. The look of devastation on his father's face nearly brought Tyler to his knees.

"You're both unharmed?" Dub spoke through clenched teeth.

He looked at his dad, but this time he didn't see the hardheaded man who criticized everything his son did. He saw a man who had lost most of his family, a man who wanted the best for those he loved but couldn't protect them no matter how hard he tried.

He took Karly's hand and moved to his father. He couldn't quite let her go yet, but he needed to get to his dad.

"Dad, I'm so sorry. I know I pulled some stupid stunts in high school. Ran away to Florida. When Mom died, I should have been here. I was in Europe when you got the news of Carol's death. And now I almost kil—"

His dad grabbed him. "You landed the airplane without an engine or runway." A sob sounded from the man who never cried. His grip tightened around Tyler's shoulders and he pulled him in for a hug.

He looked over his dad and saw Karly crying again, but this time she had a faint smile. Dub finally stepped back and rubbed his face dry with his callused hands.

John joined them. "I've talked to the sheriff. Apparently Anthony cut the line then went to grab Bryce, but couldn't do it. He said he had called to stop you, but it was too late. He called the police. The sheriff says he's a mess and for us not to touch anything out here. It's a crime scene now."

Karly started trembling again. He could see the guilt she held over her face. His hand moved up and cupped her jaw. "You're strong. You handled dropping from the sky like a pro. Anthony can't hurt you."

John nodded. "Y'all need to go by the office and let them interview you about the incident. He says they've call the FFA and they're going to send someone out to take pictures and do whatever they do at a crime scene."

Tyler shook his head. "I feel as though we're in a bad CSI show. This is so surreal. Karly, let's get you to Bryce. You ready to see your son and give him a huge hug?"

"That sounds like the best offer I've ever gotten."

How would she respond if he offered himself up to her? He was probably better off not knowing.

* * *

Opening the car door before Tyler turned off the engine, Karly jumped from the cab. Her legs threatened to give out. The door supported her while she took a few deep breaths.

Tyler stood by her side. "You need to be careful. You're still wobbly."

"I'm fine." She hated feeling weak.

"Ha. Now you sound like Dad." He put his arm around her as they moved to the front door.

"There are worse people to sound like." Winking at him, she stepped ahead of Tyler.

"That's what I'm learning." He stayed right behind her as she went up the steps. The door swung open.

"Momma!" Bryce lunged at her. He'd been hanging out with Celeste too much; jumping on people in greeting was a new habit.

"Easy does it, Cowboy. Your mom had a rough day." Tyler put out a hand to keep Bryce from knocking her down.

Karly went to her knees, sitting back on her heels, arms so tight around her little man Tyler was sure he couldn't have separated them if he had wanted to try.

"Momma, are you okay?" Little hands patted her back.

Karly started crying.

Tyler couldn't stand there watching. Bryce's bright eyes, so much like his mother's, were huge. Tyler dropped to his haunches, all of his weight balanced on the front of his boots. One hand on Karly, the other on Bryce. "The plane ride got a little rough. She missed you, but she's okay now." He leaned in closer to Bryce.

"You know how moms just need to hug you and cry sometimes?"

Bryce twisted his neck so he could see Tyler. He nodded with the understanding of a little boy who had experienced too much. "Did someone hurt her? Did you do something to make her cry?" Tyler's heart twisted at the thought of Bryce feeling the need to protect his mother.

As a kid, Tyler had been so safe and protected his whole life. How had he ended up ungrateful for everything he had been given? Selfishness was truly ugly.

Karly lifted her head and cupped Bryce's face. "Oh, no, baby. Tyler was great today. You know what? He found out we have family in Hawaii, and they want to talk to us. Grandparents, aunts, uncles and cousins."

"Really? Your mom's family?"

She nodded. "We can talk to them over the internet. What do you think about that?"

"I think that's cool. Is that why you're crying?"

"No and yes." She laughed, picking up her son and holding him so close an ant would have been squashed.

From the edge of his sight, Tyler saw John and his dad hanging back, giving Karly time with her son. "Hey, guys, why we don't go in the house? I could use a nice warm cup of hot chocolate. This is getting hard on my old knees."

Karly laughed and stood. "Yeah, your old knees." Still holding Bryce, she shifted him to her hip and smoothed out some of his more unruly hair. "So tell me what you were doing while I was flying over the hill country." She carried Bryce through the door, his nonstop chatter bringing a smile to her face.

The scene hit Tyler hard. He wanted them in his life every day. He wanted to see Karly and Bryce every

morning at the ranch table. The thought of not seeing them was scarier than living the rest of his life in
Clear Water.

Chapter Seventeen

The night she had been working toward for weeks now had finally arrived. It was Christmas Eve. Karly pulled the sheet of cookies out of the oven. They smelled right, looked perfect. The real test would come when she gave them to Tyler and Dub. Did they taste like the cookies Cindy had made for them?

During Christmas Eve service, one of Dub's favorite mares had gone into early labor, so all of the boys had headed out to help as soon as they got back to the ranch. Tyler assured her Bryce would be fine with them, and it worked out for her.

It gave her time to get all the food out and to bake the special cookies she had made last night. She hadn't been able to sleep after being interviewed by the sheriff and the Texas Rangers, then talking with her mother's family on Skype. There had been so many tears and questions answered.

Years before, Karly's relatives in Hawaii had hired a private investigator to find her mother. Learning she had died of a drug overdose, the PI had talked to Anthony. He'd told them she had lost the child she'd been carrying before she left Hawaii. They stopped looking for any child.

Believing Anthony lied to them was easy, but she still had a hard time understanding how he could cut the fuel lines. The idea that he'd tried to kill her and Tyler so he could grab Bryce... Well, no wonder she was having problems sleeping.

She took a deep breath. He couldn't hurt her anymore.

Dear God, please give me peace and let me lay my worries at Your feet. You are my refuge and strength.

She heard voices coming in through the back door. Wiping her hands on the red-and-green ruffled apron, Karly checked the food she had laid out on the island. Tamales from the church fund-raiser filled two steamers. Chili, sausage balls and a sweet corn casserole sat next to them. At the other end of the island she had trays filled with assorted pickles, olives, cold cuts and cheeses. Queso and guacamole with chips and breads sat in the middle. Karly had made everything Cindy had listed as the Christmas Eve essentials, plus the pigs in a blanket Tyler had requested.

"Christmas Eve gifts!" Celeste was the first through the door, bags in each hand. Right behind her, Rachel, Lorrie Ann and Pastor John followed. They each carried a wrapped dessert from Maggie's house. Oh, her cookies had some tough competition. She hoped they could hold their own.

Lorrie Ann set down her containers and hugged Karly. "You should have let us help with the food."

Karly could not tell if her statement was based on doubts she could cook real food or a pure desire to help.

Maybe both mingled up together. "I wanted to serve you after everything you've done for Bryce and me."

Pastor John grabbed a sausage ball and popped it in his mouth. "This reminds me of the spread Cindy had every Christmas Eve."

Karly's stomach knotted up. "I found her recipe box and used her notes on what everyone liked. She had your names on the card for those."

Everyone laughed as he stopped his hand midway to his mouth. He grinned and ate another one. "These were my favorites. Thanks, Karly."

With her apron twisted in her hands, she looked over the food. "I hope it's okay. I don't want to upset anyone. I threw in some of Bryce's favorites, too."

Lorrie Ann hugged her again. "It's all about being together. You did a great job. Now, where are the boys?"

"One of the mares went into labor a couple weeks too early. They're at the barn. I wanted to set up the kitchen without people watching."

"I want to see the new baby horse!" Celeste grabbed her father's hand. "Please, Daddy. Let's go to the barn."

"I want to see the foal, too." Rachel looked at her father.

"I'm not sure they want us all out there." Pastor John glanced at Karly. "What do you think? Should we go?"

"Everything's already here." She slipped off the Christmas apron and hung it on the hook in the pantry. "I think we should join the boys."

"Yay! Come on, Rachel. Let's go." Celeste grabbed her sister's hand and ran for the door.

"Easy, girls," their father called after them. "We don't want to upset the mare."

Karly followed them to the barn. The light from the

barn shone like a beacon, welcoming new life to the ranch. Inside, they followed the sounds of the hushed whispers to the far end of the barn.

Standing outside the stall, Tyler held Bryce on his shoulders. Dub leaned against the metal bars that ran from the half wall to the ceiling. Mia, Adrian's daughter, stood on her toes.

Celeste went straight to her grandfather. "Is the baby here yet?"

The small group turned and looked at them. Adrian stepped out of the stall door. "Y'all are just in time to see the little guy stand."

John picked up Celeste so she could see over the wall.

Karly gasped. A long-legged colt lay in the bedding, his mother nudging him, nickering softly as she cleaned him off. He was dark red with black legs, except for one white sock on the left leg that stretched out in front of him.

"He's beautiful." Rachel's hushed voice expressed the awe Karly was feeling.

They all watched as the little guy struggled to stand. The spindly legs would give out and he would try again. They would gasp when he fell. In less than fifteen minutes, he was standing, looking for his mother's milk.

Karly couldn't believe it. "That's amazing that he can walk so soon."

Tyler smiled at her. "He's got heart. How about we leave the new family alone so they can settle?"

As a group they turned back to the house. "Adrian, you want to join us for dinner?"

"Thanks, Tyler, but Mom will get upset if I don't get Mia back in time to open the gifts. See y'all later."

The kids chatted all the way to the house, the excitement of the new foal overshadowing the bitter cold and Christmas Eve dinner.

Dub and Tyler both stopped at the entryway into the kitchen. "Santa must have stopped by early. Look at all this food." Dub walked to the stack of Christmas plates. "Haven't seen these since…" He looked at Karly. "You did this?"

"I'm sorry. I didn't mean—"

Tyler had his arm around her before she could finish. "It's perfect. Thank you. You did all this while we were in the barn?"

"What are these?" Dub picked up one of the sausages wrapped in croissant dough.

Tyler took it from his dad. "My new favorite Christmas Eve food."

Dub's scowl made her laugh. Then he turned it on her. Spine straight, she bit down on her lips. He winked. He got another and chewed slowly, before nodding. "Well, I think they're my favorite now. You have to make them next year."

Next year. Two words that made her want to cry and dance at the same time. She wanted to grab him and dance a grand waltz. Those two little words changed her world. She had spent her whole life getting through the night or worried about the next day. Plans for next year with people she loved made her heart sing.

"Yes, sir." She settled for giving him a smile.

Everyone filled their plates. With nerves on edge, she watched Bryce place a pile of everything on his dish that precariously balanced on his stubbed arm. Several times she had to stop herself from taking it from him. Tyler was right—she needed to let him fail and succeed without her intervention.

At the table, everyone joined hands for the prayer. Bryce didn't even hesitate to hold his short arm out to Tyler. She had forgotten to make sure to sit on her son's right side.

Tyler looked at her and winked before bowing his head for prayer. Pastor John's words of praise and thanksgiving never had seemed truer than right now, right here surrounded by people that were good and true, not out for themselves.

Thank You, God, for bringing these people into my life right when I needed them most. Thank You for Tyler and showing me a man can be a friend and protector without using me. Please hold my heart when he leaves. Let me lean on You.

Dub squeezed her hand. Everyone was looking at her, waiting for her to finish her private prayer. "Sorry."

Pastor John's warm brown eyes glimmered with a smile. "Sometimes we need a little extra time with God. Tonight is a good time for that. Now, on to the tamales." Stacks of the corn husks covered the table—not the traditional meal she dreamed of serving, but this was better than her dreams. Laughter filled the room along with the scent of vanilla and pine.

Dub told stories of his childhood and of Carol and Tyler when they were small. "The rivers were raging after the flood, and Tyler thought he could build a raft like Huck Finn. I knew then we were going to spend a great deal of time praying for that boy."

"Uncle Tyler, you seem to have been in trouble all the time."

"My curiosity got the better of me time and time again." He sat back and grinned. Karly had to smile. He didn't seem to regret his Huckleberry past.

Celeste rested her chin on her hands and nodded. "I must take after you, Uncle Tyler." Her sweet little face was serious. "I try to stay out of trouble, but it never works."

Her father leaned over and kissed her on the head. "Hey, I hear there are a few gifts under the tree for some good girls and boys."

Celeste dropped her head to the table. "Does that mean I don't get one?"

Tyler went to her and picked her up. "From one adventurer to another, I guarantee you there are boxes with your name on them."

"What about me?" Bryce asked. "Do you think there is one for me, too?" His dark eyes widened, filled with worry.

"Oh, I saw two or three."

"Really?"

"Ready to go find out, or do you want another round of dinner?"

Dub sat back and patted his stomach. "I think I want more tamales."

Celeste dropped to the ground and rushed to her grandfather's side. "No. You can get more after we open gifts. Please, Grandpa."

John narrowed his eyes. "That's not how you act, young lady."

"I'm sorry." She lowered her eyes.

"I'm just teasing." Dub hugged her. "Let's see if your uncle Tyler got coal this year."

In a whirlwind the dining room was empty. Karly started gathering the plates and taking them to the kitchen.

Everyone had left but Tyler. He leaned against the archway, arms crossed. "What are you doing?"

"I thought you were salutatorian of your class." She held up the dirty dishes.

"Ha-ha. The table can be cleared later." He walked over to her and took the dishes out of her hands. "The family is waiting and the kids are about to storm the castle. So come on, Cinderella, the party can't start without you." He tangled up his fingers with hers and led her toward the living room.

"Wait a minute. I have something I'd like to give you before everything starts." It was her turn to take charge. Pulling him into the kitchen, she lifted the cover off the cookies she had been working on for over a month now.

She wouldn't let herself get discouraged by the brief cringe she saw on his face before he planted a bright smile on his face.

"You're still determined to make cookies?" He took one and winked at her. At first he took a small nibble, probably afraid of a full commitment after the last one he'd eaten.

She wasn't insulted by his look of surprise as he took a bigger bite.

His face stopped in midmotion. His eyes wide and full of questions, he stared at her. Holding the sugar cookie up, he swallowed. "Where did you get these?"

All of a sudden her excitement turned to dread. What if she'd messed up? "I found your mother's recipe box." Karly pulled on her earring. "I've been practicing until I thought I got it right. I'm sorry it was a bad id—"

"No, it was a shock. They taste just like my mom's." One corner of his lips pulled up, creating a dimple. "This is one of the most special gifts I've ever received."

He stepped closer, so close that his nose was mere inches from hers. "Thank you." Lowering his head, his lips touched her cheek, and then he stepped back.

She followed. He might have promised not to kiss her again, but she had not made the same vow. Standing on her toes, she wrapped her fingers around his biceps to steady herself. Before she closed her eyes, she saw the look of surprise on his face.

She moved in to join their lips. She pressed closer. His hands surrounded her waist.

He leaned into the kiss, taking over. Tentative, gentle and soft, as if she was a precious gift he didn't want to break. Her hands moved up to his shoulders. No space remained between them. The pressure of his kiss went deeper, and she could taste the sugar cookie.

A loud cough caused them to jump apart.

Tyler actually turned red. She couldn't stop her smile. He was so cute.

Dub had one eyebrow raised.

Tyler glanced at the ceiling. "There was some mistletoe. It was right there. Who moved it?" He grabbed Bryce, who stood right behind Dub, and tickled him. "Did you move the mistletoe?"

Bryce giggled. "I didn't take it." They all laughed.

Tyler had Bryce in one hand and reached out to her with the other. "The family's waiting."

Chapter Eighteen

Karly took the last sip of her hot chocolate. Tyler sat next to the tree with her favorite story in his lap. He closed the book and took a drink from his snowman-shaped mug. Pastor John and his family had left over an hour ago, and Dub had gone to bed. Bryce was too hyper to go to sleep, so Tyler suggested one last story under the tree.

"Well, Cowboy, I think I'm done for the night. What about you?"

He yawned. "One more."

"We could, but what if Santa comes by and we're still awake? There'll be more presents tomorrow." Tyler stood, stretching out his long legs. He held out a hand to her and helped her to her feet. "Karly, this has been a perfect night. Thank you."

She didn't know what to say. They had made all her dreams come true and he was thanking her. She went to unplug the lights from the tree and glanced out the window. "Tyler?"

"What's wrong?" He walked over to her and looked

over her shoulder. "I can't believe it." He turned to look at her son. "Bryce, I think you got your wish for snow."

Bryce ran to the window and pressed his face to the glass. "Snow!" Before she could say anything, he had run out the door.

The door slammed and she was right behind him. Snow. There was actual snow falling from the sky. Small soft white flurries danced on the air, zigzagging to the ground.

She stood on the porch, staring with wonder at the light frosting covering the ground. Tyler stood behind her, his hands resting on her shoulders. "I can't believe we're getting snow."

He gently squeezed. "It's not going to last."

"It'll live here forever." She laid her hand flat on his chest. His heart jumped against her hand. "God has given us this gift, so we have to celebrate it, enjoy it and savor it. Later we can pull it out and relive the wonderful blessing we had in this moment in time—when the world was perfect and we had everything we wanted."

"How did you get so wise?" His eyes softened, and he moved to kiss her.

She ran backward and laughed. "Hard knocks and love." Her eyes lit up. "Let's dance in the snow." She joined Bryce and they swung each other in a circle.

"It's so beautiful, Momma." He stuck his tongue out before running around in a large circle, stomping on the snow.

Karly started after him, but Tyler took her hand and said, "Marry me."

She froze. "What?"

"Marry me."

"Tyler, I'm flatter—"

He put his fingers on her lips. "Don't say anything right now. I get why you're hesitant. You've jumped in before only to find fire. I've waited a long time. I can wait some more. No rush." He tapped her nose. "We have to celebrate all the gifts God gave us. You and Bryce are a gift I want to cherish."

She couldn't talk, couldn't find the words to form a sentence. She swallowed, trying to clear the tightness in her throat. "I want to say yes now. I do. I've said yes too many times to too many losers. I don't think you're…"

He kissed her. Lifting his head, he kept his arms around her. "I know you don't want a relationship. But I'm here. I'm moving home, and I want to prove to you I'm worth the risk. I love you, Karly—completely and absolutely love you with my whole heart. You are an amazing woman. I also want to be Bryce's father if you'll let me."

She looked into those surreal blue eyes and thought of all the arguments she had for not saying yes. Before she could manage one word, he started talking again. He was adorable.

"I'll understand if you want to wait a year or two. That's fine. The good thing about my job is I can live anywhere." Cupping her face, he leaned his forehead against hers. "I know I want to marry you, so when you're ready, all you have to do is ask me and I promise to say yes. Deal?"

She nodded.

"Momma, Tyler, look—the snowflakes are getting bigger." He jumped, trying to catch the white flakes. "Do you think we can build a snowman in the morning?"

"If it keeps snowing, we might be able to manage a Texas snowman."

"What's a Texas snowman?"

Tyler knelt down and picked up a handful of leaves and twigs. "It takes a little snow, a little earth, a few leaves and some twigs to make a Texas snowman."

"Cool." Bryce looked up and twirled with his tongue out. "Momma, come taste the snow! Tyler! Look I have one on my... Oh, it melted."

Tyler pulled her into a waltz pose and started to spin. "Come on, Karly! Let's dance in the snow. You asked for it and you got it."

Bryce turned and twirled, laughing in the night. "This is the best Christmas ever!"

"Yes, it is." She looked up to the sky as he spun her around the music in her head. God had given her everything she dreamed of, so why was she afraid? "Tyler Childress, will you marry me?"

He stumbled briefly, but recovered and lifted her high as if she was as weightless as one of the snowflakes. "Yes! Yes! Yes!" he roared. She was sure they heard him across the entire canyon.

Not much later the front door opened. Dub stood with his cane in the porch light. "What is going on out here? Is that snow? In December?"

"Yes, but even more special, Karly asked me to marry her and I said yes."

"Karly asked you? What?" He threw his head back and laughed. "I knew she was a smart girl. Now, boy, that is the best news I've gotten in years. Welcome to the family, Karly."

Bryce jumped on them. "Yay! This is the most wonderful Christmas ever. Snow, and Tyler will be my dad! Do you think tomorrow I'll get a horse?"

Tyler laughed. "We'll see, Cowboy. Now that I'm going to be your dad I'm sure we can work something out."

Karly said, "Wait a minute, Mom still has the last vote in that decision." She went to Dub and kissed him on the cheek. He had tears in his eyes.

His voice was low and hoarse with emotion. "I can't tell you how happy I am. Thank you."

"Thank you for raising such a wonderful man. I hope I can do half as well with Bryce."

"Momma, come dance with us!"

Dub waved her on. "Go join your family. Believe me, they grow up too fast." After one last kiss on his cheek, Karly jumped down the steps and ran through the falling snowflakes. Tyler met her in the yard and swung her around.

"I can't tell you how happy you've made me. So how soon can we say I do?"

"Would it be okay if we wait a while to actually say I do? Maybe June, here on the ranch?"

Moving closer to her, he leaned in for a kiss. She would take that as a yes.

Bryce made a face. "Ugh, Mr. Childress, they must have found more mistletoe. They're kissing again."

"I'm gonna be your grandpa now, so no more 'Mr. Childress,' and you might as well get used to the kissing. We'll probably be seeing more of that stuff."

Bryce sighed. "I guess we'll have to get used to it if it makes Momma happy."

* * * * *

THE DOCTOR'S CHRISTMAS WISH

Renee Ryan

To my fabulous, incredibly smart, savvy editor, Melissa Endlich. I'll treasure your kindness, insight and generosity for many years to come. You deserve only the best in life.

Trust in the Lord with all your heart and lean not on your own understanding; in all your ways submit to him, and he will make your paths straight.

—*Proverbs* 3:5–6

Chapter One

The house phone rang at 10:33 p.m. on the Sunday after Thanksgiving. The high-pitched sound yanked Ethan Scott's attention away from the television screen and the football game he'd carved out time to watch live, no distractions.

Who would be calling at this hour?

The hitch in his breath was born out of a hidden fear he kept tucked deep inside his soul. When his parents were killed in a fatal car crash, Ethan had been the first to get the news. As the oldest of four, he had to identify the bodies, to inform his three younger siblings and to handle all the funeral arrangements.

He'd completed each task without hesitation, and had been forced to repeat an eerily similar process a year and a half ago when another deadly car accident had taken his fiancée.

The incessant ringing continued.

Like a shock wave, old memories rippled across new. Ethan's previously easy, relaxed mood spiraled into something darker.

He debated ignoring the call. Few people had his

home number, and any medical emergency would either go to his answering service or come through on his cell phone.

The ringing stopped.

Banishing unwanted memories and the emotions they brought, Ethan sat back to enjoy the game. The Broncos were about to score a touchdown.

The ringing started up again.

Ethan's gut took a hard roll. Surely the Lord wouldn't deal him another blow, wouldn't make him suffer through another unexpected goodbye. He'd had enough sorrow for one lifetime. He put the game on mute, then made the short trek from living room to kitchen.

The sound of doggy toenails clicking on the tile floor alerted him that his treasured black Lab had followed him. He patted Baloo on the head and then glanced at the caller ID.

Keely O'Toole. Ethan's gut took another hard roll, for an entirely different reason this time.

His neighbor was one of the few women in town he tended to avoid, for reasons he didn't want to explore tonight. Or ever.

Since Keely made a habit of avoiding him as well, he figured whatever had incited her to call the house—twice—on the landline—had to be important.

He snatched up the telephone receiver. "Ethan speaking."

A short, tense pause sounded on the other end of the line, followed by a weary female sigh. "Is Ryder around? He's not answering his cell phone."

"Hello to you, too, Keely."

She sighed again, the sound filled with frustration. "Is Ryder home or not?"

"Not. He's working the night shift at the hospital."

"That's unfortunate."

Something in her voice put Ethan on alert. He could practically feel Keely's agitation coming through the phone. Both his younger brothers were doctors. But where Ethan was a primary care physician and Brody was working for Doctors Without Borders, Ryder specialized in emergency medicine.

If she was calling Ryder this late at night…

"Talk to me, Keely. What's going on?"

"I need your help."

Four words Ethan never expected to come out the woman's mouth, at least not directed at him.

Something must be seriously wrong. "Are you hurt?"

"It's not me. It's Felicity. She's really sick and I don't know what to do. Should I take her out in this weather, to the ER waiting room, or do I hold off, pray it'll go away? I'm really, really worried."

She was also rambling. Another first.

Ethan mentally sorted through her words, stopping on an unfamiliar name. *Felicity.* Who was Felicity? His mind went blank. Then he remembered the little girl who had moved in with Keely over the holiday weekend. He didn't know the whole story, only that Keely was the child's legal guardian for an indefinite amount of time.

"What's wrong with her?"

"She's complaining of stomach pain."

In full doctor mode now, Ethan digested this piece of information. "Any vomiting?"

"Just once, about an hour ago."

"When did she last eat?"

"Around six."

He checked his watch, did a mental calculation between regular dinner hours and now. "What did she eat?"

"A hamburger, fries, oh, and a cinnamon roll. I know they aren't the healthiest choices, but she starts school tomorrow and I took her to the mall to buy her some new clothes. You might think it's odd I'm putting her in school two weeks before Christmas break, but I wanted her to meet other kids before—"

He cut her off. "Hold up. Does she have a fever?"

Keely blew out a loud hiss. "I checked it right before I called Ryder's cell phone. The thermometer said 99.7 degrees. Can you… Ethan, please, can you come over and look at Felicity?"

"On my way." He hung up the phone and headed for the mudroom just off the kitchen.

Baloo trotted past him and took up position at the back door, a hopeful expression in his coal-black eyes. Normally, Ethan would indulge the dog. He and the black Lab had been through a lot of hard times since Ethan rescued the animal during his tour in Afghanistan.

"Sorry, buddy, you can't come with me."

Baloo whined, the sound pitiful and well honed from years of conning Ethan.

"Hang tight, old boy. This shouldn't take long." Ethan scrubbed the animal's face between his hands. "I'll let you out when I get back."

The dog's ears drooped, but he obediently lowered himself to his haunches and rested his chin on his paws.

Ethan grabbed his coat and trod through the three inches of snow that had fallen throughout the day. He didn't have far to go. The backyard of Keely's childhood home spilled into his. They had that in common, both living in the houses they'd grown up in, having inherited them from their parents. Ethan, after his had died. Keely, after hers had moved to Arizona.

He was on her back stoop, stomping snow off his boots, when the door flung open. "What took you so long?"

Since she sounded like a terrified new parent, he forgave her for her rudeness. "Came as fast as I could."

"Don't just stand there. Come inside."

Holding his tongue, again, he climbed the steps. As was becoming a habit whenever they were up close and personal, he reminded himself this was Keely. Once upon a time she'd been just another skinny kid hanging out with his younger sister.

Despite growing into a beautiful woman with long, gorgeous red hair, amazing green eyes and a figure that jealous peers had once compared to Jessica Rabbit's, Keely was still that same annoying girl Ethan tolerated because she was his sister's BFF.

Except, lately, things had changed between them. Their relationship was morphing into something new, something charged with tension and awkward pauses. The initial shift had started nearly a year ago, right after she'd left her big-city life in New York and settled back in Colorado.

Ethan moved deeper in the house.

The inevitable kick in his gut came right on schedule, as it always did whenever his gaze locked with Keely's. Tonight, the sensation hit him hard. It wasn't an altogether awful feeling, kind of reminded him of danger-induced adrenaline.

Precarious territory. "Where's the patient?"

"Her name is Felicity."

"Right." Ethan shed his coat, tossed it on a nearby bench. "Where is she?"

"Upstairs in her room."

Ethan recognized the panic in Keely's voice, which was mirrored in her wide, almond-shaped green eyes. Her long, wavy hair was also disheveled, as if she'd dragged both hands through the now tangled strands more than a few times.

At the obvious signs of her distress, everything in him softened. He gently touched her sleeve. "I'm here, Keely. I'll take care of the child."

She drew in a few unsteady breaths, her legendary hostility toward him diminishing with each exhale. "I... I believe you."

He dropped his hand. "One last question before I have a look at her. How old is she?"

"She turned seven last month."

His throat squeezed shut. His eyes began to burn.

What were the odds? He swallowed, hard. He'd barely regained his equilibrium when Keely took off at a clipped pace.

Ethan followed after her. They moved at the speed of light from kitchen to living room to stairwell. The smells of home filled him, a mixture of floral scents, furniture polish and freshly baked bread.

He hadn't been inside this house in years. Like a good neighbor, he'd left Keely alone. She'd done the same for him, a situation that worked for them both.

But now, as he followed her through the house, Ethan wondered why he'd kept his distance. He liked the grown-up Keely, sometimes, when she wasn't being snarky or unnecessarily antagonistic. A couple of unfortunate incidents from the past didn't mean they couldn't find a happy rhythm going into the future. Maybe they could even be friends. Now that she was twenty-nine and he thirty-four, their five-year age gap didn't seem so large.

At the top of the stairs, she stopped outside the second room on her right. Hand on the doorknob, she swung her gaze to his. *Slam*. He told himself he was imagining the body blow. But, of course, he wasn't.

"Keely, after I'm through examining the child I'd like the two of us to—"

A little girl's whimper cut off the rest of his words. Ethan's pulse picked up speed. Blood rushed in his ears. Memories yanked at him, emptying his mind of everything but a miserable sense of grief and loss.

He hadn't expected this strong reaction. He saw kids every day at the office. No problem. Yet here he was, his heart pounding and his breath speeding up. He fought the urge to close his eyes. If he did, he'd be back at Fort Bragg, back to the time when he thought he would be a husband and a father. A split-second swerve to miss a skunk had taken away that future.

This wasn't about him.

Mouth grim, he shoved aside the unwanted memories and walked into the room.

Keely couldn't figure out why Ethan's shoulders were bunched as he made his way toward Felicity's bed, or why he seemed overly tense. She'd take his behavior personally, but now that she thought about it, she realized he'd been relatively relaxed when he first entered through the back door. He'd only grown silent and progressively distant as she'd guided him through the house.

A tall, broad-shouldered man, he moved toward Felicity at the slow, steady pace of a graceful jungle cat. With his glossy black hair and pale blue eyes, Ethan Scott was entirely too good-looking for his own good. The two days' worth of scruff on his well-defined, square jaw gave him a dangerous edge.

Keely had no problem imagining him in the Army Ranger uniform he'd once worn. She shook away the thought, and lifted up a silent prayer that Ethan proved to be the capable doctor everyone in their small town of Village Green, Colorado, claimed he was.

With heavy, lumbering steps, Keely joined him beside Felicity's bed. Tonight he looked more like a regular guy than a former soldier turned successful doctor. He wore faded jeans and a long-sleeve T-shirt that read Of Course I Don't Look Busy. I Did It Right the First Time.

Typical Ethan, the big, bad, frustrating bane of her existence.

"You must be Felicity," he said to the little girl in a low, rough voice that sounded slightly tortured. What was up with that? "I'm your neighbor Ethan. I'm also a doctor."

In her unnaturally pale face, Felicity's big blue eyes rounded. "You don't look like a doctor."

"That's because I keep my white coat at the office." He drew in an audible breath, then carefully sat on the edge of the bed, his eyes running over the child, gauging, measuring. "I understand you're not feeling well."

Felicity's blond curls bobbed up and down. "My tummy hurts real bad."

"Can you tell me where it hurts?"

She whimpered. "Everywhere."

He went still for a beat, his expression bland, giving nothing away. Keely had no idea what was in his head, but she knew what was in hers. Concern for the little girl she'd agreed to take into her home. The transition from carefree single woman to legal guardian of a seven-year-old had begun months ago, only becoming official this week. She was still reeling.

"Okay, Felicity, I'm going to—"

"You can call me Flicka." Cheeks bright pink, the little girl lifted a skinny shoulder. "But only if you want to."

The easy, affectionate smile Ethan gave the child was very different from the tight, barely tolerant ones Keely received.

"Okay, Flicka, I'm going to perform a few tests. When I press on your stomach, I need you tell me if it hurts."

The little girl nodded again. There was nothing but trust in her eyes, even while her hands clenched around the bedcovers as if she were preparing to embark on a wild amusement park ride.

Incredibly gentle, Ethan pressed on her stomach. "Any pain?"

"Nope." Felicity's death grip released, as did Keely's fear. But when Ethan moved his hands to the lower right portion of Felicity's abdomen, Keely's breath caught in her lungs.

"How about now?" he asked. "Does it hurt when I press here?"

"Not really."

"You're doing great, Flicka. Just a little bit longer and we'll be through." Ethan continued the rest of the exam with a firm but gentle manner.

When he held Felicity's ankle with one hand and her knee with the other, then rotated her hip, the little girl simply watched him in silent fascination. No gasp of pain. No clenched fists in the comforter.

Keely nearly cried in relief.

Eventually, Ethan stood, said goodbye to Felicity, then motioned for Keely to follow him into the hallway.

The moment they were alone, she asked the question burning in her mind. "Is it her appendix?"

"Nothing indicates that particular diagnosis."

What kind of cryptic, unhelpful answer was that? "Are you certain?"

"She's not experiencing swelling in the abdomen or pain in the lower right region. At this point I don't believe an ultrasound or additional lab work is necessary."

He'd pitched his voice low, as if to calm her fears. Keely wasn't appeased. "If it's not her appendix, then what's wrong with her?"

"She has a stomachache."

His matter-of-fact tone increased her distress. "Is there something you can give her to make her feel better?"

"For now, there's nothing to do but continue supportive measures. Keep her hydrated and resting. If the symptoms persist or worsen, call me and I'll come back over."

Why was he so calm? Didn't he understand how worried she was? "I can't bear seeing her in pain."

"Keely, relax. Flicka has a stomachache, probably brought on by stress or the consumption of junk food or both."

"You're saying this is my fault because I let her eat junk food."

"That's not what I'm saying. Kids suffer stomach-aches all the time. I'm confident she's going to be okay."

Why didn't she feel better? Why this terrible spasm of guilt in the center of her heart? "I feel so helpless."

"You did the right thing calling me."

Actually, she'd called Ryder. Ethan's younger brother by two years was so much easier to take. Though he was just as good-looking as Ethan, nearly identical actually, with Ryder there was none of the friction and hostility she experienced in the company of this particular Dr. Scott.

"I mean it, Keely. You can call me anytime, no matter how late."

She gaped at him. "Why are you being so nice to me?"

"Because I'm a nice guy." The grin he flashed her was full of the teenage boy she remembered, the one she'd spun a few girlhood dreams around, not the one who'd humiliated her in front of his friends, twice.

"Seriously, why?"

"I'm giving you a pass because you're new to this parenting thing." His eyes sparked with genuine compassion.

No fair. The man had amazing eyes, long-lashed and full of secrets. She saw sorrow there as well, more prominent than usual.

It wasn't the first time she'd noticed that look in Ethan's eyes. Their paths crossed a lot, primarily because he often came into her restaurant, Senor O'Toole's, on his lunch break.

He might be the big, bad, frustrating bane of her existence. But the lone wolf image didn't ring true, not tonight. Hardly ever, if she was being honest with herself. The raw vulnerability simmering under that tough exterior made Keely want to reach up and smooth away his pain.

She resisted. "Felicity's really going to be all right?"

"For now." He looked about to say more. He even opened his mouth, but then closed it and headed down the stairs.

Keely hurried after him, catching up just as he was shoving his arms through the sleeves of his coat.

He reached for the doorknob, then paused. "Call me," he said. "Anytime, for any reason."

There were so many ways to take that suggestion, even more ways to respond. She chose the most sincere. "I will, and thank you for coming over so quickly. I really appreciate your help tonight."

"You're welcome." He gave her a warm smile.

Her heart stuttered. It *actually* stuttered.

"Good night, Keely."

"Night, Ethan."

Still smiling, he swung open the door. And disappeared into the night.

Chapter Two

Keely waited until Ethan was out of sight before she shut her back door. The rhythmic sound of the dishwasher sloshing through the rinse cycle accompanied her return journey through the kitchen and then into the living room.

Now that her initial fear for Felicity's well-being was put to rest, Keely's mind wanted to linger on the man who'd eased her worries. She'd hardly recognized her neighbor.

Ethan had instilled a sense of calm. He'd been unspeakably gentle with Felicity and Keely was grateful for that. But now she was left feeling confused and edgy and not quite herself.

With his quicksilver smile and excellent bedside manner, Ethan had prodded awake the loneliness she kept stuffed behind a healthy dose of busyness. She'd always thrived on filling her days with activity, to the point of barely having a free moment to herself. Better to be busy than to open herself to ridicule or, even worse, another heartbreak.

At some point in the past year since her broken engagement to William Cutter Sloan III, Keely had convinced herself that activity helped heal her pain, making her feel vital, needed, wanted even. In reality, she'd been sleepwalking through life, burying her pain and humiliation in work, work and more work.

Well, she was wide-awake now, thanks to the seven-year-old little girl she'd taken into her home.

A sense of purpose swelled as Keely mounted the stairs. She was determined to raise the child to the best of her ability. The days ahead would require faith, hope and love.

It all started with love, as her pastor often said. Keely now understood exactly what he meant.

She paused outside Felicity's bedroom and drew in several tight breaths. Ethan claimed the little girl's stomachache wasn't serious. Keely hoped his diagnosis proved accurate.

She'd never forgive herself if something happened to her cousin's daughter. Keely had promised Juliette she'd take care of Felicity until she was once again free to do so herself.

Who knew when that would be? Six years, nine, the full twelve? It was up to the Colorado Department of Corrections and contingent on Juliette's good behavior.

For a brief second, Keely stood rooted to the spot by a deep, painful ache in her chest. Her cousin had made a terrible mistake. She deserved forgiveness. Yet Keely couldn't help wondering why Juliette hadn't come to her for help, or gone to any of their other family members. Including Keely's twin brother, Beau, who was dripping in money from his days as a world-class professional skier.

By letting pride rule her actions, her cousin had not

only lost her freedom. She'd lost the chance to raise her daughter. As a result, Keely would be responsible for Felicity during the child's most formative years.

Lord, help me to be a good influence. Give me the wisdom to guide Felicity from child to young adult.

Releasing a sigh, Keely took one last deep breath and entered the bedroom.

Felicity lay resting on her side, eyes shut, her hands clasped together beneath her chin. She looked so sweet, so innocent. Keely had to swallow several times to release the lump lodged in her throat.

Nothing had prepared her for this melting of her heart, this wondrous, piercing mix of fear, resolve and deep devotion for a child she'd only met three times before Saturday. She hadn't expected to care this much, this fast. Maybe she was capable of loving again after all. For the past year, she'd wondered.

As if Felicity sensed her presence, her eyes slowly blinked open.

"Hey, kiddo." Pasting on a smile, Keely moved deeper in the room. "How are you feeling?"

"Better, I guess." The words came out raspy. "I'm thirsty."

"I bet you are." Keely sat on the edge of the bed and retrieved the cup of water she'd brought to her little cousin earlier. With her free hand she helped the girl sit up and take a few sips.

When she'd had enough, Felicity collapsed back on the bed with a sigh.

Letting out her own whoosh of air, Keely set the cup aside and brushed back a tangle of blond hair from the pretty face that was a tiny copy of her mother's. "Here's hoping by tomorrow you'll be good as new."

"I don't think I'll be better by morning." Felicity stared at Keely in open terror. "I mean, you know, not completely. Not good enough to go to school."

Keely bit her lower lip. Ethan had been right. Felicity's stomachache had been brought on by stress or, more specifically, by worry over starting another school, her third in the same number of months.

Poor kid. She'd experienced a lot of upheaval since her mother was caught embezzling money from her employer. Sent to live with her grandmother during the trial, then with Keely once the verdict was carried out and the paperwork for legal guardianship was complete, Felicity had undergone too much inconsistency in her young life. A little coddling was in order.

"I've been thinking about that." Keely cleared her suddenly thick throat. "It's late and you haven't had much sleep. Let's push your start date back a few days."

"You really mean it? I don't have to go to school tomorrow?"

"No school tomorrow."

Felicity's entire face lit up, her O'Toole heritage already evident in her pretty, petite features. According to family lore, their ancestors had been world-famous Shakespearean actors known for their extraordinary beauty and charm as much as their talent.

Keely hadn't caught the acting bug, but she'd traded on her looks for about a second and a half when she first arrived in New York City right out of high school. It had taken all of three weeks to realize her talents were better suited for the business office of the modeling agency, rather than the runway.

She'd really loved her job as a booking agent but was happy to be home after a ten-year absence. She had her brother here in Village Green. Her lifelong best friend Olivia Scott, now Olivia Mitchell, also lived in town, and Keely had a little girl right here in her home, depending on her.

"Keely?"

"Hmm?"

A moment of silence passed, and then came a very small, very sad sigh. "Do you think my mom misses me?"

Even knowing this conversation was coming, Keely still felt a pang of dread. What if her words instilled fear rather than calm? "Of course she misses you."

"Do you think she's lonely without me?"

"Your mother loves you," Keely said truthfully, if somewhat evasively. "We'll visit her next month. In the meantime you can write to her."

Although Juliette would eventually be able to see her daughter weekly, she wasn't allowed visitations during the first month of her incarceration.

The holiday season was going to be difficult for Felicity. Since her father had signed over custody before her birth, Juliette was the only parent the child had ever known. Keely was determined to give her sweet cousin the best Christmas of her life. It wouldn't take away Felicity's pain or sense of loss, but it would certainly offer her a lovely distraction.

"I know having your mom gone is really hard, but I'm here for you now, and always."

Choking out a sob, Felicity flung herself into Keely's arms.

With a fierceness that grabbed her by the throat, she pulled the child close and once again silently promised to make this Christmas season one the girl would remember for years to come. "Oh, sweetie, I'm going to take really good care of you, I promise."

Felicity clung for several, long seconds. Keely gently rocked the child back and forth. Once she felt Felicity relax, she eased her back onto the bed. It was hard not to look at her without seeing Juliette. Mother and daughter had the same cornflower-blue eyes, attractive dimples and exotic tilt to their features.

"Will you read to me before I go to sleep?"

"I would love that." Keely sorted through the stack of books she'd placed on the bedside table this afternoon.

"Do we want one of the American Girls, or should I read from—" she picked up the book at the bottom of the pile "—*My Friend Flicka*?"

Keely couldn't help smiling as one of the mysteries from earlier in the evening was now solved. *You can call me Flicka*, Felicity had told Ethan.

Her dimples flashing prettily, the child pointed to the book in Keely's hand. "That one, please."

"*My Friend Flicka* it is." Still smiling, Keely opened the book and began reading about a boy and his horse. Her mind was only partly on the words, mostly on Felicity.

She was a sweet child with an inherently kind nature. Not too many years in the future, she would steal young boys' hearts without even trying. Keely only hoped Felicity's life took a happier route than Juliette's.

Now that she was Felicity's legal guardian, Keely would ensure that her little cousin made wise choices. Keely would start the process by loving her, and creating a stable home and, of course, raising her in the church. *Train up a child in the way he should go: and when he is old, he will not depart from it.*

With the verse from Proverbs convicting her, she turned the page and continued reading. By the time she made it to the end of the first chapter, Felicity was sound asleep.

Keely spent the rest of the night on the phone clearing her calendar and ensuring that her managers were okay running the restaurant a few more days without her. Then she texted her brother and asked him to check in periodically during the afternoon and evening shifts. With his ski shop, the Slippery Slope, next door to the restaurant, it shouldn't be a problem.

The next morning, Keely woke feeling better about her role as a surrogate mother to her cousin's daughter. Maybe, just maybe, she'd get it right with Felicity.

Please, Lord, let it be so.

Just after sunrise, the child herself came into the kitchen when Keely was sipping her first cup of coffee for the day.

"Hey there." She set her steaming mug on the counter. "I was just about to run upstairs and check on you."

Rubbing at her eyes, Felicity smiled around a jaw-cracking yawn. "I'm hungry."

Which answered Keely's next question. Obviously, the child was feeling better this morning. "How do pancakes sound?"

"Yummy."

While Keely mixed up the batter, she and Felicity discussed their favorite foods, which led to the popular chocolate-versus-vanilla debate. Chocolate won, of course.

She made a mental note to stop by her best friend's brand-new chocolate shop with Felicity in tow. If they went in one afternoon this week, perhaps her cousin could meet Olivia's twin daughters, Megan and Molly, who were Felicity's same age and attended Village Green Elementary. It was an excellent way to help the child make new friends in a safe, comfortable environment.

By the time Keely set a full plate in front of her, she knew she'd made the right decision to keep Felicity home for the day.

She was just about to dig into her own stack of pancakes when a knock sounded on the back door.

Thinking she knew exactly who was standing outside her house, Keely chewed on her bottom lip. She wasn't sure she was ready to face Ethan again, not before she'd consumed at least two more cups of coffee. The animosity between them she could handle. It was familiar, comfortable, but this sudden getting along, even if only for a child's sake? Well, that confused and intimidated her.

Another knock came, louder and more insistent.

"Aren't you going to see who it is?"

The question spurred Keely into action. "Be right back."

She felt a catch in her throat when she opened the door to a very different man than the one she'd interacted with last night. He'd ditched the casual T-shirt, jeans and—sadly—the scruff. He now wore a pair of dark blue dress pants and a crisp white button-down. He was also rocking a beat-up leather jacket and aviator sunglasses.

Keely sucked in a breath, wondering why her pulse sped up whenever the man came within five feet of her.

Not much got to her. In truth, very little got to her.

But a clean-shaven Ethan Scott decked out in professional attire and really cool shades?

Oh yeah, that got to her.

Ethan removed his sunglasses, only to realize his mistake the moment his unhindered gaze connected with Keely's. He should have called instead of coming over to check on Flicka in person. Too late to change his mind now. He was tethered to the spot by a pair of sea-green eyes.

Why had he never noticed how long and full Keely's lashes were? How had he missed the flawlessness of her complexion?

He tried to look away. He really tried. But then the doctor in him took over and he noted the tiny lines of stress around her mouth, the purple smudges beneath her eyes.

She'd had a rough night.

"Is Flicka still experiencing stomach pains?"

"No, she's fine. She's—"

"Dr. Ethan, Dr. Ethan, you're here!"

Charmed by the enthusiastic greeting, he peered around Keely and smiled at the girl. She was smaller than he'd calculated, skinnier, too, but utterly adorable as she frantically waved a hand over her head.

"Hey, Flicka."

He'd barely shifted around Keely when the little girl launched herself at him. He caught her and held her close for one beat, two, then slowly set her back on her feet and studied her more closely. "Looks like someone's feeling better."

"I am." She bounced from one foot to the other. "My tummy doesn't hurt at all, not even a little bit. Are you here for breakfast? Keely made pancakes and they're really, really good."

As he sorted through the rapid-fire speech, Ethan's mind hooked on one word. Pancakes. His favorite. He shot a questioning glance in Keely's direction. "Is there enough for me?"

"Sure, why not?" Face as grim as her tone, she headed toward the kitchen without another word.

Hardly a warm invitation. But there was one thing Ethan had learned since Keely moved back to town and took over her family's restaurant: She'd inherited her mother's gift in the kitchen. He'd take whatever she was serving, with whatever prickly attitude she adopted. Her cooking was *that* good.

Flicka took his hand and dragged him deeper into the house. "I didn't think I was ever going to see you again, ever, at least not for a few more days."

He chuckled. "I'm your neighbor. Our paths will cross often, maybe every day."

Keely made a soft sound of protest in her throat, barely audible, but Ethan caught it. "Got a problem with that?"

Her pause told its own story. But then she lifted a careless shoulder that didn't ring true with her tight expression.

"Not at all." She blessed him with a sugary sweet smile. "I enjoy your company, Dr. Scott."

They both knew that wasn't true, but Ethan decided to be an optimist this morning. Maybe he and Keely really could set aside their differences and become friends. Neighbors were supposed to be friendly, weren't they? Wasn't that the same as being friends?

Flicka carried the conversation while Ethan dug

into a large stack of fluffy pancakes. He hadn't shared breakfast with a single mother and her daughter in nearly two years.

Technically, he wasn't doing so now. Flicka wasn't Keely's child. Still, he had to focus on his food, and the girl's excited chatter, rather than the unease he felt. The cozy setting felt too familiar, a taste of the life he'd had and then lost so abruptly. Out of sheer survival, he shut his mind to everything but the plate of food in front of him.

Holding painful memories at bay was hard work. By the time he finished his pancakes he was exhausted. He needed to vacate the premises stat. Unfortunately, he'd only dealt with one of the reasons he'd made the short journey across their adjacent yards. He said goodbye to Flicka, included a promise to stop by soon, then asked Keely to walk him out.

At her challenging stare, he tried not to show his impatience. He wasn't in the mood for one of their legendary arguments this morning. "I have something I need to run by you."

"All right, fine."

Once they were alone on the back stoop, he allowed himself a good long look at his neighbor. What he saw put him immediately on edge. She was especially beautiful in the morning light, her hair several warm shades of red, gold and copper.

She'd tamed the long strands in a sleek ponytail. The simple style highlighted her stunning features. Even with her face free of cosmetics, Ethan could easily picture her on the cover of a fashion magazine.

"What did you want to speak with me about?"

A muscle knotted in his chest at her wary tone. The progress they'd made last night was gone.

"First off," he began as calmly as possible, "I didn't come over to mooch breakfast, although I certainly enjoyed every bite. So, thanks."

"Oh, uh…you're welcome."

Her faltering voice told him he'd caught her off guard, as if she didn't expect a compliment from him, which made Ethan wonder why he didn't do it more often. There were many things he liked about Keely. Her smile, her eyes, her quick wit, her smile, her…

What had he come over for again?

Thankfully, Keely filled the conversational void. "You were right, by the way."

He felt his eyebrows travel toward his hairline. "Although I never tire of hearing that, especially from you, it's so rare. But I'm one step behind. What was I right about?"

She made a face. "Felicity's stomachache. It was definitely brought on by stress. Her recovery started almost immediately after I told her she didn't have to start school today."

The comment brought him to the other reason for his visit.

"I'd like you to bring her into the office for a complete exam." Last night had been an emergency, but Ethan didn't normally treat patients unless he knew their history. "I assume you have access to her medical records."

She nodded. "The school required them for enrollment."

"Bring them with you to her appointment."

"Okay. Ethan, I…" She hesitated, clearly debating whether to argue the point.

He cut her off before she could begin. They were in his wheelhouse now. "Keely, the child needs a primary care physician."

"You're right, of course." She gave him a firm nod. "I'll call the office later today and make an appointment."

"Good." They were on the same page.

"But I think it would be best if I made it with one of the other doctors in your practice."

"Why not me?"

"I… It's hard to explain."

"Try."

She dropped her gaze and sighed again, softer this time. "I guess it's because we're neighbors. It could get awkward."

Nearly everything about their relationship was awkward. But this wasn't about them. Or was it?

"Is it because of what happened at the Young Professionals mixer last year?"

"Of course not."

The response came too quickly. He lifted a single eyebrow.

"All right, yes," she admitted. "It's *partly* the reason."

Something inside him went ice-cold. "You're still holding that against me?"

Her gaze snapped with familiar annoyance. "You embarrassed me in front of Parker Thorpe and two of his associates."

Of course he'd stepped in. For good reason. "The guy was married."

"And that matters why?"

"Married," he reiterated.

"Parker and I were just talking." She huffed out the words in obvious frustration.

Ethan resisted the urge to hiss out his own frustration. He and Keely had done this dance too many times to count in the past year.

Yet, no matter how he explained his side of the argument, the woman refused to believe he'd actually been looking out for her. At the time of the mixer, she'd been new to town and had no idea what kind of guy Parker really was beneath the dentist-enhanced smile and hundred-dollar haircut.

"Look, I'm not saying the conversation wasn't innocent, at least on your end." He held her stare. "But it wasn't on his."

"You can't possibly know that for certain."

"Parker Thorpe is, was and always will be a player."

"As I recall, you said the same thing about Kenny Noble."

Ethan frowned at the reminder. "Kenny was eighteen. And you were twelve."

"I was thirteen. And, besides, I was just talking to him."

"You were still too young to be hanging out with a senior in high school. You were only twelve."

"Thirteen," she corrected again, this time with an exaggerated eye roll. "There was no need to tell him how old I was—"

"I beg to differ."

"—in front of half your stupid football team."

Okay, she had a point there. Ethan ran a hand over his jaw and went on the defense. "I was trying to protect you, not just from Kenny but from all the guys."

"That's your argument? You were protecting me? By humiliating me in front of your friends?"

That hadn't been his intention. Several of the guys had made derogatory remarks about her curvy figure. Ethan still felt a simmering rage whenever he remembered some of the names they'd called her.

He started to explain himself, again, but she cut him off. "I have to get back inside. Felicity will be wondering where I am."

She turned to go.

"Keely, wait."

She spun back around. "What now?"

"Don't forget to call and set up Flicka's appointment. Make it with me or Connor, it doesn't matter, as long as you—"

He was talking to her back.

"I mean it," he called after her, raising his voice over the wind. "The kid should see a doctor for a complete exam."

She stopped, sighed, slowly nodded. "I'll take care of it today."

Despite her reasonable tone, Ethan sensed she was still upset. And that bothered him. A lot. Keely wasn't a woman who held on to petty grudges. If she was still this twisted up about the past, then he'd clearly hurt her and would have to make it up to her.

If only he knew how.

Chapter Three

The rest of Ethan's morning went about as smoothly as his conversation with Keely. Before he saw his first patient, he had a stack of lab reports to review and phone messages to return, nearly all of which required his immediate attention.

He prioritized. Then took action, tackling the refills from pharmacies first, the more involved problems next. Halfway through dictating a letter on a patient he was referring to a specialist, his computer screen went blank. "Not again."

He pounded at a few keys, only to lose most of the work he'd completed in the past hour. Good times.

Mouth grim, he tried to focus, but an image of breakfast with his neighbors flashed in his mind. He hadn't realized how much he missed being part of a small, happy family.

Logically, he knew he'd been living in limbo too long, running in place, moving neither forward nor backward. He wasn't ready for another relationship; perhaps he never would be, but it was time to stop spinning his wheels. Time he got connected in the community and did his part for the town.

Decision made, he opened his email program and fired off a message to a former classmate and the newly elected mayor of Village Green. If there was a volunteer opportunity in need of Ethan's particular skills, Hardy Bennett would hook him up.

Ethan sat back. Why didn't he feel better? Why couldn't he shake the notion that the need for his skills was much closer to home, literally next door? He'd seen something in Flicka's eyes, a sense of loss he recognized on a soul-deep level.

Clearly, the story behind the little girl's arrival in Village Green was an unpleasant tale. Because he knew how it felt to have the future yanked away without warning, the unsettling sensation in his gut dug deeper.

His nurse stuck her head in the office. The Santa hat sitting at a jaunty angle on her head, along with the jingle-bell earrings she wore, was a visible reminder that the Christmas season had officially begun. "Your first patient is here, Dr. Scott."

He glanced at his watch, frowned. Tasha Dupree was ruthless when it came to keeping Ethan and his partners on schedule—one of the many reasons he valued her—but she was way ahead of herself this morning.

"My first patient isn't due until nine." He raised a hand to keep her from interrupting. "I marked off the extra time this morning to answer phone calls and update patient charts."

"It's a walk-in. And before you tell me to hunt down one of our other doctors, the patient specifically requested you."

Ethan made his way around his desk. Tasha gave him

a big, toothy grin. He eyed the nurse more closely. She definitely had an amused look in her dark brown eyes that were the same color as her hair.

Somewhere in her late twenties, Tasha was known for her quirky sense of humor. He had a bad feeling about this walk-in appointment.

"You gonna tell me the name of the patient?"

"I'd rather let you find out for yourself." She handed him the tablet she'd brought with her.

Ethan gave the screen a cursory glance, and groaned when he noted the name of his early-morning walk-in. Lacy Hargrove.

No denying the young divorcee was beautiful. She was also on the prowl for husband number three. Word around town was that she planned to bag herself a doctor this time around. Ethan was currently at the top of her list now that his medical partner Connor Mitchell was newly married to Ethan's sister, Olivia.

Tasha gave him a sympathetic pat on the arm. "Want me to join you in the exam room?"

"Does a chicken have wings?"

The question earned him a dry laugh. "Of all the birds you could have referenced, I find it interesting you chose a chicken."

Ignoring the wisecrack, Ethan scanned Lacy's complaint. When his eyes landed on a familiar word—*stomachache*—his mind went to last night's patient.

Ethan liked Flicka. But she reminded him of the little girl he'd thought would become his stepdaughter. Samantha had been just as sweet, just as charming. With his mind poised between past and present, he experienced a moment of utter grief before tucking away the emotion and focusing on work.

Blinking the screen back into focus, he finished reviewing the notes on Lacy's ailment. Mouth pressed in a flat line, he handed the tablet back to Tasha and spoke in an even tone. "Where did you put the patient?"

"Exam room 3."

"Let's go."

"Right behind you." Adopting his same professional manner, Tasha followed him down the hallway in relative silence, if he didn't count the tinkling jingle bells.

After determining that Lacy's stomachache was simply indigestion, Ethan gave her the name of a good antacid, bolted from the room and continued seeing patients throughout the day.

By half past six, he was back at his desk, staring at his computer without really seeing the screen. He'd been feeling off since last night's unplanned house call. The encounter with Keely had opened old wounds. This morning's homey breakfast had only made the pain that much more real.

As he leaned back in his chair, Ethan's gaze landed on a photograph from his army days. He was in full battle gear, his arm slung over Tracy's shoulders. He'd been sent to Afghanistan to treat high-value patients. Tracy, an experienced helicopter pilot, had been assigned to fly the injured soldiers in from the battlefield.

It was love at first sight for them both. Following regulation, they'd held off dating until they were back in the United States. Tracy had been a single mother. Her daughter, Samantha, had stolen Ethan's heart nearly as quickly as her mother had.

He'd proposed to Tracy six months after their first official date. She'd died three weeks later in a freak accident eerily similar to the crash that had taken his parents.

Samantha's biological father had shown up at the funeral and taken her away immediately following the service. Ethan's heart had been ripped out not once, but twice.

The loss of so many loved ones had left its mark. Life was fragile and could be gone in a blink. Too much pain came with loving and then losing. He would not willingly fall in love again, wouldn't—couldn't—go through another funeral.

Yeah, okay, he knew it was irrational. He loved his siblings, didn't he? He could lose them, just as he had lost all the others. But why cloud the issue with logic, when he was perfectly happy living in the great state of denial?

Ethan didn't blame God for his many losses. That would give the cold, distant deity too much power.

Needing to get away from his maudlin thoughts, he abruptly rose and left the office building. Once he was sitting in his SUV, the engine idling, he checked the time on the dashboard. Ryder would have left already for his shift at the hospital.

Ethan wasn't especially looking forward to going home to an empty house. At least Baloo would be there waiting for him. Man's best friend.

Fifteen minutes after pulling out of the office parking lot, Ethan swung his car onto his street. His neighbors had begun decorating their houses. Lights blinked from roofs. Man-made snowmen, plastic reindeer and Santa sleighs adorned the snow-coated lawns. He'd been dropped in the middle of Christmas Town, USA.

Instead of soothing his dark mood, the decorations

reminded him of the family he'd lost, the plans he'd had for the future.

Once he was safely inside his garage, he told himself for the third time—or was it the fourth?—that he was perfectly fine with Baloo's company for the evening. He actually preferred to be home alone with his dog most nights. He couldn't experience any more grief if he didn't let any more people into his heart. He had his siblings. They were enough.

He could practically hear his mother sighing in disappointment, and Tracy telling him that was no way to live. Yeah, well, they'd both left him. Not by choice, but he felt the hole in his heart, and his life, anyway.

Baloo greeted him with a series of exuberant barks.

Ethan scratched the animal behind the ears. "Bet you're ready to go outside."

Rising to his full height, Ethan glanced briefly out the window and noticed Keely's house ablaze in light.

His throat cinched up tight. Since when did his neighbor turn on all her lights? Maybe Flicka was sick again. Or was she afraid of the dark? The thought tugged at the part of him that had nearly become a father.

There was something about the kid, something in her eyes, a lost look that reflected his own pain. He'd sleep easier knowing she was all right.

And while he was checking on the child, he'd point out to Keely—with extreme patience, of course—that she'd forgotten to make the appointment for Flicka's wellness visit. It was the responsible thing to do.

Ethan was nothing if not responsible.

Because Keely was standing at her kitchen sink, looking out the window while she washed vegetables, she noticed the exact moment Ethan exited his house with a rambunctious Baloo.

Against her better judgment, she allowed herself to observe man and dog. Halfway between their yards, Baloo bounded into a snowdrift, then popped up with a ball in his mouth and white flakes clinging to his black fur. Keely could hear Ethan's uninhibited laughter as he brushed off his snow-covered dog.

She never saw this side of him. She couldn't help wondering why. She sensed something tragic had happened to him before he returned to Village Green. There were times when they weren't sniping at each other that she saw the grief in his eyes. Thanks to Cutter, she knew that look of loss well.

Though Keely didn't know any details, she sensed Ethan's heart had been shattered by the loss of a woman.

Had it been a death or a bad breakup?

Either scenario indicated a man unwilling to let go of something, possibly someone, from his past. A good reminder, she told herself, that Ethan wasn't the man for her.

That didn't mean Keely couldn't enjoy watching him now. Riveted by the sight of all that masculine energy unleashed in a game of fetch, she continued to stare.

As if sensing her eyes on him, Ethan paused in the middle of his windup. The smile he shot in her direction reached deep inside her heart and squeezed.

Gasping softly, she moved away from the window and that heart-tugging grin. No doubt about it, she was in serious trouble.

What was it about the man? He was good-looking, and sure, she liked good-looking men. What woman didn't? He was also single, financially stable and a successful doctor.

But she also knew he could be arrogant, bossy and treat a woman—Keely—like a twelve-year-old girl instead of the adult she'd become. Added to her suspicions as to why he didn't date, she knew to keep up her guard.

Minutes later, even prepared for the resounding knock, Keely still had to lock her knees and gulp for air.

Felicity rushed into the kitchen. "I heard a knock at the back door. Do you think it's Dr. Ethan?"

The kid had excellent hearing. Keely filed away that piece of information with everything else she'd discovered about the little girl today. Turned out, Felicity enjoyed dance classes and ice-skating as much as Keely had at her age.

She also disliked playing soccer, tennis and other organized sports. Again, just like Keely.

There was still so much to discover about her cousin. At least she'd made considerable headway today. Unfortunately, whenever the subject of school came up, or Keely broached the possibility of meeting new friends, Felicity's face turned gray and the complaints of not feeling well began.

Keely was concerned there might be a larger problem brewing than the child's simple reluctance to attend a new school and meet other girls her age. *Please, Lord, let this be a normal part of the transition into my home and not a symptom of something bigger.*

A second knock sounded. Felicity gave Keely a look of impatience. "Can I see if it's Dr. Ethan at the door?"

"Go ahead."

The door squeaked on its hinges mere seconds before Ethan's low chuckle rumbled in response to the child's excited hello. Clearly, Felicity wasn't shy around their handsome neighbor. The thought gave Keely hope for the girl's future.

"I brought my dog over to meet you," she heard Ethan say to Felicity. "His name is Baloo."

A series of happy barks mingled with delighted little-girl squeals. "He's so pretty."

"Don't let him hear you say that." Ethan spoke the words in an amused stage whisper. "Baloo's sensitive about his gender."

"Oh, sorry. *He's* so *handsome*," Felicity cooed. "You're a handsome boy, aren't you?"

It wasn't long before the child invited their visitors to come inside the house.

Baloo bounded into the kitchen first, tail wagging fast as a whip. Keely smiled at the handsome black Lab. "Hey, big boy."

All but quivering with excitement, the dog leaped at her. Ethan caught hold of his collar just in time.

"Sit," he ordered.

Baloo whined pitifully but immediately obeyed, then politely offered a paw to Keely.

Charmed, she obliged the dog by giving him a hearty handshake.

"That's so cool," Felicity announced, moving in for a better look. "Can I try?"

"Go for it." Keely stepped aside so the little girl could take her place in front of Baloo.

With the same patience he'd displayed the previous evening, Ethan showed Felicity a series of tricks that Baloo could do. Sit. Shake. Lie down. "Now you try."

"Okay."

Only after Felicity took over issuing the commands

did Ethan shift his attention to Keely. *Oh boy*. She blamed the stutter in her pulse on those piercing blue eyes. When Ethan zeroed in on a woman, she knew it, all the way down to her toes.

He'd changed clothes since this morning. The five o'clock shadow provided a dangerous, appealing edge. He wore a different T-shirt, but the slogan was similar to last night's: Here I Am. What Are Your Other Two Wishes?

The man really was annoying. Snorting in exasperation, she lifted her head, found herself caught once again in his gaze. She really wished he'd quit staring at her with…*those eyes*.

"Hey," he said with a knowing smirk.

Unable to speak, she hummed out a quick response.

His smile turned into a muffled chuckle. The slightly condescending sound increased her unease. Then came the familiar frustration. Antagonism was one step away. But giving in to the emotion would be childish.

"I, uh…" Keely grabbed the remaining scraps of her dignity. "I wasn't expecting you to stop over again tonight."

"Came to check on my patient." He broke eye contact—finally—and focused on Felicity.

The little girl was running Baloo through his repertoire of tricks a second time around.

"How you feeling this evening, Flicka?"

"Huh?" Hand wrapped around Baloo's outstretched paw, the little girl looked up. "Oh… I'm good. I didn't have to go to school, so Keely and I spent all day baking cookies and making care packages for the Youth Center's Christmas party."

"Sounds like fun."

"It was super fun. In a few days I have to meet Keely's best friend, Olivia, and her daughters, Megan and Molly." The child's eyebrows pulled together in a worried frown. "They're my age and Keely says they can't wait to meet me."

"If Keely said that, then it's true."

"I guess so." She heaved a sigh, the little-girl worry evident in the sound. "Hey, can I take Baloo into the other room and see if he'll play tug-of-war with a sock?"

Though innocently asked, the question brought a complete change over Ethan. His smile dropped, his shoulders tensed, his gaze went distant. It was as if he'd been transported to another place, at least in his mind, somewhere not altogether pleasant.

He cleared his throat, twice. "It's one of his favorite games, especially with little girls on the other end of the sock."

As the two hurried off, an awkward silence fell over the kitchen. Keely couldn't understand why Ethan's entire demeanor had changed simply because Felicity wanted to play tug-of-war with Baloo. She remembered a similar change in him last night.

In the days leading up to their broken engagement, Cutter had looked much like Ethan now. The memory made her doubly wary of the man standing in her house.

Nevertheless, she couldn't stop herself from worrying about Ethan. *He needs me.* The thought surprised her. Ethan Scott was the most capable man she knew. And the most annoying.

And yet…

She placed her fingertips on his arm. "Are you all right?"

Shrugging away from her touch, he blinked slowly,

squared his shoulders and drew in a long breath. Once again he was Mr. Cool, Calm and Casual.

"Something smells good."

Now that they were back to polite small talk, a surge of complicated emotions spread through her. The sense of relief was easy enough to understand. The agitation, not nearly so much.

"I made chicken à l'Orange and baked sweet potatoes. And a healthy salad." *Don't ask him to stay for dinner. Do. Not. Ask.* "You're welcome to eat with Felicity and me. There's plenty."

He looked about to turn down her offer. But suddenly, inexplicably, Keely very much wanted him to stay.

"Consider it payment for not teasing me over how I overreacted last night."

"You didn't overreact."

She frowned. "I thought Felicity had appendicitis."

"Given her symptoms, it was a logical concern."

For the second time in so many days, Keely stared at Ethan as if he were a stranger. In many ways, he was. She felt as if they were meeting for the first time. She decided to pretend the change in their relationship didn't matter. But it did.

And that scared her far more than she was willing to admit. The man had too many secrets, none of which he seemed willing to share with her. *Been there, done that, have the remnants of a broken heart to prove it.*

"While we're on the subject of Flicka." He pointed a finger at Keely. "I noticed you didn't make the appointment yet."

She blinked at him in shock. Ethan was arrogant, and the big, bad, frustrating bane of her existence, but he wasn't a micromanager. His office staff handled scheduling. "How can you possibly know whether or not I made an appointment for her?"

"I checked."

Of course he did.

"It's important, Keely. Flicka needs a primary care physician. Make the appointment."

"Felicity really took to Baloo tonight. What do you think? Should I get her a dog for Christmas? Would it help ease the transition for her?"

"Changing the subject, are we?"

"You better believe it."

He laughed. Despite her irritation at his bossy manner, the deep rumble made her smile in return.

Knowing he was right, again, Keely stopped resisting. "I'll make the appointment tomorrow."

"I'm going to hold you to it."

As if she didn't know that. "You never answered my question. Are you staying for dinner?"

His hesitation returned. But this time it lasted only a few heartbeats. "Yeah, I guess I am."

He looked mildly surprised by his acceptance.

That made two of them.

Felicity's laughter rang out. Keely's throat constricted at the happy sound, so different from the groans of pain last night. In that moment, Keely knew she was in over her head. How was she supposed to parent a child she barely knew?

All the fears she'd held at bay since she'd begun taking over legal guardianship shot to the surface. A gasp of utter panic leaked out of her.

Misinterpreting the sound, Ethan's gaze narrowed

over her face. "I don't have to stay for dinner. You can take back the invitation and I won't hold it against you."

"It's not that."

Concern etched across her face. "Then what?"

"I… Oh, Ethan, I want to take good care of Felicity, but what do I know about kids? I spent the last decade working in a world of fashion models."

"Keely, listen to me." The epitome of calm confidence, Ethan took hold of her shoulders and gently turned her to face him. "You're doing a great job so far."

Instead of calming her fears, his unexpected words of praise had the opposite effect. "What if I fail her?"

Hands still on her shoulders, he tweaked her nose in a big brother sort of way. "You're exhausted from last night. Once you get some sleep, everything will look better in the morning."

"You're probably right."

"Of course I'm right. I'm always right."

The arrogant comment did what no kind words could have done. She bristled. Prepared for a fight, she snapped her gaze to his, felt her anger melt at his compassionate smile.

That look had her abandoning her pride and admitting, "I'm really scared."

"It's okay to feel scared. It means you care."

Two nights in a row the man had shown her unspeakable kindness. Defeat settled on her shoulders. Because if history had taught Keely anything, it had taught her that a truce between her and Ethan never lasted.

Chapter Four

Now that the emotion of the moment was over, Keely told herself to step back, take a breath, and put some distance between her and Ethan. Things were changing between them, their relationship morphing into something different.

Step. Back.

Instead of heeding the internal warning, she held her ground, drawing strength from the man's solid presence.

She should probably feel embarrassed for admitting her fears to him, knowing he could use them against her one day. Though he'd never been that small and petty. Argumentative, yes, but never unkind. And so she stayed rooted in the moment.

It felt good, she silently admitted, allowing Ethan's confidence in her abilities to chase away her worry. A sob of gratitude slipped past her lips.

He tugged her into a friendly hug. "That's it. Let it out, sweetheart."

Sweetheart. The endearment spread warmth through her chilled limbs.

"Flicka seems to adore you. That's half the battle in these types of situations."

Drawing on his assurance, Keely stepped out of his embrace. To her horror, a rogue tear escaped. Tenderly, almost affectionately, he wiped her wet cheek with the pad of his thumb.

She could hardly stand his casual show of kindness. Any moment she was going to break down in sobs.

Taking another step back, she searched for another topic. *Think, Keely, think.* "I'm determined to make this Christmas special for Felicity. I plan to pull out all the stops, whatever it takes to make her feel comfortable in her new home."

"Tell me what I can do to help."

His immediate offer of assistance didn't mesh with the Ethan Scott she knew, the man who'd turned avoiding her into an art form. So much had changed in two short days.

As she stared into Ethan's blue eyes, she saw the secrets he kept inside him, remembered the way he kept everyone but his closest family and friends at arm's length.

A timely reminder. Never again would she weave dreams around a man who couldn't be completely open with her. And now that Felicity was in her life, she had to think of her, as well.

Bottom line, falling for Ethan Scott was far too risky. Even a friendship between them carried complexities she didn't want to explore.

And yet she found herself asking, "You truly want to help me give Felicity a memorable Christmas?"

"Isn't that what I just said?" He sounded more than a little insulted.

And they were back to familiar territory, just as she'd feared their tenuous truce a thing of the past. "Somehow I can't see you trimming a tree, stringing popcorn or pinning up stockings to the mantel."

Instead of his rising to her provocation, a look of sorrow came and went in his eyes. It was the same expression she'd seen right before he stepped into Felicity's room last night. Had he lost someone he cared about, someone he'd done all those things with in the past?

"I was thinking of something more manly," he said, not quite smiling. "You know, like hanging your outdoor lights."

Her twin brother usually did that, but with the Slippery Slope's extended hours during the holidays, Beau's free time was limited. "That would be lovely, Ethan. Thank you for offering."

She'd text Beau the good news later tonight.

"No problem, happy to do it."

As they stared at each other, something quite wonderful passed between them. Keely opened her mouth to say something, but Ethan spoke first. "How does Sunday sound?"

She blinked, trying to picture him on a ladder, hanging Christmas lights. The image was entirely too homey for her peace of mind.

This had to stop, this thinking of Ethan Scott as anything other than a distant acquaintance. Thankfully, she remembered she'd invited him to dinner, which was only half done. "I'll finish up in here while you go see if Felicity and Baloo need anything."

Ethan's features softened into what might be considered affection, with a twinge of amusement around the edges. Somehow, after she'd spilled her guts only moments before, that look was far worse than a sneer.

And then he smiled. "Trying to get rid of me, O'Toole?"

No. *Yes.* "Maybe."

He laughed, a deep, masculine rumble in his chest.

Something actually fluttered in her stomach, and her knees threatened to give out. She frowned at her reaction.

"Right," he said, still laughing. "Off I go."

Keely grimaced after his retreating back, trying feverishly to isolate the exact moment when things had changed between her and Ethan. Long before Felicity had moved into her house.

Forcing her breathing to calm, she gathered all the ingredients for making a salad. She'd just retrieved her favorite wooden bowl when her cell phone rang.

A quick check of the screen had her wondering why the newly elected mayor of Village Green was calling her. She put the phone up to her ear. "This is Keely O'Toole."

"Keely. Hardy Bennett here. I'm glad I caught you."

Her frown deepened at the overly friendly note in his voice. The man was usually all business when they spoke, which was often, since she was the coordinator of Village Green's annual Christmas parade. "Hardy, what can I do for you?"

"It's what *I* can do for *you*." He laughed at his own joke. "During our previous conversation you hinted that your committee was short on staff."

"Well, yes, we could use at least one more member."

Two would be better, but with the parade only three weeks away, Keely didn't hold out much hope for finding volunteers at this late date. Hardy, proving why he'd won the mayoral election in a landslide, offered up a solution to her dilemma.

"I have an updated list of potential volunteers. I'm shooting an email with the names to you..." She heard the click of computer keys. "*Now.* Once you've reviewed the list, let me know who you'd like to fill the open position."

He spoke as if it was as simple as picking a name off the list and putting the person in place. "I'll take a look and get back to you in the morning."

"Good enough." Hardy ended the call.

Keely opened the email app on her smartphone and absently thumbed through the potential candidates for the hole in her committee. She'd barely begun when a familiar name popped out at her. She snorted. "Yeah, right."

She moved on. Backed up. Stopped. Considered. *Not him, Keely.*

No, she decided, definitely not him.

She scrolled to the end of the list. Then looked again, drawn once more to the third name from the top.

The sound of purposeful footsteps had her jumping in surprise. She bobbled the phone from one hand to the other, then lost her grip entirely.

With catlike reflexes, Ethan reached out and caught the phone before it hit the floor. He started to hand it over but then glanced at the screen and froze.

"What is my name doing in an email from—" he scrolled to the top of the page "—our illustrious mayor?"

"Apparently, Hardy is under the impression that you're interested in getting involved in the community."

"Well, yeah, I sent him an email just this morning asking him to plug me in somewhere." Confusion dug across his forehead. "But why is he forwarding my name, and these others, to you?"

"Because I happen to have the perfect volunteer opportunity for your particular skill set."

He shot her a wary glance. "What sort of opportunity?"

"Village Green's annual Christmas parade needs you."

Silence met her words.

"The committee is short at least two members."

More silence.

Keely searched his face, but the man was good at hiding his emotions when he wanted to be. At least he hadn't said no. *Yet.* She gave him her sweetest smile. "Don't you want to give back to your community? Wasn't that the point of your email to Hardy?"

"How much time are we talking about?"

"Just over three weeks."

"Uh-huh." His gaze neutral, he passed the phone back to her. "What would I be doing on this committee, precisely?"

"That would be up to the parade coordinator to decide."

"Who's the coordinator?"

She beamed at him. "Me."

His eyes widened. "So I'd be putting my life in your hands for the next three weeks?"

"A bit of an exaggeration but yes, in a manner of speaking that's precisely what you'd be doing."

He leveled her with a dark look, no doubt meant to intimidate her. The gesture had the opposite effect.

Keely would probably wonder over her nerve for years to come, but in that moment, she couldn't help herself. She moved in close, lifted herself onto her toes and pressed her lips to his ear. "Afraid?"

"Not even a little," he clipped out, sounding as though he was forcing the word past jagged glass.

She'd clearly hit a nerve, which had been her goal. Gloating would be in poor taste. So she stepped back and, deciding to soften her approach, explained that much of the work was already done. "We're just finalizing details at this point."

He appeared to consider her request. That was when Keely knew she had him.

This is crazy, she told herself. She needed to spend less time with Ethan, not more. It wasn't too late to let him off the hook, to let them both off the hook.

Instead she found herself nudging him along. "So, I can count on you?"

He nodded.

Giving him no time to change his mind, she shot out her hand. "Welcome aboard, Dr. Scott. Our first meeting is Wednesday night, seven o'clock sharp."

The following afternoon, Ethan took a break between patients and escaped into his office with the idea of reducing the never-ending stack of unanswered phone messages.

He'd barely read through the first one when his mind wandered back to a single moment from last night. In Keely's kitchen, when she'd asked him to stay for dinner. He hadn't planned on accepting. He still wasn't sure why he'd agreed to stick around.

One moment he was introducing Baloo to Flicka. The next, he'd been transported to another time, another home, another *life*. Every instinct had urged him to grab his dog and bolt, before the memories became unbearable.

And yet he'd accepted her invitation.

Things had gone downhill from there.

Now he was committed to working on the town's annual Christmas parade, in a position that would require him to take orders from Keely. Part of him couldn't imagine a worst-case scenario. Another part actually looked forward to watching the woman in action. Something about Keely intrigued him.

She ran her restaurant with efficiency and poise. Whenever a problem arose, she simply dug in and did what was needed. He was becoming more comfortable around her, thinking of her in familiar terms. Not quite friends, nothing so simple.

Then there was Flicka. She was a sweet kid, yet full of a silent, underlying despair that made him want to erase her pain.

A portion of the ice around his heart chipped away, leaving him feeling raw and vulnerable, missing the family that had been ripped away from him.

He spun his chair around and took in the view of his hometown. Village Green was all dressed up for the holidays, a virtual winter wonderland straight off the front of a Christmas card. Along shoveled walkways, storefronts were decorated with garland and twinkling lights.

The festive decorations did nothing to ease Ethan's gloominess. This would be his second Christmas without Tracy and Samantha. Still wallowing in grief from their sudden deaths, he'd found last Christmas lonely and depressing.

Admittedly, Ethan wasn't as sad this year. Yet he wasn't at peace, either. He couldn't shake the notion that he was at a crossroads in his life. The sensation had been growing over the past few months.

A rustling sound from the doorway had him spinning back around. His medical partner Connor hovered on the threshold of his office, his attention engrossed on the tablet in his hand.

"Got a minute to discuss a patient?"

Ethan checked the watch he'd worn in the military and continued to wear as a symbol of where he'd been and how the past had shaped the man he'd become. "Sure."

His next patient wasn't due for twenty minutes.

"I'll keep it brief." Connor stepped fully into the office, then shut the door behind him.

Ethan felt his jaw tighten. He recognized that look on the other man's face. He'd seen it often enough during their long-standing friendship to know whatever Connor had to say, Ethan wasn't going to like it.

He made his way around the desk. Stuffing his hands in his pockets, he leaned back on his heels and waited.

Connor dropped his gaze back to the tablet. Ethan studied his partner's bent head as he punched at the screen. They'd been friends longer than Ethan could remember. They'd played on the same sports teams and run in the same crowd.

But while Ethan had alternated between keeping his siblings out of trouble, working two jobs and earning his college degree before joining the military, Connor had taken the traditional route of college, medical school and marriage to his childhood sweetheart. Sheila's death had hit Connor hard, leaving him to raise his twin daughters on his own, until he'd found happiness a second time around with Ethan's sister, Olivia.

Throughout the years, even with time and distance between them, Connor and Ethan's friendship had remained strong.

When Connor became a widower, Ethan had been there for him. After Tracy's accident, Connor had given Ethan a reason to come home, by selling him half of his already thriving medical practice.

At last, the other doctor lifted his head. "I saw a new patient this afternoon. Felicity O'Toole."

Ethan's heart thumped extra hard as two simultaneous emotions moved through him. Relief that Keely had brought Flicka into the office. And insult that she'd made the appointment with Connor and not him.

With Connor being the father of twin daughters Flicka's age, it made sense Keely would want him to be the child's primary care physician. Nevertheless, if Ethan had any doubt as to whether the woman still held the past against him, he now knew she did.

He was suddenly regretting his agreement to work on the parade with her. If she wanted to, she could make his life difficult, or at least uncomfortable. Except Keely was never spiteful and he'd given his word.

Surely the next three weeks wouldn't be too terrible.

"Keely specifically requested that I let you know she'd followed through her with her promise." Connor shifted his stance, angled his head at a curious tilt. "Want to tell me what that means?"

Ethan gave his partner a brief explanation of Sunday night's events, then finished with "I insisted she bring the child to the office for a complete exam."

"All of which she told me. And yet she made the appointment with me instead of you?" Connor's eyes filled with bafflement. "Why do you think she did that?"

"No idea." Hearing his own heartbeat pounding in his ears, Ethan drew in a tight, audible breath. "Maybe you should have asked Keely."

"I did. She got all nervous and tongue-tied. What *is* it with you two? One would think…"

He fell silent.

"One would think *what*? Spit it out, Connor."

The other man waved away the question. "Not relevant to the conversation."

Since dropping the subject worked for Ethan, he refocused on the practice's newest patient. "Did you discover anything in Flicka's medical history I should know about, in case I have to make another house call?"

Connor's eyebrows pulled together. "Who's Flicka?"

A smile tugged at Ethan's lips. So the kid only wanted him to call her by the nickname. But the warmth that spread through him immediately turned to ice. Only heartache resulted when a guy got too close to a woman with a sweet kid. "I meant Felicity."

"She likes to be called Flicka?"

"Yeah, she does." At least by Ethan.

"I'll make a note of that." Connor typed in the change. "You can read her chart later, but basically the child is healthy and up to date on all her shots."

Good. That was good.

"She's also extremely fond of you. Throughout the exam, it was Dr. Ethan this and Dr. Ethan that, with a little Baloo thrown in to mix things up."

Ethan chuckled.

"Given everything she's been through," Connor continued, "I suggested Keely create an environment of consistency and—"

"Hold up." Ethan lifted a hand in the air to stop Connor. "What *situation* are you talking about?"

"Keely didn't tell you about the girl's mother?"

"She did not."

And Ethan hadn't asked. *Why* hadn't he asked? Because he hadn't wanted to get too close, or overly involved with the child and her pretty guardian.

No better way to keep things on the surface than by not asking too many personal questions.

"Felicity's mother is Keely's first cousin." Connor went thoughtful again, but only for a moment. "She's in prison serving a twelve-year sentence for embezzlement."

The words echoed in Ethan's head.

Prison. Embezzlement. Not what he'd expected. Even if Flicka's mother served a third of her sentence, and was released on good behavior, she would miss out on a lot of her daughter's life, possibly even the important preteen years.

No wonder Keely was concerned about her role in the child's life. Ethan's estimation of his neighbor went up five notches. Dangerous ground, since he was perfectly happy keeping the woman at a distance.

"It's been a hard year on the girl. Village Green Elementary will be her third school in as many months."

"That explains the stomachache Sunday night."

Connor nodded. "That would be my diagnosis."

They briefly discussed the rest of the child's medical history. Prior to Sunday night she'd had the usual childhood illnesses, nothing out of the ordinary.

Even though Ethan had access to Flicka's chart, he appreciated Connor giving him the information firsthand. "Thanks for the update."

Connor swung open the door. "No problem."

In the hallway, Ethan fell into step beside his partner. His head was still full of Keely and her little cousin. Now that he understood the situation more clearly, he felt a driving need to make things right between him and his neighbor.

Keely had a challenging road ahead. She would need a friend. Why not Ethan? He could think of a thousand reasons why not. Most of which kept him from making the trek across their backyards later that night.

Chapter Five

Ethan arrived at City Hall ten minutes early. He took a circuitous route to the conference room that led him past Hardy's office—empty, of course—and then to a soda machine that was currently out of his favorite flavor. He told himself he wasn't stalling. He was just killing time.

After a bit of meandering, he located another soda machine at the back of the building. He fed a dollar into the designated slot.

He wasn't stalling, he told himself, even as he popped open the can, and took a long, slow swig. He tossed the can in the recycle bin, then followed the sound of laughing female voices.

At the threshold of the conference room, he looked around and immediately zeroed in on Keely. She was dressed in casual jeans and a green sweater the same color as her amazing eyes. She was setting Flicka up at the end of a long conference table with paper, crayons, kid scissors and several other supplies.

He watched the two interact. They were certainly easy with each other, comfortable even, as if they were already finding their temporary roles as mother and daughter a good fit. The kid's transition wasn't without problems, and could possibly get worse before it got better, but Ethan had no doubt she would settle nicely into her new home. Keely was that determined.

Confirming his suspicion, she said something that made Flicka laugh, which had Keely leaning over and kissing the child's head. There was something unbearably sweet in the gesture and a sense of longing for all he'd lost echoed through him, pressing the air from his lungs.

Ethan tore his gaze away from the charming scene and glanced around the room again. He knew all the people in attendance by name, their various connections to each another and how long they'd lived in Village Green. That was the way of a small town, and why he loved living here, certainly one of the reasons why he'd come home after Tracy's funeral.

It took him a second to realize he was the only man on the committee. Hardy Bennett had some explaining to do. As did Ms. Keely O'Toole.

He moved deeper in the room and was immediately surrounded by seven—he counted—women. Two had been friends of his mother, two were local business owners and the last had sat beside him in high school chemistry.

Flicka came to his rescue, by waving at him and calling him over. With great relief, he said, "Excuse me, ladies, I'm being summoned."

Keely met him halfway across the room. She smiled, soft and sweet, and the expression made him smile in return.

"Ethan, I'm so glad you made it."

"I don't suppose it's too late to back out?" He'd meant it as a joke. But instead of her laughing, Keely's eyes turned serious, even a little desperate.

"Please, please, say you're kidding."

"Of course I'm kidding." He slapped a hand to his heart. "I'm wounded you have to ask."

"Don't tease me like that, okay? I really need your help."

He shouldn't enjoy hearing those words come out of her mouth. But he did, entirely too much.

This was when he usually bit back at her, when he met frustration with frustration, impatience with impatience. But he saw the concern in her eyes and gave her a break. "I made a commitment, Keely. You can count on me to follow through."

She gave a slight wince, so slight that if he hadn't been standing this close he would have missed it. But her expression was full of gratitude.

"Thank you," she whispered, touching his arm to punctuate her point.

He inclined his head. "You're welcome."

"Dr. Ethan, over here," Flicka called out to him.

"Hey." He drew alongside the kid. "What're you doing?"

The girl's eyes sparkled. "I'm making a Christmas card for my mom."

He inspected her handiwork. "Looks like you've got a great start."

"Want to help me?"

"Sure." He settled in beside her. "Better make it an easy task. I have to pay attention to the meeting, too."

"Oh, okay." She thought for a moment, moved around a few items, then pulled out a sheet of Christmas stickers. "You can put these around the border."

"You got it." As soon as he peeled off the first sticker, a sprig of holly and berries, Keely called the meeting to order.

Ethan wasn't surprised she attacked the agenda with the same competence she ran her restaurant. After introductions were made, apparently for Ethan's sake, they hashed out the rules for the parade floats.

Crepe paper, yes; toilet paper, no. Motorized and animal-and man-powered vehicles were allowed, except unicycles because of a disastrous event three years ago. The committee then finalized the list of participants.

Individual reports were next. From where Ethan sat, it seemed most of the work had already been completed and now it was a matter of tackling the various unfinished details. Maybe, just maybe, it wouldn't be so bad working on the parade. It might even be fun. He was so confident of this that when Keely put him in charge of coordinating the parade route, he didn't even flinch.

"No problem." Especially since Keely had already filed the necessary permits with the city.

As the meeting wound down, not only was Ethan comfortable with his agreement to work on the parade, but he was feeling smug.

But then an outrageously late committee member came rushing into the room, a whirlwind of designer clothes, five-inch heels and expensive perfume. To his dismay, it was none other than Lacy Hargrove.

Ethan sank low in his chair, grateful the divorcee hadn't noticed him. Actually, she hadn't bothered looking at any of the committee members. She was too busy discarding her coat and showing off her dress, which was better suited for a gala than a town hall meeting.

Then she dramatically announced, "We have a problem."

Keely eyed Lacy with impatience. "What sort of problem."

"The camels are a no-go."

"Camels?" Ethan blurted out, realizing his mistake a moment too late. All eyes were on him now, most notably Lacy's.

The woman's face split into a wide smile. "I simply can't believe what I'm seeing. You really have joined our little committee."

Ethan boldly held her stare. "I'm looking forward to helping my community."

She started to respond, but Keely cut her off. "Lacy, what do you mean the camels are a no-go?"

"Our supplier has already committed his animals to a neighboring town. I asked him for the number of another traveling zoo, but all the names he gave me don't have camels. We'll have to go with plan B."

Not sure what plan B was, and thinking the lack of camels was a good thing, Ethan quickly scanned the list of parade participants. "I don't see camels mentioned anywhere. Why do we need them?"

The woman on his left answered his question. "To pull Santa's sleigh, of course."

"Why not stick with, I don't know…reindeer?"

Keely shot him a warning look. "You've lived in this town long enough to know it's a Village Green tradition to mix things up when it comes to Santa's sleigh."

"Yeah, okay, but why camels? They're pack animals."

"They don't actually pull the sleigh. It's motorized. We use silk cords to look like reins."

It was good to know no animals would be hurt, but still. "Trust me on this when I say they're a really bad idea."

He knew this from personal experience. Throughout his time in the Middle East, he'd never met a camel that hadn't spit on him.

"We've never had camels before," Alice Wainwright said by way of defense. "It'll raise the bar from last year's zebras."

"Perhaps that's true," he allowed. "But camels are notoriously stubborn and—"

"Ethan." Keely said his name in a clipped, no-nonsense tone. "A quick word in the hallway, please."

Fully prepared to make his case, he followed her out of the room. The sound of chairs scraping against the tile floor told him the rest of the committee had hopped out of their seats, probably hoping to overhear his and Keely's…discussion.

Once they were out in the hallway, Keely spun around, parked her hands on her hips and glared at him. "I don't appreciate you questioning this decision. The committee has already decided this issue by a democratic vote."

"Well, I didn't get a vote or an opportunity to make a case against camels, so I'm making it now. You don't know what you're getting into, Keely. I do."

"The decision is made, Ethan." Scowl firmly in place, she took a step toward him. "Let it go."

He took his own step toward her, going toe-to-toe with the ornery woman. "I've had personal experience with camels. They grumble, bellow and grunt. They're beyond stubborn. They bite. And, Keely." He leaned in so close their noses were practically touching. "They spit."

Holding perfectly still, she refused to back away or give an inch of ground. "You're making at least half of that up."

"I'm telling the truth and I don't appreciate you questioning my integrity."

She glowered harder, but still didn't budge on the issue.

"You're going to regret this decision," he warned. "And I'm going to enjoy saying 'I told you so' the day of the parade."

"This discussion is over. You can either get on board with this or walk away."

The woman made him crazy. Barely an hour earlier she'd told him she needed him. Now she was daring him to leave her in the lurch. "I have half a mind to do just that."

"Don't go." The request came from a small, vulnerable voice. "Please, Dr. Ethan, please don't go."

In a flash, he was on his knees in front of the kid. "Hey, hey, Flicka, there's no need to cry." He wiped her wet cheeks with his thumbs. "I'm not going anywhere."

She sniffled. "But you and Keely were fighting."

"We weren't fighting." Keely joined him on the floor, ran a hand over the little girl's head. "It was just a discussion, but all's well now. Right, Dr. Ethan?"

He tried not to sigh. "Yeah, we're good."

They rose and simultaneously put out a hand to the little girl. Smiling through her tears, she took both and let them lead her back into the room.

How was it, Ethan wondered, that he'd successfully kept his relationship with Keely O'Toole superficial and distant for an entire year, and yet, after a single late-night phone call to help out a sick kid, he was deeply embroiled in her life, and she in his?

A bittersweet pang washed over him. They didn't get along any better than they ever had. But, for the sake of the child clinging to their hands, Ethan promised himself he would try to keep things light and easy between him and Keely. At least, whenever Flicka was with them.

As far as the other times their paths crossed? No problem. He'd simply deal with those on a case-by-case basis.

Keely woke early the next morning to the sound of Felicity crying out her name between loud, gasping sobs. She scrambled out of bed, grabbed her robe and rushed down the hallway in her bare feet.

"I'm here, Felicity." Flinging open the door, she dove into the semi-darkened room, then skidded to a stop at the edge of the bed. Breathing hard, she said again, "I'm here."

The little girl blinked up at her with big, watery eyes above tearstained cheeks. "I... I... I...had a bad dream."

"Oh, baby." Keely sank on the bed and pulled the child into her arms. "I'm so sorry. You're awake now and I'm here."

She choked on a sob. "I... I think I'm going to be sick."

There wasn't time to get to the bathroom. Keely pulled back, looked frantically around for a towel, but reacted too late.

Felicity got sick across the front of Keely's robe. "Oh, you poor little girl."

"You…you're not mad I threw up on you?"

"Not even a little bit. These things happen."

"I'm really, really sorry."

"Hush now, hush. There's no need to apologize." She paused to wipe a strand of hair off the child's face. "Do you feel better, or do you think you'll be sick again?"

"I… I think I'm better."

"Let me know if that changes." Working quickly, Keely shed her soiled robe and set about cleaning up the rest of the mess. She had to duck into the bathroom for a moment.

Seconds later, she returned with a glass of water and a wet washcloth, which she used to wipe the child's face. Even when she was finished, tears continued leaking out of the big round eyes.

"What's wrong, sweetie? Still upset about your bad dream?"

"No, I…" Felicity whimpered. "I miss my mommy."

Despair pooled in Keely's stomach. For a dangerous second, she was overcome with the magnitude of what she'd undertaken by bringing this child into her home. She knew nothing of parenting, even less of what it took to help a young child feel safe and protected.

"I know you miss your mom, and I'm sure she misses you." Perched on the side of the bed once again, Keely took the glass of water and brought it up to Felicity's lips.

After she took a tentative drink, she rolled stricken eyes up to Keely. "I don't want to forget her."

In that, at least, she could ease the child's mind. "I won't let that happen, I promise. In fact, I'll take you to visit her in a few weeks and then every week after that until she's free to come home."

"I… I think I'm going to be sick again."

Better prepared this time, Keely placed a towel across the child's lap and a small plastic bucket beneath her chin. When she was finished, she collapsed back on her pillow. Her face looked unnaturally pale and her eyes were enormous against her now colorless skin.

Hands trembling, Keely carefully removed the bucket and towel, then tucked the covers around Felicity's tiny shoulders. In the soft, dawn light her cousin looked incredibly young.

She deserved a *healthy* childhood, deserved a chance to create happy memories that would stay with her forever. Keely wanted to play her part but feared she was already failing.

Reaching down, she swept another lock of hair off the child's forehead. The skin beneath her fingers felt disturbingly hot. Fear replaced every other emotion.

What if Felicity's stomachache was caused by more than simply missing her mother? What if she was really ill? Keely wouldn't be able to live with herself if she didn't find out.

"I'll be right back."

She raced into her bedroom, hurriedly changed into jeans and a sweatshirt, then retrieved her phone. If Ethan refused to help her, and she wouldn't blame him after the way she'd spoken to him last night at the parade meeting, then she'd take Felicity to the ER.

Bottom lip caught between her teeth, she punched out his number. He answered on the first ring, with a curt, "Dr. Scott."

"Ethan, it's me. Keely. I…it's Felicity. She's sick. Her forehead's hot to the touch and she's thrown up twice."

"On my way." He disconnected before she could

thank him, which was just as well. She'd rather do that in person and then apologize for last night. She'd pulled out the *I'm in charge* card, which hadn't gone over well, big shocker.

Hurrying down the stairs, she swung open her back door at the same moment Ethan climbed the final stair. He was already dressed for work in black dress pants and a gray button-down beneath his leather coat.

Thankfully, he didn't waste time with pleasantries. "Any other symptoms I should know about?"

As she led him through the house, she filled him in on the events of the morning. "She woke up about half an hour ago, crying out for me. She'd had a bad dream, got sick, then mentioned missing her mom and got sick again."

They mounted the stairs together, but at the top, Ethan moved in front of Keely and entered Felicity's room ahead of her. His entire demeanor softened. "Hey, Flicka, I hear you're not feeling well again."

The little girl gave a pitiful whimper. "I threw up all over Keely and she didn't get mad or anything."

His response was too low for Keely to hear, but it had Felicity laughing softly and looking less pitiful.

Sitting on the edge of the bed, he went through a similar process as he had Sunday night. But this time he spoke to Felicity about other things besides the tests he was performing on her.

Felicity slowly relaxed and, little by little, her pinched expression released. When the conversation turned to her mother, her lower lip trembled, her face paled, but she didn't cry.

At last, Ethan rose and motioned for Keely to follow him into the hallway. She searched his face, saw a combination of toughness and tenderness that gave her an odd little jolt at the center of her heart.

"It's not her appendix."

The news came as a huge relief. "Okay, good. Any idea what *is* causing her stomachaches?"

"Hard to say, but my guess would be a mix of loneliness and fear, neither unexpected, given her situation."

His words made Keely's throat burn. "I wish I knew how to make things easier for her."

"I've been thinking about that and I have an idea, one you mentioned in passing the other day." His hand closed over hers, squeezed gently. "You can get her a dog. Having a pet to care for will keep her busy and her mind off her worries."

Keely liked the idea, but she wasn't exactly in a position to run out to the pet store this morning and pick one up.

As if he read her mind, a slow, attractive smile spread across his face. "I'll loan you Baloo for the day, as a sort of test run."

Inexpressibly touched, she felt a smile move across her face. "You'd do that for Felicity?"

"And for you, Keely. I'm doing this for you, too."

She felt it again, that jolt in the center of her heart.

It wasn't fair. Just when she was ready to write him off as the frustrating bane of her existence, he did something like this. "When you put it that way, how could I possibly refuse?"

Chapter Six

Later that night, Keely stared at the man standing on her back stoop. He'd changed out of his office clothes and was once again wearing a more casual look, day-old scruff on his jaw included. Thick black lashes framed dazzling blue eyes that sparkled with unexpected warmth.

Not only was Ethan smiling, he'd come bearing gifts from his sister's gourmet chocolate shop, as evidenced by the two bags in his hand. Keely felt herself sigh, which she immediately replaced with suspicion.

What was the man up to now?

Ethan had never given her a gift. Perhaps both bags were for Felicity. Even still, the man standing before her didn't mesh with the man she'd always known, the one who had given her nothing but push back last night at the parade meeting.

"Hey," he said, breaking the lengthy silence.

"Hey, back." *Brilliant response, Keely. That's the way to get the man to view you as a smart, savvy woman.*

Which wasn't even the point. If she ever dated again, Ethan wasn't the man she would choose. He had secrets that showed in his eyes, right before he put up invisible barriers as thick as the winter coat he wore now. Keely had learned the pain of thinking she could get past those kinds of obstacles. She knew to keep up her guard.

However, after he'd lent Baloo to Felicity for the day, she'd come to the conclusion that she should at least attempt to be friends with the man. They were neighbors. Their paths crossed often, and he'd made two house calls for Felicity.

"You're here to pick up Baloo?"

He nodded. "You gonna invite me in?"

"Of course." She stepped aside to let him pass.

There wasn't a lot of space in the mudroom. While Baloo had slept, Keely had taken Felicity shopping for Christmas decorations. The spoils of their efforts littered most of the floor.

Ethan maneuvered his big, rangy body through the cramped quarters. Twice, he bumped into Keely. Both times, he paused, studied her with a closed expression, then went back to peeling off his coat. His expression held something different tonight, something kinder. Maybe even tender. Who was this man? And what had he done with the Ethan Scott she knew?

He took a step toward her. "Keely."

The way he said her name sent apprehension traveling up her spine. She had no idea what to do with this newer, kinder version of the man. He was being too nice. Too likable.

Unaware of her internal battle, he took her hands. His palms were still warm from the gloves he'd recently removed. "It's long past time I apologized properly."

Apologize? Oh no. He didn't get to take the high road before she could do so herself.

"You made several valid arguments about the camels last night," she admitted, if a bit grudgingly. "And I could have handled the situation with more poise, but the decision has already been made and it's final."

"I'm not talking about the parade meeting. I was speaking about the past, *our* past."

"I...oh."

"I never meant to hurt you, not the time I stepped in with Kenny Nobel when we were kids, or last year with Parker Thorpe. My goal was to protect you."

"I know that, Ethan." She'd been wrong to hold the two incidents against him for so long. "I *know* you meant me no harm."

His lips tilted in a lopsided grin. "So we're good?"

"We're good." She tried to pull free of his grasp.

He wouldn't let her go.

"Now that we're friends, would this be a good time to ask you to change your mind about the camels?"

She felt her lips twitch at the hopeful note in his tone. "I never pegged you for a sore loser."

"Who said I lost?" He leaned in close, giving her a whiff of his spicy, masculine scent. "It ain't over till it's over."

"It's over when *I* say it's over."

He heaved an exaggerated sigh. "Seriously, Keely, camels are a bad idea."

"What is it with you and camels?"

"I thought I made myself clear last night. They spit."

Ethan would know, especially after his tour of duty in Afghanistan. Nevertheless, Keely wasn't giving in. She couldn't. "The committee voted. It's a done deal."

"Don't say I didn't warn you."

An odd, silent message spread between them, something complicated and full of meaning she didn't quite understand.

Ever since he'd embarrassed her in front of his high school buddies, Keely had thought of Ethan as arrogant, bossy and close-minded. Her opinion had been confirmed a year ago at the Young Professionals mixer.

But lately, she'd caught glimpses of a different man. Beneath the competent exterior were hints of vulnerability and sadness, the same raw emotions she'd witnessed in Cutter at the end of their relationship.

Wasn't that telling?

Ethan rarely dated, and only for occasions that required him to bring a plus-one. Not for the first time, she wondered if he'd lost someone he loved, a woman perhaps? It would explain a lot. But no one was talking, not Ethan, or his sister, Olivia, who normally told Keely everything.

Whatever haunted the man, it was sad and grave. Her heart softened even more. "It's my turn to give you an apology."

"For…?"

"For wrongfully accusing you of trying to humiliate me. For that I'm truly sorry."

At last, he let go of her hands. "Apology accepted."

Keely was the first to look away, but not before she took a quick head-to-toe assessment.

Ethan looked good tonight. The faded jeans and combat boots were familiar. The T-shirt was new, and read I'm a Bomb Technician. If You See Me Running, Try to Keep Up.

A smile came despite her best efforts to stop it. "Where did you get that?"

"Olivia's Sweet Shoppe." He retrieved the shiny pink

and brown bag he'd set on a nearby bench. "Where else would I buy chocolate but from my favorite sister's new store?"

Olivia was his only sister. Still, Ethan's love of family was unmistakable, and something Keely had always admired about him.

"I meant the T-shirt." She pointed at the black fabric stretched across his muscled chest. "I'm assuming that one's from your days in the army."

He looked down at his shirt. "Probably."

"You don't know?"

He lifted a shoulder. "I can't remember."

Sighing again—why couldn't she stop sighing around the man?—she directed him to follow her into deeper into the house.

"Is Dr. Ethan here?" Felicity's pounding footsteps accompanied the question.

The moment she rounded the corner, Ethan greeted her.

"Dr. Ethan." The little girl practically flew at their neighbor and wrapped her arms around his waist. Before he could do anything but choke out a laugh, she hopped out of his embrace and launched into a detailed account of her day.

When she finally took a breath, Ethan seized the moment to conduct a subtle yet thorough medical exam, mostly questions, then a look at her eyes, ears, nose and throat.

Seemingly satisfied with what he found, or rather didn't find, he presented a bag from Olivia's Sweet Shoppe to the little girl.

And so began another round of hugs. "I love chocolate."

"Who doesn't?"

They eventually moved into the living room and Felicity's chatter wore down. Her energy, however, remained high, as evidenced by the fierce game of tug-of-war she instigated with Baloo and the knotted sock the dog retrieved from beneath a chair.

Keely smiled at their antics, relieved to see the little girl looking so happy, so…normal. The day had started quite differently, all because Keely had introduced the topic of school yet again. If only she could figure out a way to help the child accept new people in her life as she had Ethan.

Give it time, she told herself. But as she watched her cousin looking so happy, Keely decided a dog was definitely in Felicity's future.

Out of the corner of her eye, she saw Ethan watching the two with a sad, nostalgic smile. He blew out a tortured breath, then turned to face Keely.

"For you." He presented another bag from Olivia's store.

"Oh, Ethan, you didn't have to—*oh*." Keely released a soft gasp of pleasure. "You brought me chocolate-covered popcorn."

"Olivia said it's your favorite."

Too choked up to speak, she nodded. *Get control of yourself, Keely O'Toole.*

How could she? She had no idea what to do with this newer Ethan Scott, the one bearing her favorite treat.

"I love you, Baloo." This, from Felicity, as she flopped down on the floor next to the dog. "So very, very much."

Welcoming the distraction, Keely took in the scene through slightly watery eyes. Felicity and Baloo were both on their backs, breathing hard, staring up at the ceiling.

The sight of them brought back Keely's smile. Expecting to see a similar expression on Ethan's face, she glanced at him.

There was no smile on his face, no tender expression, nothing but an intense look of longing, as if he wanted something so far out of reach he'd lost hope of ever achieving it. Keely had lived in a similar place for months after Cutter withdrew his marriage proposal.

A verse from the book of Proverbs came to mind. *Hope deferred makes the heart sick.*

She desperately wanted to offer Ethan words of comfort, but she didn't know what to say without prying into his past, a past he'd never once shared with her.

"Hey, Dr. Ethan, are you and Baloo staying for the movie?"

"What movie?"

"It's called *Miracle on 34th Street*. Keely says it's a classic." Felicity grinned. "Want to watch it with us?"

"Uh." He cleared his throat. "I—"

"Please say yes. We're making real popcorn, and Keely saved some of the cookies we baked yesterday and…say yes." She placed her hand on his arm. "Say yes, say yes."

Against her better judgment, Keely silently chanted along with the little girl in her head. *Say yes, say yes.*

"Sure, why not?" There was a strained note to his voice, as if it had cost him something very personal to give in to the little girl's request.

"Ethan." Keely touched his arm. "We don't want to impose on your time. Feel free to—"

"I'd like to stay." He gave her a wan smile, the gesture belying his words. "I mean it."

She wanted to believe he was sticking around for all the right reasons. But she just didn't know. She'd called Olivia earlier and gently grilled her friend about Ethan's past. His sister had been surprisingly closed-lipped, only saying that it wasn't her story to tell.

Keely had to trust that Ethan would share his past with her when he was ready, which was probably never.

Some things, she thought with a heavy sigh, never changed.

With only a bowl of popcorn separating them, Ethan lounged on the overstuffed couch beside Keely. What was becoming a startling new habit, he'd accepted an impromptu invitation to stick around with his neighbor and her little girl.

He still wasn't sure why he'd agreed. If pushed for an explanation, he'd blame it on not wanting to disappoint Flicka.

That had only been one of the reasons.

The other was sitting on the couch beside him.

The more time he spent in Keely's company, the less alone he felt, the less haunted, as if he were slowly waking from a bad dream. Maybe letting down a bit more of his guard wasn't a terrible idea. But if something happened to Keely and Flicka—

He cut off the rest of that thought and hardened his heart. He couldn't—*wouldn't*—suffer another loss. The risk was too high.

He made a point of not looking at Keely, though he was fully aware of her presence. A pleasant feminine scent wafted off her, a girly mix of lavender and orchids. He didn't know what perfume she used, but he'd always liked it.

Breathing in, feeling a bit light-headed, he risked a glance in her direction, thankful her attention was on the screen.

Even in profile, her features were stunning. She had the kind of classic beauty of an actress from the Golden Age of cinema. Rita Hayworth came to mind.

Captivated, Ethan stared, once again feeling something come alive within him. Something he thought he'd buried with Tracy.

He quickly looked away, darted his gaze around the room. The large space, with its comfortable furniture and handcrafted cabinetry, would look good decorated for Christmas.

The season celebrating the birth of the Savior had always been Ethan's favorite. Many of his happiest memories from childhood were from this time of year. He'd wanted to recreate many of his family's traditions with Tracy and Samantha.

God had other plans.

Ethan wasn't really angry at God anymore. But peace still eluded him. Instead of welcoming Christmas with his own family, in his own home, he would spend the day with Olivia, Connor and the twins. It would be nice, but not what Ethan really wanted.

He wanted a family of his own, a wife, children, but he wasn't willing to take the risk of losing them. He shut his eyes against a wave of sorrow, opened them, then zeroed in on a spot at his feet.

Flicka had chosen to view the movie sprawled out on the floor, her head resting lightly on Baloo's back. As he watched his dog so content in the little girl's company, Ethan was dragged back in time, to another living room.

Breath clogged in his throat, Ethan shifted his gaze, this time to a spot on the far wall. He couldn't risk losing himself in memories, most of which he'd tucked away for good. Grief and loss would always be a part of him, but he'd let Tracy and Samantha go. Or had he?

Shouldn't his life look different than it had a year ago?

Keely swiveled her head in his direction. "You say something?"

"Nope."

Her eyebrows lifted. "You were mumbling under your breath."

He forced a smile, grabbed a handful of popcorn, paused before stuffing the kernels in his mouth. "Anyone ever tell you how much you look like the heroine of this movie?"

Keely's eyes widened in disbelief.

"I'm giving you a compliment, Keely. This is the place in the conversation when you say thank you."

"Thank you."

The words came to him inside a soft whisper. He felt a small crack open in his heart, followed by a moment of utter panic. Not Keely. Not her. If he let her in, then lost her, he didn't think he would survive.

"You know, Dr. Scott, you project this carefree image to the world, but I'm not fooled." She poked him in the chest. "You need to learn to lighten up."

"I know how to relax. Just last weekend I went skiing with your brother." Even with his shoulder injury still giving him problems, Beau O'Toole was a force on the slopes. Ethan had been happy just to keep up with the hotshot skier. "The weekend before that I went sky-diving with Ryder."

"Oh, well, then, you're not overly intense at all. Don't know where I could have gotten that idea."

Smirking, she returned her attention to the TV screen.

He stuffed popcorn in his mouth, chewed thoughtfully, willing his heart rate to return to normal. Not until the movie credits rolled across the screen did the muscles in his back release.

"Hey, Dr. Ethan." Flicka sat up and rubbed at her eyes. "Can I give Baloo a doggy treat before he has to go to bed?"

Hearing his name, the black Lab lifted his head and gave Ethan a hopeful look. "Sure, but only one."

"Come on, Baloo." Flicka hopped to her feet. "Let's get you a treat before your daddy changes his mind."

The dog dutifully followed her out of the room.

Expecting Keely to follow, Ethan was surprised to find her watching him closely. He held her stare without wavering. Any minute, she would get up and leave the room.

One beat passed, then two, and by the third she blessed him with a slow, sweet smile. His mind went blank, a black void of nothing.

"Thank you, Ethan, thank you for bringing over Baloo this morning. And for working on the parade, even though we both know you don't want to, and for sticking around tonight." Her smile softened, reaching all the way to those remarkable eyes. "Felicity would have been disappointed if you'd said no."

"It was my pleasure." He was shaken to discover he spoke the truth. Nothing much surprised Ethan, or caught him off guard, but everything about tonight had done both.

He was stepping into a minefield of complicated emotions. His heart was thawing, opening up to possibilities he'd hadn't allowed himself to consider for well over a year. The risk was too great, with far too much to lose, maybe more than ever before. The thought made his shoulders bunch.

Flicka's laughter rang out from the kitchen, followed by Baloo's happy bark.

A smile tugged at Ethan's lips, and then moved into his heart, thawing another chunk of ice. "I think my dog is in love."

"Felicity has that way about her."

There was no denying that.

"Oh, Ethan." Her face grew suddenly serious, her expression grave. "I really, really want to do right by this child. But she's not transitioning as well as I'd hoped, as evidenced by her stomachache this morning."

Thinking only of reassuring her, of erasing that worried scowl, he took her hand. "The situation is still new for both of you. You're doing great, Keely, making all the right choices on Flicka's behalf. Like I've said before, consistency and routine will build her confidence. The quicker you can get her on a regular schedule, the better."

A frustrated hiss whooshed out of her. "How can I do that if she refuses to go to school?"

"Give it time, Keely. Do your best and leave the rest—"

"To the Lord."

Not even close. Blind trust had never come easy for Ethan. It had been harder since Tracy's death.

Battling back a bitter response, he forced himself to stay in the moment. It was easier than he would have thought, thanks to a pair of sea-green eyes staring at him with a combination of worry and hope. It was the hope that got to him, the realization that she trusted him enough to seek his advice.

With his free hand, he reached up, brushed a lock of hair off her face, then tucked it behind her ear. Another little-girl giggle had them both jumping.

Keely drew in a shaky breath, let out a tremulous laugh. "Felicity is definitely getting a puppy for Christmas."

Ethan homed in on the change of topic as if it were a suture to a gaping wound. "As I said this morning, it's not a bad idea. Taking care of another living creature will teach her responsibility and help keep her mind off her own problems."

"That's what I discovered today with Baloo. Thanks again, by the way, for loaning him to Felicity."

"I'm sure Baloo enjoyed the company." Uncomfortable with the way she was looking at him, as if he was a superhero, he changed the subject. "So, any ideas about the breed you want to get for Felicity?"

"Not really." A thoughtful expression crossed her pretty features. "I was thinking of getting a dog from the animal shelter."

And there she went again, reaching inside his chest and giving his heart a good, hard tug.

Caught in a haze of admiration, he found himself offering his personal assistance. "Want help picking the dog out?"

"Actually…" She paused. "Yes, I believe I would."

"If we don't have time to speak after the parade

meeting tomorrow night, I'll call you in the next few days to set up a time that fits both our schedules."

"Sounds good."

Yeah, it did. A little too good. He was going under, drowning in a deep green sea the color of Keely O'Toole's eyes.

Ethan told himself not to panic. Keely was struggling in her new role as a parent. She needed a friend right now. Once Flicka was more settled, then his neighborly duty would be complete. He could pull away in good conscience.

It was a brilliant strategy for everyone involved. If he stuck to the plan, Ethan told himself, no one would get hurt.

Chapter Seven

Ethan arrived at his second official parade meeting determined to play nice with Keely. Not only because Felicity would be in the room, watching them closely, but also because Keely deserved a break. She'd had a rough couple of weeks and Ethan didn't see the point in adding to her stress.

Now that he knew what he'd gotten himself into, he came more prepared for this meeting than he had been for the last. Laptop in one hand, a to-go mug of strong coffee in the other, he entered the conference room and commandeered the empty seat beside Flicka. "Hey, kid, how you feeling tonight?"

A smile cut across the child's face. "Better. Keely got me this coloring book today and I've been working to get at least ten pictures done before bedtime."

"Nice goal." He'd barely had time to admire the three pages she'd already colored when Keely passed out the evening's agenda and called the meeting to order.

"Lacy isn't coming tonight, but she sent me her report," Keely informed the committee, her mouth thinning as she glanced at her computer screen. "According to her notes, she still can't find any camels and is all out of ideas."

Ethan held back a knowing smirk. As if she could hear his thoughts, Keely looked at him sharply. "You got something to say?"

"That's, uh, too bad?" At her grimace, he added, "Imagine I said that with enthusiasm."

"Yeah, you seem real broken up."

He let his silence be his reply.

Mrs. Colchester, the woman sitting on his left who'd once been his mother's dear friend, tapped him on the shoulder. "Instead of offering platitudes, why don't you fire up that fancy computer of yours and see if you can locate us some camels?"

Before he could respond, the lady on her left leaned forward and gave him a pointed look. "I second that idea."

With a straight face, Keely said, "Couldn't hurt."

"I can help you," Flicka offered, scooting her chair close to his and peering at the computer with wide, eager eyes.

Seeing no easy way out, he said, "Sure, no problem."

While the rest of the committee gave their reports, Ethan halfheartedly surfed around on the internet. Flicka proved incredibly proficient with the search engine, which made her a little too helpful for Ethan's taste. But he was impressed enough not to hinder her efforts.

Keely called for a short break.

Flicka announced she needed to go to the bathroom. One of the other ladies offered to take her, which left Ethan the only one still sitting at the table. Keely came up behind him and glanced over his shoulder. "How's it going?"

Her floral scent had his mood edging into annoyance. "Nothing so far."

"Are you even trying?"

Flicking a cool-eyed glance over his shoulder, he said as calmly as possible, "Yes, Keely, I'm trying."

"I'm delighted to hear that."

She didn't sound delighted. She sounded wary. "Out of curiosity, let's say, I fail to locate camels. What's plan B?"

Her eyebrows knit together. "You don't want to know."

"Oh, but I do."

She closed her eyes and gave a slight, shuddering sigh before opening them again. "Go-karts."

He threw his head back and laughed. "You're actually considering the idea of go-karts pulling Santa's sleigh?"

He was horrified to think she might be serious.

"There was a lot of debate, mostly from me, but I was outvoted seven to one." She worked her hands together at her waist. "So now you understand why I'm pushing so hard for the camels."

"I will get you camels. Whatever it takes."

"I think you actually mean that."

"I do."

After a long hesitation, she closed her hand over his shoulder. "You pull this off and I'll owe you one. Any favor, name it and it's yours."

"With that kind of incentive, I better get to work."

Felicity had been in Keely's home nearly two weeks and the girl was still balking at starting a new school.

Though she truly sympathized with her cousin's concerns, Keely couldn't coddle Felicity indefinitely. It was time to take action.

One phone call to her best friend and a new plan was set in motion. When she informed Felicity that they were eating breakfast with Ethan's sister and her twin daughters the next day, Felicity had seemed a bit wary, but not altogether resistant.

But now, as they headed into the heart of Village Green, she second-guessed herself. Was she pushing Felicity too hard, too fast?

She would know soon enough.

"Even though I know there's no such thing as Santa, can we put out a plate of cookies anyway?"

Keely squeezed Felicity's hand. "Absolutely. It's an O'Toole tradition. We're going to get a tree, too. Not a plastic one, either, but a real live one, which is another family tradition."

"Can we take a picture and send it to my mom?"

An invisible fist squeezed the breath out of Keely's lungs. "I think that's a lovely idea."

The poor child had been through a lot of trauma because of Juliette's actions. Keely was even more determined to provide a wonderful Christmas for the girl, with as many family traditions as possible.

"Can we put up stockings for me and you, and maybe Baloo and Dr. Ethan, too?"

"I don't see why not."

Felicity caught her bottom lip between her teeth. "I'd like to hang a stocking for my mom, too, even though she won't be here. And we'll want to put one up for cousin Beau."

"He'd like that."

Although her brother would never admit it, Beau needed family, especially now that his professional career was over. He'd made the most of the situation, by opening his own ski shop and giving lessons to locals, but Keely sensed his restlessness.

Beau clearly missed the life that had been ripped from him after one disastrous training run. He'd been the rising star of winter sports, touted as the David Beckham of downhill skiing.

"Where did you say we're having breakfast?"

"The Turkey Roost."

Felicity wrinkled her nose. "That's a weird name for a restaurant."

Although Keely didn't disagree, she came to the diner's defense. "It's no weirder than the name of my restaurant."

"Senor O'Toole's isn't weird, it's supercool."

Keely's family's restaurant served Irish food with a Mexican flair, a none-too-subtle nod to ancestors on both sides of her family.

With the song "White Christmas" playing on the car radio, Keely pulled her Jeep into an empty parking space and cut the engine. She glanced at the little girl in the seat beside her.

Doubt once again consumed her.

Felicity hadn't complained of a stomachache in days, nor had she thrown up or had any bad dreams. Surely this breakfast with Olivia and the twins would bring the child another step closer to settling into her new life.

"I'm so happy you want to meet Megan and Molly." Keely intentionally put a positive spin on the morning.

Felicity said nothing until they were both out of the

car and heading down the sidewalk toward the restaurant. "What if they don't like me?"

Keely didn't immediately try to talk the child out of her fear. She'd spent much of her own childhood feeling shy and awkward. Making friends had been difficult. At thirteen, things had gotten worse when, practically overnight, she'd transformed from a skinny, gawky kid to a fully developed young woman.

"When I spoke with Olivia she assured me the girls are excited to meet you." Smiling to punctuate her point, she pulled Felicity into her arms for a brief hug. "But if you feel uncomfortable, or want to go home, tell me and we'll leave."

"Okay." The little girl visibly relaxed. "While we're in town, do you think we could maybe visit Dr. Ethan at his office?"

And they were back to Felicity's favorite topic.

Though she'd never admit it out loud, Keely shared the little girl's fascination with their handsome neighbor. Now that they were inadvertently spending so much time together, she wondered if they were on the road to becoming friends. *Don't get ahead of yourself, a lot of water under that bridge.*

"I don't know when we'll see him again. Maybe not until the next parade meeting. Dr. Ethan is a very busy man." She said the words as much for herself as the little girl.

The disappointment in the child's eyes mirrored a similar emotion whirling through Keely, an emotion she absolutely refused to acknowledge.

"Come on. Let's go meet some new friends."

The little girl resumed chewing on her bottom lip,

even as she heroically lifted her chin and fell into step beside Keely.

A bell attached to the front door announced their arrival. Feet gliding across the checkerboard flooring, Keely took in the 1950s vibe. The yellow Formica tables were paired with pink-and-blue plastic chairs, and the authentic jukebox was playing retro music.

Olivia waved at them from the back of the restaurant. She'd commandeered a large table and had spread out an array of art supplies. Touched by her friend's quick thinking, Keely took Felicity's hand and steered her toward the table.

As they wove their way through the restaurant, Olivia smiled broadly. There was no denying the woman was Ethan's sister. Though her hair was a shade lighter than her brother's, the eyes were the same shape and color, the nose similar, as well. But where Ethan's face was distinctly, undeniably male, and could have been chiseled out of granite, Olivia had softer, rounder, more feminine features.

Glowing with newlywed happiness, she rushed forward and yanked Keely into one of her customary hugs.

"Thanks for doing this, Olivia," she whispered, emotion causing her voice to rasp. "I owe you."

"You owe me nothing. I wouldn't have missed meeting Village Green's newest resident for all the money in the world." Olivia stepped back and smiled at the little girl clinging to Keely now. "You must be Felicity. Come meet my daughters."

On cue, the twins abandoned their art project and rushed over to greet the timid child. "I'm Molly and this is my sister, Megan. We're identical twins."

Felicity looked from one girl to the other, the tension in her shoulders visibly disappearing. "I sort of figured."

"I know, right?" Molly grinned, revealing a missing front tooth. "Kind of hard to miss."

All three girls laughed.

"Do you have any pets?" Megan asked, joining the conversation slower than her sister but with equal enthusiasm.

"No." Felicity shook her head. "But I want one real bad."

"We have a dog." Molly took over the conversation once again. "Hey, Mom, can I have your phone so I can show Felicity pictures of Samson?"

While the three girls huddled over the tiny screen, Keely felt her own shoulders relax. With their blond hair a full shade lighter than Felicity's, the Mitchell twins looked like their father. They had sweet, delicate features and what everyone in town called "Mitchell eyes," an unusual pale amber color that looked like finely spun gold.

Once they showed off their dog, Molly asked Felicity if she wanted to make a holiday box.

"What's that?"

"It's for school. We're going to make greeting cards for everyone in our class and then put them in the boxes during the holiday party."

"You mean like Valentine's Day?"

"Exactly," Molly confirmed. "Mom brought enough supplies for all three of us."

Megan took her hand and pulled her toward the table. "We'll help you get started."

Keely felt her eyes blur with tears of relief. The Mitchell girls were such kind, caring children and Felicity already seemed comfortable around them.

If anyone could understand some of what her cousin was going through, it would be Molly and Megan. They'd lost their mother to cancer when they were four. Connor had done an excellent job raising them on his own. But then Olivia had returned to town and stepped in as a temporary nanny when his housekeeper had busted up her knee.

The two had fallen hopelessly in love within months. Keely didn't begrudge her friend one ounce of the happiness she'd found with Connor. And yet she felt a pang in her heart whenever she was around the newlyweds. Their obvious joy in each other gave Keely a sense of deep, hopeless yearning for something she'd almost had with Cutter—almost, but not quite.

She only wanted a smidge of her friend's happiness. And despite her heartbreak, she still wanted to build a life with a man she loved, who loved her in return. Cutter hadn't been that man. Next time she gave her heart away, she would make sure the man was free to love her.

The tinkling bell attached to the front door heralded a new arrival. Keely glanced over her shoulder and felt her breath catch in her lungs. She watched Ethan enter the diner with his long-legged, rangy stride. He saw her and smiled. The gesture sent set her heart tripping over itself. Stupid heart.

Chapter Eight

Once a week, Ethan picked up breakfast for his office staff as a thank-you for keeping the practice running smoothly. Six months ago, he'd changed the day to earlier in the week when he discovered his sister and her friends—primarily Keely—met for their scheduled Bible study on Friday morning.

Which raised the question, what were they—*Keely*—doing at the Turkey Roost this morning? Maybe she hadn't noticed him.

Unlikely, since his gaze was locked with hers. He watched, intrigued, as Keely purposely relaxed her stance. He didn't buy the casual pose; too many emotions flitted across her face.

She took a faltering step toward him, then stopped.

His gaze zeroed in on the tiny lines around her mouth, and the purple smudges beneath her eyes. Was Flicka sick again? Or were those signs of stress due to Keely's concerns about her new role in the child's life?

Ethan felt a powerful need to put the woman at ease, to attack her concerns with logic and reason. She'd already proven herself a capable stand-in mother. He had no doubt Flicka was in excellent hands. Still, he sympathized with Keely's worry.

The child was in her care indefinitely, with no real idea when her tenure as guardian would end. That had to weigh heavy on her heart, not knowing when she would have to say goodbye to the child she so clearly loved.

Ethan's gut twisted. He knew the loss she would suffer when that day arrived. His breakfast order forgotten, he headed toward the back of the diner.

A little-girl squeal had his feet grinding to a halt. "Dr. Ethan, Dr. Ethan, you're here. You're really, really here."

Deserting the table and whatever art project she'd been working on, Flicka practically broke out in a run to meet him halfway across the diner.

Her excitement was so genuine his heart slammed against his ribs. "Hey, kiddo."

He barely had time to brace himself before her skinny arms shot out and wrapped around his waist. He had no defense against her uninhibited show of affection. And yet he knew it was a mistake to get too close.

She pulled back and grinned. "I didn't know when I was going to see you again. Keely said it could be days and days."

"She said that, huh?" He shot a glance at the woman in question.

A rush of color hit her cheeks. "You're a busy man."

"Not that busy."

Her only response was a quick shrug.

"Hi, Uncle Ethan."

"Well, well, if it isn't Squirt One." He ruffled Molly's hair, then repeated the process with her sister. "And Squirt Two."

The girls grinned at the nicknames he'd given them long before Olivia married Connor. They were cute kids, sweet, outgoing, and now he understood the reason for this early-morning breakfast. Keely was attempting to introduce Flicka to other children her age, in a neutral setting that would help put her at ease. Clever.

Molly pulled on his sleeve and, with no small amount of pride, said, "We were just showing our new friend pictures of Samson. She thinks he's cute."

"He's *really* cute," Flicka confirmed, an unmistakable look of longing in her eyes.

"Have you met Baloo yet?" Megan asked her.

Felicity gave a fast head bob. "I love Baloo. He can sit and lie down and shake hands and he really likes to play tug-of-war with a sock."

Ethan started to tell Flicka she could play with Baloo again tonight, but Olivia broke into the conversation. "Girls, we need to order breakfast soon, or you'll be late for school."

With the efficiency reminiscent of their mother, Ethan's sister herded all three children back to the table while also motioning for the waitress. He noticed the various supplies on the table and figured one of the women had thought to keep the girls occupied with some sort of art project.

"Want to join us for breakfast?" Olivia asked him.

Tempted, he eyed his sister. He had time, as long as he ate quickly. However, if he knew Keely—which, surprisingly, he was beginning to think he did—he would guess she was helping Flicka make friends. His presence might hinder the process.

His suspicions were confirmed when a silent appeal entered Keely's gaze. Odd that he knew exactly what that look meant.

"Sorry, Liv, can't. Gotta get back to the office."

As if they'd practiced for this moment all morning, the three girls begged him to stay, their voices ringing out in perfect harmony, hitting a high note only Baloo could hear.

"Next time," he promised, touched by the adorable display. He turned to go, then stopped beside Keely. "Got a sec?"

Confusion covered her face, followed immediately by annoyance.

"I'm kind of in the middle of something here." She looked pointedly look at Felicity. "Can it wait until later?"

Of course, it could wait.

But something in him wouldn't let it go. "I'll be quick."

By the sound she made in her throat, half frustration, half protest, he expected her to refuse. She surprised him by saying, "I'll walk you out."

At the door, he touched her arm. "Hang tight."

He veered back to the cash register, picked up his standing order, then opened the door for Keely to exit ahead of him.

As she moved to a spot beneath the heated awning, Ethan studied her more closely. She wore her red hair in long, soft, curling waves. Her dark-wash jeans looked new, as did the green and gold sweater that highlighted her eyes, simple yet elegant, just like the woman herself.

Ethan realized he'd seen her in a dozen different ways, everything from formal to casual, from runway-ready to sweatpants sloppy.

His gut dipped at the insight that he was this aware of his gorgeous neighbor. What was it about Keely that got to him?

He wanted to say it was tied up in their long, tumultuous history, but that wouldn't be completely accurate. Something new was growing between them, something complex. There was an appealing innocence about Keely O'Toole, a vulnerability that called to the protector in him.

Not that he thought of her as weak. The woman was no pushover, as she'd proven in her role as the parade coordinator. Her inner strength was refreshing.

"You wanted to speak with me?" she asked.

When he didn't respond right away, she smiled the secret smile of woman. That was all it took to scramble his thoughts.

She moved a step closer and suddenly he could smell her shampoo, made from ingredients he couldn't quite pinpoint.

The day he arrived in Afghanistan, his CO had told him he had one job to do, treat the wounded to the best of his ability. Simple instructions, complex task. That was similar to the way he felt around Keely. Simple interactions, complex emotions.

Further complicating matters, she was a mother now, a package deal. If Ethan allowed himself to fall for her, and subsequently for Flicka, he would have to accept that he could lose them, as he had lost so many other people he'd loved. If he kept that salient point in mind, every decision he made concerning Keely and Flicka would be easier.

Her smile turned into a little laugh. "Tick tock, Ethan. I need to get back to Felicity and the girls."

His lips twitched. Bossy, take-charge, snippy Keely was one of his favorites. "I thought we'd set the date to go dog shopping."

"You want to firm up our plans? That's what couldn't wait?"

When she put it that way…

He dug in his heels.

"As you told Flicka, I'm a busy man." He used her own words against her. "If we don't figure out a time soon, we may never coordinate our schedules, and then you could miss out on a really great dog."

Something flashed in her eyes and he suddenly remembered their standoff at that first parade meeting. He'd felt something shift inside him that night, away from hostility toward something far more pleasant. The sensation slammed into him now.

He, Ethan Scott, a man who'd been to war, who'd been twice tasked with burying loved ones, was done in by a pretty scowl. Not on his watch.

"You know I'm right," he said, driving home his point with a challenging grin.

"Let me check my calendar and get back to you later today."

He tapped the tip of her nose. "You do that."

With nothing more to say, he headed down the sidewalk.

Keely's frustrated sigh followed in his wake.

He looked over his shoulder and shot her a wink.

She blushed prettily.

Now, that, he decided, was a fine way to start his day.

At 3:25 p.m., Keely pulled into the carpool line at Village Green Elementary. Her plan to introduce Felicity to the Mitchell twins had proven far more successful than she'd hoped. Her only goal had been to help the little girl make friends, and thereby settle into her home with greater ease.

But once breakfast was finished and it was time for Megan and Molly to head off to school, Felicity had begged to go, too. With the paperwork already complete, it had been a simple matter of checking her in at the office.

As the guidance counselor escorted Felicity to her classroom, the little girl had practically skipped down the hallway. She hadn't looked back at Keely once.

Ethan had been a far different story this morning.

Keely let out a long, exasperated sigh. The wink had been unexpected. Her breath had stalled in her lungs, and all she could do was stand there under the awning, watching him stroll down the street with that ambling, loose-limbed gait.

Any man that good-looking, that strong and capable, should come with a warning label.

The school bell buzzed. Swarms of children soon spilled out of the front door. Keely climbed out of her Jeep and hurried to stand on the sidewalk so Felicity would see her. She'd half expected to get a call from the school nurse, but the child had made it through the entire day. Progress.

Keely waved at Olivia sitting in the carpool line three cars back, then set her gaze back on the front doors. Any minute now, she would see Felicity.

She exited with several other little girls, the Mitchell twins included. They scattered onto the sidewalk. One by one, each girl sped away from the group toward a waiting car.

Felicity looked around, and then her gaze converged with Keely's. She lifted a hand in greeting.

A smile split across the child's face. She said something to the Mitchell twins and then rushed ahead of them. "I had the best day ever. I can't wait to tell you everything."

"I can't wait to hear everything." Heart full of relief, she opened the door for the girl to scramble into the Jeep.

Keely hadn't even pulled away from the curb before Felicity began regaling her with the events of her day.

"I learned so much. I'm not behind or anything. I think math is going to be my favorite subject." She took a breath. "Oh, and the other kids were really nice to me. Well, except Kale Rivers, but he's mean to everyone." She took another breath. "I love my new teacher, Mrs. Donnelly. She said she was going to call you tonight. I'm not in trouble or anything. She just wants to touch base with you."

Trying desperately to keep up with the child's monologue, Keely took a right turn and caught sight of Felicity's lively face out of the corner of her eye.

There was such joy in her gaze. Keely's stomach fluttered with a mixture of happiness and sorrow. Happiness for all she would share with Felicity, sorrow for Juliette. She would miss so much of her daughter's life. Keely had to swallow several times to dislodge the ache in her throat.

"The best part of the day was recess. Molly and Megan introduced me to their two best friends, Hailey and Brenna. They're my friends now, too."

Oh, thank You, Lord. Perhaps Felicity's transition would be easier than she'd originally thought.

Only as they entered their neighborhood did the child wind down long enough to notice the packages in the back of the Jeep. "Hey, what's in the shopping bags?"

"See for yourself."

Felicity swiveled in her seat to get a better look. "It looks like school supplies and art stuff. Why art stuff?"

"For your holiday box."

Felicity swung back around. "Can we work on it as soon as we get home?"

Home. The word melted Keely's heart into a puddle. Maybe, just maybe, they were past the rough patch.

Thank You, Lord. Thank You for the privilege of caring for this child, no matter how temporary.

"Do you have any other homework?"

"Only the holiday box," Felicity said. "It was due today, but I get extra time because I'm new."

"Then let's get to it as soon as we unpack our supplies."

She hit the button for the garage door and nosed the Jeep forward. After cutting the engine, she grabbed a handful of bags and led the way inside the house. The project was nearly complete when a light snowfall began.

Distracted, Felicity danced to the window. "It's snowing."

"So it is."

The child's voice turned wistful. "I *love* playing in the snow."

Keely did, too. Feeling a surge of excitement, she joined Felicity at the window, took note of the fat flakes clinging to barren tree branches.

"Should we build a snowman?" she asked Felicity.

"Oh, can we?"

The excitement on Felicity's face gave Keely renewed hope they were on the right path. "Absolutely."

They quickly dressed in their coats, hats, scarfs and gloves, then hurried into the backyard, talking and laughing.

Keely tested the snow to make sure it was packable. The tiny clump in her palms was soon perfectly round. With Felicity bouncing on her toes, Keely kept adding snow until the mound was nearly too big to hold.

"Okay." She set it on the ground. "Help me roll this across the yard."

Felicity moved in next to her. Tongue caught between her teeth, the little girl went to work. Apparently, Keely's cousin took her snowman-building seriously. Another trait they shared.

Felicity rolled while Keely added, packed and molded until the snowball gained a sizable girth. They turned and headed back in the opposite direction just as Ethan's back door creaked. Keely looked up to see Baloo vault out of the house. The excited dog danced in frantic circles around his owner.

Felicity stopped midroll and pointed. "Look. It's Baloo and Dr. Ethan."

At the sound of his name, the dog did two full spins, then sped across the yard, snowflakes flying in his wake. Baloo greeted Felicity with happy barks.

Caught in the sweet moment, Keely laid a hand on her heart. So captured by the scene, she forgot that wherever Baloo went, Ethan soon followed.

She glanced over her shoulder, allowing herself one long look into piercing blue eyes, then felt her own narrow. *Oh no.*

Ethan reached down and scooped up a large handful of snow.

"Don't you dare," Keely warned, hands on hips, scowl firmly in place. "Don't even think about it."

"What?" His grin flashed, quick and devastating. "Can't a guy create a perfectly round masterpiece of snow without someone questioning his motives?"

"I mean it, Ethan. Put down the snowball and walk away."

She spoke a heartbeat too late.

"Consider this payment for conning me into working on the parade with you." Ethan's perfectly round masterpiece sailed in a wide, looping arc.

Keely took off at a dead run, and felt the snowball hit her in the middle of her back.

Sputtering in outrage, she quickly ran for cover. "This means war, Dr. Scott."

Chapter Nine

While Keely hid behind the thick trunk of a cotton-wood tree, Ethan packed another snowball with quick, sure hands. Then, when she made the mistake of abandoning cover to issue a series of ridiculous threats, he fired.

It skimmed her right shoulder. She stammered out another warning, but then wisely retreated behind the tree.

"You have no idea who you're up against." The dire threat lost its impact, primarily because it was uttered from behind a tree large enough to hide a small SUV.

Ethan laughed, even as he sent three more snowballs at Keely in rapid-fire succession.

She pelted him with her own arsenal of snowballs. The woman had impressive aim. He dodged to his left, bobbed to the right, but still took one in the chest, another in his left kneecap.

It wasn't until the fight was in full swing that Flicka realized she was missing out on the fun.

Ethan immediately claimed the kid for his team. "You make the snowballs," he said. "I'll throw them."

"Great idea." She dropped to her knees and got to work.

"Hey," Keely called out from behind her tree. "No fair, that's two against one."

"You can have Baloo," he offered, lobbing a slow pitch over the animal's head. The dog caught the snowball midair.

"Gee, thanks, Ethan, how kind of you to even out the odds."

Baloo took another leap, this time catching the snowball Keely fired at Ethan. "I rest my case," she shouted, but he heard the humor in her voice.

Ethan switched jobs with Flicka. After the kid got in a few solid hits, and took one herself, Ethan called a truce.

Keely sauntered out from around her side of the tree. "Giving up already?"

"Brave words from someone covered in snow." He swaggered in her direction, hands out, palms facing her.

Adopting a similar pose, she made her way toward him. When only a few feet separated them, she casually lowered her hands and reached inside her jacket. Smiling sweetly, she lifted herself onto her toes and smashed a handful of snow in his face.

"That's for not fighting fair," she whispered in his ear.

Torn between laughing and revenge, he chose something in between. Roping his arms around her waist, he pulled her flush against him.

"What...what are you doing?"

The words came out a little breathless, egging him on in ways he couldn't begin to describe. "Payback, Keely."

"Ethan, I'm warning you—"

"Yeah, yeah, heard that one before." Blinking snow out of his eyes, he gave Flicka a sidelong glance. "Want to learn how to make a perfect snow angel?"

"I do, I do."

"Your cousin has agreed to demonstrate the proper technique."

Keely gasped. "Ethan, no. Don't. I… I'm…"

"You…you're…what?"

"Cold."

"Nothing like a little physical activity to warm you up. Trust me on this," he whispered in her ear. "I'm a doctor."

Hooking his foot around the back of her knees, he dumped her gently atop the snow-covered ground.

Flat on her back, she glared. "You will pay for this."

The threat was issued as both a challenge and a promise. The woman made him smile.

Hands on hips, he leaned over her. "You're supposed to move your arms up and down, your legs side to side, kind of like jumping jacks on your back."

"I know how to make a snow angel."

Flicka moved in beside him, adding her own words of encouragement. "Come on, Keely, you can do it. Move your arms and legs like Dr. Ethan said."

Lips pressed tightly together, she went through the motions, finishing up by pressing her head back into the snow.

"Well done," Ethan praised, earning him another fierce expression. No doubt about it, Keely O'Toole had a lovely scowl, the kind that made a man stop and take notice.

"You going to stand there grinning at me like a big sap, or help me up?"

He was *really* starting to like this woman.

"Now, pay close attention, Flicka. Making a perfect snow angel is all in the dismount."

Reaching out, he waited for Keely to accept his assistance. She remained unmoving.

He wiggled his fingers.

"Fine." She placed her hands in his, set her heels atop his toes. He yanked her up, catching her against him before her feet touched the ground.

For a dangerous moment, his mind went blank but for the woman in his arms. The world melted away.

"My turn," Flicka declared.

A little mournfully, Ethan set Keely on the ground and then turned to the bouncing child beside him. "Let's find a clean spot in the snow."

Near the property line between the two houses, he dumped the girl gently in the snow, encouraged her to move her arms and legs, then hauled her up.

Back on terra firma, she spun around and studied her snow angel with fierce concentration. "Mine's smaller than Keely's."

"But just as pretty."

"You think so?"

"I know so."

She smiled, her eyes shining from beneath her bright pink ski cap. The child was so sweet, so trusting, so much like another little girl he'd once loved like a daughter. Feeling the pull of memories, Ethan forced himself to stay in the moment.

"Want to help us finish the snowman Keely and I started?"

He pulled in a hard breath. "Sure."

Anything to keep his mind off the past.

Head down, he focused on the mechanics of stacking three snowballs on top of one another, largest to smallest. Keely and Flicka packed snow between the gaps. Baloo offered his assistance by dancing around and eating snow.

"Time to bring the snowman to life." Keely disappeared inside her house and returned with a cowboy hat, a Christmas bandanna, and assorted other items.

They let Flicka do most of the work, and then they all stepped back and admired the finished product. The cowboy hat and bandanna gave the snowman a Western look that somehow worked with the rugged mountains as a backdrop.

"Best snowman ever," Flicka declared, clapping her hands.

Keely met Ethan's gaze. There was something in her smile. Gratitude. Relief. Understanding the sentiment perfectly, he held out his hand for a fist bump, then repeated the process with Flicka. "We make a great team."

"Who wants hot cocoa?" Keely asked.

Ethan wavered between acceptance and retreat. He was already in too deep, grasping for a dream that belonged to his former life, the portion of himself he'd buried with the woman he'd lost on a North Carolina highway.

"We have the tiny marshmallows," Flicka added.

Ethan had no defense against all that little-girl innocence. "Tiny marshmallows are my favorite."

They stomped into Keely's mudroom. Ethan dried off Baloo's paws. Only once he was sure the dog wouldn't track in any unwanted snow or mud did Ethan shed his coat and gloves.

A soft, feminine laugh slipped out of Keely. "Okay, there has to be a story behind that one."

She pointed to his chest when he simply stared at her.

Realizing she meant the slogan on his T-shirt, he looked down. My Favorite Number of the Alphabet Is Blue.

"Olivia gave this to me on my birthday, something about my mind working differently than most."

"So true."

Keely punctuated the statement with a laugh. The sound had Ethan clearing his throat. "Someone mentioned hot cocoa?"

"Follow me."

He paused on the threshold of the kitchen, took in the table speckled with colorful ribbons, wrapping paper and so many sparkles he thought he might have contracted retina-burn.

"Hate to tell you this, Keely, but, uh…" He blinked. "…a glitter bomb went off in your house."

Her snort of amusement was drowned out by Flicka's excited explanation, something about holiday boxes and handmade Christmas cards. The kid spoke fast, but his mind hooked on one word. "You went to school today? That's awesome."

"I'm in Megan and Molly's class."

"Even better."

"I know." She absently petted the dog glued to her side. "Hey, can I take Baloo in the other room and give him a doggy treat?"

The topic change was so swift, Ethan was pretty sure he had whiplash. He managed a nod.

"Great. Come on, Baloo."

The besotted animal followed after the little girl.

Ethan felt a wave of fondness wash over him. "That's one awesome kid."

"She is, isn't she?" Keely maneuvered in beside him and they stood side by side in companionable silence.

Something almost peaceful filled him. "Did you check your calendar?"

"Why?"

"For our trip to the—" He cut off his own words, craned his head around the doorjamb, then whispered, "Animal shelter."

"You still want to help me pick out a dog for Felicity?"

He couldn't understand why that surprised her, but clearly it did. "Well, yeah."

"I'm only available during a small window Friday morning," she said, not quite meeting his eyes, "after I drop Felicity at school and before the lunch crowd descends on the restaurant."

"Friday morning works for me."

Her gaze whipped to his. "Don't you have to see patients?"

"I'll rearrange a few things."

She continued staring at him, as if she couldn't quite believe he wanted to help her. He hated that she thought so little of him, that he'd given her a reason to distrust his motives in their long, complicated relationship. "So, are we a go?"

"We're a go." It was her turn to clear her throat. "I'll…uh, make the hot cocoa while you go check on Felicity and Baloo."

"Trying to get rid of me, O'Toole?"

"What? No. What gave you that idea?"

He laughed at her uneasy tone, a deep, low rumble

in his chest that felt entirely too good. A surge of guilt reared, as if he was betraying Tracy by having so much fun with Keely.

The sensation was all too familiar. "This is becoming a habit," he muttered.

And he didn't only mean the sense of betrayal, but also his desire to hang out with Keely and Flicka when there was no real reason to do so.

His heart was thawing, as if slowly letting go of the family he'd lost and grasping for the one right in front of him. But with caring came too much risk; with love came pain and grief. As long as he kept things shallow between him and Keely, no one would get hurt.

With that in mind, he stayed only long enough to consume one cup of cocoa, then he made his excuses. Keely didn't try to stop him from leaving. In fact, she'd all but rushed him out the door.

It was a good thing, he told himself, they were on the same page. Wasn't it?

The next morning, Keely woke up feeling groggy from a lack of sleep and even more confused over Ethan's speedy retreat after one cup of hot cocoa. She'd sensed him pulling back before he'd taken the first sip. Out of self-preservation, when he'd started making noise about needing to get home, she urged him quickly along.

Shoving the disturbing man out of her mind, she focused on getting Felicity ready for school. The task was far more stressful and chaotic than feeding half the town on St. Patrick's Day. When she eventually steered into the school's carpool line, she discovered she'd forgotten to pack Felicity a lunch.

"I'll do better tomorrow," she promised as she handed over a five-dollar bill. "But you'll have to eat the school's food one more day."

"No worries. A lot of kids buy their lunch."

Not kids with mothers who owned a successful restaurant. Making a lunch was a way to show the little girl she meant to be more than a glorified babysitter. The Lord had brought Felicity into her life, and Keely would honor the privilege of mothering her by being, well, a good mother.

After she dropped Felicity off, the rest of Keely's morning went by quickly. She worked at her restaurant, falling back into a comfortable rhythm with her staff.

By the time most of the lunch crowd had cleared out, she was ready for a break. Actually, what she needed was chocolate.

"I'll be back in fifteen," she told her kitchen manager on her way out the door. She crossed Main Street at a trot, then ducked inside Olivia's Sweet Shoppe.

The aroma of handcrafted chocolates beckoned her further inside. A cluster of café tables encouraged customers like her to sit, sip hot cocoa or enjoy the various chocolates and other treats available to the sugar enthusiast.

Busy helping a customer, Olivia looked modern and chic in her brown twill pants and a pink, fitted T-shirt with the store's logo scrolled across the front. Keely made eye contact with her friend, and then headed to the display case while she waited for Olivia to finish up with the sale.

The pleasant scent of chocolate flowed over her, making her aware she'd skipped lunch. As she snagged a sample of peppermint chocolate bark, her phone vibrated with an incoming text.

She glanced at the screen and shook her head at the message from Ethan, asking if he could skip the parade meeting tonight because Baloo will get lonely if I leave him on his own that long.

Choking on a laugh, she keyed in her response. Don't even think about bailing on me.

His return text had her rolling her eyes. Cut the poor dog a break. He's feeling needy lately.

She fired off another message. Are you still pouting over the camels?

I don't pout, was his reply.

Her fingers flew over the keyboard as she dared him to prove it, by coming to the meeting and actually behaving himself for once.

Her phone rang a second later, the tune from the movie *Jaws* blaring out its ominous two-note warning. She punched the talk button. "I mean it, Ethan. You agreed to be on the committee and I'm not letting you back out now that the real work has begun."

A very low, very masculine sigh filled her ear.

"What's wrong? Got a hot date?" She regretted her words as soon as they came out of her mouth. Now he was going to think she was interested in him in *that way*.

"As a matter of fact..."

She could hear the snarky grin in his voice.

"I do."

"Oh." Disappointment rocked through her, which was really irritating. Ethan might be young, single, successful and good-looking, but now that she thought about it, Keely hadn't seen him with a woman outside of work-related events. She wondered what had changed.

"My date is with a large pepperoni pizza, my needy dog and the rest of the Broncos game I have recorded on my DVR."

The relief she felt came fast and hard, which irritated her even more. All she could manage was another breathless, "Oh."

His amused chuckle did annoying things to her heartbeat. "As much as I hate to admit this, Ethan, I really need you to pull your weight on the committee. The parade route is long and winding, and you know Village Green better than most."

He paused for a long moment. "Fine," he said at last. "I'll be there."

"Don't make me come looking for you."

"I'm half tempted to skip the meeting, if only to see if you'd actually hunt me down."

"You wouldn't like it."

"Says you."

"Ethan—"

"Don't worry. I'll be at the meeting. I'll even bring pizza for the troops."

"You're a good man, Dr. Scott."

"About time you said so."

Both laughing, they disconnected the call at the same time.

What, she wondered, was that? If she didn't know better, she'd say Ethan had been flirting with her, and she with him.

She was still staring at the black screen when her friend came up beside her and pointed to the phone. "Bad news?"

"No." Keely lifted her head. "Why do you ask?"

"You're frowning."

She forced a smile that clearly failed to convince her friend. "Is it Felicity?" Olivia queried.

"No, she's good, and one of the reasons I stopped in." She juggled the phone in her hands. "I was thinking we could set up a sleepover for the girls this Saturday night."

"What a lovely idea." As they discussed the particulars, Olivia's worried expression stayed firmly in place.

"Keely? Are you sure there's nothing bothering you, something you'd like to share with your very best friend?"

"I'm fine. Just a little tired, if you must know."

"I don't doubt you're exhausted." She closed her hand on Keely's arm. "It's just… I don't quite know how to put this, so I'll say it plainly. I'm worried about you."

In that, at least, Keely could put her friend at ease. "My life has changed completely since Felicity moved in with me. And the transition hasn't been completely smooth."

"The change started before your cousin arrived." Olivia took both her hands. "Tell me what's made you so…distracted."

How did Keely explain something she hardly understood herself? Not without sharing the shift in her feelings for Ethan, feelings she was ruthlessly trying to restrain. "It's parade stuff, nothing I can't handle."

Sympathy replaced the worry in Olivia's eyes. "I take it my brother is still giving you a hard time about the camels."

"How on earth do you know about that?"

"Blame it on modern technology." Olivia laughed. "The Village Green Facebook page has several posts about your argument. But don't take my word for it, see for yourself."

Keely thumbed open the appropriate app on her phone and scrolled through the posts. The comment about Ethan putting up a fight over camels pulling Santa's sleigh had three hundred and seventy-eight likes, fifty-nine comments and twelve shares. There was another post with an accompanying picture of Keely and Ethan standing toe-to-toe, caught in the middle of a stare down.

Oddly, instead of looking angry, they looked as if they were having fun, as if they were flirting instead of arguing. The post coined their conflict as *Camelgate* and asked the question *Will we see camels walking the streets of Village Green this Christmas Eve? Or will the good doctor get his way?*

There were four hundred and thirty-two comments already debating the issue, most siding with Keely.

Shaking her head, she closed the app. "People in this town have way too much time on their hands."

"All right, out with it." Olivia pointed an accusing finger at her. "How did you scam Ethan into working on the parade?"

Keely didn't like the implication that she'd twisted Ethan's arm to get him to cooperate. Sure, she'd all but dared him, but he was his own man. He could have said no at any point. "You've got it all wrong. It was your brother's idea to give back to the community."

"Nope, not buying it, what do you have on him?"

"Nothing."

"Oh, it's something, all right."

Irritated on Ethan's behalf, she frowned at her friend. "You're not being fair to your brother. He's devoted to pulling his weight on the committee."

"Look at you, taking up for him. I simply don't know what to think."

"What does that mean?"

Olivia cocked her head. "As long as I've known you, you've never once come to my brother's defense before."

Was she really that contrary when it came to Ethan that his own sister found her defense of his character suspicious? The question haunted her long after she left the chocolate shop.

En route back to the restaurant, Olivia's words floated around in Keely's head. *You've never once come to my brother's defense before.*

Sadly, her friend was right. For years, she'd chosen to see Ethan through the eyes of a humiliated teenager. The hostility hadn't been completely one-sided. But, to his credit, Ethan had made the first step toward reconciliation. It was now up to Keely to adjust her attitude toward the man.

It helped that he'd shown her a new side of himself recently. He'd trudged through a blanket of snow, twice, to check on a sick child, then lent that same scared little girl his dog just to keep her from feeling lonely.

Keely recognized the flutter in her heart. She'd felt it before. She'd been thirteen, infatuated with a boy five years older than her. Falling for Ethan—again—could very well end just as badly as before. With her humiliated and Ethan completely clueless.

No, thank you. Not only wouldn't she do that to herself, but she wouldn't drag Felicity through the emotional maelstrom, either. Perhaps, one day, Keely would fall in love again, with a man who loved her as much as she loved him.

That man would not be Ethan Scott.

Chapter Ten

Not long after disconnecting with Keely, Ethan's phone buzzed again. His gut rolled at the familiar name and number blinking across the screen. He hadn't spoken to Tracy's mother in months, and only three times since the funeral.

Between their last conversation and now, he'd spent more time thinking about his lovely neighbor than the woman he'd vowed to cherish all his life. He felt like a coldhearted jerk.

Nevertheless, he let the call go to voice mail and shoved his past in the dark recesses of his mind. He spent the rest of the afternoon seeing patients. Though he had no idea why, several of them thanked him for his service before he redirected the conversation back to them.

Curiosity had him stopping Connor in the hallway. "What's with all the outpouring of public gratitude for my service?"

Connor's eyebrows shot up. "You're really getting outpourings of gratitude?"

Ethan nodded.

"Then let me add my thanks to the mix, because, dude, when you step up, *you step up*. Man to man, what made you do it?"

Ethan had no idea what Connor was talking about. "Define... *it*."

"Word around town is that you're officially working on the Christmas parade."

"It's true, I am...now, wait just a minute. How do you know this? I've only attended two meetings." As soon as he said the words, he remembered this was Village Green. Gossip traveled faster than the speed of light.

"Village Green's Facebook page is a plethora of information." Connor said this with absolutely no sarcasm in his voice.

It was all in his eyes.

"Village Green has a Facebook page? Why?"

"I would think it's self-explanatory," Connor said, chuckling. "You should check it out sometime. There are even pictures from a parade meeting. One in particular has the town talking, for good reason."

Ethan stared at his partner, partly baffled, partly horrified the Village Green's grapevine had gone digital. And there were pictures. He shuddered. "I'll pass, thanks."

"If it was anyone else, I'd say our newly elected mayor engaged in a fair amount of arm-twisting." Connor shook his head, obviously baffled. "So, tell me, what happened?"

"Wrong place, wrong time."

"I'm thinking there's more to the story, and your lovely neighbor is at the heart of it."

When it came to him and Keely, there was always more to the story. Ethan had been denying the truth of that for months, avoiding her in an attempt to keep her out of his head, and possibly even his heart.

"Well, however it came about, I'm glad you're getting reconnected in the community. It's been a long time coming." Connor clasped his shoulder. "Welcome back to the living."

Ethan flinched. "What's that supposed to mean?"

"You know exactly what it means. Take it from someone who knows, you've been among the walking dead long enough."

Ethan bristled. "It's called mourning. I lost the love of my life." He clenched his teeth. "It's only right to honor her memory."

"By not living your life? By holing yourself up in your house every night, going out only when it's required? That's not honoring her memory, it's living in fear."

"What do you know about it?"

As the words slid past his lips, Ethan knew they were a mistake. Of course Conner understood Ethan's private pain. His friend had lost his wife to cancer, and had spent three years living solely for his daughters and not for himself. Only after Olivia came into his life did things change.

"You want to honor Tracy's memory," Connor said, his tone sympathetic, "start living again, Ethan. It's the best advice I can give."

He knew his friend was probably right. And yet he couldn't help thinking this conversation was somehow a betrayal to everything Tracy had been to him. "I didn't ask for your advice."

"No, you didn't." Connor blew out a sharp breath of

air, started to say more, but Tasha chose that moment to poke her head out from exam room 5.

She pointed at Ethan, then Connor. "Move it, boys. We have patients waiting and a tight schedule to keep."

Duly chastised, Ethan and Connor went their separate ways. Despite the busy afternoon, Ethan left the office with plenty of time to feed and walk Baloo before the parade meeting.

On his way to City Hall, he stopped in Pizza Italiano to pick up the promised pizzas. As he waited for his order, Connor's words came back to him. *You want to honor Tracy's memory, start living again.*

Wasn't that what he was doing? By serving on the parade committee?

Somehow he didn't think that was what Connor meant.

Ethan arrived on time. Flicka saw him the moment he entered the conference room.

"Dr. Ethan. Dr. Ethan." She skidded to a stop inches from him, then eyed the stack of boxes in his hands with obvious interest. "What kind of pizza did you bring?"

He set the boxes on the table. "There's one cheese pizza, one with everything on it and two with pepperoni."

"I looooove pepperoni." Clearly delighted, Flicka thanked him with a fast hug full of little-girl ferocity.

Emotion simmered just beneath his oh-so-calm surface, battling its way to freedom. *Start living again.*

His heart ached with a twinge of yearning, as though what he really wanted was within his grasp, if only he had the courage to reach for it.

He carefully set the girl away from him and focused

on opening the lid of the first pizza box. The rest of the committee swarmed around the food.

Happy for the distraction, Ethan swapped greetings, surprised at how comfortable he felt around these women, solidarity through their joint efforts to put on the best parade the town had ever seen.

He took a quick head count and noticed a glaring omission. He sent a hopeful look in Keely's direction. "Lacy not coming tonight?"

"Oh, she's coming, but she's running late, as usual. If she's not here in ten minutes, we'll start without her."

Nancy Watson, a middle-aged woman once friends with Ethan's mother, went in search of plates and napkins. Mrs. Sweeny, his high school geometry teacher, took orders for anyone who wanted a drink from the soda machine.

As Ethan interacted with the rest of the women in the room, he thought he heard a click that sounded like the camera app on a smartphone. He remembered Connor's words about the Village Green Facebook page. *There are even pictures.*

Feeling mildly violated, Ethan claimed his usual seat beside Flicka. He quickly concluded she was feeling okay. Her color was good and her eyes clear. He felt it safe to ask, "How was school today?"

"Great." She beamed at him. "Did I tell you that Keely and I are going to pick out our Christmas tree this weekend? We're not getting a plastic one, either, but a real live one."

"Make sure it's a Colorado blue spruce, or nothing at all."

"Okay." She dropped her gaze to her lap, but not before Ethan caught the agony in her eyes.

He'd seen the same expression in the mirror in those early weeks after Tracy's death. Sorrow, pain, lost hope. Poor kid.

He wanted to pull the little girl close and tell her everything was going to be all right. But he didn't know that for certain, and he didn't make promises he couldn't keep.

"What's wrong, Flicka?"

She glanced up, her watery eyes glistening under the lights overhead.

"I want to get my mom and Keely Christmas presents." She whispered the words so softly he had to lean forward to hear. "But I don't know how I can."

Relief washed through him. The problem had an easy solution. "I'll take you shopping."

The storm clouds disappeared from her expression. "You…you don't mind?"

"Not at all." Actually, he hated shopping, and couldn't think of a worse activity than flitting from store to store in search of a perfect gift. But the kid had a dilemma and Ethan was in a position to solve it.

"We'll go Saturday. It's my turn to see patients in the morning, but after that I'm free the rest of the day."

"Oh, Dr. Ethan, thank you. Thank you so much."

"You're welcome." He shifted in his chair, wondering how he'd managed to get himself in this deep, this fast.

Panic tried to take root. He'd done nothing out of the ordinary, he told himself. His offer to take the kid shopping wasn't personal. It was what he did. He solved problems.

Keep telling yourself that, Doctor.

Fortunately, Keely called the meeting to order. "The route coordinator and I will do a walk through town next week." She caught Ethan's eye. "If that works for you."

He nodded.

"Great."

The individual reports were next. Because he was the newest member of the team, Ethan went last. "I've met with the Village Green police and fire departments. We're good to go on security and ready for any unforeseen emergencies. The route is also confirmed."

He had Flicka pass out copies of the route map, then wrapped up his report and smiled at Keely. "Back to you."

"Where are we on the camel situation?"

A hush fell over the room and all heads turned to him. "Same as we were last time you asked, and the time before that."

"You haven't even tried to find them, have you?"

"Actually, I have." He lifted the lid of his laptop and opened his email. "As of this morning, I've found a company willing to lend us camels for the day. I'm waiting to hear on the cost for transportation before I commit."

Fully aware all gazes were fixed on him and Keely, he shut the lid of his laptop and smiled smugly at her.

She held his stare. "When will you know for certain?"

He gave a quick, succinct answer. "Soon."

"Give me a ballpark."

The woman was relentless. "Two to three days."

"We're running out of time, Ethan."

Her distress was evident and Ethan realized getting the camels was important to her. "I'll make it happen, Keely." This time, his smile was sincere. "I promise."

A few female sighs filled the room.

"Thank you, Ethan. I trust you won't let me down."

When she looked at him that way, with confidence and respect, he knew he'd pick up the camels himself if that was what it took to have her think that highly of him.

The door swung open and Lacy rushed into the room, drawing all eyes in her direction. The woman certainly knew how to make an entrance. She tossed down her purse. "We have a problem."

"What sort of problem?" Keely asked in a strained voice.

"We no longer have a Santa."

"Oh no!"

Ethan couldn't blame Keely for that small moment of alarm. Santa was the highlight of the parade. First the camels, and now Santa?

"What happened, Lacy? Ralph Donovan has always done such a great job in years past. He—" Keely broke off, then glanced at Felicity. "Sweetie, would you mind getting me a soda from the machine?"

"Okay."

Once the child left the room, a dollar bill clutched in her palm, Keely addressed Lacy once again. "You told us at the last meeting that Ralph was confirmed."

Lacy lifted a silk-clad shoulder. "He wants nothing to do with a sleigh being pulled by camels. He says they spit."

Ethan gave Keely an ironic tilt of his head. It took everything in him not to say I told you so.

Hips swaying, Lacy maneuvered around the table and then sat in Felicity's empty seat. "You know, Ethan, I'm thinking you could rock a Santa suit."

Caught completely off guard by such a ridiculous

suggestion, he gaped at the woman a full two seconds. Mistake.

Warming to the idea, the committee began talking over one another, delightfully hashing out the possibility of Ethan taking over for Ralph. They tossed out a large number of pros, a few cons, then a whole lot more pros.

Keely attempted to regain order. She even tried to explain why Ethan couldn't possibly be the route coordinator *and* Santa, without success.

Short of coming off as a Scrooge, Ethan was stuck. The news was probably already up on Facebook. He didn't know whether to say ho-ho-ho or bah humbug.

"You okay with this?" Keely asked him over the excited chatter.

He shrugged.

"Okay, then, problem solved. We have us a Santa after all."

Cheers erupted in the room.

Two days after the disastrous parade meeting, Ethan still wasn't sure how he'd ended up with the conspicuous job of Santa, in a sleigh pulled by camels. Camels he was now tasked with finding because he'd promised Keely he wouldn't let her down.

The woman standing beside him outside Village Green's animal shelter had to realize this was her fault. She'd clearly lost control of her committee. By the glances she threw his way, no doubt Keely was waiting for him to back out at any minute.

Ethan could ease her mind, let her know he would follow through on his word, but what would be the fun in that?

Just to annoy her, he released a long-suffering sigh.

"I'm really sorry, Ethan. If you don't want to be Santa I'm sure I'll find someone else."

There was a note of desperation in her voice. Obviously, locating another Santa at this late date wouldn't be easy.

"It's no big deal, Keely, a couple hours on a parade float." He'd made a promise. He would follow through, unless he could con Ryder into filling in for him. One Scott brother was the same as the other.

Keely blinked up at him, her eyes soft, a little dreamy. Had he put that look on her face?

"Come on. Let's get out of this frigid wind and pick out Flicka's Christmas present."

They entered the animal shelter in silence. The foyer was decorated with pinecones, garland, red poinsettia plants and a large wreath on the front of the welcome desk.

The place might look like Christmas. It did not smell like Christmas. The scent of industrial cleaner failed to mask the fragrant odor of Eau de Wet Dog.

"Oh, Ethan, I have no idea how I'm going to choose."

"That's why I'm here."

Nodding, she started for the desk.

Ethan stopped her with a hand on her arm. "Before we go any further, I want you to repeat after me. 'I can only get one.'"

She made a face. "Is that really necessary?"

The innocent question told him she'd never been inside an animal shelter. He had an instant need to protect her, to bundle her up and hustle her out of the building. With her big soft heart, this process was going to be hard on her. For days, maybe even weeks, her dreams

were going to be haunted by all the little furry faces she had to leave behind.

"Say the words, Keely." He pressed his face inches from hers. "'I can only get one'."

"Oh, honestly." She rolled her eyes. "'I can only get one.'"

"Again, and this time with conviction."

"I. Can. Only. Get. One."

"Now you're ready." He stepped back. "After you."

Head tilted at a haughty angle, she approached the welcome desk and stated her desire to adopt a dog. The teenage girl behind the counter handed them over to an older woman with a wiry build, thick glasses and gray, springy hair. She introduced herself as Margo.

"I'm Keely and this is Ethan."

"Follow me." As Margo escorted them into the kennel area, she fired off several initial questions, then asked, "Is there a specific type of dog you're looking for?"

"Not really. I originally thought I wanted a puppy, but I'm open to other options."

"That's good to know. Sometimes the older dogs get ignored this time of year." Margo unlocked a gate and led the way into a long walkway with wire kennels on either side.

Keely entered next, Ethan right behind her.

Even from this distance, they were confronted with a menagerie of breeds, sizes and ages. Ethan couldn't stand the neediness, the sorrow, the silent plea for rescue. He hardened his heart to their plight. Either that or Baloo would have a sibling before nightfall.

Evidently facing her own struggles, Keely muttered, "I can only get one. I can only get one. I can only get one."

He took her hand. "We can come back another time."

"No." She drew in a sharp breath. "I want to do this, for Felicity."

"For Felicity," he repeated, even as he felt the tug of a dozen conflicting emotions in his gut.

Like so many of the animals behind the cage doors, Ethan felt abandoned, with an empty future ahead of him. He could never reclaim the dreams he'd lost. But maybe, like some of the animals here, he could reach for a new one.

Was he ready to take the risk? To confront the possibility of another loss, for the sake of what he could gain? He thought maybe he was. But if he took the leap, what would it mean to Tracy's memory?

If he were a praying man, now would be a good time to lift up a petition for clarity.

Keely pulled her hand free, took a deep breath and then began the arduous process of choosing a dog. She moved from cage to cage, stopping, assessing, then repeating the process on the other side of the aisle.

Ethan felt her internal battle as if it were his own.

They came to the end of the kennel area. Keely retraced her steps. On this second pass, she paused at only one cage. For several seconds she studied the brown-and-white dog with the long, shiny coat and soulful black eyes. He—or she—wasn't quite a puppy, but not fully mature, either, probably somewhere between five and six months old. The handwritten placard on the kennel read Cupcake, Male, Mixed Breed.

Keely lowered herself to her knees and started speaking softly to the docile animal. The poor little guy had a distant look in his eyes and a collapsed posture, clear signs of mistreatment from his previous owner.

"I don't know, Keely, he seems pretty timid. If he's been abused he could prove difficult to train."

Waving off his concerns, she swung her gaze to Margo. "What's his history?"

When the woman gave Keely a glowing report, Ethan asked the most pertinent question. "How long has he been here?"

"Nearly three months," she admitted.

Not a good sign. Ethan expressed his concerns.

Margo glowered. "I blame it on the internet. There are too many how-to-pick-a-dog articles out there warning people off timid animals like Cupcake. All he needs is a little love, a safe environment and some patience."

Ethan wasn't convinced.

Reading his hesitation accurately, Keely parked her hands on her hips. "Remind me again about the day you found Baloo in Afghanistan."

On one of his many lunch breaks at Senor O'Toole's, Ethan had told Keely how he'd found Baloo in a burned-out hut, cowering in a corner. The dog had been even more timid than Cupcake.

"I seem to remember you saying something about Baloo blossoming once he knew he was safe and loved."

Point taken. Three years later, Baloo was one of the friendliest dogs in Village Green. He never met a person—or animal—he couldn't get along with, including cats.

Keely leaned into his personal space. "You think Baloo knows he was rescued?"

The woman was—no pun intended—like a dog with a bone.

"You win." Ethan lifted his hands in surrender. "It's your choice."

She pointed to Cupcake. "I'd like to take him into one of the get-to-know-you rooms."

An hour later, paperwork complete, Ethan drove away from the animal shelter with Flicka's new dog tucked in a borrowed carrier on the backseat of his SUV.

They made a stop at a local pet store, then were back on the road. Halfway into their neighborhood, Keely placed a hand on his right biceps. "Thank you again for agreeing to keep Cupcake at your house until Christmas morning. Felicity will be so surprised when you bring him over."

Ethan had tried to talk himself out of making the offer. Yet he'd made it anyway. "Baloo can use the company."

"It's not too late to change your mind. I can ask Beau to keep Cupcake at his house." She pulled out her cell phone, waved it back and forth. "Just say the word."

"Don't call your brother. It's less than two weeks to Christmas. What could possibly go wrong?" A thousand things, he knew, but a lot could go right.

Tucking her phone back in her purse, Keely relaxed. "At least let me come over and take care of him."

That was precisely what Ethan didn't want. Having Keely in his house daily was too cozy, too couple-like.

"You'll hardly know I'm there," she persisted.

He opened his mouth to volunteer Ryder for the job, but found himself saying, "I'll get you a key to the back door."

Chapter Eleven

After a few sniffs and a handful of circling each other, Cupcake and Baloo became fast friends. It seemed the puppy's transition was going to be easier than Felicity's. That was something to celebrate. Wanting to share her pleasure with Ethan, Keely glanced over at him.

He wasn't watching the dogs. He was watching her, closely. And yet his expression was carefully neutral.

"Thanks again for letting Cupcake bunk at your house."

"No problem." He flashed a smile, the one that turned her stomach into a trampoline for an entire family of butterflies. "I kind of like the little guy."

Reaching down, he scratched the puppy's head.

"Don't get too attached, Dr. Scott. Cupcake is an O'Toole man through and through."

Ethan's smile moved into his eyes. "Please tell me you're going to change his name."

"I'll let Felicity decide."

"I suppose that makes sense." Eyes locked with hers, he straightened. He took a step toward her, just one, yet the air in the room suddenly changed, becoming charged with energy.

Their relationship was shifting into new territory, though she doubted neither of them would admit that out loud.

He took another step. She took one herself, until they were standing face-to-face, mere inches apart, so close that she could see the countless shades of blue in his eyes.

"Is this a bad idea?" she asked him.

"Probably."

Not sure if they were talking about the puppy, or something else entirely, she held her position.

Ethan remained unmoving, as well. The tension was thick in the air between them, but not altogether unpleasant.

"We should head back to work."

Breathless for no good reason, Keely nodded. The silent standoff continued. Neither of them moved.

Then Ethan's head drew a shade closer. He was going to kiss her. She didn't know whether to be overjoyed or terrified. Holding her breath, she remained steady, waiting, watching.

His lips touched hers, barely a whisper; then he snapped back and put a polite distance between them. "I'll…uh, get that key I promised."

She choked on a breathless sigh. "I'll wait here."

The air felt lighter with him out of the room. Staring at nothing in particular, she reached up and touched her mouth. Ethan had barely pressed his lips to hers and yet the moment had felt special, life altering.

Needing something to do with her hands, she reached

down to pet the puppy. Ethan returned with the key and handed it to her.

Their fingers were still touching when Ryder shuffled into the kitchen. Keely jumped back, away from Ethan. She didn't know why she felt so guilty. Ryder hadn't even noticed her yet.

Sleep-rumpled, his hair sticking out from nearly every angle, Ryder let out a jaw-cracking yawn. He wore faded jeans that looked a million years old, an equally ancient sweatshirt and a tired grimace.

The Scott men looked alike, but this one favored Ethan the most. They had the same cobalt-blue eyes, long black eyelashes and bold slash of eyebrows beneath a full head of black hair.

Ryder swept a glance over the room in general. "Morning."

Voice strained, Keely responded in kind.

"Keely?" His gaze narrowed, and he glanced from Keely to Ethan and then back to her. "What are you doing in my kitchen?"

"She's with me." Ethan maneuvered to stand slightly in front of her, as if to shield her from his own brother.

"Let me get this straight." Ryder stared at his brother. "You're in the same room with Keely…willingly?"

Well, ouch. Didn't take a rocket scientist to decipher the meaning behind Ryder's shocked reaction.

Keely didn't know why she was so surprised. Prior to her call for help with Felicity, Ethan had made a point of keeping his distance from her. She'd avoided him, as well.

Still, Ryder's words hurt.

She told herself the opinion of others didn't matter. She didn't need to win earthly favor. Only what God thought of her truly mattered. Except there were times when Keely did care what others thought of her. What did that say about her?

Not liking this insight into her character, she cut a quick glance at Ethan. His eyes were on his brother and he'd flattened his lips into a hard, grim line. He looked as though he was about to tear into Ryder. On her behalf.

How utterly fascinating. And really, really sweet.

She choked out what she hoped was a mild laugh and adopted a casual stance. "Come on, Ryder. Ethan comes into my restaurant at least three times a week."

"Sometimes more than that. I enjoy Keely's company."

Ryder scoffed at this. "Since when?"

Keely flicked another glance at Ethan. Quiet, calm, expression closed, he held her gaze.

She shifted her attention back to Ryder. He was leaning against the counter, eyes on her. But where Ethan's gaze was inscrutable, Ryder's was full of brotherly concern. For her.

"Don't read too much into this, Ryder. Ethan and I were just dropping off my little cousin's Christmas present."

On cue, a happy yip cut through the tension in the room.

Ryder zeroed in on the canine wrestling match at his feet. "Either I'm seeing double or there are two dogs at my feet."

"Ryder, meet Cupcake." She reached down and picked up the puppy, holding him as much as a shield as a means to give the man a better look. "Felicity's Christmas present."

Ryder's face went blank. "Who's Felicity?"

"Keely's cousin. I told you about her." Ethan's words were meant as an explanation, but sounded more like a scold. "She's the little girl that moved in with Keely last weekend."

"I thought her name was Flicka."

"Felicity *is* Flicka. They're one and the same."

"Right, got it." Yawning, Ryder ran a hand over his tired face. "What time is it, anyway?"

Ethan glanced at the chunky black watch on his wrist. "Quarter till eleven."

"Earlier than I thought. No wonder I feel like someone parked a tractor on my head."

By the gravelly quality of his voice and the half-glazed eyes, it was clear they'd interrupted Ryder's sleep. Keely winced in chagrin. "Tell me we didn't wake you."

"Nope, hunger woke me." He reached for an apple, took a loud, crunching bite. He continued staring at Keely, then Ethan, then Keely again. "You two, together in the same room. Huh."

Ethan made a sound in his throat that was just short of a growl. "Go back to bed, Ryder."

Apple in hand, Ryder headed toward the living room, then paused in the doorway. His gaze dipped to the dog in her arms, then returned to her face. He appeared about to say something, then seemed to change his mind. "Bye, Keely."

"Bye, Ryder."

She waited until he was out of earshot before breaking her silence. "That was awkward."

"A little bit."

Sighing, she hugged the puppy closer. He gave her

chin a swipe of his pink tongue, then settled comfortably in her arms.

"Ryder's been working the night shift all week. His internal clock is way off. He probably won't even remember seeing you this morning."

She let out a mirthless laugh. "A gal can hope."

He took the puppy from her arms and gently set him on the floor. "Let's finish getting Flicka's dog settled in and then I'll drive you back to the restaurant."

As if by silent agreement, they said nothing more about the kiss that, from Keely's point of view, wasn't really a kiss. Like a well-oiled machine they worked in tandem making Cupcake comfortable in his temporary home.

Back in her restaurant, Keely walked into the kitchen and did what she did best. She took charge. Elbow deep in orders, she told herself nothing had changed between her and Ethan.

Deep down, she knew that wasn't true.

Everything had changed.

At the memory of being wrapped in his arms for those brief seconds, feeling warm and safe and cherished, her eyes shut of their own accord. Ethan's lips had barely touched hers, but she'd felt treasured on a level she hadn't realized existed.

Had Ethan experienced a similar connection?

The question unsettled her. Because whether or not her handsome neighbor had been affected by her, she'd been affected by him. There could be no going back to the way things were between them. Of course, that didn't mean Keely couldn't try.

With renewed resolve, she opened her eyes and went to work feeding the hungry lunch crowd.

* * *

Saturday morning dawned cloudless and bitter cold. Although Ethan would rather stay in bed, he had two dogs requiring his attention. He dressed quickly, then trudged down the stairs and into the kitchen. Pink-tinted light bathed the room in a soft, welcoming glow.

Not yet fully awake, he glanced at the thermometer as he filled the dogs' empty food bowls. Overnight, the outside temperature had dipped to an inhuman five degrees Fahrenheit.

Once they'd consumed their breakfast, both animals gave him identical expressions of need. "Hang tight, boys."

He pulled out his phone and texted Keely, asking if the coast was clear. She sent him a quick thumbs-up emoticon, followed by three smiley faces.

"We're good to go."

Shoving his arms in his heaviest coat, he opened the back door and stepped back. Baloo and Cupcake bulleted past him. Both dogs seemed oblivious of the dangerously cold air. Blowing into his cupped palms, Ethan pulled up the hood and huddled deeper inside his coat.

The sun had barely made its appearance in the east, but the sky was already a spectacular explosion of color. Ethan might not be on the best of terms with the Lord, but that didn't mean he couldn't appreciate the artistry of His handiwork. Looking at the wonder of God's creation, he didn't doubt He existed.

What he had a harder time grasping was why the Lord allowed some people to die young, and others to live into old age. Why cancer ravaged an otherwise healthy body, yet a person with terrible eating habits never got sick.

It all seemed so random. Ethan couldn't begin to comprehend God's unfathomable ways, or understand why the Lord allowed tragic car accidents to happen to good people. *Why, Lord?*

He'd asked the question a thousand times, had received the same silent response. Familiar agitation reared. He tried to pace off the sensation in the thick snow. The troubling doubt only grew, stretching and snapping inside his gut.

The creak of door hinges had him looking across Keely's backyard. Bundled in a thick, oversize coat and snow boots, she exited her house and trotted over to him. Welcoming the interruption, he focused solely on the woman approaching him with a smile.

Keely's face was free of cosmetics, and her hair was a red, flaming cloud of curls framing her exquisite face.

She'd never looked more beautiful. The last time they'd been this close, this alone, Ethan had pulled her into his arms and briefly kissed her. He'd tried to put the moment out of his mind, had nearly succeeded, but now that she stood barely a foot away he could think of nothing else.

"Hey," he said around the lump lodged in his throat.

"Hey."

They stared at each other for several beats. Her eyes were warm, full of unspoken words. His heart squeezed.

She shifted her stance. "You ready for tonight?"

He lifted an eyebrow.

"The walk-through of the parade route."

"Right, yeah, sure. Flicka coming, too?"

"She's spending the night with Molly and Megan. It'll just be the two of us."

He didn't know whether to be pleased or worried. The

kid acted as a nice buffer. Cupcake, misjudging speed and distance, slammed into Keely's booted ankles.

"Well, hello there." She scooped up the puppy.

Clearly happy to see her, the animal showered her with doggy kisses. Her throaty laugh added to Ethan's agitation.

He looked away, fought for control, searched his mind for an innocuous topic. "Where's Flicka?"

"Fast asleep." She dodged another round of sloppy dog kisses, then set the puppy on the ground. "It was nice of you to offer to take her Christmas shopping, but it's not necessary. I'm free this afternoon. I can—"

"She asked me for a reason, Keely." He watched, mildly affronted, as her smile dropped into a scowl. "You got a problem with me spending time alone with Flicka?"

"I trust you with her, it's just…" Sighing, she twisted the tails of her scarf between her fingers. "I don't understand why she asked you to take her shopping instead of me."

"Think about it, Keely. Why wouldn't she want you to take her Christmas shopping?"

"I don't know, I—Oh." She lifted her hands, let them flutter to her sides. "*Oh*. She wants to buy me a gift."

He tapped her on the nose. "Bingo."

"And you agreed to help her pick out my present?"

"Two for two."

"Oh, Ethan." She gave him a watery smile. "How completely, utterly sweet of you both."

Giving him no chance to respond, she leaped forward, planted a brief kiss on his lips, then bounced out of reach.

His heart took a direct hit.

He'd always had a soft spot for Keely. Even as kids, he'd considered it his duty to look out for her, to protect her. But this warmth spreading through him felt like something more than duty, something more than friendship, something…lasting.

Every muscle in his back tightened.

"I should get back inside, before Felicity wakes up and comes looking for me."

Cheeks bright pink, she gave him a smile that nearly brought him to his knees. At her back door, she paused and then pulled out her phone. Her thumbs tapped across the screen.

At the same moment she lifted her head, his phone buzzed with an incoming text. He didn't have to guess who it was from.

Smiling like a sap, he retrieved his phone and read Keely's message. Thanks for being so wonderful with Felicity. xoxox

The fact that she put her gratitude in writing, where he could see it for as long as he kept the text on his phone, touched him in ways he couldn't explain. But it was the *x*'s and *o*'s—hugs and kisses—that really got to him. His heart pounded so hard he felt each beat at the base of his neck.

He looked up, expecting to catch her watching for his reaction, but she'd already vanished inside her house.

He lowered his head again, noticed the voice mail from Mrs. Jenkins still waiting for him. After herding the dogs back inside the house, then making sure they had fresh water, he forced himself to listen to the message.

Bracing himself as if heading into battle, he punched the screen, then pulled the phone up to his ear.

Unmistakable sadness flowed through him as the familiar voice said, "Ethan, hi, it's me, Phyllis, Tracy's mother."

She spoke with a tentative rasp, as if there were a possibility he would forget who she was and how they were connected.

He listened to the rest of the voice mail like a man facing a firing squad. It wasn't until he put the phone back in his pocket that he realized the magnitude of the woman's request and what it would cost him. Tracy's mother wanted him at yet another memorial service for her daughter. She also wished for Ethan to be the one to scatter Tracy's ashes over her favorite lake.

He'd already said goodbye to his fiancée at her military funeral. He couldn't go through a second ceremony. He shouldn't have to, *none* of them should, which was why he'd urged her family to scatter her ashes that day. Her mother had protested, claiming she wanted her daughter with her a little while longer.

Now, nearly eighteen months later, Phyllis was finally ready to let Tracy go. Ethan was happy she was seeking closure, but he wanted no part of the process. He deleted the message.

The rest of the morning, he focused on work. He gave his patients his full attention. Whenever he found himself with a free moment, his thoughts wanted to dwell on the past. Yet every time he thought of Tracy, he struggled to bring up a clear image.

To make matters worse, Keely's likeness kept encroaching at the oddest moments. More and more he saw past the bristle and droll humor to the sweet, vulnerable woman beneath.

He shoved both women out of his head.

At five minutes to noon, he saw his last patient for the day. Mrs. Collier was an eighty-eight-year-old woman with a bad heart, struggling to survive on Social Security, and had a penchant for making him cookies as payment for his services. The old girl couldn't hear half of what he said. But he liked her.

When she left his office Ethan was in possession of a dozen cookies and a lighter heart. He walked the block and half to Senor O'Toole's. The place was swarming with customers, which suited his purposes perfectly. He stole Flicka away after a quick, perfunctory conversation with Keely.

One block later, he escorted the little girl into the first, and hopefully last, shop of the day. The Emporium was touted as Village Green's premier gift shop, specializing in everything from vintage tea sets to antique hair clips to all things female.

According to Ethan's sister, this was *the* place to buy a special gift for a woman. Flicka seemed to agree. Her delighted chatter filled the store.

"There are so many choices," she breathed.

That was an understatement.

It took less than two minutes for Ethan to realize he was in over his head. He was just about to call in the big guns, aka his sister, Olivia, when a teenage girl with a mouthful of braces approached him and Flicka. "How can I help you?"

Ethan let out a breath of relief. "We're looking for a Christmas gift for a woman."

"Actually, we're looking for two gifts," Flicka corrected. "One for my mom and one for my cousin Keely 'cause I love her and she's getting me a real tree. Isn't that cool?"

"Very." The salesgirl asked a few questions about both women, then began guiding Flicka through the store.

Happy to hand over the reins, Ethan wandered around on his own. A display of porcelain dolls caught his eye. Impressed with the intricacy of their clothes, he moved closer. One in particular pulled at him. The curly blond hair and big blue eyes looked so much like Flicka it was as if the kid had personally modeled for the doll-maker.

"Hey, Flicka, look at this." He plucked the toy off the table and presented it to the girl.

"She's super pretty." With tentative fingers, she reached out and touched the lacy green dress. "Hey, she kind of looks like me. Can we get her for my mom?"

He had no idea if a woman in prison was allowed such a luxury, but this was Flicka's decision. They'd figure out the logistics later. "If that's what you want."

She considered the doll with a thoughtful expression.

"Did you know my mommy is in prison?" Dropping her hand, she rolled her big, innocent eyes up to him. "She stole money that wasn't hers."

At the matter-of-fact delivery of this piece of information, Ethan's gut twisted so hard he had to swallow to catch his breath. "I'm sorry, Flicka."

"Me, too." She heaved another sigh. "Keely says everyone makes mistakes and my mommy is real sorry for what she did."

"I'm sure she is."

"If we get this doll for her, then maybe, when she's lonely and misses me, she can hug her real hard and not be so sad."

Throat thick, Ethan smoothed a hand over the bent

head. The kid might as well have reached inside his chest and ripped out his heart. "That's a nice thought."

"So I can get this doll for my mom?"

"Consider it done."

The very corner of her mouth turned up. "Now I just have to find something for Keely."

As she headed over to a table with women's scarves and jewelry, Ethan fully understood Keely's desire to make this Christmas special for Flicka. She was such a great kid, with a tender, thoughtful heart. She deserved the best in life and definitely a great holiday season.

Maybe he could help with a little recon. He drew near the kid. "Have you thought about what you want for Christmas?"

"Oh, yes. I think about it all the time." Her eyes settled on him with a clarity that gave him a bad feeling in the pit of his stomach. "I want a daddy of my very own."

"Is that so?" he croaked out.

"I've never had a daddy before." The wistful look she sent him shot past every defense he'd erected around his heart.

Ethan desperately wanted to make this child happy, but he couldn't give her what she wanted. It would be wrong to lead her on for even a minute. He tried to diffuse the situation.

"With Christmas only a few weeks away," he said slowly, choosing his words carefully, "it's kind of short notice. I don't think we'll be able to find you a daddy by then."

"I guess that makes sense." Shoulders slumped, head lowered, she rummaged through the scarves with lifeless flicks.

The kid's sorrow twisted Ethan's gut in all kinds of

knots. Something stirred inside him, something stronger than frustration. Panic, or a desperate desire to fulfill her wish personally?

That kind of thinking would only end in disappointment for them all, especially Flicka. Again, Ethan redirected the conversation. "What else is on your Christmas list?"

Her hand paused. "Well...if I can't have a daddy, then there's only one other gift I want."

"What would that be?"

"A puppy."

Chapter Twelve

"Have fun, sweetie." Keely waved to a grinning Felicity as the child climbed into Olivia's SUV behind the Mitchell twins. Felicity's blond curls were loose and blowing across her face, her expression full of excitement for her sleepover.

So different from the little girl Keely had picked up at the Denver Airport the day after Thanksgiving. Felicity had come off the plane wearing dark shadows beneath her sad, red-rimmed eyes. She'd been wary of Keely at first, full of pain, but determined to make the most of her situation with the resilience that only came from the innocence of youth.

Barely three weeks in Village Green and Felicity was starting to look and act like a normal child, no dark circles under her eyes, much less hidden pain in their depths, and for that Keely lifted up a prayer of thanksgiving.

As Olivia's black SUV turned the corner and the taillights disappeared from sight, Keely went back inside her restaurant.

Checking her watch, she gasped. She barely had

time to get home, tame her unruly hair and apply fresh makeup before Ethan picked her up to walk the parade route. As she hurried home, she admitted, if only to herself, that she was looking forward to spending the evening with him.

A little hum of excitement sounded in her throat. Her relationship with her neighbor was long and complicated, made up of tension and laughter and a slew of emotions difficult to describe. There was a lot of water beneath their bridge, spiked with hurt feelings on her side, masculine wariness on his.

Keely didn't blame Ethan for her perceived hurts from the past. Well, okay, she didn't blame him anymore. Sighing, she stared at her image in the mirror of her bathroom, seeing the child she'd been, not the woman she'd become.

She'd grown up shy and awkward in her own skin. Her twin brother had been the opposite. Beau had been born cool, with an easiness that people gravitated toward.

Not Keely. She'd struggled with low self-esteem, the condition exacerbated when her body had developed earlier than other girls her age. She'd received instant attention from older boys with impure motives. She knew that now, as she looked back on those days with the eyes of a woman.

Ethan hadn't treated her as his equal back then. But he hadn't been cruel, either. He'd shown her genuine respect and had looked out for her when others had only wanted to cause her harm. And…and…

No, oh, Lord, no. Not him, not now.

Keely's face drained of color as the truth settled over her. She was falling in love with Ethan. Maybe she was already there. Hope bloomed beneath the shock and panic, but she denied the emotion, fought for air. For several, long seconds she forced her mind to calm, her breathing to slow.

How had she let down her guard? *When* had she let it down?

Had it been that Sunday night he'd come over to her house to check on Felicity? Had it been sometime after, or perhaps even before? What did it matter?

Miserable, she stared at her unnaturally pale reflection. Her emotions were there, in her eyes, making them appear a bright, brilliant green. A dozen thoughts fluttered like hummingbird wings through her mind.

Ethan must not be allowed to know the change in her feelings for him. Tucking away her fears, she freshened up her makeup, fluffed her hair, then went in search of the man who'd battered down her defenses without her permission. Typical Ethan.

When she opened the door to him, he gave her a boyish grin and her stomach hit her toes.

Why did he have to be so good-looking? He wore faded jeans and yet another T-shirt—Never Trust an Atom. They Make Up Everything—beneath the heavy coat he'd just unzipped.

"Good evening, Keely." Genuine affection threaded through the words. "Ready to take a walk through town?"

Unable to speak with her tongue stuck to the roof of her mouth, she smoothed a hand over her hair and simply nodded.

"Great. Let's go." He took her hand and guided her to his car.

Once they were in town, standing on the sidewalk that paralleled Main Street, she washed out her lungs with deep, calming breaths. The night was cold and clear and a paper-thin moon was visible above the mountain peaks. The buildings in town sparkled with thousands of tiny Christmas lights. The storefronts were decorated with garland, holly and wreaths. She breathed in again. This time the scent of pine filled her.

Proving he'd come prepared, Ethan dug into his pocket and whipped out a map with the parade route outlined in red. "I figure we can start our walk-through outside the Turkey Roost, since that's close to where the parade will begin."

"Works for me."

As he refolded the map, a gust of wind lifted hair off his forehead, revealing the granite-hard features that had become so dear to her. An odd feeling went through her, the kind of heady sensation that teenage girls got when they had a crush.

Get control of yourself. He's still the same big, bad, frustrating bane of your existence.

Keely attempted to smile, was pleased to see him return the gesture. Ethan Scott had an amazing smile. When she continued staring at him, he cocked an eyebrow and waited with a mock patience that sent her temper spiking.

"Go ahead," he urged. "I'm waiting."

"For what?"

"For the snarky comment. I can see it in your eyes. Let's have it, O'Toole." He leaned over her, his eyes glinting with familiar challenge. "Hit me with your best shot."

Her muscles went taut at the teasing note in his voice. And then a funny thing happened. She relaxed.

This was Ethan. *Her* Ethan, the man who came into her restaurant regularly. The man who calmed her fears over a sick child. The man who took her to the animal shelter, and then held her hand through the process of choosing just one.

"I've got nothing."

"Nothing? Give me a pen. I have to write this down."

A flash of affection swept across her soul, which she transformed into a smile. "Ha-ha."

His eyes went serious. Reaching up, he ran the pad of his thumb across her cheek. "You're beautiful, Keely."

He'd never called her beautiful before, and because she saw the sincerity in his eyes, everything in her softened. "That's the first time you've ever said that to me."

"That can't be right. Are you sure?"

"Positive."

"Well, then." He dropped his hand. "I look forward to rectifying that gross injustice as often as possible."

"Oh, Ethan."

She no more conquered the emotion welling inside her when he draped his arm over her shoulders. "Come on, O'Toole. Let's check out the route, look for any potential snags, then, if you're really nice, I'll buy you dinner at Pizza Italiano."

"Sounds like a plan."

They fell into easy conversation as they walked the two-mile parade route through town.

Ethan told her about his college days and how tough it had been juggling school and work while also raising his three younger siblings. Keely told him about her job at the modeling agency and how she'd loved working in the business office so much she'd taken it upon herself to earn her business degree by attending night classes.

A light snowfall began as they drew near the parade's finish line. The good news was that they were less than a block north of Pizza Italiano. The restaurant was known for serving the best lasagna in Village Green.

Once again, Ethan issued his dinner invitation with the sincerity of a man asking a woman on a date.

Under the circumstances, with her emotions riding just below the surface, there was only one answer to the question. "Yes, Ethan, I would love to have dinner with you."

Pleased Keely had accepted his invitation, Ethan placed his hand on the small of her back and guided her across the street. With Christmas barely a week away, the crowd of holiday shoppers was thick on the sidewalks. People came and went from store to store, laughing and calling out to friends.

Carolers dressed in period costumes wove their way through the tangle of humanity, their voices lifted in perfect harmony as they sang the most popular songs of the season. The mood was festive, happy, and Ethan found himself humming along to "Silent Night." Keely joined him.

He took her hand, smiled into her sea-green eyes, then glanced up. The sky was midnight silk. The multitude of stars sparkled like diamonds on the black velvet backdrop. A blast of cold air managed to sneak under his collar.

Ethan reached around Keely, opened the door and waited for her to enter ahead of him. With her usual grace, she glided past him, head high, shoulders square. Her scent of lavender and wild orchid lingered in her wake, even as the unmistakable smells of tomato sauce and fresh-baked bread wafted on the air.

The place was busy, but there were still seats available. As they were led to a table for two, Ethan noticed how Keely's hair sparkled with melting snowflakes under the restaurant's lights. The woman fascinated him. This vivid awareness worried him, even as a wave of emotion washed through him.

There was a tenderness in him he'd experienced for only one other woman, a willingness to sacrifice his own needs for hers, to go the distance no matter the obstacles.

His shoulders felt heavy, as did his feet. A part of him was tired of fighting his attraction for Keely—his neighbor, his friend. Even as the thought formed, guilt whipped through him. Tracy's private memorial was in a few days and even though he had no plans to attend, Ethan's mind wasn't supposed to be on another woman.

Keely smiled at him from over her shoulder and he felt a portion of his burden lift. He'd said goodbye to Tracy. She'd want him to move on. Could he take another chance at love, knowing how precarious life was, how quickly he could lose everything? He shifted around Keely and pulled out her chair.

"Thank you," she whispered.

"My pleasure." Without thinking too hard about what he was doing, he leaned forward and pressed his hand over hers. "Hope you're hungry."

"Starving." She rotated her wrist until their palms were touching. For a brief moment, he saw his own tumultuous feelings reflected in her eyes.

Could they be more than—

Did they dare try to—

Cutting off each thought before it fully materialized, he rounded the table and took the chair facing Keely.

The waiter soon arrived and took their orders. Lasagna for them both.

As the waiter walked away, Keely smiled.

Ethan felt another burst of attraction, stronger than the one before. "I like you, Keely." He took her hand again. "More than I think you realize."

"I like you, too, Ethan." Her voice was wistful, wary. "I've enjoyed our time together these past few weeks, more than I thought possible."

He laughed at the grudging admission. "I don't know if you mean that as a compliment or an insult."

"Maybe a little of both." She pulled her hand free, cocked her head to the side as if she could see straight through the inside of his brain. "You do a good job of keeping people at a distance. For all the time we've spent together, I still don't feel as though I truly know you."

Picking at the tongs of his fork, he thought through her words, as if glimpsing himself for the first time from another's perspective. He saw a man alone, needing no one, seeking no one's help. The words from a long-ago sermon came to him. *Man is made to be in community.*

"You're right. I do keep others at a distance," he admitted for the first time in his life. "I have since my parents' car accident. From the moment I was forced to identify their bodies, I've always been the one others turn to for help."

"Who do you turn to?"

"No one."

"Sounds like a lonely existence."

His life was lonely. Or rather it had been, until Keely had called the house phone in a panic. Nothing had been the same since, and he wasn't entirely sorry for the change in his life.

"I suppose there is a certain loneliness in knowing

that every decision I make carries a burden, and a consequence."

He felt the enormity of what he said crashing in on him. Even ignoring Phyllis's many calls held repercussions, not only for him but also for Tracy's mother, for her entire family. He was suddenly tired, the kind of exhaustion that couldn't be slept off.

"You aren't alone, Ethan." Keely's words came at him as if she were speaking to him from behind a wall of water. "You have your family. And you have…me."

He should have expected the declaration. He and Keely were friends now. Yet his pulse sped up. And he found himself speaking the truth in his heart. "You have me, too, Keely."

Something sad slid into her gaze. "Do I?"

"Yes, you do." The moment felt bigger than the words they were speaking.

"Oh, Ethan." She smiled, but a pensive light still lingered in her gaze. "I need to tell you something about my time in New York, I—"

Her phone buzzed, cutting her off midsentence. She glanced at the screen, lifted panic-stricken eyes to him. "It's Olivia."

"Answer it."

She lifted the phone to ear. "Olivia, what's wrong? Is it Felicity?"

Face grim, she listened to whatever his sister said in response to the question. "Oh. Oh, the poor thing."

She listened for several seconds longer, shared a worried look with Ethan. He could hear Olivia's muffled voice. Keely frowned. "Is she crying?"

More of the one-sided conversation passed. Then Keely said into the phone, "Tell her I'm on my way."

She ended the call and stuffed her phone back in her purse. "I have to go. Felicity's homesick."

"I'll drive you over to Olivia's." Before she could argue, he held up a hand to stop her. "It's closer than taking you home."

"You don't mind?"

"Not at all." He motioned for the waiter, gave an abbreviated explanation and requested the check.

As he helped Keely into her coat, and escorted her out onto the sidewalk, he noticed her valiant attempt to ward off tears. "I can't help thinking this is my fault, that I pushed her too hard to make friends."

"Lots of children her age experience separation anxiety." He opened the car door, waited until she climbed in, then leaned his forearm on the roof. "This isn't abnormal behavior for a seven-year-old."

She let out a weighty sigh. "I hope you're right."

Taking a shortcut through town, he made it from the restaurant to Olivia's house in record time. He'd barely pulled his SUV to a stop when Keely dashed out of the car and up the front steps. By the time he entered the house, he was confronted with three sobbing little girls.

"Please don't hate me," Flicka wailed.

"We don't hate you," one of the twins said while the other rubbed her back and added, "We get homesick sometimes, too."

Their kindness seemed to make Flicka cry harder.

"If it's okay with Keely, you can come back tomorrow afternoon," Olivia suggested. "And you can finish watching the movie with the girls then."

"I… I'd like that a lot." Her little voice trembled with a mixture of misery and tempered hope. Ethan's heart broke for the kid.

"Then that's what we'll do," Keely confirmed, pulling the child into a hug. "But for now, I think we all could use a good night's sleep. Things will look better in the morning."

Goodbyes were said, hugs were given, more tears flowed and then, finally, Ethan and Keely were back on the road with Flicka bundled up in the backseat. Her soft whimpers cut deep.

Having never been through anything quite like that before, Ethan was as emotionally wrung out as the little girl in his car. Parenting, he decided, especially parenting little girls, wasn't for sissies.

As Ethan pulled his SUV into her driveway, Keely glanced over her shoulder. Sometime during the ride home, exhaustion had caught up with Felicity. "She's sound asleep."

"Not surprising. She's had an exhausting evening." He turned off the engine and twirled the keys around his finger before stuffing them in his pocket. "I'll carry her inside."

The offer was both unexpected and greatly appreciated.

"That would be really helpful, thanks." She waited for him to pull the child into his arms before reaching in and gathering up Felicity's overnight bag.

They entered the house in silence, managing to get the child upstairs and in the bed without waking her. Grateful for his assistance, Keely walked Ethan to the front door. "Thank you for your help."

Shadows covered most of his face, but she was able to read the intent in his eyes a second before he gathered her close. Setting her head on his chest, she resisted the urge to cling.

"She's going to be okay, Keely. Even children from stable households get homesick."

"I pray you're right."

She could feel the rise and fall of his breathing beneath her cheek. The emotion of the evening was catching up with her and she didn't know what to do, what to say, so she just stood there, drawing on his strength.

Eventually, his hold loosened. Tenderly, with great care, he tucked a stray piece of hair behind her ear. "Call me if you need me to come back over."

"You don't have to do that."

"I'm here for you, Keely. You aren't in this alone. Okay?"

She nodded.

"Call me," he reiterated, in a soft, serious tone. No smile. No teasing banter.

This wasn't a game for him. Well, it wasn't for her, either. It was real and complicated and she thought she might cry, because she was in over her head. With Felicity. With Ethan. She'd never felt this out of control in her life.

"Good night, Keely." Taking her face in his hands, he kissed her gently on the lips and then he was gone, leaving her to gaze after his retreating back.

Mind reeling, she shut the door behind him, pressed her forehead to the wood and let the tears come, let them trail down her cheeks unfettered. She was falling in love with Ethan Scott, the big, bad, frustrating bane of her existence and one of the kindest men she knew.

Love was supposed to make her happy, wasn't it? Yet Keely had never been more miserable in her life.

Chapter Thirteen

Ethan was greeted at the back door by two tail-wagging, rowdy dogs, one of which had a shredded throw pillow clamped between his teeth. The other had the telltale signs of feathers clinging to his black fur.

Evidently, the dogs had thrown a party in his absence.

Torn between amusement and annoyance over the mess he now had to clean up, he pointed an accusing finger at the culprit holding the pillow in his mouth. "Looks like you killed it dead."

As if presenting a hard-earned trophy from an epic battle, Cupcake—they seriously needed to change the animal's name—dropped the pillow at Ethan's feet.

Giving into a laugh, he petted the puppy. "Good dog."

Baloo woofed softly to remind Ethan he had another animal in the house that required his attention. In the hopes of saving the rest of his pillows, he said, "Let's go for a walk."

Still dressed in his winter gear, Ethan snapped leashes into collars, then herded the dogs out the front door.

He steered the animals in the direction of Hawkins Park. The going was slow. Between the two of them,

Baloo and Cupcake managed to sniff every bush and tree trunk on the block.

From the depths of Ethan's back pocket came the sound of his cell phone ringing. Gripping both leashes in one hand, he dug out the phone with his other. A quick look at the name on the screen and he let the call go to voice mail again.

He knew he was putting off the inevitable, but he didn't want to hear Tracy's mother continue to make her case for why he should attend the private memorial ceremony.

Back at the house, as he refilled the dogs' water bowls, conscience got the better of him. He pulled out his cell phone again. There were nine missed calls, all from the same South Carolina number. Giving in, he scrolled to the oldest and waited for the inevitable plea.

"Ethan, this is Phyllis again. Please call me. I want to discuss the particulars of Tracy's memorial service with you."

He hit the delete button.

The next two messages were variations of the first, each one making a case for Ethan to attend a ceremony that included scattering Tracy's ashes over her favorite lake. *Delete.*

Phyllis eventually quit identifying herself, preferring instead to get straight to the point. "Ethan, you have to come to the memorial. Tracy was as much yours as she was ours. She would want—"

Delete.

There was no reason to listen to the rest of the messages. He knew what Mrs. Jenkins wanted from him. He would eventually call her back, but not tonight, not until he had his argument for turning down her request formulated in his mind.

Sinking onto the couch, he closed his eyes and desperately tried to call up Tracy's image. Her features weren't crystal clear anymore and that felt like the biggest betrayal of all.

Abruptly, he rose, went to the bookshelf in the study off the den. He fished around until he found the professionally made photo album her mother had sent him a month after the funeral. Taking the book with him, he returned to the living room.

The dogs sat at his feet, looking at him with adoring eyes. He dropped a hand to each of their heads, heaved a tight breath.

He felt empty inside. The sorrow was there, but so was a healthy dose of annoyance. He'd said goodbye to Tracy at her military funeral. He'd come home and built a new life for himself, away from the military, away from the memories.

He'd surrounded himself with the familiar, yet had remained distant from the ones he loved most. It had been easier that way, not getting too involved, not stepping out on faith. Simply existing.

Feeling as frozen inside as the snow on the ground, Ethan opened the album, placed his finger on a picture of him and Tracy. His hand shook violently on the page as the weight of grief overwhelmed him.

"I can't do this right now." He tossed the book of photos on top of the coffee table.

Picking up the remote, he flicked on the television and settled in to watch whatever football game he could find. His goal was simple, to numb his pain, to forget.

To focus on anything but the woman he'd lost and the life that had almost been his.

At twenty minutes to nine on Sunday morning, Keely sent Felicity upstairs to brush her teeth and took the opportunity to call Ethan. She told herself she simply wanted to inform him that Felicity was feeling better and actually wanted to go to church this morning. But that wasn't entirely true. Keely also wanted to make sure they were still…what?

Friends? Something more?

Mildly annoyed with herself, she keyed in his number.

He answered on the third ring. "Good morning, Keely."

Was he pleased to hear from her? She couldn't tell by his neutral tone.

"Hey," she said in a breezy voice, all cool and casual. "I wanted to let you know Felicity's better this morning."

"That's a relief."

"In fact, she and I will be leaving for church in five minutes."

"She's good with that?"

"It was her idea. Anyway, I'm telling you this in case you want to let the dogs out while we're gone."

"Ah."

Biting down on her lower lip, she glanced out the kitchen window, wondered if Ethan was also in his kitchen, looking out in her direction. "You wouldn't want to come to church with us, would you?"

A long, tense silence met the question.

"Ethan?"

"I'd planned to start putting up the Christmas lights on your house this morning."

"Oh," she said, her breath rattling in her throat.

The man was just being neighborly, following through on an earlier promise. Except…she could feel her pulse picking up speed. And last night, even before they'd picked up Felicity, she and Ethan had crossed some sort of invisible line.

If she closed her eyes she could see him on a ladder, wearing one of his sardonic T-shirts while he strung lights along her roofline. Another scene flitted across her mind, replacing the first. She and Ethan were sitting by the fire in her hearth, a dark-haired toddler or two playing at their feet, a couple of dogs snoozing away and a—

Whoa. She'd been barely on speaking terms with the man two weeks ago. Thinking in terms of anything beyond friendship was getting way ahead of herself.

"Thanks. I'll leave the garage door open. The lights are in the large box next to the tool kit. Should be easy enough to find what you need."

"I'll figure it out." A short pause followed the remark. "Will I see you and Flicka later this afternoon at my sister's?"

Even before they'd married, Connor and Olivia had started a tradition of feeding family and friends every Sunday afternoon. They lived in a rambling old house on the edge of town that had once been an orphanage—of sorts—in the Old West for children born to prostitutes.

The Scotts and Mitchells had direct connections to Charity House. So did Keely's family, as well as half a dozen others in town. "Felicity and I have plans to head over after church."

"I'm bringing Baloo with me, but Cupcake has to stay behind for obvious reasons."

Keely hated that the puppy had to be left at Ethan's, but it couldn't be helped. She didn't want to spoil Felicity's surprise. "Poor little guy."

"Speaking of the poor little guy, I really have to insist on an immediate name change, especially now that he's bunking with us Scott men."

"What? Cupcake's not masculine enough for you?"

Ethan's derisive snort was answer enough. "From now on, I'm calling him…" He paused as if contemplating various possibilities. "…Tank. Has a nice ring to it, don't you think? Says I'm tough, don't mess with me."

She bit back a laugh. "No, not Tank."

"Okay, how about… T-bone?"

She kind of liked that one, but it wasn't up to her. Or Ethan, for that matter. The dog was Felicity's Christmas gift. "Not T-bone, either."

"Axel, Spike, Razor Blade?"

"No, no and definitely not."

"Come on, Keely, work with me here."

She switched the phone to her other ear, lowered her voice to a whisper. "I thought we agreed to let Felicity decide."

"Right, muddy the waters with logic."

Her heart stuttered at the amused response and she admitted she'd lost objectivity. She'd let down her guard and Ethan had slipped beneath her defenses.

"Geronimo, Hank, Rawhide?"

"I'm hanging up now." She disconnected the call on his deep chuckle.

Moments later, Felicity entered the kitchen, dressed and ready for church. "Molly and Megan promised to sit with me at Sunday school this morning. They really aren't mad I left last night. They both said so on the phone just now."

Keely made a mental note to buy those sweet girls each a very special Christmas present this year. "Well, then, we certainly don't want to be late."

It took three go-rounds for Keely to find an empty space in the crowded church parking lot. She dropped Felicity off in the second grade Sunday-school room, put her phone on vibrate and then entered the main sanctuary.

From a pew near the back, Olivia waved at her over. "Connor and I saved you a seat."

"Thanks."

She smiled. "Felicity's feeling better this morning," she told both her friends.

"I'm glad," they said in unison just as the worship band kicked off the first song.

With Christmas a week away, the sermon was on the power of God's love given in the form of His Son. "We haven't done a thing to earn this gift, freely given."

The young preacher paused, glanced over the congregation, making eye contact with several people, Keely one of them. "All we have to do is receive. Not easy, especially when we're also taught that it's better to give than receive." He paused again. "But if we don't first receive God's gift, we will have little to give others when the time comes."

The message resonated with Keely. She thought back over the year since she'd come home. She'd arrived with a shattered heart. She'd buried her pain with activity, working hard at the restaurant, volunteering at the church and around town.

She'd given her time, but not herself. She'd kept busy serving others, but never stopped long enough to receive back from them. Because receiving required vulnerability, and opening herself up to another heartache. She'd allowed Cutter's inability to let go of his past to keep her from claiming a future for herself.

How was she supposed to guide Felicity to live a healthy, functional life if she didn't model it herself?

"Keely." Olivia's hand touched her arm. "Are you okay?"

Opening her eyes, she smiled at her friend. "Yes, of course. I'm fine."

She wasn't, not really. But she would be, after she made some changes in her life. She would do it for Felicity. And maybe even for herself. She thought of her mother's favorite saying, *Begin as you mean to go.*

The sermon came to an end and Keely bowed her head for the closing prayer. She discovered during the announcements that the men's ministry was putting on a father/daughter dance Wednesday night in place of youth group.

Her first thought was of Felicity. Would she want to attend? Probably, especially if the Mitchell twins were going with their father. Who would take Felicity?

Ethan came immediately to mind, but Keely couldn't see herself asking him. There was another option. Her brother.

Then why didn't that feel right?

Why, when she shut her eyes, could Keely only picture Ethan escorting Felicity to the father/daughter dance?

Chapter Fourteen

With Baloo riding shotgun, Ethan arrived at Connor and Olivia's place just after noon. Pulling his SUV in behind Keely's Jeep, he studied the gigantic, newly renovated house. There was history here, family history for the Scotts and the Mitchells and several others in town. Ethan was pleased that the brick and stone structure still had an old-fashioned charm that spoke of days gone by.

He cut the engine, noted the number of cars already in the drive. Ready to eat, Ethan snapped Baloo's leash into his collar, then let the dog out of the car. Ryder's pickup pulled to a stop behind Ethan's SUV.

Still dressed in scrubs, his brother hopped out of the truck, stretched his long legs as if working out invisible kinks. His face held signs of a stressful night in the ER.

"You just getting off work?"

"There was a bad accident out on the highway just as my shift was ending. I stuck around to help out. Hey, boy." Yawning, Ryder leaned down and gave Baloo's head a good scrubbing. "Hope Liv made extra mashed potatoes. I'm in the mood for some serious carbs."

After a cursory knock on the front door, two men

and a dog entered the house to the sound of organized chaos. Children's laughter mingled with adult conversations, the clinking of dinnerware accompanied a popular Christmas song wafting on the air from invisible speakers built into the wall. People milled about with plates overflowing with food.

"I see dinner is served." A grin slid across Ryder's face.

Ethan gave him a fist bump. Announcing their arrival, Baloo let out a single, loud *woof.*

The Mitchells' dog, a fat-bellied pug-and-beagle mix, came wheeling around the corner at warp speed. The two dogs greeted each other with the familiarity of old friends.

"Well, well. Look who the dogs dragged in." Dressed in jeans and a cable-knit sweater, Connor joined them in the hallway. "Hope you came hungry."

"Need you ask?"

Laughing at Ryder's question, Connor led them into the dining room where an elaborate buffet was set up. "We're informal today. Fill a plate and sit wherever you like."

"On it." Ryder made a beeline for the food.

Ethan hung back, taking in the eclectic mix of people already assembled. He'd known everyone in the room since grade school. Nodding at familiar faces, he circled his gaze around the room, checking for two people in particular.

"Last time I checked, Keely and Felicity were in the kitchen helping Olivia and the girls."

"Who said I was looking for Keely and Flicka?"

"Weren't you?" Connor's voice held no small amount of irony. "My mistake."

Deciding there was no good response, not without opening up another conversation about the way he was living his life, Ethan moved toward the food table.

Ham, thickly sliced tenderloin and several other kinds of meat shared space with a dozen side dishes, including Ryder's hoped-for mashed potatoes. Another, smaller table in the corner held desserts, one of which was Ethan's favorite, pecan pie.

Connor clapped him on the back. "Have at it, my friend."

"Don't have to tell me twice." He picked up a plate and began moving counterclockwise around the table. He nodded to Keely's twin brother, who was working his way around in the opposite direction.

Beau O'Toole was the polar opposite of his hard-working, serious sister and the quintessential poster boy for Colorado ski country. The man's startling green eyes were identical to Keely's, but where her hair was a fiery red, Beau's was a sun-tipped bronze.

They met up at the plate of ham.

Ethan eyed the man, noticed the signs of strain on his face, the kind that came from battling physical pain. "You haven't been in the office for weeks. How's the shoulder?"

"Fine." The one-word answer came out clipped and irritated, belying the easygoing stance and overly casual tone.

Ethan took another inventory of the guy, this time with the eyes of a doctor. Beau filled his plate with his left hand. Telling. The former world champion was right-handed. The shoulder wasn't fine. "Make an appointment, Beau."

"My shoulder is good, Ethan. Let it go."

Not going to happen. When they'd gone skiing last week, Beau had tackled the slopes with unusual aggression. He was clearly paying the price now. "Still doing your rehab exercises?"

Darkness filled Beau's gaze. "No point. My career's over."

"Competitively speaking, but it doesn't mean you can't ski for fun and go as hard at it as you did last weekend and—"

Beau cut him off. "I'll make an appointment if you'll stop talking."

"My job here is done."

"Excellent." Beau finished filling his plate.

As he left the room, Ethan fell into step beside him. Muttering something about pushy friends, Beau broke off toward the living room. Ethan slowed his steps, debating whether to follow. He'd made his point.

As he hovered in the doorway, he watched Flicka in an animated discussion with Connor's twins, something about a dance later that week.

Ethan's first instinct was to turn and walk away. He had good reason to put distance between him and the kid. She'd made it clear she wanted a father, with a look in her eyes that warned Ethan he was at the top of her list. It wouldn't be fair to let her spin hopes and dreams around him, as if it was possible he could fill that role in her life.

"I can't go to the dance," Flicka said, her voice small and vulnerable, her head hung low. "I don't have a father."

Molly patted her on the back with an obvious show of sympathy. "My daddy is taking both my sister and me, I'm sure he'll take you, too."

Flicka lifted her head. "You really think so?"

"I don't see why not."

Ethan struggled with a vortex of emotions, sadness, remorse, a yearning to provide the little girl with something real and lasting, something that went far beyond a dance at the church. His soul was being ripped to shreds. This was the type of pain he'd been avoiding since Tracy's death, for good reason.

Seeking escape, he melted into the shadows, found an empty chair in the hallway. He set his untouched plate on the small table beside him and shut his eyes. He regretted the move.

He was back in Tracy's apartment, early in their relationship, wearing the tux he'd bought for the father/daughter dance at Fort Bragg Army post. Tracy's daughter, Samantha, was beaming up at him with the adoration of a daughter. The memory was fresh, and too, too real, as if the dance had been just yesterday, rather than two years ago.

Something inside him broke.

He couldn't breathe, couldn't think, couldn't stay in this chair, in this house, another second.

Blinking open his eyes, he reminded himself that what he'd lost could never be recovered. Tracy was dead. Samantha was living with her biological father. Ethan was probably only a distant memory to the little girl.

Grief came hot and fast, clawing at him.

He needed air—now. He abruptly rose, left the hallway with clipped, purposeful strides.

Someone called his name.

He kept walking, not stopping until he was outside in the backyard, bent at the waist, drawing in large gulps of air. He blamed his reaction on Flicka's desire for a father, but that wasn't the full truth. He'd had Tracy and Samantha on his mind ever since he listened to Mrs. Jenkins's voice mail yesterday.

Everything he'd put behind him gnawed at his composure with fresh vigor.

"Ethan?" Keely's voice was soft, so soft it almost wasn't there, like a whisper in his head.

"Ethan." Her hand touched his sleeve. "Talk to me. Are you ill?"

He took a shuddering breath, continuing the process until the fire in his chest eased and the air didn't catch in his throat. "I…" He swallowed, once, twice. "I'm good now."

"No, you're not."

Two more breaths, a slow blink, and he was feeling calmer.

Keely moved her hand down his arm, clasped her fingers with his. "You were caught in a panic attack."

He nodded, surprised at the relief the silent admission brought him. He'd kept the past locked inside him for so long, ignoring it, pretending all was well. It was a relief to admit that the pain was still with him.

"Did something happen in Afghanistan, something you've never shared with anyone?"

The question brought him up short. She thought he was suffering from PTSD?

"I'm okay, Keely." He pulled their joined hands to rest against his heart, the rhythm steadier for the connection. "I just needed some air."

She studied his face for several long moments. "Will you tell me what happened to make you run outside, away from your family and friends?"

He recognized the concern in her eyes and desperately wanted to share his past with her. The words were there in his mind, struggling for release, but they stalled halfway up his throat. "I'm sorry, Keely. I…can't."

Not yet.

But in that moment he knew Connor was right. Ethan needed to start living again. He needed to make peace with Tracy's death. He would eventually tell Keely everything about his life with Tracy. It was the right thing to do, the only thing to do.

The realization brought a new level of calm. Finally, he was able to breathe easier. Something came and went in her eyes, something that looked like sadness, with a twinge of disappointment, maybe even pity.

Pity was the last thing he wanted from her.

What do *you want?*

Ethan didn't know. All he knew was that this woman was in his mind, maybe even his heart. Living again would somehow involve her.

How had he let this happen? How had he allowed another woman and her child slip past his guard?

Even knowing the danger, he felt affection awaken in his chest. Affection for Keely. He didn't want that, not here, not now. Or maybe he did, maybe he needed to feel something again. And maybe Keely was just the woman—

No.

He hadn't fully let Tracy go. He knew that now, confirmed by his inability to stop thinking about her since her mother's phone calls.

Instead of exploring the complicated feelings racing through him, Ethan changed the subject. "Have you ever made ice cream from snow?"

* * *

Keely blinked at the startling shift in topic. Standing before her, his gaze dark and turbulent, Ethan Scott stole her breath. He looked so vulnerable. Regretful and sad.

Longing to erase his pain, she lifted her hand to his face.

He stepped out of reach.

"Well?" He tilted his head to one side. "Have you ever made snow ice cream?"

Her heart started beating out of control. She was sure he heard it. Unable to look directly into his eyes, she lowered her gaze and concentrated on the slogan on his T-shirt. If Things Get Any Worse, I'll Have to Ask You to Stop Helping.

Message received.

And yet everything had just gotten a whole lot more complicated. Keely couldn't stay detached any longer. She couldn't pretend indifference, or a lack of caring. Ever since Cutter, pushing others away had been her modus operandi. Now she was the one being pushed away.

"I get it, Ethan. You don't want to talk about whatever is bothering you."

His eyes went flat.

Wonderful, she'd made him angry. "I'm sorry. I'll leave you alone with your thoughts."

She made to leave.

He caught her by the arm. "Don't go."

The emotion in those two simple words hovered on the air between them. Ethan's pain was so real, so thick, Keely nearly choked on it.

Somewhere overhead, a plane crossed the sky. She

looked up at the clear, brittle blue, but found no inspiration to help her break through his barriers. "You don't have to tell me—"

"I want to, Keely, but not here, not yet, not today."

An unspoken promise hung in his words. He would eventually tell her what was weighing so heavy on his heart. She should be relieved. She felt only despair. She'd heard similar words from Cutter two weeks before he retracted his marriage proposal.

Only in hindsight, as she'd reviewed their relationship with a fresh perspective, had Keely recognized the signs of a man still pining for his dead wife.

Ethan had those same signs now.

She thought she might cry. "When you're ready, then."

He nodded, clearly relieved she let the matter drop. "What do you know about the father/daughter dance at the church?"

The lack of transition to the new topic dragged a gasp from her. Had Felicity asked him to take her? It would certainly explain the wariness she detected in his stance, the pinched expression on his face.

She gathered her racing thoughts. "The dance is this Wednesday night, given by the men's ministry at our church. They've scheduled it in place of regular youth group. It's a Christmas theme, of course."

"Is there an age limit for the kids attending?"

"I don't believe so. I heard Mr. Larson telling Pastor Rick that he's taking his daughter again this year." She couldn't help grinning. Abe Larson had recently turned ninety-eight and his daughter Alma was well into her seventies.

Ethan finally cracked a smile. "Do you think your brother will take Flicka?"

"Probably." Why was Ethan asking so many questions? "Do you know something I don't? Something to do with the dance?"

Looking uncomfortable, he rubbed a hand across his jaw. "I'm pretty sure Flicka wants to go. I overheard her telling the twins."

With this new piece of information, Keely would definitely be bringing up the topic with her brother.

"There's more."

Keely didn't like what she heard in Ethan's voice. "All right."

"When Flicka and I were out shopping yesterday, I asked her what she wanted for Christmas."

Dread took up residence in Keely's heart. "What did she say?"

"A father."

Poor, dear, sweet Felicity. Her mother was in prison; she was living in a strange town, starting a new school and spending Christmas with people she hardly knew. Her one and only wish? A father. And she'd shared that information with Ethan. It didn't take a psychology degree to figure out why.

"That had to have been awkward for you."

"You have no idea."

"How did you respond?"

"I told her it was pretty short notice and it would be difficult to find her a father this year."

"That's certainly true."

"She seemed a little disappointed, but I think she expected my response. I then asked her if there was anything else on her list." He shifted his stance, stuffed his hands in his pockets. "She said a puppy."

Keely wanted to break out in song. "Well, that's something."

"Bruiser is going to be a big hit Christmas morning."

"You mean Cupcake."

"Bullet?"

Keely's lips twitched at his hopeful expression. *"Cupcake."*

"Maximus?"

She was laughing now, and so was he. Ethan Scott was frustrating, annoying, with far too many secrets swimming in his eyes, but Keely was starting to like him, in a way that had nothing to do with friendship.

"Cupcake, and that's the end of it."

Silence fell over them.

At least the mood was lighter now. For that, Keely was grateful. She still wanted to know what had set Ethan off. Had it been talk of the father/daughter dance? She didn't think so.

There was so much she didn't know about the man, so many missing pieces.

He bent down, scooped up a handful of snow and studied it with quiet fervor. "Since you have evaded my question twice, I'm going to assume you've never made snow ice cream."

Hands twisted at her waist, she concentrated on the snow nestled in his palm. She could feel his gaze on her, watching her closely. "Your assumption would be correct."

"It's time for a cooking lesson, Ms. O'Toole." He dumped the snow back on the ground.

"By all means, Dr. Scott, educate me."

* * *

They were in the kitchen, deep in the middle of her cooking lesson, when Beau entered the room. "Hey, sis, came to say goodbye."

Ryder was one step behind him, suffocating a yawn behind his hand. "I'm heading out, too."

Both men's gazes landed on the colorful candy sprinkles Ethan had set on the counter.

Proving he still had the sweet tooth of a ten-year-old boy, Beau's eyebrows shot up. "Are we about to miss something good?"

"Not good. Great." With one hand holding a bottle of vanilla extract and the other reaching for a bag of sugar, Ethan tossed a negligent glance over his shoulder. "I'm teaching Keely how to make snow ice cream, thereby completing her culinary education."

Moving deeper in the room, Ryder gaped at his brother. "Since when do you know how to do anything in the kitchen more complicated than ordering takeout?"

Giving a dismissive snort, Ethan spread the ingredients out on the counter. "All I need is fresh snow and a whisk."

"You know how to use a whisk?" Beau looked duly impressed.

"I'm not a complete Neanderthal."

Ryder peered at the ingredients scattered across the counter. "Snow ice cream is a kid's treat. Where did you learn how to make—" He cut his own words off, winced. "I mean…ah, man. I didn't mean to bring up a sore subject. I—"

"Shut up, Ryder." Ethan growled the words.

"Shutting up. Shutting up right now." Palms raised,

Ryder backpedaled toward the door he'd previously come from.

Keely looked from one Scott brother to the other. Unease had fallen over the entire room. Even Beau looked uncomfortable.

What was she missing?

Felicity and the Mitchell twins rushed into the room. Molly spoke for the group. "Daddy says you're making snow ice cream. We've come to help."

Chapter Fifteen

Snow ice cream was a huge success. Not long after the last batch was served, a mass exodus from Olivia and Connor's house began.

Keely had promised Felicity they would shop for their Christmas tree that very afternoon, but she needed to speak with her brother first. She caught up with him in the foyer.

"Can you stop by the restaurant and make sure Sylvia put today's receipts in the safe?" Keely trusted her manager, but the Sunday lunch crowd was heavy during the holidays and she'd feel more comfortable knowing for certain that the money was locked up. "I could do it myself, but it's out of my way."

"No problem." He jammed a ski cap on his head. "I was heading in that direction anyway."

Squinting in the darkened hallway, she assessed her brother, her *twin* brother, wondering why their connection wasn't as strong as it had been when they were younger. As kids, they'd been close, practically able to read each other's minds. The link had continued into adulthood.

But lately, whenever Keely looked in brother's eyes, she saw a stranger. He'd been different since moving back to Village Green, still her brother and yet…not. She blamed the gulf partly on herself. She hadn't taken the time to reach out enough. It was another unfortunate consequence of Cutter's change of heart, another circumstance of allowing his past to influence her future.

"Felicity and I are picking out a Christmas tree this afternoon. Want to come over later and help us decorate it?"

"Sorry, I have plans."

Keely sighed. Her brother hadn't even attempted to come up with a plausible excuse. Though she desperately wanted to press for details, she didn't dare. Not when a potential audience could enter the foyer at any minute.

Beau turned to go, then swung back around. "I meant to tell you earlier, but I got distracted by ice cream."

She laughed. "Understandable."

"Yeah, well, Felicity mentioned the father/daughter dance Wednesday night. I'd be happy to take her." He sounded sincere.

It was nice of Beau to offer, and yet Keely had really hoped Ethan would step in. She knew it wasn't fair to expect that of him. He was only their neighbor, and probably still reeling from his "daddy" conversation with the little girl.

Since Beau was family, there wouldn't be any expectations beyond the event. "The dance is formal."

Annoyance whipped across his face. "I own a suit."

"*And* a tie?"

"The tie could be a problem," he muttered.

She started to say something snarky about him being

the quintessential ski bum, but the sound of footsteps had her holding her tongue.

"I can loan you one." Ethan's voice came from behind her.

Keely spun around.

"Don't look so surprised, O'Toole. I own nice clothes."

"I can get my own tie," Beau growled at him.

Ethan lifted empty hands in the universal show of surrender. "Just making a friendly offer to save you time and unnecessary hassle."

"Thanks, but I'm good."

An odd strain fell over the two men. It grew thicker when Ethan drew alongside Keely, putting them shoulder-to-shoulder.

Beau's eyes narrowed. He shifted his gaze to Keely, then back to Ethan.

Something passed between the two. Keely wasn't sure what, only that it was not a pleasant meeting of the minds. There seemed to be more going on between them than the issue of a tie.

"Walk outside with me," Beau asked Ethan, not Keely. "I have something I want to run by you."

"All right." Ethan whistled for Baloo, who appeared seconds later in the hallway, tail wagging. With his hand on the dog's collar, he made a deliberate show of giving Keely his undivided attention. "I'll see you later?"

"Sure."

Beau gave her a brief nod and then stepped outside with Ethan, Baloo following behind him. As she watched, Keely couldn't tell what they were discussing, but it seemed serious.

At least Felicity would be attending the father/daughter dance at the church with Beau. Keely clung to that happy thought as she went in search of the little girl. She found her playing a board game with Molly and Megan on the living room floor.

For a moment, Keely watched Felicity. She appeared comfortable, animated and fully in the moment, a sure sign she was over whatever had made her homesick last night.

Deciding to give her a bit more time with her friends, Keely slipped out of the doorway and moved into the kitchen, where Olivia was stacking plates in the dishwasher. "What can I do to help?"

"Not a thing." Olivia smiled at her from over her shoulder. "Connor and I are nearly finished."

Her husband entered the kitchen from the dining room, set several empty bowls in the sink. "This is the last of them."

"Splendid."

Grinning, Connor moved in behind his wife, wrapped his arms around her waist. "You are a treasure, Mrs. Mitchell. Have I told you how much I love you?"

Olivia sighed against him. "Not in the last half hour."

"A terrible oversight." Seeming not to care that Olivia's hands were wet and full of soapsuds, Connor whipped her around to face him, then waltzed her through the kitchen, humming a tune from another time.

As she matched her husband step for step, Olivia smiled up at Connor with such love in her eyes Keely felt a moment of pure envy. *I want that, Lord. I want to love and be loved without reservation, without conditions, without someone from the past standing between us.*

She thought she'd found it with Cutter. The widower

had said all the right words, made all the right promises. When he spoke of his dead wife, he'd been reverent and wistful, but had assured Keely he was over the loss of her.

Keely had made the assumption that the joy he'd found in his first marriage was a sign that he knew how to love, how to commit totally to a relationship.

What neither of them had understood at the time was that his heart still belonged to his dead wife. Tragically, he'd only accepted the truth *after* he gave Keely an engagement ring.

The retraction of his marriage proposal had been painful for them both. Keely actually felt sorry for Cutter. He would never truly be able to live a full life until he was able to let go of his wife. Keely hoped he could find the courage to do so. He deserved to be free, to find happiness.

But then, so did she.

The next time she gave her heart to a man, he would not be pining for the woman he'd lost.

Connor swept Olivia into a deep dip, then bent over and kissed her square on the mouth. They both came up laughing and smiling into each other's eyes, as if the world had slipped away, leaving only the two of them. Olivia was Connor's second chance at love. Keely took hope in that.

"I love you," he whispered to his wife.

"Oh, Connor, I love you, too."

Feeling as though she was intruding on a private moment, Keely silently slipped from the room.

Felicity met her in the hallway. "The game's over. Molly won, but I'll get her next time."

"I'm sure you will." She ran her hand over the little girl's head. "Ready to go pick out our Christmas tree?"

"Yes, please."

They were soon on the road, heading to the north end of town. Everyone in Village Green knew that the best trees were sold at the tree lot managed by the coaches from the local high school.

Keely pulled into the lot and smiled at the extensive inventory still available. As she unbuckled her seat belt, Felicity informed Keely that, "Dr. Ethan told me we should get a Colorado blue spruce, or nothing at all."

Sounded like something he would say. Hiding a smile behind a cough, Keely met her cousin at the front of the Jeep. "Well, then, let's hope they have an assortment of blue spruces to choose from."

"They have to be *Colorado* blue spruces."

"Of course."

With help from John Weston, the football coach and one of Keely's former classmates, they located the perfect tree. It was nearly seven feet tall, with full branches, a straight trunk and no bald spots. It was also a Colorado blue spruce.

"For an additional ten dollars," John informed her, "we'll deliver the tree within the next twenty-four hours."

"Done." She paid for the tree and delivery in cash.

On the way home they stopped at a store that carried children's clothing and picked out a new dress for Felicity to wear to the father/daughter dance.

At home they discovered two surprises. The first was Ethan on a ladder, hanging outdoor twinkle lights. The other was their Christmas tree perched against the front porch.

"You ladies have excellent timing." Ethan waved at them from his perch near the edge of the roof. "I'm nearly done."

He looped the string of lights around a hook connected to the overhang. He then stuffed some sort of manly looking tool in his back pocket and climbed down the ladder.

Though it was barely dusk, the sky a pretty purple-gray, he suggested they checked out his day's work. He fiddled with the timer a moment, and then plugged the main cord into an outdoor socket.

The house burst into light.

"It's wonderful," Keely breathed in pure delight.

Felicity responded with more enthusiasm, clapping her hands while also singing the chorus of "Jingle Bells" at the top of her lungs. Smiling over the child's head, Ethan and Keely joined in.

It was a perfect moment, full of joy and hope and everything good about the Christmas season.

Eyes less distant than they'd been this afternoon, Ethan jerked a nod toward the house. "I see you followed my recommendation."

Not sure what he meant, Keely angled her head. "How so?"

"The tree." He clasped her shoulders and turned her toward the front of her house. "That is most definitely a Colorado blue spruce."

She laughed.

He shoved his hands in his pockets. "Need help getting it inside?"

Wiggling her recently manicured fingernails, she gave him a droll eyebrow lift. "What do you think?"

"I think…" He made a grand show of studying her outstretched hands. "You are a girly girl."

"I'll take that as a compliment."

"What about me?" Felicity scooted between them so she could gain Ethan's attention. "Am I a girly girl, too?"

"You, my dear Flicka." He ruffled the child's blond curls. "Are the girly girliest of them all."

Ethan wrestled the tree inside Keely's house, careful not to bump the walls or leave too many pine needles on the floor. He was pleased to discover that while he'd been outside securing a stand to the tree's trunk, Keely and Flicka had been busy clearing away furniture in front of the large picture window that faced the street.

He set the tree in the now empty spot, then moved it around until Keely was satisfied with its position.

Stepping back, he removed his gloves, and studied the overall effect. "You made a good choice," he declared.

Flicka added her agreement.

Keely simply nodded. "Coach Weston assured me this was the best Colorado blue spruce on the lot."

At the mention of the high school football coach, Ethan felt a spurt of irritation. Odd. He liked John Weston. Everyone in town liked him, especially women. The guy was young, single and, by all accounts, a man of integrity.

Had the football coach hit on Keely?

Something churned inside Ethan, something directly related to the smiling woman standing beside him. Each moment in her company made him feel alive, like he was finally home.

This afternoon, when her brother had point-blank asked him if he had his eye on Keely, romantically, Ethan hadn't said yes. But he hadn't said no, either. Instead he'd swiftly changed the subject, insisting the guy come into the office so Ethan could check his shoulder properly.

And that had sufficiently ended their conversation.

There was no denying Ethan had feelings for Keely. But what was he going to do about them?

"Okay, Keely. Are you in the white-lights-only camp or do you prefer colored lights? Think hard before you respond." He swiveled his head toward hers. "There is only one right answer."

With her expression giving nothing away, she reached inside a plastic bin and pulled out a string of lights. Hiding the bulbs from his gaze, she walked over to an outlet, plugged in the strand and an assortment of bright colors sparkled at her feet.

"We can now remain friends."

Laughing, she made a grand show of wiping off her forehead with the back of her hand. "Phew."

Flicka, already rummaging through another plastic bin, grabbed a box of ornaments. "Are you going to stay and help us decorate the tree?" she asked him.

The last time he'd decorated a tree had been with Tracy and Samantha. He didn't want the past encroaching on the present. He'd had enough of that for one day. He wanted to live in the moment, with Keely and Flicka.

But if he spent more time in their company, it would be that much harder to pull away after the holidays. He couldn't give either of them what they needed, though a part of him wished he could.

Perhaps he should leave now, before he got in too

deep. He was working up an excuse when Flicka offered him a box of shiny red and gold ornaments.

"You can put these on the tree while I string the popcorn Keely and I made last night." Her eyes were full of little-girl innocence. How was he supposed to say no to that look?

Before he could stop himself, he was reaching for the box and saying, "Works for me."

Despite his concerns, the next two hours were pleasant. The three of them worked well together. When the last ornament was hung, they stepped back as a single unit.

"It's the best tree ever," Flicka declared with no small amount of pride.

Ethan eyed the massive amounts of lights and twice as many ornaments. The result should have looked overdone and chaotic. Yet, somehow, with its mix of old-fashioned and modern bulbs, store-bought and homemade ornaments, the tree actually worked. "It does have something special about it."

Caught in the moment, Ethan found himself accepting Keely's invitation to stay for leftovers and cake.

"But I need to feed the..." He paused, barely stopping before he gave away Flicka's Christmas surprise. "...Baloo, first. Then I'll come back over."

Giggling, Felicity pressed a hand to her lips. "Is that what you call him now? *The* Baloo?"

The kid missed nothing. "He's only *the* Baloo on Sundays."

"That's just silly." She lowered her hand. "Can I come with you and help you feed *the* Baloo."

Keely came to his rescue. "Actually, little miss, you need to set the table."

The girl grumbled, but at Keely's reminder the task was one of her daily chores, she didn't argue further.

Dinner went well, as it had gone every other night Ethan dined with Keely and Flicka. The three of them were sliding into a nice rhythm. In fact, Ethan felt so comfortable that he didn't balk even when the kid invited him to stay for another movie night, *The Muppet Christmas Carol*.

Thus, he found himself sticking around until nine o'clock.

As the final credits rolled across the screen, Keely announced it was bedtime for Flicka, since she had school in the morning. "Two more days and it'll be Christmas break."

The child hopped to her feet and looked directly at Ethan with big, round, hopeful eyes. "Will you say bedtime prayers with me tonight?"

A tide of panic washed through his beleaguered soul. Yet no excuse came to mind.

"We can say them right here in the living room, because God hears us wherever we pray."

Consumed with indecision, Ethan shared a look with Keely. Her eyes had gone watery with emotion. The sight made him feel all kinds of things he hadn't felt in a year and a half.

He reached out and briefly touched her hand. "Okay." He turned back to Flicka. "We'll pray right here."

The kid wiggled onto the sofa between him and Keely. Squeezing her hands tightly together, she shut her eyes and rested her forehead on her knuckles.

Feeling as if he were coming apart from the inside out, Ethan adopted the same pose.

"Dear God," Flicka whispered, "please take care of

my mommy in prison and let her know I'm okay living with Keely and Dr. Ethan. Can You also tell her they're taking super awesome care of me and that I'll see her real soon? Oh, and if there's a puppy out there who needs a home, can You bring him to me so I can love him? And… I think that's it. Amen."

Ethan was done in by a seven-year-old's sweet, heartfelt prayers.

"Now it's your turn," Flicka said.

Keely's soft voice said, "Dear Lord, thank you for bringing Felicity into my life."

His eyes squeezed tightly shut, Ethan listened to the rest of her prayer with his stomach tying into knots inside knots.

She included requests for her family and friends, mentioned the poor, the hungry and the hurting. Then he heard his name. "I pray You guide Ethan's hands as he treats his patients. And let him know he's cared for—"

"And loved," Flicka added.

"And loved," Keely said after a brief pause.

"Your turn, Dr. Ethan."

"I…don't…" He heaved a sigh. The pain in his throat made his voice deeper than usual.

"It's okay," Flicka whispered, nudging him with her shoulder. "There's no right or wrong way to pray."

"Lord," he rattled out, "I pray You keep Flicka and Keely safe, always. And take care of the rest of my family. In, uh… Your Son's name, Amen."

He opened his eyes and caught Keely watching him with soft eyes. In that moment there was no shadow covering his soul, no pain, no sense of terrible grief. There was just Keely and this moment of incredible peace.

Flicka shifted beside him, then jumped to her feet, sufficiently breaking the mood.

"Night, Dr. Ethan." She kissed him on the cheek.

He swallowed past the golf-ball-sized lump in his throat. "Night, kiddo, sleep tight."

Eyes sparkling with little-girl satisfaction, she repeated the process with Keely.

The moment she headed upstairs to brush her teeth, Ethan stood. "I have an early morning. So I should probably—"

"You don't have to explain anything to me." She took his hand and led him to the back door. "Good night, Ethan."

Still holding on to him, she pressed a tender kiss to his cheek. The longing for something more was so powerful it stole his breath.

He stepped back and put physical distance between them. "I found the camels we need for the parade."

Her reaction was priceless, a mixture of utter shock and skepticism. "You're really through fighting me on this?"

"A smart soldier knows when to remain in battle and when to retreat." Though he hadn't meant to speak in subtext, his words had a double meaning. By the sad look in her eyes, Keely caught both of them.

He'd hurt her again. It seemed inevitable whenever they got too close, whenever things between them seemed to take a step toward something real and lasting.

Not sure how to breach the awkwardness, not even sure he should try, he said good-night and then strode across their snow-covered backyards. He swerved around the snowman still wearing the ridiculous Christmas scarf and cowboy hat, the memory of the snowball fight clear in his mind.

The evening had been a turning point in his relationship with Keely, a glimpse of what his life could be like with her and Flicka in it.

He could see it now, the three of them sitting around a Christmas tree, a couple of dogs running wild, another child on the way...

He immediately pushed the image out of his mind.

What was the point of reaching for that kind of happiness when it could be lost at any moment?

Chapter Sixteen

With his mind in chaos, Ethan entered his house through the back door. He immediately dealt with the dogs. The brisk walk did nothing to calm his racing thoughts.

He'd enjoyed his time with Keely and Felicity. Whenever he was with them he felt at peace, finally whole again, a sensation that had been missing in his life since losing Tracy.

Tracy. He tried to draw up her image. But it was Keely's face he saw, Keely's long red hair and sea-green eyes. His beautiful neighbor challenged him with her wit, engaged his mind with her intelligence and sparked his humor with her snarky comments.

Guilt reared and he accepted the truth at last. He was falling for Keely O'Toole. He might already be in love with her.

His breath turned cold in his chest, a sensation that had nothing to do with the frigid night air. If he let himself love her, and then lost her, he'd never survive. But if he never loved her, would he really be living? He couldn't help thinking the life the Lord had planned for him included Keely.

"Let's go home, boys."

He retraced his steps, the dogs trotting happily beside him, blissfully ignorant of Ethan's inner turmoil. As he directed the animals back inside the house, he caught sight of his face in the hallway mirror. His eyes looked hollow. They matched how he felt inside. He trudged into the kitchen, filled the dog's water bowls with hands that were no longer steady.

Returning to the living room, he sank onto the couch. Too exhausted to do anything but watch television, he reached for the remote. The photo album on the coffee table caught his eye. He'd left it open to a picture of him and Tracy. Samantha had taken the shot. It was off-center and slightly blurry and that much more charming for the imperfections.

His hand hovered over the page. An ache spread through his chest. He turned the page, studied the assortment of photos. They were mostly of Tracy and Samantha, but Baloo had worked his way into several of the images.

Memory after memory slammed into him. He let them come, let them take him back in time, to another place, another life. He turned the page. Somewhere halfway through the album, the process became less painful, more cathartic.

You want to honor Tracy's memory, start living again.

He paused at the picture of him and Samantha at the father/daughter dance. He wouldn't regret taking her, wouldn't regret filling in for her real father, if only temporarily.

Head down, he finished looking through the album. He flipped to the final page, paused. It was the same candid shot of him and Tracy in Afghanistan he kept on his desk at work.

Beside the photo was Tracy's favorite Bible verse. "And we know that all things work together for good to those who love God, to those who are the called according to His purpose."

Ethan's eyes burned over the perfectly timed message. It felt as if Tracy was giving him permission to move on.

"I love you," he whispered to the image. "You will always be in my heart, but it's time I said goodbye."

The never-ending sorrow that had lived inside him for well over a year released its tight grip. *Thank You, Lord.*

It wasn't an elegant prayer, but it was full of sincerity, the first step on his journey back to retrieving his faith, to taking back his life.

He leaned his head back, closed his eyes and let the peace that transcended all understanding fill him. At some point he must have fallen asleep, the album still on his lap.

The sound of his cell phone ringing startled him awake. He recognized the hospital's number. Setting aside the album, he answered on the fourth ring, "Dr. Scott."

"Ethan, it's me, Ryder."

The concern in his brother's voice had him snapping awake. He rubbed a hand over his face. "What's wrong?"

"Alma Collier was brought in by ambulance. She's had a heart attack."

The last of his grogginess vanished. He'd just seen the elderly woman on Saturday and had feared this moment was coming. "I'll be there shortly."

Ending the call, he checked the time, discovered it was just shy of 6:00 a.m. He showered, took care of the dogs, then, seeing lights on at Keely's house, sent her a text.

Heading to hospital. Emergency. May not be able to run home before work. Can you check on dogs later this morning?

Her response came immediately. Absolutely.

He texted his thanks.

A long pause followed, making Ethan think she wouldn't respond. He was already in his SUV, shoving his key in the ignition when her next text came through.

No words, just symbols. xoxoxo

Hugs and kisses. Despite the seriousness of the situation, and his concern for Mrs. Collier, Ethan drove away from his house feeling less alone than he had in a year and a half.

Ethan's text hadn't given Keely much information concerning the emergency that had called him away. Halfway between their yards, she lifted up a prayer for both doctor and patient.

As she stepped onto the back stoop, she couldn't help noticing the lack of Christmas decorations. No sparkling lights, no garlands, not even tacky lawn ornaments scattered in the front yard.

The Scott house looked sad, as sad as Ethan when

his gaze went distant and he erected an invisible wall around himself.

What's your story, Ethan? What aren't you telling me?

Using the key he'd given her, Keely entered the house through the back. Two happy dogs greeted her. "Hello, boys."

She gave each head a pat, then pulled both animals into a group hug. Ethan's text hadn't mentioned if he'd fed them this morning. "I'm thinking a small bowl of kibble can't hurt."

She got no argument from the dogs.

As she entered the kitchen pantry, she moved with the ease of someone familiar with every corner of this house. Of course she was familiar. She'd spent considerable time here as a child. Even at the worst of her teenage years, when she'd been wrongfully labeled a terrible flirt by jealous peers, Olivia had stood by her.

Smiling, she set the bowls on the ground in front of the dogs. Baloo, polite and well trained, calmly went about eating his snack. Cupcake, on the other hand, needed a few lessons in manners. The puppy proceeded to inhale his food.

To the sound of canine crunching, Keely glanced around the kitchen. There didn't seem to be many signs of use. Such a pity. Especially since someone had gone to the trouble of updating the appliances, flooring and decorative tile.

Running her fingertips along the granite countertops, she itched to dirty things up a bit. Kitchens were meant to be used. Keely could do a lot of creating here. She could see herself feeding an entire family of kids, Ethan coming up behind her for an impromptu waltz and—

She cut off the rest of that thought and picked up

the now empty bowls. Then she took the dogs outside.
When they'd finished their business, she ushered them
back into the house. Cupcake initiated a game of tug-
of-war with Baloo and an ancient sock.

While the older dog indulged the puppy, Keely expanded her tour beyond the kitchen. The moment she
stepped into the living room, she realized Ethan had
forgotten to turn off the lights. Or perhaps Ryder was
home from the hospital.

Doubtful. The house had an empty feel. Nevertheless, she called out, "Ryder?"

No answer.

She strolled fully into the room, glanced around at
the masculine decor. The brown leather furniture and
bold, solid-colored rugs were of excellent quality but
lacked imagination. "Anybody home?"

Still no answer.

Keely couldn't help herself. She worked her way
through the room, shutting off lights as she went.

As she was nearly finished with the task, her gaze
fell on the coffee table, zeroing in on what looked like
a scrapbook, or maybe a photo album. Keely sat on the
sofa and studied the book without actually picking it up.

The various pictures depicted a happy family caught
in candid poses. The father had dark hair cut military
short. The mother had long golden blond hair. The
young daughter was full of smiles. There was even a
family dog, a black Lab, about the same age as Baloo,
and—

What, exactly, had she stumbled upon? Whose family was this?

Maybe the album belonged to Ethan's youngest
brother, Brody. It was certainly possible. Brody was

in some foreign country working for Doctors Without Borders. He could easily have left something this personal behind for safekeeping.

As she leaned forward for a better look, a sob rose in her throat. That wasn't Brody in the pictures. It was Ethan.

She yanked up the album, focused on one of the images. Ethan's arm was slung over the beautiful woman's shoulders. She was smiling up at him. The love in their eyes was evident. The little girl, a miniature version of the woman, had her hand on Baloo's back.

Caught up in the joy that leaped off the pages, Keely continued flipping through the album. It didn't take her long to realize this was no casual relationship. Had Ethan been married?

There were no wedding pictures. And yet the people in the photographs were the very essence of family.

Hands shaking now, Keely turned to the back page, to a picture of Ethan and the woman in matching battle fatigues. Unable to stop herself, she started back at the beginning, this time stopping on several images of the woman in a flight suit, posing in and out of a helicopter.

Despair filled Keely. She thought she and Ethan were growing close, maybe even building the kind of connection that would last a lifetime. She'd been wrong, so wrong. Here, in her hands, was evidence that she knew very little about her neighbor, and nothing of the man in this album.

"What happened to you?" she whispered to the woman smiling up at her. Something tragic; nothing else explained the sadness she often sensed in Ethan.

Keely had fallen for a man she hardly knew, a man who still held on to a woman from his past.

Feeling like an interloper, she set aside the book and closed her eyes. She'd been in this place before, in love with a man who still clung to the woman no longer in his life. She knew how this ended. In heartache. *Her* heartache.

It was exactly the wake-up call she needed.

After leaving the hospital, with Mrs. Collier in critical but stable condition, the rest of Ethan's morning remained busy. On his lunch break, he made his usual trip home to let the dogs out.

As soon as he entered the house, he knew Keely had followed through with her promise to check on them this morning. All the lights were out, something neither he nor Ryder ever remembered to do. As the dogs danced around him in a tail-wagging frenzy, the fine hairs on the back of his neck prickled.

Something felt…off.

Unable to pinpoint what, he moved into the living room and froze. The photo album wasn't where he left it.

Had Keely moved it, or Ryder?

The easiest way to find out would be to wake up his brother. Yeah, like that would go over well.

Leaving Ryder to his sleep, Ethan took care of the dogs, then drove back to town, determined to get answers, even if they weren't the ones he wanted. It would be tempting to return to his office, ignore the nagging sensation in his gut, pretend the pulse beating in his ears meant nothing.

Ethan was through taking the easy way out. No more putting off the inevitable. He made the trip from parking lot to Keely's restaurant with ground-eating strides.

The moment he pushed into Senor O'Toole's, a wall of heat and noise hit him.

The restaurant was full of holiday shoppers. There wasn't a free table in the place, but the stool at the counter where he usually ate remained free. Weaving his way through the crowd, he claimed his regular position. Keely had her back to him as she manned the soda machine, filling drink glasses with the speed and efficiency he'd grown to expect of her.

As if sensing his eyes on her, she glanced over her shoulder. The shaky smile she gave him was a haunting echo of the wariness he himself felt. The way she held her shoulders, at a cautious angle told him all he needed to know.

She'd seen the photo album.

Ethan's gut rolled, his heart filled with remorse. He should have told Keely about Tracy long before now.

Keely's smile remained stiff around the edges, her eyes filled with what almost looked like pain.

Yeah, he should have told her about Tracy.

Drawing in a bracing breath, he got straight to the point. "We need to talk."

She flinched at his abrupt tone. But after only a brief hesitation, she motioned for one of her waiters to take over at the soda machine and approached Ethan.

With the counter a physical barrier between, they stared at each other for a long moment, neither speaking, neither moving. Then, as if coming to a hard decision, Keely reached out and closed her hand over his.

Ethan wanted to whisk her away, to protect her from the pain he saw in her eyes, the pain he'd unwittingly inflicted on her. "Keely, I realize you saw the—"

She stopped him midspeech with a gentle squeeze to

his hand. With her hand still linked with his, she said, "I owe you an apology."

She was apologizing to *him*?

"When I was in your house this morning, I noticed you'd left all the lights on in the living room. Long story short, I saw the photo album you left on the coffee table and looked through it. I'm sorry, Ethan."

"There's nothing to be sorry for."

Breaking eye contact, she pulled her hand away, worked the edges of a bar towel between her fingers. "I didn't mean to intrude on your privacy. There's simply no excuse."

"I should have told you about—"

"Keely!" a masculine voice bellowed from the kitchen, sufficiently cutting off the rest of Ethan's speech. "Get in here, quick."

She gave him an apologetic grimace. "I'll be right back."

When she returned, she had a difficult time meeting his gaze. Their conversation was clearly making her uncomfortable. Ethan pressed on anyway. "I should have told you about Tracy."

"Tracy." She spoke the name so softly he wasn't sure she'd actually said it out loud. "Is that the woman in the photos?"

"Yes."

The muscles in her jaw bunched and her fingers shook as she continued to pick at the towel in her hand.

"I want to tell you about her. But you're busy. And I have to get back to the office soon. I'll come over later this evening, after Flicka goes to bed, and we'll talk then."

"It'll be late. Tonight is the father/daughter dance at the church."

The dance. He'd forgotten all about it. "Text me when she falls asleep."

"Okay." She opened her mouth to say something else, but was once again called into the kitchen.

As Ethan watched her make her way through the swinging doors, he desperately wanted to tell her they'd work things out and maybe even find a way to be together. Not as friends or neighbors, but as a couple.

Was he willing to set aside his fear of losing her? He wanted to try. With love came loss, but without love life was nothing more than existing. He was tired of just existing. He wanted more and wanted it with Keely.

But he wasn't free of the past just yet. There was a ragged loose end that needed tying up first.

Having lost his appetite, he returned to the medical clinic without eating lunch. He waved off questions, stepped into his private office and shut the door firmly behind him.

Working on his laptop, he searched for the proper website and booked a flight from Denver to South Carolina for Friday afternoon, with a return flight two days later. The cost was ridiculous and he'd be gone just over forty-eight hours. But when Ethan pulled into his driveway Sunday evening, the night before Christmas Eve, he would be free to begin the rest of his life.

Would Keely be a part of it?

For the first time in a year and a half, he wanted to take a leap of faith. It would take courage and prayer to commit to another woman. He lifted up a petition to the Lord, for guidance, clear direction and the courage to step out into the unknown future.

After his last patient was gone, he returned to his office, pulled out his phone and made the call he'd put off long enough.

Phyllis Jenkins answered on the first ring. "Ethan, I'm so happy to hear from you."

"I'm coming to the memorial," he said without preamble.

"Oh, that's…" A sob sounded in his ear. "…so very…" Another sob. "…wonderful."

"Thanks for inviting me."

"It wouldn't feel right without you."

They talked for another fifteen minutes. He disconnected the call to the tune of female tears of gratitude. Setting the phone on his desk, he continued to stare at the blank screen.

A scratching on his doorjamb had him looking up and staring into a pale, taut face, the very embodiment of physical pain.

Ethan quickly rounded his desk. "Sit down, Beau, before you fall over."

The stubborn man remained propped against the doorframe, practically turned inside himself, cradling his elbow in his palm. Ethan took the bulk of his weight and guided him to a chair. "Let me guess, you went skiing this afternoon."

"If you're going to say I told you so," Beau gritted out, "I suggest you pause and reflect."

Not intimidated in the least, Ethan gave his friend a long look. "You gonna tell me what happened?"

"I went skiing this afternoon. I took a turn too tight and had to overcorrect and might have tweaked my injury a bit."

"Tweaked your injury," Ethan repeated, amazed at the guy's gift for understatement.

"Look, Ethan." Beau blew out a hard, frustrated hiss of air. "I'm on a time crunch here. Give me a shot of cortisone or whatever it takes to help me manage the pain long enough to dress for the dance and we're good."

The dance. Right, that was tonight. "What time are you supposed to pick up Flicka?"

"Just before seven." He ground out the words through clenched teeth, gasping for air as Ethan helped him stand and then steered him down the hallway.

Clearly, the guy was in a lot of pain. That he came into the office spoke volumes.

"Well?" Beau gave him a hopeful look reminiscent of Baloo begging for a dog treat. "You gonna hook me up with something to help me get dressed without collapsing?"

"No can do. I'm not that kind of doctor."

Beau frowned. "I thought you were my friend."

"I am. Which is why we're doing this right, starting with X-rays."

He set the world champ of pigheadedness in exam room 1 and then tracked down Tasha.

"We have a last-minute patient."

"Let's get to it, then. I have date in an hour."

One look at the X-rays told Ethan that Beau wasn't going to make the dance. He gave him the bad news, plus a prescription for pain medication.

"No pills," Beau ground out.

Proving he meant business, he tore the prescription into shreds. Even that simple task took effort, if the sweat pouring down his face was any indication.

"But you're in pain."

"I'll gut it out."

Ethan shook his head. "What about tonight?" he asked. "You gonna gut out the entire dance?"

"The dance isn't the concern. Dressing for the event…" He sighed heavily. "That could be a problem."

The guy wasn't only stubborn he was delusional. "I'll cover for you tonight."

"Wow, Doc, aren't you the stand-up guy?" Beau's tone was full of irony, but did nothing to deter Ethan now that the idea was in his head.

Later, as he stood in his bedroom, working the black tie hanging around his neck into a respectable bow, he thought of Tracy, of her favorite Bible verse scrolled on the pages of the photo album. "And we know that all things work together for good to those who love God, to those who are the called according to His purpose."

It was as if God had been leading Ethan to this moment all his life. Every heartache, every tragedy, every loss had brought him to this place, at this time. Tracy would always be in his heart, but he couldn't keep living in the past. As a pastor once told him, and Connor reiterated, clinging to the dead was no way to live.

The future was within his grasp. All he had to do was reach for it. Did he have the courage?

Chapter Seventeen

Keely's cell phone dinged with an incoming text, but as her hands were busy wrestling Felicity's hair into a complicated updo she could only glance at the screen. It was from her brother.

As she twisted, twirled and bent locks of the little girl's hair, she lifted up a silent prayer that whatever Beau had texted wasn't bad news.

She ignored the phone a bit longer. She'd had quite enough troubling news for one day, starting with the photo album she'd stumbled upon this morning and Ethan's promise to discuss Tracy with Keely later tonight.

A wave of intense jealousy tried to take hold. Keely refused to give in to the emotion. So Ethan had a past. Well, Keely did, too. Not many people made it into their late twenties without some kind of romantic history trailing after them.

She cared for Ethan, maybe even loved him. Nothing he said would change that. Unfortunately, what he said could affect their future and whether there was a chance for them to be together.

Her phone buzzed again, obnoxiously reminding her she hadn't opened the text from her brother.

"You want me to get your phone for you?" Felicity asked from her position in front of the mirror. "I can reach it if I stretch out my arm real far."

"No need. I'm just about finished." Keely tucked the last strand of hair beneath the crystal tiara, bobby-pinned it in place, then nodded in satisfaction. "It's official. I've still got the touch."

"Can I see?"

"Absolutely." She handed Felicity a small mirror, turned her around, then showed her how to position the glass so she could view the back of her head.

"I love it! It's the best hairstyle ever!"

Keely bit back a laugh. Apparently, Baloo was the best dog ever. Out in the backyard stood the best snowman ever. They'd picked out the best Christmas tree ever, and so on.

Well, as far as Keely was concerned, Felicity was the best kid ever. She pressed a kiss to the child's cheek. "Time to get into your dress."

"Yay." She skipped and twirled out of the room.

Now that she was alone, Keely picked up her phone and frowned at the message from her brother. Change of plans. Ethan filling in for me tonight. He'll pick up the kid at your place.

Worry for her brother had her typing out a quick text, asking him if he was okay.

I'm fine.

The cryptic response only added to her worry. Thumbs flying across the screen, she asked if he needed her to come over.

His curt, one-word answer—don't—ended the conversation, but not Keely's determination to find out what had happened to her brother. Seeking answers, she texted Ethan next.

His response was nearly as curt as her brother's. She huffed out a breath. "Doctor-patient confidentiality, indeed."

Beau had obviously blown out his shoulder again.

Keely was half tempted to call her mother and tattle on him, but her brother was a grown man.

Sighing, Keely debated whether to tell the little girl about the change in plans, then decided to let her be surprised when Ethan arrived on their doorstep.

"Felicity?" she called out. "Need help getting dressed?"

"Nope. All done." Felicity's door swung open and out she twirled, her red-and-green Christmas dress sparkling in the overhead lights.

She spun again, and again and again, then finally stopped. "So? How do I look?"

"Oh, Felicity." Keely sniffled back a wave of emotion that felt suspiciously like maternal pride. "You look absolutely beautiful. Like a fairy-tale princess come to life."

"I feel like a princess. Thank you." She threw herself at Keely. "Thank you for being my mom while mine is gone. I love you so much."

"I love you, too, baby, with all my heart." The doorbell kept her from blubbering all over the child.

Keely let Felicity open the door.

The little girl's squeal of delight matched her own reaction to the man standing on their front stoop, holding a wrist corsage of tiny red roses in a clear plastic box.

Okay, it was true, nearly every man on the planet

looked good in a tuxedo. But Ethan, with his black hair, masculine features and startling blue eyes, took the sophisticated suit to a whole new level.

"Is that for me?" Felicity asked, pointing to the corsage.

"It is." He stepped inside the house, shut the door behind him and gave all his attention to the little girl.

Felicity twirled.

"Wow, Flicka. You look like a princess."

She twirled again. "Keely just said the very same thing."

Eyebrows raised, he glanced at Keely over the child's head. There was something in his expression, something besides warmth, a silent promise her heart understood but her mind couldn't quite grasp.

The look in his eyes said that Ethan cared for her in a way that went beyond friendship. Was it possible his feelings for her were as strong as hers for him?

She nearly wobbled, forced her knees to lock. "I'll get your coat, Felicity."

When she returned, Ethan was telling Felicity he hoped they played the chicken dance song at least once.

"What's the chicken dance?"

"I won't spoil it for you, but let's just say you're in for a treat." As he helped the child into her coat, he smiled over at Keely. "What time's our curfew, Mom?"

Her heart dipped to her toes. Could this man be any more charming? Playing along, she gave a stern wag of her finger. "Ten o'clock, sharp. Not a minute after or you'll answer to me."

They all laughed.

Before leading the little girl outside, Ethan pulled

Keely into his arms for a brief hug. "I'll see you later tonight."

"I'll be here waiting."

"Good, we have a lot to talk about, you and me."

Oh, boy, did they ever!

At precisely three minutes shy of 10:00 p.m., Ethan guided Flicka up Keely's front walk. Ever since climbing into his SUV in the church parking lot, the kid had been a nonstop chatterbox, going on and on about the fun she'd had at the dance. "Did you have fun, Dr. Ethan?"

He slung his arm over her shoulder. "I did."

Far more than he'd expected.

There'd been a moment, right after they first entered the all-purpose room at the church, when memories of another father/daughter dance had hit him. But then Flicka had caught sight of the area where formal pictures were being taken. Unaware of his turmoil, she'd grabbed his hand and begged to get a photograph with him.

The joy in her face had pulled him back into the moment, where he'd stayed the rest of the evening. The men's ministry had gone all out. There'd been games, line dances with helpful instructions from the older girls, an excellent dinner and, to top off the evening, the infamous chicken dance.

"What was your favorite part of the night?" he asked.

"Oh, that's easy. The chicken dance."

That had been his favorite part, too.

Without knocking, the kid burst through the front door and sped into the living room as if she lived there, which, of course, she did. But the ease and familiarity of the move weren't lost on Ethan. Every day the child was becoming more comfortable in her new home. There was, indeed, hope for the future.

"Keely! Keely, where are you?"

The woman in question entered the room, her gaze landing on the child's face. "Well? Did you have a good time tonight?"

"It was the best dance ever!"

A secretive smile spread across Keely's features. "Somehow I knew you were going to say that."

Flicka laughed.

"Hey, Keely, look what I can do now." An enthusiastic rendition of the chicken dance, tune included, followed the command.

Keely dutifully watched and clapped along and even hummed several bars of the song. The affection in her eyes was unmistakable, as were the tears she valiantly fought off with several fast blinks.

It was a full ten minutes before the kid wound down. By then Ethan thought his heart might explode with love for the woman and child who had come into his life one cold Sunday evening nearly a month ago. He didn't want to lose them.

"Dr. Ethan and I got you this." Flicka dug into the goody bag she'd received at the end of the night. She rooted around a bit, then produced the photograph they'd taken upon first arriving at the church.

"It's…oh, it's lovely."

While Keely battled another bout of tears, the excitement of the evening finally caught up with Flicka. Her loud, jaw-cracking yawn was followed by a second one, and then a third.

Smiling softly, Keely brushed a hand over the little girl's cheek. "Time for bed, sleepyhead."

"I am pretty tired." With one last surge of energy, she launched herself at Ethan, gave him a fierce hug. "Thanks for being my daddy tonight."

"You're welcome." His voice came out low and gruff. He wanted desperately to make promises that he would be her daddy for years to come, but something held him back. A mix of loyalty to his former life and a need to find closure before making promises.

"I'll never forget the fun we had tonight."

"Neither will I." He kissed the top of her head, then set her away from him. "Sleep tight, sweetheart."

"Okay."

Thanking him with her eyes, Keely ushered the child toward the stairs and told Ethan to make himself comfortable.

True to her word, she returned fifteen minutes later. By the time she joined him on the couch, Ethan had shed his coat and suit jacket, pulled loose his tie and propped up his feet on a nearby ottoman.

"She's already asleep. Oh, Ethan, I think she's finally settling into her new life."

"That would be my diagnosis."

She laughed. The relief in the sound was unmistakable and Ethan felt the last of the ice around his heart melt away. He patted the empty spot beside him. "Come sit down and we'll have that talk I promised."

Her gaze wary now, instead of settling in beside him, she chose the chair on the other side of the coffee table. The lights of the Christmas tree sparkled behind her, adding a soft, homey feel to the room, and to the moment, bringing the surety of what Ethan wanted, what he craved.

"Will you tell me, that is…" Her gaze darted around the room. "Will you tell me about Tracy now?"

"Yes." He lowered his feet to the floor, leaned his elbows on his knees and held her stare. "But now that the time is here, I'm not sure where to start."

Keely's face turned soft, kind. "Who was she to you? Your girlfriend?"

"My fiancée."

The revelation didn't seem to surprise her. But her shoulders bunched and she crossed her arms around her waist. "The little girl in the pictures. She was Tracy's daughter?"

He nodded, and then, in a voice without inflection, he told the story of the woman he'd lost. "I met Tracy in Afghanistan. It was love at first sight for us both, but we didn't date until we were stateside."

Now that he'd begun, the words spilled from his mouth. He told Keely things he'd never told anyone, not even his siblings. With each revelation, he could feel the past releasing its grip.

"I proposed six months after our first date. I was completely committed to becoming a husband to her and a father to her daughter, Samantha."

He detailed his and Tracy's plans to stay in the army. Then, with his mind poised between past and present, no longer able to sit, he took to pacing the perimeter of the room.

Keely held silent, watching him closely yet giving him the time he needed to gather his thoughts.

In a halting voice, he told her about the car accident that had taken Tracy's life, about the terrible call that had been eerily similar to the one he'd received the night of his parents' crash. All the grief and agony he'd once felt reared up, threatening to tug him under.

At some point, Keely had jumped to her feet and crossed the room to where he now stood frozen in memories. She drew him into her arms and held on, saying nothing, simply allowing him to calm his breathing.

"I'm sorry for your loss," she whispered, her cheek pressed against his bent head.

For several seconds he simply stood in the circle of Keely's comforting embrace, allowing her kindness, her understanding—her very presence—to erase another layer of the pain he'd buried deep within his heart. The final step toward healing, toward letting go of his past, still eluded him.

"Tracy's mother called me." Stepping back, he explained about the memorial service and what Phyllis requested of him.

"Are you going to scatter her ashes?"

"I need the closure."

He admitted that now, as he stared into Keely's eyes, wanting to take a chance on her, on them, but not yet fully free to do so. "I fly out Friday afternoon and, barring any delays, will be home Sunday night. I'll miss the last parade meeting, but not the parade itself."

"I understand."

He took her face in his hands. It wasn't solely her outward beauty that called to him, that made him want to wake up, to live again, to risk another loss for the sake of love. It was Keely herself, her sly wit and the warm heart that lurked beneath her snarky exterior.

"Do you understand why I'm telling you about Tracy?"

Eyes unspeakably sad, she nodded very slowly, very carefully. "You want me to know how much you still love her."

"Of course I still love her. I'll always love her. She's a part of me." He held her gaze, wanting her to hear the truth from him, only him. "I'm the man I am because of knowing her."

With each word he spoke, he felt the last of his grief lifting, the past finally releasing him. But instead of joy filling Keely's eyes, instead of understanding and relief, she looked defeated, devastated even, as if he'd taken a scalpel to her heart and was carving away. "I've hurt you."

She nodded, tears filling her eyes.

"I'm sorry." He didn't know what else to say, so he addressed the issue head-on. "Tell me how I can fix it."

Chapter Eighteen

Keely's heart was breaking, shattering at her feet, because of the man standing before her. And just like every other time in their tumultuous past, Ethan had no idea of the impact his words were having on her. But this time, she would tell him. No more evasion, no more jumping to conclusions.

His words echoed in her mind, torturing her. *I still love her. I'll always love her. She's a part of me.*

Keely forced back a sob. She'd heard a variation of those words once before, the day Cutter had taken back his proposal.

Ethan might as well have stuck a dagger in her heart. In that moment, Keely knew she loved him, but he would never be hers, not completely. The tears she'd ruthlessly held at bay demanded release. She gave up the fight and let them come.

She spun around, presenting her back to the man she loved. Not for one more second could she look into Ethan's intense blue eyes, eyes shadowed with memories from his past.

"Keely." He came up behind her, drew her back against his broad chest. "Talk to me."

For one, blissful second she allowed his strength to swallow her grief.

She would have given him her heart, her future, her everything. They would have been good together, happy, if only his heart was free to love her in return.

His hands closed over her shoulders, and he slowly turned her around to face him. "I've hurt you. You must realize that was never my intention."

"Oh, Ethan, I know that."

He placed a knuckle beneath her chin and applied gentle pressure until her gaze once again met his. "Would you rather me not have told you about Tracy?"

"No." She said the word in a rush of air. "I'm honored you shared your past with me. I'm sorry for your loss, Ethan, so very sorry. You've suffered a great tragedy." He'd lost the love of his life in a car accident, just as he'd lost his parents. How did he bear it? How did he make it from one day to the next?

His strength humbled her.

"Tell me why you're crying. Why do I get the feeling I've just broken your heart?"

Honesty goes both ways, she reminded herself. "You shared your past with me. It's only fair I share mine with you."

The look of utter shock on his face would have been comical under any other circumstances.

"I'm nearly thirty years old, Ethan. Did you think I made it through my twenties without a single relationship or heartbreak?"

He speared a hand through his hair. "I don't know

what I thought. But when you put it that way, it makes sense you would have experienced at least one breakup."

"It was far more devastating than a simple breakup."

Hand clasped in his, she led him back to the couch, waited until they were both settled to tell him about her disastrous romance with Cutter.

When she finished the tale of how they met—at a party thrown by mutual friends—she paused to gather her words. "We were perfectly suited for each other. Our goals for the future were the same and we really got along, better than most friends and certainly better than most couples we knew."

"If you were that good together, why aren't you with him?"

"It's complicated."

"You listened to my story. Give me a chance to hear yours."

It was only fair. "I knew Cutter was getting ready to ask me to marry him. He'd even taken me ring shopping. Then, when he told me he was taking me to dinner at our favorite restaurant, and that I should dress for the occasion, I knew he was going to pop the question."

"Did he ask you to marry him that night?"

Pain slashed through her heart. "During dessert. We were happy for a time, a few weeks, but I could feel Cutter pulling away emotionally. And then…" She couldn't get the words out. They simply vanished.

Ethan took her hand. The gesture gave her the strength to continue. "And then, one day, Cutter asked for the ring back."

"Did he give you a reason?"

Sorrow and humiliation filled her. "He said he wasn't ready to get married, because he wasn't over his wife."

"He was divorced?"

"A widower. His wife died of cancer two years before we met." She slowly pulled her hand free, lifted her chin, held his stare. "When he asked for the ring back, his exact words were 'I'm not ready to marry you. I still love Pamela.'"

"Keely, listen to me." Ethan's voice took on a desperate note. "I told you about Tracy because I'm ready to let her go. I'm ready to move on. With you. I want to be with you and I think you want to be with me. Am I wrong?"

She shook her head, unable to lie about something so important.

"That's why I'm going to the memorial service, to deal with the past, so I can move into the future. I hope to do that with you."

His sincerity was real. But would it last?

Would he go to the memorial service and realize he wasn't ready to move on?

She couldn't take that kind of blow again.

"It's late." She shifted out from under his touch. "It's been an emotional night for us both. Let's take a break, talk again tomorrow, or the day after that, or maybe next week."

Like a boulder cemented to concrete, Ethan held his ground. "We can table this discussion, if that's what you want. But I'm not going to change my mind about you, or us."

The promise was there in his eyes, yet no words of love.

"I'm tired, Ethan. Please, go home, we'll talk again soon."

"I'm *not* going to change my mind," he repeated, taming a stray wisp of hair behind her ear. The tenderness in the gesture teased hope to the surface. She ruthlessly shut it down. He himself said he needed closure.

Keely desperately wanted to believe Ethan. Cutter had been equally sincere. He, too, had meant the words he'd said, until he took them all back.

"I'm leaving for Tracy's memorial Friday afternoon. When I return, we'll talk." He pressed a light kiss to her temple, her cheek, then her lips. "Think of me while I'm gone."

How could she not?

Ethan wordlessly picked up his jacket, then his coat, then walked out the front door.

The soft click of metal meeting metal told Keely she was alone. Very alone. More alone than she'd ever felt in her entire life.

Keely didn't think about Ethan for the next three days. She didn't think about him when she gave the all clear signal to Ryder so he could let the dogs into the backyard.

She didn't think about him at the final parade meeting where she and the committee addressed last minute details. She didn't think about him when she and Felicity built another snowman, or when they made snow ice cream or…

Who was she kidding? she asked herself, as she prepared dinner for her and Felicity. Keely did nothing *but* think about Ethan. And every time she did, she prayed for him. *Lord, give him the closure he's seeking.*

He would be home late this evening. Would he call her? He said he would, but what if he didn't? Sighing, she looked out the window, noted that snow was coming down heavier than forecasted.

"Keely?" Felicity hovered in the doorway, her face pinched in pain. "I don't feel so good."

She forced her legs to move quickly, then crouched in front of the child. "Is it your tummy?"

Hand pressed over her mouth, she nodded. "Will you call Dr. Ethan and ask him to come over?"

"I can't, baby. He's still out of town."

The child's big blue eyes flickered with despair. "But…but… I really miss him. Can't you make him come home?"

If only it were that simple.

"He is coming home, but not for several hours yet." If the storm worsened and they closed the airports, he might not make it home until tomorrow, or the day after that. Information Keely did not share with her little cousin.

"Let's get you in the bed until you feel better."

They barely made it three steps before Felicity's face went dead white and she lost the contents of her stomach on Keely's shoes. Her first instinct was to call Ethan, but he wasn't home. And Ryder was working the night shift at the hospital.

Helplessness danced a chill up her spine. She had two choices, stand here wringing her hands, or take Felicity to the ER. Keely knew what she had to do. As she helped the child in her car, then backed out of the drive, she could hear nothing but the sound of her pulse drumming in her ears.

Keely took the quickest route to the hospital, around town, instead of through it, where there would be no stoplights or ridiculously slow speed limits.

Snow came down hard, making visibility nearly impossible. She didn't see the black ice, had no way to correct her course by time she did. The steering wheel jerked out of her hands. The Jeep went into a fast skid, too fast. She steered into the turn, but couldn't regain control.

As her car slipped toward an embankment, Keely's first thought was of the child in the backseat. She prayed Felicity wouldn't be hurt. *Please, Lord, keep her safe.*

Her next thought was of Ethan, and what this accident would do to him. And then…

Everything went black.

On the drive home from Denver International Airport, Ethan concentrated on the road. The snow was coming down hard, but he wanted to get home, needed to get home. To Keely, the woman he loved. As he thought back over their relationship, he recognized that the two of them had been building to this moment for nearly a year.

In the silence of his SUV, he practiced his speech, reviewing what he would say to convince Keely he was ready to commit his future to hers.

He got the call from Ryder a mile out of town. His brother's voice came to him as if from a long, dark tunnel. His mind latched on to two words. *Car accident.*

Then two more. *Keely* and *Felicity.*

His heart turned cold as ice and empty as the night. He couldn't lose Keely and Flicka. He thought of all the time he'd wasted, holding them both at a distance, when he could have enjoyed them more, loved them more, given them his entire heart.

The spiral of regret and fear threatened to pull him under. He pulled his own SUV to a stop and asked, "How badly are they hurt?"

"They're fine, Ethan. Mostly bumps and bruises, but I thought you would want to know about the accident."

"You were right. Tell Keely I'll be there in ten minutes."

"I thought you were out of town."

"Just got home." No, he wasn't home, not yet. Not until Keely was with him, and Flicka. Only then would he be home.

He disconnected the call and pulled back onto the highway.

The ten minutes it took to make the journey from the edge of town felt like an eternity. Patience ready to snap, he burst into the ER, found Ryder, who took him to where Keely was filling out paperwork and Flicka was nowhere in sight.

Was she all right?

Anticipating his question, Ryder told him, "Felicity's fine. One of the nurses took her to get Jell-O in the cafeteria."

His brother's explanation poured warmth over his cold fear. Relief nearly buckled his knees. He made his way toward Keely, ran his gaze from her head to her toes, saw nothing but the bumps and bruises Ryder promised.

"Keely."

"Ethan." She cast aside the clipboard and rushed into his arms.

He held on to her for a long, wordless moment. With her wrapped in the circle of his arms, and his hand stroking over her silky hair, he felt a moment of incredible peace. Spending the rest of his life without her by his side was no longer an option. "Don't ever scare me like that again."

"Oh, Ethan, I scared myself." She sobbed into his shirt. "What if I'd killed Felicity?"

"You didn't." The idea was too terrible to contemplate.

"She was feeling sick and I didn't know what to do. So I bundled her up and drove her to the hospital. But there was a patch of black ice on the road and…and…" She trailed off, clutched at his shirt. "I lost control of the Jeep."

A sudden image of a similar crash insinuated itself in his mind. He ruthlessly shoved it aside. "What matters is you're both okay."

He said the words as much for himself as for her.

"I'm so sorry."

"I am, too." He lowered his head, pressed his lips to hers. It was more than a kiss he gave her, but also a promise.

When he pulled away, she blinked up at him with her heart in her eyes. He saw the love shining in their depths, and the fear, the hope, all the same emotions swirling inside him.

"I don't want to go another day, wishing I had said this one moment sooner. I love you, Keely O'Toole."

"I love you, too, Ethan."

Wanting privacy for what he had to say, he drew Keely into an alcove off the waiting room, pressed another kiss to her lips. "When I came home to Village Green, I was convinced I would never love again. In my life, love came with loss and I didn't want to ever experience grief again like I did when Tracy died."

The pain that flashed in Keely's eyes had him wanting to sugarcoat the rest of his speech. That wouldn't be fair to either of them.

"My heart was locked in the past with Tracy. But then you showed up. You, Keely, with your wit and humor and snarky personality, and despite our shaky beginning, I've come to believe God Himself had a hand in drawing us together."

"And yet you avoided me for nearly a year."

He winced at the accuracy of her claim. "I avoided you because you made me uneasy, made me want to grasp for something I'd lost, to build new dreams in the place of old."

Bare your heart, Ethan. Give her your truth.

"I will always love Tracy. I won't dishonor her memory and say otherwise. But I'm not looking to replace her." He knuckled an errant curl out of her eyes. "I want to start something new, with you. What we build together will be different than what I had with Tracy, yet just as wonderful, just as genuine and lasting."

"I want that, too. But I come as a package deal."

"Flicka's a great kid and I want to help you raise her, no matter how long she's in our care."

Eyes shining, she smiled. "I'm pretty sure that can be arranged."

There was so much more he wanted to say, so much he wanted to tell her, to proclaim and promise. But he didn't want to bear his heart in a hospital waiting room. And they had a little girl probably wondering where they were.

"Then let's find Flicka and go home."

"I like the way you think, Dr. Scott."

Ethan showed up for breakfast at Keely's the morning of the parade, at precisely 6:00 a.m. Keely opened the back door and ushered him out of the cold.

"You have to eat fast," she said. "We're due down-town in thirty minutes."

"Good morning to you, too." Humor tinged his words, while intent wavered in his eyes. A second later, he swooped in for a kiss.

She let herself linger in his arms. The moment he'd arrived at the hospital after her accident, every doubt in her heart had vanished. Ethan loved her. And she loved him in return. "I love you, Ethan. I—"

Felicity's voice coming from the kitchen cut her off. "Please tell me you two aren't kissing out there."

Laughing, Ethan took Keely's hand and dragged her with him into the kitchen. "Maybe we were, and maybe we weren't."

The little girl made a gagging sound, but it was clear by the happiness in her eyes that she was pleased they were together.

The next two hours went by in a blur.

After eating a quick breakfast of yogurt and protein bars, they left the house and arrived downtown two hours prior to the start of the parade. Ethan and Keely went their separate ways.

Once she'd done all she could as the parade chair, Keely set aside her micromanaging tendencies and left the remaining details in the hands of her competent team. Walkie-talkie turned on to the proper channel, she guided Felicity to a spot on the sidewalk one block from the finish line.

They'd barely settled in when the Mitchell twins rushed over and begged Keely to let Felicity watch the parade with them. The little girl gave her a hopeful ex-pression. "Can I?"

"Where are your parents?"

"Over there." Molly pointed across the street.

Olivia and Connor waved.

Making her decision for her, the walkie-talkie went off with a request for her immediate assistance at the Rotarian float. "Okay, you can go, but don't leave the area until I come get you after the parade."

As soon as the girls raced across the empty street, Keely climbed into her golf cart and sped back to the starting line.

Other than the minor issue of a broken part easily fixed on the Rotarian float, the parade started on time and proceeded without a hitch.

The crowd roared with laughter when the last float started down the course. Santa's sleigh being pulled by camels received the expected cheers and applause.

Ethan, otherwise known as Santa, waved to the cheering spectators while several prominent members of the community dressed as elves tossed out miniature candy canes. Keely willed him to look in her direction. The moment he noticed her, she lifted her hand, froze midwave.

That wasn't Ethan giving the crowd a jolly ho-ho-ho. It was his brother, Ryder. "Where's Ethan?" she wondered aloud.

"Right behind you."

She spun around and stared into the smiling face of the man she loved. She attempted a scowl, but couldn't quite pull it off. He looked far too handsome with that sheepish grin on his face. "Why aren't you on the float like you promised?"

"Although I do kind of like it when you scold me, Ryder volunteered to take my place."

"How much did you pay him to volunteer?"

"Aw, Keely." He placed a hand to his heart, staggered a step back. "I'm wounded you would think I'd do such a thing."

"How much?"

"Let's just say, my brother is doing me a favor that will require a large one in return."

She couldn't help it, she laughed at him. "Oh, Ethan, I love you. Don't ever change."

"Only for the better, babe."

It was a promise she would treasure for the rest of her life.

"I love you," he whispered for her ears only. "I want to grow old with you."

"I think that can be arranged."

"I'm not giving you a chance to change your mind." He took her hand, pulled her around the corner and then, once they were shielded from gawkers, dropped to one knee. "Keely O'Toole, will you marry me?"

"Yes. Yes, Ethan, I'll marry you, as soon as we can set a date."

Still holding her hand, he rose to his feet, pulled her in for a quick kiss. "God has blessed me with love twice in my life. It's more than I deserve and nothing I take for granted. I love you, Keely, with all my heart."

She believed him. "I love you, too, Ethan."

"I promise to spend the rest of my days loving you with all that I am. I will protect you and keep you safe and build a happy, fulfilling life with you."

"I'll do the same, Ethan." She rose onto her toes and kissed him on the mouth. "I will love you until the day I die."

Epilogue

Ethan's Christmas morning started an hour before the sun made its initial appearance over the horizon. By six thirty he was showered and dressed in jeans and a red sweater. He opted out of shaving. Rubbing his hand over the day-old stubble, he padded down the stairs in socks, no shoes.

It took him another ten minutes to feed the dogs.

While they gobbled up their breakfast, Ethan shoved his feet into a pair of combat boots and grabbed his coat. He let the animals out the front door, where Felicity's Christmas present joined Baloo in sniffing every bush and barren flower bed within a fifty-foot radius.

At five minutes to seven, Ethan was through waiting for the sun to rise. It was Christmas morning. He had presents to deliver and two females to spoil.

It took him considerable effort tying the shiny red ribbon around Cupcake's neck. Apparently, the animal thought Ethan had invented a new game.

"Hold still, you furry mutt." Sometime overnight the dog had turned into a greased pig. "I mean it. Stop squirming, Cupcake."

The puppy perked up at the sound of his name and swiped his tongue across Ethan's chin.

"Enough." After a bit of unnecessary roughhousing, he finally managed to tie the ribbon into a respectable bow. "You look very pretty."

Cupcake gave him a doggy grin.

Ethan grabbed the engagement ring he'd fished out of the safe last night, then turned his attention onto the dogs. "All right, boys, let's go spend the best day of the year with our two favorite girls."

Minutes later, the puppy tucked under his arm like a football and Baloo standing politely by his side, Ethan knocked on Keely's back door. It opened with a whoosh.

"What took you so long?" The impatience in her tone was reminiscent of the last time she'd uttered the same words, the night he'd come over to check on a sick child. The night his life had changed forever, and certainly for the better.

He grinned, probably looking as dopey as the puppy in his arms. "Came as fast as I could."

As if caught up in the same memory, Keely gave him a dreamy smile and said, "Don't just stand there. Come inside."

Heart bursting with love, he climbed the concrete steps, each one taking him closer to the beautiful woman with the long, gorgeous red hair and sea-green eyes who would soon be his wife.

Today, he would make their engagement official, by sliding his grandmother's ring onto her finger.

Keely stepped aside and Ethan moved deeper into the house. He set the puppy on the ground and gave the hand signal to stay. Cupcake sat obediently at Ethan's feet.

Baloo did the same.

"Where's Flicka?" he whispered.

"Waiting for us in the living room, all but busting with impatience."

"Wait." He stopped her from turning away with a hand on her arm. "I want to give you your Christmas present first."

"Now?"

"Definitely now." He slid the antique, two-carat diamond ring onto her finger. It was a perfect fit.

"Oh, Ethan. It's…it's beautiful. I love it." She lifted misty eyes to his face. "I love you."

"I love you more."

She yanked him against her and kissed him hard on the lips. "Well, I love you most."

He laughed, knowing his life with this woman would be chaotic and loving and full of challenges. He wouldn't want it any other way. "Fair warning, Ms. O'Toole, I'm not a fan of long engagements."

"That makes two of us."

They were finally on the same page, for all the right reasons, ready to step into the future together, as husband and wife. After another, longer kiss, the puppy lost his patience and barked.

"Is that Dr. Ethan and Baloo?" Flicka called out.

"It is," Keely called back. "And they brought your Christmas present with them."

"Really? What is it?"

"Come see for yourself."

Pounding feet sounded seconds before Flicka entered the mudroom. Her shriek of pure delight had both dogs barking and Ethan resisting the urge to cover his ears.

The little girl kissed Baloo on the head, then dropped

to her knees in front of the puppy. She touched the big red bow around his neck. "Is...is he for me?"

"Merry Christmas, Flicka."

She burst into tears, which set off more barking and a canine lovefest. Baloo nuzzled Flicka's cheek. The puppy licked her face.

Sighing over the happy scene, Keely looped her arm through his. "Merry Christmas, Dr. Scott."

"Merry Christmas."

They moved the celebration into the living room, where they spent the rest of the morning laughing, eating cookies and opening presents. The dogs focused all their efforts on pile-driving through the discarded wrapping paper and boxes.

The sweet chaos filled Ethan with unspeakable joy. After losing one family, the Lord had blessed him with another. He would never forget Tracy and Samantha, they would live in his heart forever, but this was where he now belonged.

He was home, ready to begin the rest of his life with Keely by his side and Flicka in their home for however long that turned out to be.

Ethan couldn't have wished for a better Christmas gift.

* * * * *